SO-ABM-201

**The year 1620.**

A little boy, fishing from the Plymouth wharf, looked up casually, and watched the white sails of a ship as it slipped out of the harbor.

"Yonder sails the *Mayflower*," he observed indifferently, and turned back to his fishing.

That was the world's comment on a gallant adventure which was to prove as far reaching in history as it then seemed mad, hazardous, impossible.

Those who sailed westward were no stodgy, venerable graybeards. They were young—men and women, almost all under thirty, many scarcely twenty—eager, fearless, and very human. And they were inspired as much by the romance of adventure as by the passion for spiritual freedom.

Della from
JHE.
X-mas. 1934.

It is the story of these people during those last frantic, excited weeks before their great venture began that Mrs. Morrow tells. *On the back flap of this jacket you'll find more about them. And on the back of the jacket, Mrs. Morrow's own story of how and why she wrote her latest historical novel.*

# Yonder Sails the Mayflower

## BY HONORÉ MORROW

A few of the characters in

## YONDER SAILS THE MAYFLOWER:—

ROBERT CUSHMAN: Tall and handsome—agent of the Pilgrims to the Merchant Adventurers of London who financed the venture. Some people thought him selfish, calculating, cold, but underneath his quiet elegance and his untiring efficiency burned the heart of a passionate idealist.

DESIRE MINTER: With violet eyes, ruddy brown hair, red mouth. She loved and was loved by Robert Cushman.

CAPTAIN MILES STANDISH: No Puritan he, but a little cock of a soldier, a veteran who prided himself on his fiery temper.

WILLIAM BRADFORD: Educated in Roman law and philosophy, he was leaving the world behind him for a wilderness because of his spiritual convictions.

WILLIAM BREWSTER: For a year and a half a fugitive from the King's wrath, he was the dominating force that held dissenting groups together.

JOHN CARVER: The Deacon, who led his flock as much by reason of magnetic personality as by authority.

CAPTAIN NUTT of the *Cushat Dove:* The notorious pirate who ravaged the west coast of England. He could not understand why Desire Minter would not give up the bleak New World and come with him to Cathay.

CHRISTOPHER MARTIN, governor of the *Mayflower:* A little man, suspicious of his betters. A born mischief-maker, he covered his own defects by bluster.

EDWARD WINSLOW: Young and passionately in love with his bride, he foresaw only Paradise in the New World, and until he got there he sang like an angel to the delight of the Pilgrims.

MARY CUSHMAN: Quick-tempered, hating the whole idea of the New World. She had never pretended to love or understand her husband, Robert.

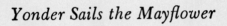

*Yonder Sails the Mayflower*

## Books by Mrs. Morrow

### NOVELS

THE HEART OF THE DESERT

STILL JIM

LYDIA OF THE PINES

THE FORBIDDEN TRAIL

THE ENCHANTED CANYON

JUDITH OF THE GODLESS VALLEY

THE EXILE OF THE LARIAT

THE DEVONSHERS

WE MUST MARCH

FOREVER FREE

WITH MALICE TOWARD NONE

SPLENDOR OF GOD

THE LAST FULL MEASURE

BLACK DANIEL

BEYOND THE BLUE SIERRA

ARGONAUT

### SHORTER FICTION

THE LINCOLN STORIES

(*Dearer Than All, Benefits Forgot,* and
*The Lost Speech of Abraham Lincoln*)

### BIOGRAPHY

MARY TODD LINCOLN

THE FATHER OF LITTLE WOMEN
(LITTLE, BROWN & CO.)

TIGER! TIGER!

### JUVENILES

ON TO OREGON!

SHIP'S MONKEY
(*with* WILLIAM J. SWARTMANN)

# Yonder Sails the Mayflower

### BY HONORÉ MORROW

WILLIAM MORROW AND COMPANY

*New York*                    *1934*

COPYRIGHT - - 1934
BY HONORÉ MORROW

All rights reserved. This book, or parts
thereof, may not be reproduced in any
form without permission of the publisher.

PRINTED IN THE U. S. A. BY
QUINN & BODEN COMPANY, INC.
RAHWAY, N. J.

# Author's Note

ABOUT a year and a half ago, an old sailor man on the River Dart said to me, "Over there, in that meadow and on that hill, the Pilgrim Fathers prayed before they went to America. The old people say they left Dartmouth, here, in a fearful storm."

I had forgotten that the Pilgrims put in at Dartmouth, so I went home and checked the old man's remark. He was, of course, correct. I returned to the Dart, tramped through that meadow and climbed the hill. So here they stood, I told myself, and this is what they saw in August, 1620! What did the Dartmouth and, later, the Plymouth delays mean to them? Why had the *Speedwell* proved unseaworthy? They were five weeks in the waters of this coast. What a trembling in the balance that long uncertainty meant for spiritual America! And what a tale the answers to these questions would make!

And so I was started on a new adventure of the mind!

There is very little authentic literature dealing with the Pilgrims. William Bradford's history, Robert Cushman's few letters and papers, Edward Winslow's account of New Plymouth; this was all I had through which to vision the characters of these people. But even these few pages were sufficient to make me discard the concept of the Pilgrims I'd always had. They were no solemn, stodgy elders, weeping and praying their way across a horrid deep. They were young and lusty and, by the very nature of the task they'd set for themselves, they loved danger and throve on risks.

Of all the Pilgrims, I liked Robert Cushman best. Why did such a man turn back? Had the failure of the *Speedwell* anything to do with his failure? Who was Desire Minter? Why did Chris Martin play the fool? Was Brewster always the preacher? Did no one make a joke? If not, why did my own Puritan grandparents possess such a biting wit?

Out of my own dream of the Fathers I have woven the answer to these queries. But the picture of the background, of the times, of the ships and shipping, and of the problems the Pilgrims met, are, I believe, authentic. More than this, my novel contains practically all that is known about the people who sailed on the *Mayflower,* up to the final sailing from Plymouth.

H. M.

*October 1, 1934*

# Contents

ix

*Yonder Sails the Mayflower*

# I

## *August 3rd, 1620*

A MIGHTY gray wall encircled Southampton. Soldiers with pikes on their shoulders and helmets on their heads tramped this wall and more soldiers guarded the city gates. This was, after Plymouth, one of the greatest seaports in England or in all Europe, for that matter. Twice the French had sacked it before the English recognized its potentialities and erected fortifications commensurate with its importance. Now it lay defiantly safe in the sun, receiving the trade of all the world, dispatching men and merchandise to the uttermost parts of the earth.

The West Gate of the city opened on the West Quay and here among a dozen other ships was tied a merchant vessel of one hundred and eighty tons, the *Mayflower*, of London. She was a fine, tall ship with a beautiful sheer from stem to stern; a roomy, comfortable vessel, eminently suited to the purpose for which Robert Cushman had bought her. Carrying a contingent of Pilgrims, she had come down from London on the last day of July, 1620, and now, at dawn of August 3rd, her master and Cushman were standing on the poop deck, watching the approach of the little sixty-ton *Speedwell*. The pinnace was coming from Holland with the exiled Pilgrims who had been living in Leyden.

"She seems sluggish, eh?" remarked Master Jones. "I wonder why with that spread of sail?" Jones was big and

3

burly and fifty and he wore a soiled velvet doublet of an agonizing purple hue. "Getting his sweeps out now. What's he going to do? No room to tie up to the quay!" He leaned over the stern rail. *"Speedwell,* ahoy! Not too near me, you cod-eyed fool!"

"Cod-eyed fool yourself!" The master of the *Speedwell* returned the compliment. He was standing on the low poop, a very fat man with a small head and enormous sea boots.

"Pull in those sweeps, ye scabbèd ham!" roared Jones.

"Don't hoyse yourself!" shrilled Master Reynolds. "I was a seaman when you were a scullion's dishwash! I'm going to work myself in between you and the galley. Silence, you people! Silence!" This, to the passengers who crowded the little main deck of the *Speedwell.* Their exchange of excited greetings with the *Mayflower's* passengers was adding to the confusion of the moment.

No one paid any attention to the order but shortly, by a miracle of seamanship and impudence, Reynolds maneuvered the pinnace into place beside the *Mayflower.* Immediately, the passengers from both ships rushed to the quay and there followed a noisy interweaving of men, women and children, friend embracing friend, stranger greeting stranger while the busy quayside gaped.

One passenger, however, remained on the *Mayflower.* Robert Cushman continued to stand on the poop from which vantage place he eyed the meeting with mingled feelings of pleasure and anxiety.

No man in all the Pilgrim group had had quite the responsibility he'd had in making this gathering possible. It marked the actual beginning of the venture which he had worked for three years to bring about, giving to it all that he possessed of talent, will power and physical en-

durance. And now, just for a moment, a sudden sense of
the complexity of the forces he had set in motion appalled
him. So he remained alone, leaning against the rail and
rumpling his hair as was his habit when perturbed.

Cushman was forty-two years old though he didn't look
it, for he was very slender and very straight in the back.
He was exceptionally tall. His face was long, with a firm
chin, a fine, disillusioned mouth and a thin, rather prominent nose. His eyes were dark blue and deep-set, beneath
very heavy, absolutely straight brows. His hair was unusual for it still was as yellow as a boy's. He wore it
parted at the side and waving over a small, well-starched
ruff.

For the rest, he was dressed in the Jacobean doublet
which was much pinched in at the waist. This was wine-
colored as were his hosen and so were the trunks which
showed through the hose-slashings. His shoes, which were
slashed at the toe, and his stockings were dark gray. He
wore a short, dark gray velvet cloak over one shoulder.
His gray hat was a little broad in the brim with a truncated
crown. Altogether, there was a look of quiet elegance
about him which had brought nasty comments from some
of the Pilgrims who had come down from London with
him. But he had made no apologies. He couldn't have
done their business for them clad in ill-fitting fustian. He
was beholden to neither Pilgrims nor any other men for
the clothes he wore. He had sold his farm in Kent to
buy stock in the colonizing project and his personal expenditures had been from this fund. Not that there had
been anything unusual in this carping from his fellows.
The three years of his service had been filled with adverse
criticisms and of these he was thinking as pipes blew on

the *Speedwell* and a long line of sailors and porters began to rush her stores aboard.

Master Christopher Jones, who had been studying the new arrivals with interest, interrupted Cushman's thoughts. "These look more Dutch than English. Twelve years' exile in Leyden! It's too long for an Englishman to stay away from home!"

"They're English enough, when it comes to complaining," said Cushman grimly. "It's the clothes that mislead you. They've adopted the Dutch knee-hosen, some of them."

"Mayhap." Jones shrugged his shoulders. "Now, how about allotting their quarters to the passengers?"

Cushman took a paper from his purse and began an explanation: "We've done our best to apportion the bunks so that everyone will be contented. Deacon Carver and I worked on the list for hours, last night. Of the nineteen married couples, we've put fourteen in the *Mayflower's* great cabin and five in the *Speedwell's*. Two of the three unmarried women are in the *Mayflower,* the third in the pinnace. The twenty-one children will remain with their parents or guardians, the little ones and the girls in the great cabins, the big lads 'tween decks with the womanless men."

"How many of the last have you altogether?" asked Jones, peering over Cushman's shoulder at the paper on which was a rude chart of the sleeping quarters of both ships and a much crossed and rewritten list of names.

"Sixty-four," replied Cushman. "Forty-two to the *Mayflower,* twenty-two to the pinnace. Most of them are young and won't mind rude quarters."

"It's to be hoped they're strong as well as young, for such a venture as this," grunted Christopher Jones.

The other nodded. "We had three hundred people in the English congregation in Leyden from whom to pick these first colonists and we took only the young and lusty with a handful of older ones for ballast. Elder Brewster, Deacon Carver and William Mullins are the only men who've reached fifty and they're as lusty as boys. Stephen Hopkins and I have reached forty. I think Deacon Fuller has too. Most of the rest are young, men and women both."

Jones laughed. "And these, with the cursing, Bedlamite crew we've pressed for the voyage, would mean we shan't lack for trouble! Well, give me the list and I'll place my passengers. We'll look things over and get an understanding while they're all on the quay. Do those who came from London with us remain on my ship?" scowling at the paper.

"Certainly not!" exclaimed Cushman. "The Leyden folk will be outraged if the Londoners don't take their equal share of hardships and they'll tell you so. They are used to saying what they think." He grinned into the ruddy face so close to his.

Jones stared at him. "They won't say what they think to me! I'm master of this ship!"

Cushman suppressed a smile. He had lived for eight or nine years in Leyden as one of Pastor Robinson's exiles. He knew every one of the Leyden passengers. He had, as he said, helped to choose them for their independent, sturdy quality. He never had seen one of them really suppressed yet! He knew the people who had come down from London less well. These had been chosen in several ways. A number of them came from a Separatist group in Billerica, in Essex, and were under the leadership of a little man named Christopher Martin, a wrangling fellow, very jealous of the Leyden folk. The Merchant Adventurers, who had advanced most of the money for the colonizing project, had sent a group of what Cushman considered rather doubtful people, very bumptious and given to loud talk. Several men, young, strong and eager for change, had applied to Thomas Weston, the chief Merchant Adventurer, for a chance in the colony, and Weston, always impetuous, had succumbed to his admiration for mere brawn and given them places as laborers. Cushman told himself that while the Leydenites were argumentative, those who'd come down from London were actually pugnacious and that Master Jones, who could not rule his passengers by brute force as he did his crew, was headed for difficulties strange to his experience.

"At the same time," Jones went on with sudden caution, "you'd better come with me to point out your arrangements. Where are your other chief men?"

"Deacon Carver is on the quay where I ought to be, greeting the Leyden people." Cushman pointed to a man who towered over the crowd. "Shall we let the people come aboard?"

"By no means yet! God bless us and so forth, I must get this landlubber's chart of yours into my head first!" The master led the way down from the poop.

The *Mayflower* was a merchantman of average size, about a hundred feet from beak to taffrail and twenty-five feet in the broadest part of her beam. Her sides sloped in from the line of her gun deck to a breadth of just over eighteen feet on her upper deck. At the forward end of this deck was the forecastle containing the cook's house and the crew's quarters. Aft of this on the same deck was an open waist about forty feet long by eighteen wide. Still aft and occupying a third of the open deck was the superstructure comprising the steerage, the great cabin and the poop. The deck below was known either as the gun deck or 'tween decks and was spacious enough, having nearly six feet of headroom and taking in the whole length of the ship.

One entered the steerage by doors from the waist. It was a room about eighteen by sixteen and contained the tiller, the binnacle and the great round bulk of the mizzen-mast. There was a companionway from the steerage to the deck above, called the half deck. From the half deck one entered the master's or poop cabin. During their conversation, Cushman and Jones had been standing on the top of this cabin, the poop deck. They now went down the ladder to the half deck and on down the companionway to the steerage, from which they entered the great cabin.

It was a large room, taking in the remaining after-end of the upper deck. The stern wall was square with two windows. Every foot of wall space remaining was given over to double tiers of bunks, each built to accommodate two persons. There were partitions between the tiers and two feet of space in front which could be curtained, giving privacy. The master referred to these tiny cubicles grandly as cabinets. There was a long narrow table running the length of the cabin.

Jones studied the layout for a moment, then he scratched his sandy head. "Now would ye suggest we write the name on each bunk and would the London passengers then have sense to shift their dunnage? Or must I speak each one softly or loudly as the case may be?"

The berths were filled with boxes and bundles. A baby was asleep in one of the upper bunks, wedged in with cloaks.

"I think you may have to speak them loudly!" replied Cushman.

Jones gave him a keen glance. "What amuses you?"

"You'll see later, my friend. The women will be the worst!" Cushman waved a swarm of flies away from the baby's face. It was that ruffian Billington's child. "They know nothing about ships and the necessities of ships. They will think of you as the landlord of an inn and won't hesitate to scold you about your accommodations." He chuckled.

"And why did you leave so delicate a matter to me, then?" asked Jones. "However, I can compass it! I've tamed the whale and the wily cod! But, at the same time, I think we'll take a look at the gun deck while I collect my ideas. You and Deacon Carver should have shewn me your distempering chart before!" Distinctly out of temper, he stamped out to the steerage again and down the ladder to the gun deck.

The great main hatch on the main deck was open and sunlight gleamed broadly into the long room, while a dancing light from the water flashed through the gun ports in the sides.

"Personally," remarked Cushman, "if I didn't have my wife with me, I'd prefer this to the great cabin; there's more air and free space to stir in."

Jones nodded. Although the three masts, the capstan, and the pumps took toll of this deck, and although the Pilgrims' shallop was stowed under the hatch, there was still room in which to bed three or four score people and for a long table with benches. Wherever space permitted, bunks had been built and those against the ship's sides had in several cases been roughly cabined in to give privacy to the married couples who might be housed there. There were hammocks, too, hanging from the beams.

"If that shallop was filled with rushes," said the master, "a score of boys could sleep there snug and happy as a litter of little hounds. I'll have that done today, just in case there are extra heads to count. None but men and boys here, I see," still frowning at the list. "But listen! The women are returning to the great cabin. Here, Master Cushman, take your list and do your own soft or loud speaking."

"No, you're king of the ship," protested Robert. "I have no authority whatever, I am thankful to say."

Women's voices penetrated to the gun deck. "The thing I fear is come upon me," groaned Jones. "Well, then, come along! I never ran from a petticoat yet!"

Back to the main deck they climbed. The people were streaming over both ships now, examining, exclaiming, protesting. In the great cabin there were no men but a dozen women were in debate over the ownership of the various berths.

"Good day to you, friends!" said the master, very stern, in the starboard doorway. "I am exceedingly busy but at Master Cushman's request, I am placing you in your proper bunks. Number One, nearest the larboard window, goes to Master and Mistress Brewster. Above them—"

"But there's too much air near the window!" declared Mistress Brewster, a tired-faced matron of middle age. "I won't take that bed. Let a young pair like the Winslows have it."

There was sudden silence in the cabin, all eyes on Mary Brewster. As the wife of the elder as well as on her own account, she was a personage among the Pilgrims. Her

pretty white muslin frock over a wheel-farthingale was
very simple, but it had a London air in spite of the fact
that she and her husband had been in hiding for a year.
They had joined the ship, the day before, after a secret
journey from London.

"And our two sons must take the bed above us," added
Mary firmly.

"You'll take bunk Number One, Mistress," repeated
Jones loudly, "and your great boys must go below.
They're men now."

"Men! They're only lads! I shall speak to my husband!" cried Mistress Brewster. "Robert Cushman, are
you going to permit such tyranny?"

"Elder Brewster approved of the list last night," replied
Cushman, "and the master of the ship has the right to be
a tyrant, dear Mistress Brewster!"

"And so I must die of the rheum!" shrieked the elder's
wife. "I refuse! I am not a member of the *Mayflower's*
crew to be bullied and blackguarded!"

"Why not let Master Jones finish reading the list," suggested Cushman, "then you women settle the matter
among yourselves? We men don't care where we sleep if
our wives are suited."

"Who says we don't?" A man's voice, so high that it
was almost a falsetto, broke in from the doorway. It belonged to Christopher Martin of the Essex crowd. He
was a tiny man, very sallow and dark bearded, all in black
save for his ruff. "Marie and I," he went on, "must have
a good place."

"Marie and you!" roared Jones, glad to deal with a
male. "You and Marie will take Number Thirteen and
keep your mouths shut!"

A fat woman with dimples in her huge cheeks stepped

from the group around Mary Brewster and shook her finger in the master's face. "You dare put me in a Number Thirteen, Christopher Jones—"

"Don't you dare 'Christopher' me, you farthingaled Jezebel!" Jones was purple. "Your first husband was a yokel and your second is a Johnny-jump-up." Words failed him.

Robert choked back his laughter and put his hand on the seaman's great shoulder. "Give me the list, Master. I'll talk it over with the people."

"No, you won't! Such presuming!" shrilled Mistress Martin, black eyes snapping.

"But why not? Surely that's a most diplomatical suggestion!" This was a new voice and of extraordinary quality. Everyone fell silent. It was as if a chorus of robins had paused to listen to the nightingale's note, so rich, so full, so thrillingly sweet.

The query came from the lips of a young woman whom Cushman had not seen before. Clad in a pale blue dress, she was standing near the linnet cage someone had hung in the window. Her eyes were violet and she had, besides, ruddy brown hair, creamy skin and a wide, deeply red mouth.

"What a wench!" Cushman heard Jones mutter. Then the master added aloud, "Thank you, Mistress! I'll give *you* the cabin list, then, as soon as I have read it to you." He cleared his throat. "In general, the parents will keep their own young children, but the orphans will go to the gun deck."

"Oh, no!" exclaimed the young woman. "Why, the More children are very babes! Look! Here's Eleanor," lifting an undersized girl of eight in her arms, "and her brothers Dick and Jasper are still more dwarfish!"

"They're mere bastards and indentured servants!" rumbled Jones. "They've been like monkeys all over my ship ever since we set sail."

"They are *not* bastards!" corrected the young woman.

"Don't *you* start arguing, Mistress!" cried the master. "I'd be loth to use hell-rake words to you."

She laughed. Her laughter was low and rich and some subtle quality in it thrilled the troubled depths of Robert Cushman's heart.

"I won't argue, Master Jones," she was saying. "I'll speak you softly enough! But even if they were bastards, which they are not, still they'd be human children with immortal souls. Come, I'll take them all in with me, wherever I am."

"And who *are* you?" demanded Jones.

"Deacon Carver's niece, Mistress Desire Minter," replied Mary Brewster, impatiently. "Read your fond, foolish list, Master. We'll dispose of ourselves after."

"Nay, give it to me now!" Desire put the little girl down and with a smile, held out her hand for the paper.

Jones succumbed with what dignity he could. "Come, Master Cushman!" he said firmly. "We'll settle that hurly-burly I hear 'tween decks." He pushed Cushman into the steerage. "What are you grinning at?" pausing at the top of the companionway.

"Well," answered the other, "perhaps at the tyranny you'd prepared for the occasion and which Mistress Minter—"

Jones interrupted. "Now there's a wench for you! What laughter! And yet when she doesn't laugh, what lovely and familiar gravity to make a man do reverence to her."

"You have other than hell-rake words in your vocab-

ulary, I observe." Cushman was touched by the rough
seaman's manner.

"I read that somewhere," confessed the master with
pride. "On my long voyages I often carry a book with me.
You don't know the girl?"

"I never saw her before," answered Cushman, "though
I've heard the deacon speak of his niece. She is not a
Separatist, I believe."

"Better still!" grinned Jones.

Both men stood staring at the binnacle with unseeing
eyes, then silently went below.

Here confusion reigned. Perhaps fifty men and boys
milled about the deck. Boys straddled the guns, leaped
in and out of the shallop, toyed with the pumps. Boys
shrieked, called, whistled, quarreled. Several fist fights
were in progress. Cushman saw his own thirteen-year-
old Tommy among the lot. Love Brewster, a plump, pink
and white lad in his middle teens, was pushing his smaller
brother, Wrestling, who looked just like him, out of an
upper berth. Nor was the uproar confined to the boys.
Many of their elders, though some looked near twenty-
five, were wrangling over the ownership of bunks, while
bundles and bales of personal belongings were being
shoved angrily from place to place. Several sailors were
adding to the noise as they coiled down ropes and made
ribald comments on the passengers.

Jones drew his silver whistle and blew a blast. There
was a pause of curiosity. "Get forward there, you of the
*Mayflower* crew!" shouted the master. "The rest of you
ass-headed fools line up, starboard and larboard, and get
your orders! You'll sleep in bunks or the shallop as I
designate. You'll keep your barest necessities here with
you on this deck. Make ready to stow the rest in the hold

by noon of today. You'll eat at this table. Your cooking you'll do in the galley or the fireplaces on the main deck. You'll not be permitted on the half deck or the poop deck, aft, or on the forecastle or beak, forward. The gun deck and the ship's waist are your proper quarters. You'll keep clear of my crew. You'll be ruled by a governor to be appointed from among your three agents and this governor will be ruled by me in all matters relating to the ship. As for me, if any man or lad wants to question my authority, now's his time."

There was silence on the gun deck. Jones sniffed, cleared his throat and read off the bunk list. When he had finished, the passengers made a rush for their belongings and after watching for a moment to make sure that peace was maintained, the master said to Cushman, "You go up to the great cabin and see if all goes well. I'll go over to the *Speedwell* with this list for Master Reynolds."

Cushman, much amused, returned to the steerage. There was a lively sound of feminine debate in the great cabin. He shook his head and went out on the main deck. Here, grouped about the starboard ladder leading to the half deck, were most of the married men of the Pilgrims' party. There was a shout of laughter as Robert Cushman appeared.

"You and Master Jones have been routed, we hear!" cried Elder Brewster.

"We were," admitted Cushman, "and I, at least, fired not a single shot. It was abject defeat, shamefully accepted."

"They'll settle it among themselves if we give them time," said Brewster, "especially as I see Desire Minter has taken charge. And while the chief of us seems guaranteed a moment of quiet, let's agree that Pastor Robinson's desire be carried out and Christopher Martin made governor of the *Mayflower*. The people will vote him in if we agree on the appointment."

There was a general nodding of heads except by Robert Cushman. Martin, observing this, scowled. Robert shrugged his shoulders. He believed, but without tangible evidence, that Chris Martin was a cheap rascal. He had told Elder Brewster so but the elder, in an attempt to avoid debate, was following all of Pastor Robinson's ideas which, Cushman had found, were not always practical.

The Pastor's reasons for this appointment were good enough. There was danger that the people from London and Billerica would feel that the Leyden Pilgrims, as the fathers of the venture, were attempting to monopolize all the important positions. The elder, the two deacons and Cushman, all were Leyden exiles. Pastor Robinson had got Martin appointed agent only about three weeks before. But this was long enough to convince Cushman that the little man was slippery and overbearing.

Brewster gave Cushman an enigmatic glance and said, "Then we'll appoint Master Martin and after the people have voted on the matter in meeting, he will be in charge of order and decency on the *Mayflower*."

"And where is the meeting to be?" asked someone.

Brewster looked about him, a little helplessly. "We shall require privacy but where we can find it, I don't know."

"Yonder on the sands, west of the quay, is a quiet spot," suggested Robert Cushman.

"Very good!" The elder nodded. "We shall want those who actually shared in the agreement with the Merchant Adventurers to be there. The six of us here had better go about notifying the others. It's now eight

o'clock.   I'll call the meeting to order at nine."   He
glanced hesitatingly at the steerage, then with a look of
resolution went in to brave the great cabin.

In spite of Master Jones' orders, Cushman did not follow him but set off with the others to round up the congregation.   This meeting would be one of the most important ever held by the Pilgrims; most important and,
Cushman feared, most unpleasant for himself.

# II

## *Tom Weston*

About half-past eight, Cushman went into the great cabin to fetch his portfolio of papers. All was harmony here. The women were arranging their beds and hanging curtains before their bunks, laughing and chatting most amicably. Mary Cushman was tucking the bedclothes snugly into bunk Number One.

"*Must* you have the portfolio?" she sighed. "I've put all your rubbish under the feather tick."

"But this is our covenant with the Adventurers, Mary!" he exclaimed. "Don't be too fond!" He grasped the tick and with one sweep of his arm rolled it back.

"Wait! Oh, you plowman!" she protested. "I'd have got it for you if— I loathe this voyage! Vile, crowded beds!"

"Hush, Mary! For very pride's sake!" whispered her husband. He seized the portfolio and thrust back the tick, now all lumpy and askew.

Mary instantly began patting and pushing the mass of feathers into shape. "See what a selfish man can do, Mistress Desire," she cried, "and be thankful you have no husband!"

The young woman's bunk was next to the Cushmans'. She did not turn her head. "I don't have to see to be thankful, Mistress Cushman!" She laughed.

Mary laughed too, and her husband, annoyed though he was, smiled and paused with the portfolio under his arm, looking from one woman to the other. They both ignored him. And suddenly, looking from John Carver's niece to his wife, it was as if Robert saw Mary after a long absence. Pretty, oh, very pretty she was, even at forty! She was fair, with hair which might be either palest blond or faintest gray. He had forgotten that once he had thought Mary looked like a Madonna and that he had supposed this look must be an index to her character; for Sarah, his first wife, had possessed this same maternal and saint-like expression. And Sarah had been his ideal of a wife—docile, kind, a little stupid (in his opinion women with brains were restless and demanding), a notable house-wife and a loving mother to their children.

In 1616, he had buried all the children, save little Tommy, and a month after the last dead baby had been laid in the Leyden churchyard, Sarah too had died and he had placed her there with their babies. In 1617, un-done by loneliness, he had married Mary who was a widow and childless. And childless she had remained. Perhaps it was as well. For Mary was not docile nor kind nor had she even pretended to love him. Well, he'd never loved her so 'twas fair enough.

She was tall and slender and she had the most lovely eyes he'd ever seen in a human head—large, black, clear like a child's, with sweeping, thick lashes and thinly arched innocent brows.

She bent over the feather bed, patting and smoothing. Desire Minter straightened from her task and looked at him. She had a candid gaze, he thought.

" 'One writ with me in sour misfortune's book,' " remarked Desire Minter.

Robert Cushman stared at her. The woman was cast-ing Shakespeare at him! And what a quotation! Did she refer to Mary or to himself? Anyhow, he disliked your forward, reading woman. He returned her smile but only because he couldn't help it and went out. Shakespeare or Ben Jonson alone could do justice to her laughter, he told himself as he stepped from the ship to the quay. Then he shrugged his shoulders and hurried on to overtake Tom Weston who was sauntering across the sands.

Tom had spent the night in Southampton, having had, he said, more than enough of the *Mayflower's* great cabin on the way down from London.

"Did you sleep well?" asked Robert, throwing his arm across his friend's shoulder.

Weston was a smaller man than Cushman. He was an ironmonger of London and he looked like one of the poets who frequented the Globe Theatre. He was small and trim with round blue eyes and supercilious clothes. He should have worn the plain dress of his calling, a grave-colored doublet and cloak and a treble ruff. Instead his ruff was single, his black doublet was slashed with scarlet and his hosen were mere loose black strips which displayed red silk trunks beneath. His red silk stockings were gartered beneath the knee with huge black bows and his hat bore a plume along its brim, while any girl would have envied him his blond curls.

He was an ironmonger, yes! But in his soul, Weston was such a man as had been Sir Walter Raleigh whom he adored; half pirate, half poet; half statesman, half politician; and wholly an Englishman.

"Did I sleep well?" repeated Tom, looking up at Robert. "No, I didn't, after all. I was a-worried about everything. I don't like the look of the fellow Martin's friends here in Southampton. It seems he's done all the purchasing of supplies while Deacon Carver's done other things, God knows what."

Robert nodded soberly. "We'll have a struggle with them but in the end their common sense will make them sign the agreement, and then the chief of us will see that they fulfill all the conditions. We'll never fail you, Tom."

"I know you won't, dear Robin, for any cause whatever. But as for the others! Well, your Elder Brewster is the soul of honor but a very babe in money matters. If a knave among you can prove to him that fulfilling the agreement is not fulfilling the Lord's will, the elder will wipe us out of his mind. Deacon Carver is the soul of honor but for reasons I don't yet understand, he's failed to grasp the situation in London. He's far more interested in your church discipline than in your money discipline. Deacon Fuller is the soul of honor. But still he wrote with those others from Leyden that he hoped he hadn't been deceived in Thomas Weston. Chris Martin, I know, has no more thought of honor than a beetle. That leaves only two among your chiefs, William Bradford and Edward Winslow. When I met them in Leyden at the time I made this colonizing proposal to you all, I thought them then the souls of honor. But since then I've read the carping, pin-sticking, ass-headed letters they've constantly written you and I tell you, Bob, I'm worried about our moneys."

"You needn't be!" returned Cushman stoutly. "Whatever Martin may be, the other four men have minds of extra quality. That's why they naturally lead the people. We'll make them see your viewpoint at this meeting and the generality will do as we five bid them."

Tom cocked a round blue eye comically at Robert. "There's no such creature as a five-headed tyrant, my

Bob! And don't forget this, that while the most of your people are almost unlettered and simple, they yet have a good opinion of their minds, and also because this matter touches their purses, they're going to be as hard to lead as pigs."

Robert gave his beloved Tom an indignant glance. After all, these same simple, unlettered Englishmen during their twelve years' exile in Holland had established a reputation for rectitude which had been attained by no other exiled church in the Low Country, French or English. They were a close-knit, law-abiding group and would permit themselves to be forced to pay their debts. And he told Tom so.

"But," insisted Tom, "there are only thirty-five of the Pilgrims who've undergone the discipline in Leyden under Pastor Robinson and your other leaders. The rest, from London, from Billerica and from—"

"Don't forget," interrupted Cushman, "that a good many of the rest have been foisted on us by you Merchant Adventurers."

"Granted!" nodded Weston. "But that only helps to prove my contention."

They were still arguing with each other when they reached the meeting place on the sands. They seated themselves a little apart so that they might continue the debate.

The Pilgrims gathered slowly, not more than fifty in all, for the women, the children and the servants formed nearly half of the congregation and not all the remainder had been able to purchase stock in the venture, so on such a question as this, they had no vote.

Elder Brewster arrived last of all and the people then

seated themselves, facing him as he stood with his back to the sea.

The elder was more than six feet in height and very gaunt. Since the summer of 1619, the King had been in hot pursuit of him for printing and smuggling into England certain highly seditious books and Brewster's natural thinness had worn almost to emaciation under the strain. He had a large, lean face with hazel eyes under straw-colored brows. His nose was Roman and his mouth thin but kindly and singularly sweet in expression. His hair, iron gray, he wore just touching the top of his ruff. His clothing was excellent in cut and all gray save that his elbow puffs and hosen were slashed with dark blue. He had worn his blue cloak and little round, truncated hat, both of Elizabethan date, during all the ten years Robert had known him and they added to his air of distinction. No one ever criticized the elder's elegance in dress. The people were proud of the distinguished early career to which his fine dress belonged.

Brewster stood before them now apparently quite unimpressed by the fact that the King's men still were searching for him and that he was in plain view of all Southampton.

"We'll first hear Master Cushman's report," he said.

Robert got up slowly. This was the first opportunity he'd had to justify himself by word of mouth and he proposed not to be hurried.

"Three years ago," he began, "you chose me, with Deacon Carver, to solicit the King His Majesty's permission to live as a distinct body in America under the general government of Virginia. Through friends we were to sue His Majesty that he grant us freedom of religion. We were to solicit the Virginia Company for permission to settle in their lands. When we had obtained the King His Majesty's sanction and the permit or patent from the Company, then we were to find the moneys to provide for our great venture. For though we sold all we possessed, it was not enough for so deep a business. Now, all these things we have done for you. We have—"

Young Winslow called out, "You've never got His Majesty's public permission to this day, Master Cushman, nor the Virginia Company's moneys!"

Robert's clear tones rose above the murmur of voices roused by Winslow and above the hiss of waves. "Yet yonder ride the *Mayflower* and the *Speedwell!*" he cried.

Their eyes followed his pointing finger but they were not going to let him think they were overimpressed.

"You've made bondslaves of us, Master Cushman!" shouted Winslow who, at twenty-five, was the mouthpiece of the younger faction. "Deacon Carver and the new agent, Master Martin, both say they didn't sign the agreement. Only you did that!"

Robert felt his cheeks redden. But still he kept hold on his tongue. During the three years their carping and nagging had been teaching him self-control and though he felt the matter of discipline had been overdone, he had, until now, not been over-resentful.

He managed to say calmly, "I've done nothing but what equity and necessity required. I explained the changes in our agreement to Deacon Carver and Master Martin who were here in Southampton purchasing the supplies. They wrote me that they agreed to the new conditions and that I must make what arrangements I could. It was too short a time to send you notice in Leyden. I'd have lost all. It's August now, my friends, and every day we spend here on the English coast adds to the dangers of the Atlantic crossing."

"We'll never confirm that agreement!" declared William Bradford loudly.

The chorus took the offered cue.

"No! Never! Never!"

"We'd better have had the Virginia Company's moneys!"

"If we were sailing for Guiana, as we ought, we'd needn't pother about weather!"

Robert looked them over, every face familiar. Fools! With no least conception of the weight of what they were undertaking or glimmer of the depth of difficulties he had overcome for them! Yet those of Leyden had been his friends when they had chosen him to represent them out of the three hundred who formed the congregation. They must have believed then that he had signal abilities. Himself, he knew he'd worked wisely for them, so far. Why couldn't they see that and trust his wisdom still further?

"We signed the agreement over a year ago with Master Weston," declared young Winslow, his round face very indignant, his brown eyes very bright. "What caused this sudden disaffection with it?"

Elder Brewster, an old hand at conducting meetings such as this, suddenly cleared his throat. It was a stentorian bugle note which never failed to bring silence. The people turned automatically from Cushman to the elder.

"I'll restate our affairs," said Brewster, "to make sure that our London brethren understand. Master Thomas Weston represents the gentlemen who have invested their moneys for the planting of our colony. He learned a year ago that we, the Leyden exiles, wished to remove to America. He knew or hoped that there were huge profits to be made by a contract with us."

"That's not wholly just!" called Weston.

Brewster ignored him. "He came to see Pastor Robinson and Master Cushman and several others of us in Holland and made his proposals to us whereby the Adventurers were to advance the moneys needed to transport us and provision us. It was, in short, a stock partnership between them and us with certain conditions which were to bind us for the next seven years. We were satisfied with this agreement and signed it and Master Weston took it back to London where, we supposed, his Merchant friends were also satisfied with it.

"But it seems the other Merchant Adventurers were unwilling to pay us money until two conditions of the agreement were changed. The earlier agreement said, among other things, that at the end of seven years, each man might keep the house and garden he'd made but that all other profits got by trade, work or fishing must be equally divided between the Merchants and the Colonists. The earlier terms also agreed that each man should have two full days a week in which to work on his own house and garden and private affairs.

"But the agreement which Master Cushman has signed says that the houses and gardens also must be yielded up for division among all and that all our time, toil and products must belong to the common stock. We're not to have even those two days."

The elder was being perfectly accurate and completely unfair, thought Robert. But he made no protest and the elder went on.

"Last month, when word reached Leyden by our pilot that these changes had been made, Pastor Robinson wrote in firm protest to both Deacon Carver and Master Cush-man. So did a committee of our brethren, violently pro-testing that we would set sail to the new world under no such terms of slavery. Yet, in spite of all this, Robert Cushman signed the agreement. And I must say that his weight with us was vastly overestimated by Thomas Weston."

Robert, who was still standing, began to feel his self-control weaken. No one knew better than William Brew-ster how near the whole migration had been to failing the past few weeks. Robert had been in constant touch with the elder in his hiding place in London and had done all he could to ease his situation while keeping him informed about all the Pilgrim business. He couldn't believe that Elder Brewster meant all that he had insinuated. Or had he?

For three years now, Robert had not been carding wool in a back alley of a Dutch city. He had been living in the great world. Was this world's view of the Separatists as men of mean spirit, back-biting, disloyal—

He interrupted his own thoughts to say, bluntly, "The hard fact remains, Elder Brewster, that Sir George Farrer withdrew his two thousand pounds because of his dislike for those two conditions and all the rest would have fol-lowed him if I hadn't altered the terms. The fact also remains that when I made the changes, all the rest paid their moneys in at once, except the four hundred pounds which Master Weston has with him now. In other words, the Merchant Adventurers have kept faith with us, but we, having spent their moneys, now propose to break faith with them."

"There's no faith about it!" exclaimed Deacon Samuel Fuller who was by way of being a leech, a stout kindly man whom everyone liked. "They're in it solely for profit. They'd take our shoes along with our houses if they could."

"And if for the matter of a house or two we'd draw back, then we're in it solely for profit ourselves," returned Robert. "And what will our houses amount to if we follow the experience of Sir Walter Raleigh and Captain John Smith? They say to build among the savages only such shelters as we can set fire to and run away from, with little grief. If we make money in the colony, we mustn't at first spend it on pomp and fine mansions. We'll employ our riches to buy more ships and men."

"Who gave you leave to tell us how to spend our shillings, Robert Cushman?" demanded a surly voice. "How do we know you haven't already put some of them on your back? Silk stockings on legs that ought to be wearing wool!" This was Isaac Allerton.

"We all believe Master Cushman is honorable!" protested William Mullins, a Surrey man. He was not one of the Leyden Pilgrims but as he had bought nine shares of common stock in the venture, he had a large voice in its affairs. "But I won't sign this new covenant," he added. "I paid over my money to him, after reading a copy of the first agreement which he showed me. I never would have paid in on the new terms—and remember this, Master Cushman, no matter what the Merchant Adventurers profit or don't profit, our hazard's greater than theirs."

"True, Master Mullins," agreed Robert. Then he asked bitterly, "But did *they* egg us on to this venture? Did *they* ask us to take the hazard? No! It was all our own idea and they made possible its carrying out with their moneys. If we didn't want to go, they'd have been quite content not to pay."

"I wish they'd kept their money!" shouted Mullins. "If only I had mine back I'd gladly go home."

"And I!"

"And I!"

"And I!"

The clamor of disaffection drowned the rising tide. Robert could have drawn his dagger and run through any of them. Traitors! But he stood rigid and silent, his eyes on the *Mayflower*. Jones was moving her away from the quay now to save the wharf fee and was anchoring her opposite their place on the sands. They were repudiating the ship, of course, along with the conditions.

They were calling him hard names now. "Fool!" "Gull!"

As if he had had any purpose in his head or heart for years but the planting of this colony where one's children's children would be English and not Dutch!

Elder Brewster again cleared his long windpipe and again there was quiet. "You realize by now, Master Weston, I hope, that we won't confirm the agreement," he remarked.

"Yes!" Indignation made Tom's voice shake. "And I realize also that you're churlish as well as mean, dull as well as dishonest! You speak of Robert Cushman as if he were a cheating apprentice. Yet yonder ships are his and his alone, for at the last, my friends and I have done business with you all only because we trusted him. The rest of you are mere Brownists, Separatists, Nonconformists; mean, pinching, scrounging! Why, if you'd cease your perpetual discussing and nagging—"

Robert caught his friend's hand. "No! No! Let me speak, Tom!"

Weston shook his head, ground his teeth, gave his tiny blond mustache a vicious twist and plunged on.

"I tell you again, that if it hadn't been for Robert Cushman's skill and sense of honorableness and his deep, true love for England, the King's Majesty wouldn't have given even his *private* consent to the planting of the colony. It was due to Master Cushman that the Virginia Company was beguiled into granting a patent and due to him that when the Virginia Company became too tedious, my fellow merchants came forward and took the business out of the Virginia Company's sluggish clutch."

Robert threw his arm over his friend's shoulder. "Dear Tom, don't give me graces I don't possess or credits I don't deserve! You'll merely change their sneers to laughter!"

Then he could bear no more. He turned and walked rapidly westward along the sands.

# III

## *Repudiation*

As he walked, everything blurred for a moment; little waves on golden sands, great blue waves dancing beyond and the pale blue English sky. Then he was conscious again of that most primal of all smells: of the sea; of the salt, dread deep; and his will-power came into its own again. He seated himself on a log at the edge of a copse, facing the vast, land-locked harbor where ships from all over the world were spread before his eyes.

Madagascar! Zanzibar! Teneriffe! The Levant! Cathay! The words sang like wind in the rigging. Sound of twisted capstan, clank of anchor chains, all the magic business of ships rang in his ears. Little crayers loaded with coastal goods, small, swift pinnaces on the King's affairs, sloop-rigged hoys in from the Low Countries, four-masted caravels, merchantmen, men-o'-war—all these ravished his eyes. For Cushman was an Englishman, nurtured in the wonder of Elizabeth's reign and the sea drew him with a witchery, peculiar and powerful.

And now! He gave a mighty groan. It looked as if the splendid voyage was not to be, for the initial expenses of the venture were the very least of it. The Merchant Adventurers were to have supported them through the first lean years of colonization, and without such support Robert believed they must starve just as the folk of Jamestown had starved. The Pilgrims seemed not to have realized that fact. Could he make them realize it? They were so out of conceit with him now that it seemed impossible for him to have the slightest influence on them. Where had he first failed them? Perhaps, he told himself, in not having foreseen this very end! He knew how poverty had eaten into the spiritual vitals of these people. He knew that although the glorification of a free God was one motive for their crossing the ocean-sea, equally powerful was their desperate need for bread. Even their children's palms were calloused! The very babes of the Leyden Pilgrims must work or starve. He had been dull to think that he could beguile such people into giving up their houses, their bits of garden.

But what else could he have done? After years of seeking, the Merchant Adventurers were their sole hope of English help. The Dutch government would have established them on the Hudson. But *Dutch?* Never, while Elizabeth's tongue was sweet! And even without knowledge of today's disaffections, the Merchant Adventurers were utterly weary of the Pilgrims; of their squabbling, their niggardliness, their priggishness. Tom Weston, himself, would be glad to be shut of them.

He was, after this dismal review, fully convinced that he could not move them to honor his signature on the Agreement. And thus, he thought, the dream ended! He shook his head, eyes wistfully on the *Mayflower*.

In all this harbor full of ships, he saw none he would have preferred for their business. She was sound and proven seaworthy by many ocean voyages and by the fact that she had been a wine-carrier. Only vessels completely sound in the hull could procure that trade. She was of medium size. He could have got a larger merchant ship but it would have been proportionately slower and harder to handle. Even the *Mayflower* required a crew of fifty men! The larger the vessel, the greater the expense. The chartering of the *Mayflower* was costing them some six hundred pounds a month. They could have afforded no more even had a ship of one hundred and eighty tons not been adequate for their needs.

He and Weston had found the *Mayflower* only after months of careful investigation. Robert had begun his search immediately following the interview with the King. James had gone to his head like too much sack! He actually had believed they would sail within the twelvemonth. This was in 1618. And yet—

For the thousandth time Robert recalled that quarter of an hour in Whitehall. The tapestried walls. The firelight on a rich rug. The tall figure with large, uneasy head.

"What," asked His Majesty, "is the purpose of this plantation?"

"To leave the Low Countries, Sire, for fear our children won't grow up to be English. We seem likely there to lose our language and our name of English. We want to go to a land where we can enjoy liberty of conscience under Your Majesty's gracious protection."

James rolled great blue eyes at his subject and Robert, perceiving a twinkle in those eyes, hastened to add,

"Of course, we could try to enlarge Your Majesty's dominions while we spread the Gospel!"

"And what of your known weakness of faith?" asked the King.

"Sire," replied Robert, "we presented to your Privy Council last year seven articles signed by our pastor and our elder in Leyden. These specifically assent to the Articles of the Established Church and acknowledge the

King His Majesty's authority and that of the bishops and other ecclesiastical officers."

Robert had heard that James could be very kind when his personal interests were not concerned. He beckoned Robert closer and leaned on his shoulder. The King liked a comely man. "That's a good and honest motion! But how shall you live? I hear it's a mere desert waste."

"By fishing, Your Majesty," answered Cushman.

The King smiled. He had a gentle smile. "So God have my soul, 'twas the Apostles' own calling!" He turned to his secretary. "Attend to this," he said.

Robert kissed the royal hand and backed out, his blood ringing in his ears. He forgot that this same King was keeping poor Raleigh in the Tower under death sentence and that with the rest of England he was furious with His Majesty. He only remembered that James, for one blinding second, seemed like an affectionate, understanding friend. Afterward—

Well, two days afterward, the King said the Pilgrims had better consult with the Archbishop of Canterbury and the Bishop of London about their freedom of worship. This, of course, would mean a stillbirth for the colony. The bishops would never swallow Pastor Robinson's and Elder Brewster's seven articles! In the shock of disappointment, Robert found courage to tell the King's secretary he'd have nothing to do with the Archbishop.

That personage nodded. "Go on with your plantation! His Majesty won't molest you if you are peaceable. But he can't give his public authority under his seal. He'd have the strict churchmen about his ears immediately."

The splendid moment was shadowed. "I was too quickly impressed by His Majesty," Robert said, bitterly. "We'll hope that his private approval will suffice!"

It did suffice. The Virginia Company granted the patent. But the meeting with the King was entered in the Pilgrims' books as one of Robert's failures.

He was musing unhappily on this ungraciousness of his fellows when Thomas Weston sat down beside him.

"Robin," said Tom, "I'm going back to London with my four hundred pounds and a sore heart. Come back with me and, by God, I'll find us a ship and we'll set out in Drake's track round the world! Just you and me and the crew!"

"I'm grieved and I'm ashamed of them," groaned Robert.

Tom laid his hand on his friend's arm. "They aren't worth what you've given them, Robin."

"But they are!" protested Robert. "That's my chiefest difficulty! Ignorant and obstinate as they are, still they're worth any effort of mine to move them over there. I could destroy them where they sit; run them through with pleasure, toss them into the sea or what you will, the niggardly, shortsighted fools! But still I know that those thirty-five from Leyden and at least a round dozen of the others are worth more than I can do for them. Not in all England is there fiber so tough. They have souls of whit-leather. Look you! The Leyden congregation was made up of three hundred English folk who were strong enough to leave their England to starve in Holland for God. And of that congregation, these are the very pick. They dare to give up safe Holland to be killed by savages across the seas, in order that they and their children may be men, not slaves. They're worth everything—the fools!"

Tom had followed him with eyes at first half angry and now gave a laugh that was half a sob. "Dear fool, yourself!" he exclaimed. "In a degree you're right. But at

the last, their whit-leather souls have failed them. They
*won't* ratify the agreement. They're wondering now how
to get their own small moneys back. Our large sums may
go hang!"

Robert gave his friend an anguished look. "What can
I do?"

Tom gave him a slight push. "You can go stand beside
your Elder Brewster and try to show the canting dullards
what you feel about this colony. Have you told anyone
but me? Oh, I know. You've prated about spreading the
Gospel among the savages who don't want it at any price,
Bob,—and never once have you shared with them your
real dreams. Do you realize that these people think of
you as selfish, calculating, cold—"

"Not cold, Tom!" protested Robert.

"What? With that withdrawn gaze and that disen-
chanted mouth? Look in your mirror, Bob! Why, I
thought that of you, myself, until we hunted ships together and I caught you with your cheek rubbing the
*Mayflower's* mizzenmast as it were a mistress's curls. Then
I had you, my Robin! By God, then I knew your very
costards! And you never could hide your poet's self from
me again! But to the rest of the world you are remote.
Come! Am I not the only human being who calls you
Robin?"

"Yes," admitted the other soberly. He was not enjoying Tom's portraiture. "But they liked me well enough
to make me their agent."

Tom grinned. "They knew you were a man of parts.
It was Brewster and Robinson who appointed you. Poor
old Bob! But look you! If only once you could tell them
your dream of an England that compasses the globe! Of
our sweet English speech—Ben Jonson's and Shakespeare's

and that darling fool Nash's—of our tongue, spoken in every spot that saw Drake and the *Golden Hind!* Go and tell them, Robert, with your eyes shining as I've seen Raleigh's shine, and they'll follow you to the Outer Shades."

"You know I can't!" said Cushman through set teeth. "I'd only make them laugh. Don't torture me, Tom!"

"You can try, you *Brownist!*" roared Tom, hurling at him the epithet he knew Robert most disliked. "You can all talk God and Christ as easily as you wipe your noses. That's your stock in trade. But the Crusades are long past. You have to give modern Englishmen, even Brownists, something more and vastly braver to move 'em over the vasty seas."

Red and angry, Cushman turned on his friend. "You're speaking of what you don't understand! How could I go before that sneering crowd and speak of the things I told you in the sacred confidences of friendship? My feelings about England are like the feelings one has for a woman loved as a man loves once or never in this life; just so intimate and to be mentioned only to the one friend." He turned away with a gesture of hopelessness.

Tom threw his arm about him. "Forgive me, Robin! But to see you so misjudged is almost as hard on me as seeing my poor moneys lost!" He grinned ruefully.

"It looks as if I as well as your pounds were lost," grinned Robert in return. "But I *can* talk pounds! I'll try that again."

He started back along the sands, followed slowly by Tom. He could state a case clearly, he told himself, as he walked. But he could no more win men with oratory than could a crow. Why, little Winslow, who was so apt to be mistaken in his judgments, could do more with the brethren with a single sentence than he could in an hour's speech.

But he drove himself toward the spot where the congregation still sat in shrill argument. And as he moved, he tried to marshal his thoughts. He would try to beguile them into taking no action on the agreement just now. If he could succeed in this, he would have all the voyage in which to work on their understanding and when they reached America and saw how essential was the support of the Adventurers all would be well. By the time he reached the elder's side he was quite hopeful again.

"What do you want?" asked Brewster. Even his patience was wearing thin. The arguments were in full swing.

"I want to ask them to take no vote on the conditions just yet. Quieten them, prithee," begged Robert.

The elder looked puzzled but obediently he cleared his throat. There came a reluctant silence.

"Master Cushman has something to say," announced Brewster.

"Look you!" cried Robert. "You've sold all you own on earth and vested it in those two ships over there. How can you get your share of money out of them without loss? And suppose you do get back to Leyden? Where you only went hungry before, you will be now taken in custody as public charges. So you *must* go to America. But you can't leave Southampton unless you pay up what you owe here, nearly four hundred pounds. Master Weston will not give you that sum unless you sign the agreement. You won't sign, you say. But why say that? Why not leave the agreement alone till we reach America? Master Weston, to be sure, will not disgorge the four hundred on the deferment but you can raise the money yourselves if you sell a portion of our one luxury, our casks of butter."

Elder Brewster muttered, "That may answer, please God!"

And even in the anxiety of the moment, Robert realized that the hunted man must be in an agony of desire to be off on the safe seas. His calm patience was beyond praise.

The people were turning Cushman's words over in their minds.

"The butter!" shrilled Christopher Martin. "You can't sell the butter! I was three weeks bargaining for it!"

Captain Standish spoke in his clean-cut quick way. He was small and fair. "Mayhap, Master Martin, if you hadn't been so hot after butter, you'd have provided every man with a sword to his side. As it is, we've butter for twice our number and arms for less than half of us."

Edward Winslow—who had not realized, Robert thought, that his vehemence against the conditions might lead to the ruination of the voyage for which he yearned second only to Cushman's self—now called out, pleasantly,

"This is the diplomacy for which Master Weston has praised our Master Cushman! We refused to support him yet he *butters* us! Let's take his excellent advice, my friends."

"You mean, Ned, that after all your hours of raving, you'll go to America thus?" demanded William Bradford incredulously. Bradford was thirty; tall, big-boned, full-faced, the scholar of the Pilgrim group.

"We aren't signing the new conditions, are we?" returned Winslow.

There was another short silence, broken by Master Mullins, who growled, "Very well, then, sell the butter."

They put it to a vote and only Christopher Martin voted nay. Then the elder dismissed the congregation.

Tom Weston, who had listened to the debate with increasing restlessness, now drew Cushman out of hearing of the rest. "But see what you've done, Robert! All this doesn't deceive *me!* *You, too, have repudiated the Merchant Adventurers.* It's unthinkable! You're mad!"

"The important thing is to get them to America, Tom!" cried Robert. "I can manage to get them to ratify it there when they face the wilderness without your backing."

"No!" roared Weston. "I don't trust them! Our moneys, Robert, our moneys!"

Cushman answered with equal violence, "We'll repay to the last shilling! I give you my word. But if you've ever loved me, lay no straw in our way. Let us go. We *must* go."

His voice startled Tom. He stared at Robert, light blue eyes holding dark blue.

"I'm so passioned for this venture," the words tore painfully from Robert, "I'm so passioned for it that sometimes I think I'm touched in the head. Let us go, Tom!"

Sudden tears softened the ironmonger's gaze. He flung up both his hands. "Get away from England quickly, then, Robin. Be safe in the Atlantic before I reach London, for they may send the bailiffs after ye!"

"Heaven knows how ashamed I am of us!" blurted out Robert. "But we *will* repay."

"As far as I am concerned, I leave it in trust to you," said Tom; "but my fellow Merchants will be furious, fit to bite collops of flesh out of your necks. But I trust *you,* Robert."

"Thank you, from my soul," whispered Cushman.

Tom took his hand and they stood with fingers entwined, looking on the glories of the harbor.

" 'To hold acquaintance with the waves,' " murmured the ironmonger. "Bob, I shall come over to you in a year or so and we'll explore all that Virginia coast."

"And collect somewhat of our debts to you in beaver and cod, mayhap?" asked Robert slyly. "Will you come now for a last look at the *Mayflower*, Tom?"

"Not I, thanks! I'm off to meet my troubles in London! The *Falcon* galley sails at flood tide so I must say farewell now."

Neither spoke further. They continued to stare with blind eyes on Hampton Waters. Then, abruptly, Tom pulled Robert's face down to his, kissed him on each cheek and turning, ran rapidly toward the ancient quay.

# IV

## *William Brewster*

A QUEER sort of dizziness which had troubled Robert, of late, now troubled him again and he sat down on a rock, burying his face in his hands. There was a twist of pain above his heart that he thought had been roused by the parting with Tom. Any unusual stress of feeling would do this; as if the pain were a chained dog, quiet till its tail was trod upon.

The dizziness passed after a time but still he sat dully wondering how he was to face the new problems of the venture without Weston at his elbow. Some day, perhaps, he would find words with which to make the elder and the other chiefs appreciate what Tom had done for them all. Certainly, he had been the very backbone of the colony on its material side. Yes, and on its gallant, lion-hearted, impetuous side, no one had given as much as this dearest of ironmongers. As for what Tom Weston had given him: of companionship, of love, of understanding, of a widened horizon, of a more beautiful vision of living, Robert never would be able to explain to anyone. But this he could say: that though there were many famous friendships in England, Sir Philip Sidney's with Lord Brooke, Beaumont's with Fletcher, or even the King's with Buckingham, still there was none nobler nor sweeter than the friendship of the unknown Thomas Weston for the unsung Robert Cushman.

He found comfort in this thought and in his mind was

writing a letter telling Tom of it, when a familiar clearing of the throat roused him. The elder had followed him to his resting place on the log and now sat down beside him.

Robert looked up at him coldly. It was hard to forgive the older man for what he believed was an unfairness amounting to deception. Nor was Robert afraid to show Brewster his resentment. Other Pilgrims might humble themselves before the elder because of his superior social position. But Cushman, too, was of yeoman stock and would bow the knee to no one of his own class. He admitted that Brewster's experiences in the diplomatic service under William Davison had given him a polish which set him apart from the farmers, craftsmen and laborers who formed the bulk of the Leyden congregation. This early experience had marked Brewster. Even the servants of Elizabeth's servants bore her impress of intrepidity and a certain elegance of address.

But Robert's three years of close contact with secretaries and privy councilors of the King and his intimacy with Tom Weston's friends, who were poets, dramatists, soldiers, politicians and wealthy merchants, had made him, too, a man of the great world. And there was no spirit of meekness in his voice when he said to the elder,

"You owe me an apology, sir!"

The elder raised his eyebrows. "For what, prithee?"

Robert gazed levelly into the tired hazel eyes opposite his. "You didn't help me make the people understand how close the whole venture came to falling down, last month, and that but for my signing those conditions, they'd still be sitting on their bundles in Leyden, their moneys tied up so that they could neither go nor stay. You said in London I'd done well. Why didn't you say so here?"

"Because, in London, you'd made me see only your side," replied Brewster. "Here, I learned how the others felt and I sympathize with them. Those conditions *are* too hard."

"I wish Pastor Robinson were here!" exclaimed Robert. "I could always make him see facts as they are."

"Better be glad that he isn't," said Brewster with a twisted smile. "He wrote me last week that the Pilgrims had made two mistakes, first, because we'd not informed ourselves well enough on all details of the venture and, second, because we'd employed Robert Cushman."

"What?" gasped Robert.

"It wasn't my intendment to tell you," Brewster's mouth was stern, "but I gathered from your talk at the meeting that you overvalued your services to us and so I think it best for you to know what a man of the pastor's parts thinks."

"Why, I thought he was my loving friend!" This was a very heavy blow to Robert.

"We're all loving to one another, certainly," the elder nodded. "But that mustn't prevent our open recognition of each other's faults, as you know. The pastor said you had an excellent ability but that you'd shewn yourself unfit to deal for other men because you were indifferent to their feelings. And for good measure, he said we'd had little from you but conditions, conditions, suppositions, suppositions."

White and shaken, Robert got to his feet. "I see nothing for me but to gather up my wife and son and leave the plantation."

"You never have taken correction well, Robert!" sighed

the elder. "You didn't tell me in London you were actually going to *sign* those conditions."

But Robert was perfectly familiar with Brewster's capacity for quibbling and he often had taken a perverse pleasure in meeting quibble with quibble. But suddenly now he was unutterably weary, body and soul.

"Come, let's end it!" He groaned. "I'm ill of the whole affair. My very bowels are turmoiled with accusations and debates." He swung on his heel and started back for the quay.

But Brewster strode after him and caught him by the arm. "No! You still have work to do for us, Robert. The congregation has agreed to that. You made a mistake based on arrogance. We agreed to forgive the mistake and humble your pride by requiring you to act as assistant to Christopher Martin in governing the *Mayflower.*"

Cushman stared at the elder. At first, he couldn't speak for resentment. Then as the absurdity of the situation cleared itself from the fog of words, he began to laugh; cynically, it is true. But it *was* laughter and Brewster looked relieved as well as puzzled.

"At any rate," gasped Robert, "you and the congregation evidently agree with me in looking on Master Martin as a scourge! Elder, either you are mad or I am!"

"Mad?" a little stiffly.

"Aye!" laughing again. "It's like a comedy! A jury of fools judging another fool!"

"Stop!" shouted Brewster. "You're not attending the play with Master Weston! Your language, Robert!"

"It's true! I'm not attending the play," agreed Robert. "But more seriously, elder, how could one as arrogant as I hope to cope with Master Martin's arrogance?"

"That's the very purpose!" nodded Brewster. "From what they saw on the voyage down, the people believe you're the only one who can cope with him. John Carver is too kindly. William Bradford and Edward Winslow are too young, and Samuel Fuller, too hasty to strive with him. No, you're our only hope!"

"As a punishment for my zeal for the venture and because I am arrogant?" Again Robert burst into laughter, but this time there was no cynicism in it. Suddenly his fellow Pilgrims seemed very children to him and the laughter wiped out his resentment. A very sweet smile transformed his thin face. "When do I present myself to my new master?" he asked.

"Ah!" Brewster sighed with relief. "We've cleared that shoal! As for when, I'll take you to visit the *Speedwell* with me, first. The master wants to talk to me and I'd like to have you present as you know more than the rest of us about ships. Afterward, we'll try to find Martin. He left in a huff over the butter and so was not present when your appointment was made."

Robert nodded and the two started again for the quay. Cushman's burst of mirth had left him depressed. John Robinson's words still stuck like a dagger in his throat. Had the pastor been right? Was he a conceited fool? There must be some reason for such concurrence of opinion. He wondered if his association with Tom and Tom's friends had changed him. They had liked him, praised him, sought his ideas. Perhaps he *had* grown arrogant. Well, he'd soon be cured! He could feel Brewster's vague distrust of his friendship with the Adventurers. John Carver avoided him. William Bradford eyed him thoughtfully. Winslow had been openly hostile. It

seemed that he was to sail without a friend among those
who so long had been his associates. His very wife was
against him, she so loathed the idea of the wilderness.
Poor Mary! Mistress Minter had cheered her though!
That lovely laughter! He found himself, in spite of his
sore heart, smiling again at the memory of it.

They were approaching the *Speedwell*. She was a pretty
little ship, flush-decked, with a very small forecastle and
poop. Tiny as she was she bore two masts and a bowsprit
and had the added advantage of the eight sweeps to move
her in calms or tight corners. Small ships fit for a sea
voyage were hard to procure and the Pilgrims had been
fortunate to find her.

Her supplies were now aboard her and were being
stowed in her hold. As the two visitors came aboard, the
master came from below to greet them. He was, indeed,
a *very* fat man and he outclothed the *Mayflower's* master.
His boots had huge embroidered cuffs out of which his
legs sprang like twin kegs. Red hosen, revealing black
trunks, met yellow stockings above the sea boots. His yellow peascod doublet, much soiled, was topped by a fash-
ionable lace collar, wired high about his ears. His head
was extraordinarily small with stringy black hair falling
to his shoulders. A little pointed black beard under a
long nose and little yellow eyes completed the picture.
He was one of the Leyden appointees and a stranger to
Robert.

"You find me ready like the Virgins, sirs," he remarked
in a very pleasant, quiet voice. "When do the rest of my
provisions come aboard? Mayhap you'll come to my cabin
to talk the matter over?"

"Your passengers are satisfied with their quarters?"

asked Robert as they followed the seaman across the ship's tiny waist to the great cabin. This comprised the entire superstructure aft, for there was no poop, and still it was just large enough for four locker beds and a table. When the three men stowed themselves around the room there was no more space left.

"No, they aren't, but what can they do or I, either?" asked Reynolds. "Ben, go and fetch some ale!" The cabin boy, an atom with dirty cheeks and frightened eyes, flew to do his bidding.

Robert sighed. "I know! Still, once you're in the *Speedwell's* hold, I suppose it's snug enough."

"The women find it too snug," grunted Reynolds. "But it's too late now to try to provide luxuries for females." He nodded to the boy who placed three dripping tankards on the table. "Tell me when to expect the rest of my provisions, friends. I have come to you about it, elder, because I can get satisfaction from no one else. Master Martin pretends to be in control of the food. He says I am now completely provisioned. I say I have but a fortnight's supply."

Brewster looked at Cushman.

Robert shrugged his shoulders. "The matter of the provisions was taken out of Weston's and my hands by the pastor," he explained. "We had planned to buy them in Kent. I was told to remain in London to receive the moneys while Deacon Carver and Master Martin did the purchasing here. Of course, each ship should be self-contained for the entire voyage."

"Right!" exclaimed the master. "When do I get the remainder of my food?"

Robert looked at the elder.

"Where's Deacon Carver?" asked Brewster.

"But he knows nothing," said Reynolds, "for he was obliged, he told me, to go to Leyden at the last and Chris Martin took over all moneys, as treasurer, and so did all the purchasing. And this is what I think of Martin!" Reynolds made a sound as of belching.

"Don't be unseemly, Master Reynolds!" protested the elder. "Master Martin's only desire is to make adequate preparation for this perilous voyage!"

"He's more likely to make the voyage perilous!" snorted the ship's master. "Feathering his own nest! The fellow's only a chapman, buying and selling God knows what!"

"Be silent!" Brewster's great voice drowned Reynolds' suave tones. "You shall have your provisions!" He took a deep drink from his tankard as did the others.

Outside the window gulls called and swooped.

"A fair share is all I ask," said Reynolds, firmly. "The question is, What does your precious Martin reckon a fair share? The most of the provisions are stowed in the *Mayflower*. All the chief men of the colony are aboard the *Mayflower*. We, of the *Speedwell*, believe that *you'll* all feed even if the *Speedwell's* passengers and crew go hungry."

Elder Brewster flushed and rose. "I'll look into this," he remarked.

Robert rose with him, ruffling his hair thoughtfully. Was there unhappy truth in the master's allegations? Well—the food was not his affair.

But Brewster paused in the doorway to look back at Reynolds. "Master Cushman will interview Christopher Martin and will let you know when to expect your victualing. I bid you good day, Master Reynolds."

Reynolds' little yellow eyes were twinkling. "Master Cushman has my sympathy!" he remarked.

The elder appeared not to hear and strode out onto the deck.

The irrepressible Reynolds continued to smirk at Cushman. "If you need any help with Chris Martin, friend, I can give you a maggot will itch him where he can't scratch!"

"I shall ask the elder to give the task to Deacon Carver," said Cushman. "I'd rather not mix in the affair."

"Of a certainty you'll ask someone else to do the mean task," still in the pleasant voice. "That's the way the Pilgrims make a plantation."

"Is it?" Robert halted in his progress toward the door. "Is it?" he repeated, but he was asking himself the question.

"What I want is food, not conversation!" Reynolds shrugged his huge yellow shoulders. "I can converse most amiably, myself, on any known subject and some unknown."

Something in the fellow's impudence amused Robert. He was one of Robinson's brands snatched from the burning. The pastor had hired him to navigate the pinnace to America and there to remain for a year. The little ship had been outfitted in Holland under the pastor's own supervision. Neither Cushman nor Carver had had any responsibility in the matter. Reynolds, they had heard, was an experienced seaman and that is all they knew about him.

"My need is for food," repeated Reynolds. "Does it require a special session of prayer to find me that?" clasping his hands and rolling his eyes heavenward with so ridiculous a face that Robert felt his lips twitch.

"I'll do my best to get your provisions for you!" he exclaimed, and hurried after the elder.

Brewster was waiting for him on the quay and they took a boat out to the *Mayflower*.

"He's an ill-bred varlet!" was Brewster's only remark on this short row.

# V

## The Speedwell

As they gained the deck of the *Mayflower,* Robert's young son rushed to meet him. Tommy had escaped the rigors of Leyden for three years so his cheeks were full and ruddy and he had lost the Dutch accent which thickened the speech of his less fortunate little mates. He was dark, as his mother had been, yet in feature he bore a marked resemblance to Robert, who doted on the lad.

"Father!" shrieked Tommy, seizing his father's arm. "We've all worked like slaves, stowing our goods, but now it's done, Master Martin won't let us go ashore! There's a bear-baiting in Southampton and a fair and King Canute's palace. And we'll never have a chance to see such again."

A noisy crowd of men and boys was standing beside the main-hatch. Christopher Martin was berating them.

Elder Brewster disappeared into the steerage. Young John Alden, hired to look after the beer casks, called laughingly, "Help! For sweet pity's sake! A rescue!"

John Billington, a huge Londoner in blue fustian doublet and hosen, one of the young married men, roared, "Lookee, masters! We are free men going to a free land! There'll be trouble if you try this on us!"

Captain Standish sauntered up. Small though he was, he was an experienced soldier whom Tom Weston had persuaded to undertake the organization of the colony's defense.

"Come, Master Martin," he cried sharply, "these young folks only want a last look at civilization! I'm going into the town, myself, and I'll see to their safe return."

"Don't dare dictate to me, sirrah!" shrilled little Martin, his pointed beard working up and down and the cast in his black eyes prominent.

A group of sailors in the forecastle door shouted with laughter. "Hear the little game cock! Whose dunghill is it, Masters?"

Martin shook his fist at them. John Billington lounged forward. He was large and sullen and sandy, not unhandsome, with a light curling beard and thick red hair. Robert glanced at Standish, prepared to help him if the captain decided to interfere.

And then interference came from an unexpected quarter. Out of the steerage minced Mistress Martin, absolutely overwhelming in a wheel-farthingale and her hair dressed high. She pushed up to Christopher and put a fat hand on his shoulder.

"Come, Chris," she said, "you have butter to sell for these fools who don't know their minds." She pushed him across the deck. "Let them go ashore and get drunk and get left behind! Now help me down into that slop-basin they call a boat."

The whole ship watched fascinated, as with immense puffing and sweating on the husband's part and with wild shrieks and scolding on the wife's, the descent into the cockboat was made.

"It's as if a great barnyard goose led a ferret by the nose," murmured Standish, smoothing his blond mustache, his blue eyes dancing. "I'm glad I'm living 'tween decks.

My wife and I have decided to try one of the cabins, there."

"I hope Mistress Standish won't find it too boisterous," said Cushman. "You must choose the largest cabin, if you can call those rude partitions cabins."

"She's a soldier's wife, every inch of her, and I've never heard her complain about anything, not even me!" smiled the captain. "As for the passengers' quarters in general, if you hear complaints, don't heed them. This ship is a doge's palace compared with what most of 'em are used to!"

Robert felt a rush of gratitude toward the soldier. "It's the first word of praise I've heard of my beautiful ship from a passenger," he exclaimed. "My thanks, captain!"

Tommy nudged his father's arm. Standish grinned. "Tommy's my first recruit. I now have an army of one! I'll take him into the town with me, unless you're going, Master Cushman."

"I am tied here," replied Robert with regret. He'd have enjoyed a junket with Standish. "Tommy, behave yourself as a soldier with the captain and no bear-baiting."

"Come along, Tommy," cried Standish, "before we're forbidden the fair too!" And pulling the delighted boy's arm within his own he sauntered off.

Cushman stood in thought. Since Martin was not available for a while, he'd embrace the opportunity to get Master Jones' opinion on the food situation. He had great confidence in Jones.

The portfolio, which after all he had not opened, was still under his arm and he crossed the steerage to the great cabin to dispose of it. There were several people here, sitting on the edges of their bunks in various occupations. Desire Minter was reading. She did not look up as Robert thrust the portfolio under his pillow. She should have risen and curtseyed as the other women did. After all, he was one of the chief men. He hoped she wasn't toploftical with her learning. He had heard that she'd been living in an aristocratic Puritan family. Women easily got above themselves.

She had taken off her cap. Her dark hair was very thick and silken; soft, one might suppose, to the touch. He stared at the open book. It was poetry! Sir Philip Sidney's sonnets! He cleared his throat. Still she did not look up, and, very indignant, he stalked out. But going up the companionway to the poop, he suddenly chuckled. Just why was he indignant with a strange female for an alleged failing for which he also was under indictment? But what lovely hair!

Christopher Jones was smoking in the poop cabin which was sacred to the ship's officers. It was very commodious, being about fifteen feet square with a table in its middle and locker beds under the several windows. Beams and walls were painted white; a pleasant room.

There were maps spread on the table. The master was poring over them. "Only the French can make maps," he growled to Robert. "The English won't take pains."

"The English travel so much and so far they have no time and must leave map-making to the stay-at-home nations," said Robert with a grin.

Jones returned the grin. "I've no good map, though, of Northern Virginia, or New England as I suppose we must call it now. I'm trying to find a probable landing place on this map of Captain Smith's. He's drawn it with great curiosity. Perhaps he did it in his sleep! I saw these shores once but they were not thus."

Robert bent over the table with him, absorbed for a

moment in the vital and still unsettled question of the location of the colony. "We must call the chiefs together as soon as we sail," he said, "and come to a decision about this. But there's a more immediate question pressing on which I need your good sense." He looked from the maps to the master, then seated himself somewhat wearily on one of the lockers.

Jones nodded and, perching on the edge of the table, took off his most cherished possession, a black Monmouth cap, two generations old, which he wore jauntily over one ear. His face was of full habit, with small, sharp brown eyes and a wide, honest, ugly mouth above a chin like the wide, honest stern of the *Mayflower's* self.

"And what's the to-do, now?" he asked. "Have the women got out of Mistress Minter's control, already?"

Robert laughed, then sobered to reply, "No, it's the *Speedwell's* trouble, this time!"

"Three married couples and one maiden in the great cabin with the officers. 'Tween decks are twenty men and boys. Don't they like it?" demanded the master.

"You've guessed wrong again," returned Cushman. "It's the question of provisioning her," and he told Jones what Reynolds had said.

The sailor scratched his red head systematically and thoroughly. "I heard Reynolds and Martin quarreling over something this morning. I suppose it was the victualing! It was a grievous pity to give such a man as Martin the governorship, let alone charge of the provisions. Reynolds is right in his demands. I heard him say he feared scarcity and I don't blame him. The amount of victualing he has taken aboard, today, is as meager as Martin's own beard! I supposed until I overheard the quarrel that the *Speedwell* had her own stores. There's a great lack of counsel in this business, on every side. Though, mind you, I think you, yourself, have done well under the circumstances."

"I'm not sure that I have!" Robert shook his head. His self-confidence had been badly shaken by Pastor Robinson's criticisms. "Captain John Smith offered to come with us as guide but I didn't encourage him because I feared we couldn't work peaceably with him. He's a known tyrant. Perhaps, though, I'd better have accepted him—that is, if my brethren would have agreed."

"They wouldn't have!" Jones refilled his pipe. "And I'd never set foot on the same ship with John Smith and his high stomach. I prefer your mistakes in general to Smith's bullying in particular."

"But twenty-eight hundred pounds should have got us a mort of food as well as other supplies," insisted Cushman. "What can Christopher Martin have done with the moneys? Or is Reynolds lying?"

Jones shook his head. "I don't know! But I do say this: The person highest in authority among you should deal with Martin. But I doubt if the elder can handle him roughly enough. He's a mean fellow who's never risen above low, cheating peddling before in his life. He's gone daft with his exaltation among you. If you'd leave him to me, I'd give him a kick in the seat of his trunk-hosen which would land him in the stocks where he belongs."

"Elder Brewster has ordered me to attend to the affair," said Robert. "He's appointed me assistant to Martin in governing the *Mayflower*."

Jones stared, then let out his great guffaw. The cabin all but burst with its reverberations. "And I'll be appointed assistant to my own cabin boy next! Well," pausing thoughtfully, "since Martin had already been made governor, perhaps the elder knew what he was about in making you assistant! You're no mealy-mouthed, praying gosling like some Brownists. Mayhap I can teach you to knock Martin down first and give him his orders afterward, as one treats a sailor!" He grinned again at Cushman, then his glance fell on something disclosed by the window beneath which Robert was sitting and he leaped across the cabin. "What's he up to now?" he cried.

Robert leaned out the window with the master. The *Speedwell,* her sails set, was being rowed away from her mooring.

"*Speedwell,* ahoy! Where are you going?" shouted Jones.

"To find the Northwest Passage!" roared Reynolds from his half-deck. "Will ye follow as my tender?"

Master Jones laughed, then eyed the pinnace carefully as she caught the wind, took in her oars and swept down the harbor. When she was lost among the shipping, both men were silent for a time. The *Mayflower,* swinging gently at her anchorage, revealed now the mighty walls of Southampton, now the long stretch of woods to the west, now only the sea; the sea, so strange, so beautiful, so seductive, so treacherous, so soon to be their all-possessing mistress.

"By God!" suddenly shouted Jones. "See her sail!"

The *Speedwell* hove in sight. She was racing one of the King's pinnaces down the channel. "She's too much down by the stern," he added. "She'll founder in a following sea."

"Don't tell me we must delay to retrim her!" exclaimed Robert anxiously.

"I couldn't tell ye if she needed trimming without study

of her," replied Jones with caution. "I suppose Reynolds knows the ship by now."

"Will you back me if I have to quarrel with Master Martin?" asked Robert.

"With pleasure!" declared Jones. "And if we can't manage him together, we'll call in Mistress Minter!"

Cushman smiled.

The pinnace hove in sight again. She had lost the wind and her sweeps were out.

"I wonder," said Jones, "if he retrimmed her in Holland. I understood she had no topsails. But she has them, now, of a huge spread, eh?"

"Would that be a good thing?" asked Robert.

"It might rack her to pieces," replied Jones, "unless she was built for such pressure." He scowled.

"Good lack!" groaned Robert. "Must I bear another anxiety! What's to be done?"

"Reynolds naturally is anxious to equal the *Mayflower* in speed," said the master. "But I misdoubt if he'd drown himself in the endeavor. Perhaps I'd better go over and have a talk with him."

"Do!" cried Cushman. "And I'll find out what my Leyden friends know about the refitting of the ship in Holland."

The *Speedwell* was making her anchorage a hundred yards west of the *Mayflower*. The master clapped on the Monmouth cap and strode out. Robert followed to look for John Carver who had been in Leyden when the pinnace was overhauled.

*ooking*

## ⁊ Cage

IT was nearing di[nner] ... he *Mayflower*. In the cook-house, next ..., the ship's cook was preparing the cre[w] ... e he flung pots about and cursed those of ... who were pestering him with pleas for th[e] ... ;ettles and griddles. The passengers' cook-h[ouse] ... ude, though stout, shelter built on a huge s ... ich was set up several cranes and a Dutch ... ood just abaft the cook's galley.

The Pilgrims did their ... The chiefs were cared for by their servant[s] ... ers managed as they could, wives cooking ... nilies, and the womanless contingent, 'twee[n] ... ing their cooks by rotation. This had been ( ... sh's suggestion and it had worked fairly wel[l] ... th trip down from London. Tom Weston ... what would happen on the rough Atlantic.

Just at the moment, thought ...ert, all was well, for a delicious smell of pottage rose from the Pilgrims' bubbling kettles. He felt half famished and looked about for Mary. But neither the Carvers nor his wife were among those on the main deck. He went into the great cabin. At first glance this seemed utterly deserted. But as his eyes adjusted themselves to the shadowed interior, he perceived that Desire Minter was standing beside the linnet's cage, half hidden by the angle of the head of his bunk, her face to the window.

Robert forgot Mary, John Carver and his dinner. He strode over to his bed and made a noisy business of hunting for a kerchief in the bag which hung above the pillows. The slender figure in the window did not move. What ailed the maid? From whom or what was she hiding? Did she need help? After all, he *was* one of those in authority! He cleared his throat.

"Are you looking for your uncle's return, Mistress Minter?" he enquired.

"No, Master Cushman," replied Desire Minter, still without turning.

She knew his voice! That was not unpleasing. He drew nearer and stood on the other side of the linnet's cage. Still, he could see only her ear and the edge of her ruff.

"I hope you're not troubled about anything, Mistress Minter? I thought you might be because of your quotation from Master Shakespeare. 'One writ with me in sour misfortune's book.' Were you thinking of me or of my wife or—do you consider *yourself* misfortunate, Mistress Minter?"

"I do, indeed!" returned Desire huskily.

She *had* been weeping then! Poor soul! What could one with so joyous a laugh find to weep about?

"And am I writ in the same misfortune?" he asked, gently. "What ill fate is it, poor child?"

She replied passionately. "This mad venture is our evil fate. It's yours because you've succeeded in leading a band of cowards into danger and they'll hate you for it. They'll ruin you, you'll see! It's my evil fate because

I'm no Separatist! I'm not even a Puritan! And I despise
your disloyal colony and your holy cant and your—"

"Stop!" ordered Robert. "In the first place, with all
their faults, these are the bravest people in the world.
And in the second place, there's no cant among us."

She turned on him now, gazing at him through the linnet cage, and he forgave her the harsh epithets because
of the misery in her violet eyes. She spoke still a little
huskily as if her throat ached from sobbing:

"You say that although you heard the women quarreling among themselves over the best beds today? And
you've heard Master Martin? And you were reviled by
those who should thank you, this morning, on the sands.
And tonight, they'll all gather at prayers and praise God
and their own godliness. I despise them for hypocrites!"

"Then why are you here with us?" demanded Robert.

"Because I'm a coward too!" she answered, her deep
voice bitter. "I must either bide with my uncle in Virginia or starve in England. And why I'm telling a Separatist these things, I'm certain I don't know. Go away,
Master Cushman, and leave me to my hates."

There was something in her voice that touched Robert's
very heartstrings. He did not move. "But since you
must go to New England," he asked, "why not go gallantly
as is your nature? If you love England, realize that you
are colonizing for England. It will solace you."

"*If* I love England!" she burst out. "*If!*" She gave
him a glance of intense scorn. "What does a Separatist
know of loving England? *'This happy breed of men, this
little world, This precious stone set in a silver sea'*—"

She recited the matchless words with a most lovely cadence in her tones. Then she added harshly, "But you
don't care if you do desert England forever. You did

that, long ago, to go to the ugly Dutch. Now you desert her for the barbarians!"

Robert protested fiercely. "You don't know what you say! Don't dare call me a deserter! England won't have me. She doesn't want a *man* now as she did in Elizabeth's day. She wants a puppet to obey the Archbishops. Well, then, I'm no puppet! I shall take England to a new world where a man can be free!"

He forgot he was talking to a woman. Women never cared for these things.

"Free!" exclaimed Desire. "There's no such thing as freedom! The freer a good man is, the more his conscience fetters him. You think you'll be free in your colony? Why, this moment you're slave to Pastor Robinson and Elder Brewster as you never were to an Archbishop or the King's Majesty!"

He frowned at her. She was logical, which a woman could not be! And what she said was true. He was silent in the face of it.

"You mustn't tarry here, talking," Desire went on shortly. "This kind of talk is no help to you. Poor man, you need praise instead of blame." She smiled at him through the cage. "It's as if we were prisoners, looking at each other through bars."

"Perhaps we are!" He was suddenly troubled by the thought that this meeting was of immense import. He was stirred as he had been the first time he had talked with Tom Weston. And this was a woman! He said again, "Perhaps we are!"

She returned his steady gaze with her candid glance and moved slowly out from her shelter behind the bed head. "I must go to my dinner," she murmured.

He nodded and in silence watched her walk out of the

cabin. He was troubled, yes; and yet, for just a breath, all the cares which weighed him down were as light as the kiss of the south wind. As Master Jones had said, "What a wench!" If one could only have her for a friend, sighed Robert.

When he went out on deck, Mary had returned from her shore junketing and called to him to come to his meal.

"We are eating out of doors, while we can," she explained, pointing out their trenchers which their servant had placed on a coil of ropes under the starboard bulwarks. There were family groups all about the decks. The sun was hot but the breeze was cool. Everyone was excited and loquacious. Perched on the stairs to the half deck were the Carvers with Desire Minter, their trenchers on their knees. Little Jasper More was waiting on them.

"I wish you'd got me an orphan," said Mary. "Where are servants to come from in Virginia?"

"We have two men," protested Robert, "and those little More children will be a great care. It's fortunate Mistress Minter takes an interest in them for the Carvers are no hands with children and Mistress Brewster has her hands full with her stepsons."

"To say nothing of the elder whom she calls her greatest baby of all," nodded Mary. "When do we sail? Everybody asks me because of you. It's shameful to have to keep explaining that you never tell me anything."

"We hope to sail tomorrow," answered Robert, ignoring the familiar jibe. "This pottage is excellent."

"Too many dried peas in it," Mary said. "I shall go into Southampton then, at once, for a last look at civilization. And I wish the ugly ship would sail without me. Let those live with savages who want to save them!"

Robert looked at her, reflectively, wondering for the

thousandth time if he were wise in forcing his will upon her. Perhaps he ought to permit her to remain with her relations in Canterbury for a year or so while he and Tommy got the home ready. Hitherto, he'd refused to listen to her protests, but now, unaccountably, he said,

"Well, my dear wife, if America is so horrible to you, I'll consent to your returning to Canterbury."

She caught her breath and every bit of color left her face. For a moment, he thought she was going to embrace him. Then slowly she shook her head. "No!" she murmured. "No! I must not, for all our sakes."

"You mean you must not kiss me?" asked Robert, smiling. "Don't you dare embrace me? Though I don't blame you for feeling shy! It's been years since you so honored me."

Mary recovered herself. "I only bestow my kisses where they're wanted. And I shall not stay in England if you go to America. Nobody shall say I deserted you when everyone else was turning against you. Yes, I heard Deacon Carver telling Mistress Catherine all about the names they called you this morning! I hope you're satisfied with your pigheadedness now even Master Weston's deserted you."

Robert was silent in helpless exasperation. Then, to his relief, he saw that Carver was rising from his meal. Cushman set his trencher aside and hurried to join the deacon.

John Carver was as tall as Cushman. Both men were just under Brewster's height. All the chiefs were tall. It was as if inches had been needed in their leadership and so nature had provided them! The deacon was a little more stalwart than Cushman and carried himself superbly. He was ruddy and smooth-shaven with a great shock of curly iron-gray hair covering a finely shaped head. His eyes were brown and deep-set, his nose strong, and his mouth, though a little heavy in outline, was beautiful in shape and expression. His chin was round and cleft. He was a handsome man and the women had made him well aware of that fact!

He wore a fine cloth doublet of a gray which matched his hair in shade. His hosen were gray also, slashed with maroon. He was not so elegant as either Cushman or Brewster but he had infinitely more charm than either of them.

"Well, Robert," he exclaimed, "I hope you find yourself alive after this morning's session!"

"Barely!" replied Robert. "I thought I was wounded to death but I crawled off and licked my wounds and now I think I'll outlast the voyage."

The two mounted to the half-deck and achieved something of privacy by leaning against the larboard rail, facing the sea.

"They've made me governor of the little *Speedwell*," said Carver. "I thank them for nothing!"

"I'll exchange with you!" grinned Cushman.

The deacon snorted. "Nay, I prefer my own evil!"

"In that case," remarked Robert, "you'll want to take over the problem of provisioning the pinnace."

"That's Christopher Martin's care, as you very well know! I turned it over to him long since," Carver returned.

"But Martin apparently proposes to starve the pinnace," said Robert, and he gave an account of his sessions with Reynolds and Jones.

"But this won't do!" cried the deacon. "I'm a patient man, I hope, but I never could abide going without food!

If I go in the *Speedwell* I don't propose to risk famine as
well as drowning! I'll go at once and see—shall it be
Reynolds or Martin?"

"Let it be Martin!" replied Robert, enthusiastically.
"You know him well, having worked with him, while I've
had him only on the voyage here."

"He's very difficult to work with." Carver shook his
great head. "I used to pray God every morning to help
me to hold my tongue and every night I had to tell Him
that He'd not given me quite enough help! It was a relief when the pastor sent for me to come to Leyden. But
don't mistake Martin, Robert. He's a braggart, but he's
keen and he is heart and soul for the colony."

"That's news, indeed!" remarked Cushman. "Frankly,
I don't trust the fellow. Since you do, deacon, will you
tell him to shift the necessary stores to the pinnace? We
ought to be able to sail at dawn tomorrow if this fair wind
holds."

"You are always our poor troubled Martha!" sighed
Carver. "Look you! You see Martin first. I must go
talk to my niece. She says she won't leave the *Mayflower*
for the *Speedwell*. A learned woman is the very pox! I
know, for her mother was my sister and learned too. She
married a barrister and they lived utterly to the world,
among playwriters and such. Now they're both dead and
this maid is on my hands. Well, I'm thankful for one
thing! There'll be no Jonson and no Shakespeare in New
England. That applies to you, also, Robert."

"Thank you," grinned the younger man.

Carver looked at him crossly. "I wasn't paying you a
compliment!"

"Aye, but you were, deacon! You were despising me

as one of the learned! But seriously, we *must* provision the pinnace."

"Certainly, we must! So you shall seek Christopher Martin out and make him disgorge. You'll likely find him in the market-place. Look for him there, anyhow." Carver's voice was hearty and he was half pushing, half pulling Robert down from the half-deck to the gangway.

Underneath his laughing manner, however, Robert felt the deacon's resolve not to take on again the responsibility he had shifted the month before. And no one ever had been known to beguile John Carver into doing what he had resolved not to do.

Half amused and more than half anxious, Cushman reached the quay, threaded his way among sailors, soldiers, sightseers and piles of goods and ships' dunnage to the city gates. He hurried under the great archway and up the little street which led to the market-place, very quiet now as the day's trading was done. The fine old church of St. Peter's lay grim in the sun and opposite, the only sign of life in the square, men hurried in and out of a handsome Tudor mansion which Robert knew to be a counting-house.

He paused and looked about him. Then luck attended him. He saw Mistress Martin sitting in the church porch and he made his way over to her. She looked at him crossly, little green eyes hostile, double chins belligerent.

"I've *not* been attending service in here," she declared, "if that's what you think."

Cushman gave her a pleasant look. "No, I didn't think that, Mistress Martin! I'm searching for your goodman."

"So am I," she nodded more amiably. "He left me here an hour ago and here I wait."

Robert seated himself opposite her. "I'll wait too."

He was glad of this opportunity for a word or two with the woman. He never had laid eyes on her until she had come aboard the ship at London and her appearance had prejudiced him against her. For, though he never would have admitted it, Cushman was a man who found it hard to like man or woman who had no claims to comeliness. And as if her ugliness were not sufficient to rouse his dislike, she had been noisy, officious and domineering during the entire week's voyage.

"I hope Master Martin will have no trouble in disposing of the butter," he said tentatively.

"He's already sold it!" She tossed her head. "He can do anything, my Chris!"

"You may well say so!" ejaculated Robert, running his fingers through his yellow hair. "It does look then as if we could sail tomorrow! There remains only one thing to be done. The pinnace awaits the rest of her provisions."

Mistress Martin, who had been actually smiling at him, suddenly pursed her mouth and said, "You mustn't presume, Master Cushman. My husband is governor and can't be told his business." She wiped the sweat from her cheeks. "He settled all that, this morning, with Master Reynolds. The *Speedwell* has got all she's going to get. Master Reynolds is a liar!"

"But we mustn't starve him for that cause!" exclaimed Robert.

"Why not?" she demanded irritably.

Robert fanned himself with his hat. She looked, he thought, like an arrogant sow and she gave him the feeling of futility which talking with a sow might give him. She went on, "And don't think you can persuade Chris to do otherwise. He never goes against what I tell him."

Uneasiness now mingled with Cushman's sense of help-lessness. Was this silly female really capable of delaying the provisioning of the pinnace? Was there no end to the accumulating of small vexations and troubles? It was as if a swarm of flies were attempting to smother the venture, each so unimportant, but the swarm so terrible. He looked out at Hampton Waters, so safe, and told himself that just beyond their placid shelter, the hungry sea waited, growing more menacing as the autumn storms approached.

He opened his lips to tell her what Master Jones had said. And at that instant, her husband came out of the countinghouse and headed for the church porch. He paused when he reached the steps, looking from his wife to Robert, very nervous as to eye and chin.

"I hope the butter sold at a good profit," said Robert pleasantly.

"Profit! I got only four hundred pounds for what I paid five hundred!" he cried, seating himself wearily. "Such a mort of butter can't be traded to advantage in a hurry."

"Yet you told me yesterday we could make twenty per cent on ours if we wished to sell!" exclaimed Robert, more and more disturbed.

"Are ye trying to make out my goodman would cozen the Pilgrims?" shrilled Marie.

Again Robert rumpled his hair. Marie had been the wife of a farm laborer before Chris married her and it looked as if this were one more detail, apparently insignifi-cant, which might prove most portentous for the *May-flower*. For Marie ruled Chris. And Marie, in her state of intoxication over her rise in society, was a silly fool. But to make her his enemy would be unwise.

He wondered whether Martin had been in the count-inghouse on his own or the Pilgrims' business but he would not antagonize them further by asking. So he said, quietly, "You mustn't put words in my mouth, Mistress! I merely want both of you to help us get our anchors weighed as soon as may be. Every moment counts! I'm certain you see that."

"We aren't fools!" nodded Marie, almost kindly. "But you needn't hold the ships hoping we'll give that bastard Reynolds more food, because he won't get it, will he, Chris?"

"What?" screamed Martin. "Nay, you didn't come asking me that! And what business is it of yours?"

Evidently, Chris had not heard of his assistant's appointment. It was on the tip of Robert's tongue to tell them but they were so absurd and the appointment so fantastical that he could not bear to break the news to them. How they would bluster! And there was bluster enough. It was like a nightmare. They were unreal. Yet real enough, it seemed, to control the sailing of the *Speedwell*. He crushed back his irritation and tried to persuade them that nothing mattered save that the pinnace reach New England; the pinnace on which their very life in the colony depended. "Give Reynolds the moon, if need be, but let the *Speedwell* sail!" he ended.

He might have been talking to the pigeons, pecking grain from between the cobblestones, except that the pigeons could not reply. And the Martins did, volubly and insolently. Reynolds, they said, was a born pirate who would overprovision the pinnace, drop away from the *Mayflower* when well at sea, and either sell her to Spain where there was a great demand for well-stocked vessels or he would turn to freebooting, himself. They had no proof they could offer, admitted Martin. But he was so certain he was right that nothing could move him to give the *Speedwell* more than the full third of supplies which were already stored in her lazaret.

Cushman after a time fell silent. It was an appalled silence. Unless the other chiefs could be persuaded to loose this outrageous little man's hold on the purse strings, he could and probably would ruin the venture. How could the pastor or the deacon ever have procured this man such a position? Robert asked himself this, as he finally rose without a word further to the two, and walked away. It occurred to him, afterward, that his silence had affected them far more than his arguments, for as he left they stared at him uneasily.

He resolved to get Brewster and Carver together, at once, and force them to see the *Speedwell's* predicament as he did. He returned to the ship forthwith.

# VII

## *Food for the Speedwell*

THE ship was very quiet, for everyone, sailor or passenger, who could get ashore, had gone. The exodus included the Carvers. Brewster, who was keeping clear of the town, was indulging in a nap and Robert retired to his favorite resting place on the poop to wait for the elder's awakening.

Southampton was very beautiful in the late afternoon sun. Had it not been for his several keen anxieties Robert would have been glad to join the others in exploring it. He told himself as he leaned against the taffrail, gazing, that it showed a lack of faith in him that when everyone else had left all anxieties to the Lord, he could not do so!

Yet, perhaps, he thought, it was not lack of faith but God's own urgency which made him uneasy, made him feel responsible for the welfare of the venture.

For every migration, there must be some one person weighted with an anxiety which never slept. There had been Abraham and Moses. Not, he sighed, that poor Bob Cushman boasted of the talents of those men! He knew he possessed neither their talents nor their authority. Aye, there was the bitter difficulty of it. It was Cushman, a mere novice, who must make all and mind all. Cushman, who must direct but without suzerainty, lead without prestige or prerogative. Well, God undoubtedly had His reasons. Perhaps in the present confused state of their business He was showing them the weakness of that

democracy which Pastor Robinson had preached so long
and which the Pilgrims were to practice in their colony.
Plain men were to rule and the will of the majority was
to prevail. Ignorance and inexperience on the throne!
If the plain Pilgrim men said that they would not sign
the agreement, that they would not provision the *Speedwell* adequately, according to Robinson, their agent Cushman could only bend the knee to them. Did God wish
him to do this, thus proving to them their own inability
to rule themselves? Nay, he couldn't believe it! Robinson or no, Robert Cushman would struggle to the last to
force them to use honor and common sense in their deal-
ings.

The long summer day was closing and the people were
returning from the town. A delicate violet dusk enclosed
the ships. Through the shrouds, Robert gazed on the
enchanting bulk of the fortifications against the bright
pink of the sky; turret and crenelated wall, square tower,
arched gates through which had marched the soldiers who
fought at Agincourt.

A sailor lighted a lanthorn and hung it on the mizzenmast. One of Brewster's servants struck the ship's bell
suspended above the half-deck railing. It was time for
evening prayer. Elder Brewster came up the companionway and stood beneath the lanthorn while the Pilgrims
gathered below him in the ship's waist. Robert looked
down into the upturned faces, so strangely spiritualized
by the afterglow. Or was this strange? Was he not seeing
them now as God saw them?

God knew there were laggards and louts among them
and braggarts and those of evil soul. But He knew, as
He was now showing Robert, that these were in the
minority. Most of the people were honest and earnest

above the average of men and women. But their unique possession, the possession which made them blessed above all other people, was their noble dream; a dream as important to them as the very life of their souls.

*They dreamed that one could have faith in the goodness and wisdom of the common man.*

And they dreamed that this faith would set them free! In their new home, across the ocean-sea, the common man would rule himself, would unfetter his body, his mind and his soul. It was God's wish. And their faith in the dream was potent enough to these men and women to beguile them into putting their lives into the hands of Robinson, Brewster, Carver and Cushman. Not docilely! Robert with a smile reminded himself that they had given themselves up only after many alarums and excursions of mind. Never would they consent to be blindfolded while their chiefs led them along the precipices. They must gape and complain and protest but always would they follow. God help him to do his share in sustaining them!

He did not hear the elder's prayers because of this, his own.

When the service was over both Brewster and Carver joined Robert on the poop deck and he made his report to them. Both of them were concerned but not as greatly as Cushman and he felt again, as he did so frequently, that their trust in Providence was greater than Providence, itself, could desire. Still the elder declared he'd see Martin when he returned to the ship and the deacon consented to see Reynolds. They agreed to meet early in the morning and take final action in the matter.

"The thing to do," remarked the elder, "is to bring Martin and Reynolds to a better understanding."

"Sam Fuller might know something about the refitting

of the pinnace in Holland," said Carver, "but why this pother? Reynolds is a known man. He has been put in charge. Why question his ability?"

"It was Master Jones who put the question," Robert reminded him.

"It's not Jones' business!" insisted Carver. "However, Robert, if it's only to prove to you how you fret over nothing, I'll look into the matter."

"But when, when, when?" cried Cushman. "The summer is passing!"

"Calm yourself, Robert! You are overtired." The elder patted his arm. "Go to bed and leave these frets till morning."

Robert threw up both his hands and strode away. He *would* put his weary body and his exasperated mind to sleep before he lost his temper utterly.

Mary had gone to bed already. She said to him as he pulled aside their curtain, "Go get your bread and cheese, Robert. We had ours while you were mooning on the poop. Tommy has it on the main deck."

Robert groaned and laughed. "I'd forgotten food! Bad temper evidently counteracts starvation." He went out patiently, though wearily, to find Tommy.

The boy was sitting in the longboat which rested on the port side of the main deck. He was eating his supper with one hand, holding his father's bread and cheese in the other. It was very dark. Cushman chuckled. "I must have scented you out like an old fox his cub. Certes, I couldn't see you! I must look at your bed below, Tommy, to see that all's well with you before I turn in. I'd forgot you almost, lad!"

"They filled the shallop with rushes," explained Tommy, "and that's where I'll sleep. Only while the nights are fine, I'd rather sleep up here alone in the long-boat. There's a many of people packing themselves into that shallop!"

"And you've been spoiled by having your own trundle bed the past three years," commented Robert.

"I don't like sleeping with a lot of people," the boy admitted. "I didn't like it in the bed above yours and mother's coming down from London, even before the other Pilgrims crowded the cabin."

Robert, who loathed crowding, too, said, "Wrap yourself well in your blankets, then; these August nights are cool."

Father and son munched their supper in contented silence, and when finished Robert helped Tommy arrange his bed; then he kissed the boy and returned to the great cabin.

Mary began talking in a whisper as soon as he had crept in beside her.

"I think we're much too near the window, but there's room for me to hang my farthingale between the sash and the head of the bed. That's why I took it. Anyhow, someone always has to be unselfish in a mêlée like this."

"I want a drink of water," said Dicky More from the bunk above Desire's.

"Hush, dear! Not till morning," came Desire's voice through the footboards.

"And certainly not water till it's purified with a little beer," said Mary Brewster from across the way. "Remember that, Desire."

"You mustn't spoil those children," cried Catherine Carver. "Remember what they are."

"All the more reason for keeping them healthy!" retorted Mistress Brewster.

Robert sighed and decided that when Mary fell asleep he'd steal out to the longboat to join Tommy.

Long before Mary ceased her desultory whispering, Elder Brewster's familiar bass snore began, and shortly Carver joined him in an uneasy choking wheeze that was very disturbing to anyone who had not heard it before. Robert, smiling in the dark, tried to estimate how many nights in the past three years he had been kept awake by John's unique slumber song. The deacon evidently was not withdrawing to the discomforts of the *Speedwell* until the last moment!

Disturbing, all this intimacy!   Truly, religion could make strange bedfellows!   How could Brewster, reared in the spacious manor at Scrooby, school himself to endure this repulsive lack of privacy?   Actually, the elder had assured Robert, after his first night's sleep on the *Mayflower*, that he found the cabin pure bliss!   He had been a hunted man and the great cabin was sanctuary!   But Robert had no such potent reason to subdue his dislikes.   He called up the memory of his father's farm in Kent; the rambling old stone buildings, his own room, opening on his mother's flower garden.   Stillness, mists, dew on harvest fields, the plenty of his mother's table, his father's horses and dogs, the peace, the trust—how had he ever forced himself to leave it all?

There was but the single answer, of course, for both himself and William Brewster.   God had willed it.

He tried to shut out all the voices of the cabin and focus his mind on the *Speedwell's* problem.   But he found himself, instead, wondering if beneath all the chorus of snores and snortings, he could distinguish Desire Minter's gently drawn breath.   Impossible, of a certainty!   And most indelicate of him!   He closed his eyes resolutely.

When next he opened them, the linnet was piping ecstatically. He peered through the curtains. It was morning but no one was stirring in the cabin. He rose and pulling on trunk and hosen, stole out, doublet over his arm.

A tiny washroom had been partitioned from a corner of the steerage for the use of those in the great cabin. Thus far it had been used informally by all. But now, to his surprise, Robert beheld rules posted on the door. They were signed by "Governor Martin." The male Pilgrims were to wash first during the early hours of the day, the females and children during the middle hours. The servants were to keep the place clean and were forbidden to use it. The male Pilgrims were to wash in order of rank: Elder Brewster, Deacon Carver, Governor Martin, Master Cushman, Master Bradford, Master Winslow and so on through the list.

Robert gave an inarticulate grunt and entered the washroom. He made a leisurely toilet, even managing to shave before there came a rap at the door. He tilted the contents of the pewter basin into the scuppers and said, "Come in!"

Deacon Carver appeared. He grinned. "What! Not obeying the governor's first pronouncement?" He edged in as Cushman edged out.

"Pooh and tush! The fellow's an ass!" exclaimed Robert.

"What's this! What's this!" It was the familiar strident voice and Martin rushed up, his hosen only half trussed, his open doublet displaying a chest as hairy as a spider's back. He glared at Cushman.

"God's life! He's shaved too!" he gasped.

"The governor's cursing!" groaned Carver solemnly. He nudged Robert in the back.

"Shaved and out of your turn!   Can't you read?"   Martin thumped the sheet of rules with a muscular fist.

"Not all words; of course, I got through my horn book but only slowly," replied Robert as solemnly as John. "And anyhow Elder Brewster tells me I am now assistant to the governor, so I ought to be granted certain privileges."

"But I don't like you," Martin gasped, "and you aren't a proper assistant!   You're fooling me."   He ran back into the cabin.   "I'll attend to you, sirrah!"

The deacon came out combing his fine crop of hair. "We shouldn't have tormented him.   We weren't kind."

"I suppose we weren't," agreed Robert.   "But how can we take him seriously and not knock him down?   And why does he pretend not to know of my appointment?"

"He didn't return to the ship till all were in bed," explained Carver.   "Stay!   Here he comes!"

Martin was returning and following him was the elder, wrapped in his blue cloak, feet thrust bare into his shoes. He looked from Martin to the other two in sleepy bewilderment.

The governor pointed at his precious rules.   "Here's a sample of what I am to expect from my assistant!   You assure me he *is* my assistant or I'd never believe it.   Look at him!   He's already washed and shaved!   And my rules distinctly say that you're first, the deacon is second and I'm third—"

"Come!   Come!   This is puling nonsense!" protested Brewster.   "I supposed from your fury that my two friends were in a fist fight.   As for your rules, suppose I don't want to wash at all on a certain day, must the whole cabin then go frowsy?   Tear that thing down!   Let me wash!   Then let's pray the Lord to teach us not to be fools!" They never before had seen him so near to losing his temper.

As the elder closed the washroom door, Martin turned on Cushman. "And that's why you were so forward yesterday! I tell you, *I'm* in charge. I've been elected by the people. Did you think you could use authority to make me give anything to Reynolds? I have all the authority!"

"Hush, for all our sakes!" exclaimed Robert. "No one should know of these matters except the chiefs." He walked out on the main deck. Carver went back into the cabin.

"God bless us and so forth!" boomed a great voice. Jones leaned over the half-deck rail and winked at Robert. "What a childish quarrel! Come up to my cabin, friends, and compose your differences over a good pull of beer."

"Do that, Robert," called the elder, "and the deacon and I will join you immediately."

Martin darted up the ladder and Robert followed slowly. The first mate and the pilot were in the poop cabin but both left at a word from Jones, who followed his guests as far as the doorway. There he paused to say, "Master Martin, you're a fool not to give the *Speedwell* her full share of stores," and closed the door before the governor could reply.

He whirled on Cushman. "So you've tattled your lies to Jones!"

Robert made a supreme effort to be patient. "I think you're acting in a prejudiced manner against Reynolds, Governor. You wouldn't heed me so I asked Jones' opinion."

It was the first time Martin had been addressed respectfully by his title. He suddenly smiled broadly and Robert had to admit to himself that the chapman had an open grin which was not unpleasant.

"Master Cushman, I'll be as kind to you as my fiery hot nature will permit," he said. "So I repeat, once for all, Reynolds has his share and he gets no more. He's only waiting to cozen us and desert us."

"But what will he do with the thirty Pilgrims aboard him?" demanded Robert.

"They won't trouble him long," returned Martin darkly. He was tying his points vigorously now. "You don't need to know Reynolds' father and mother to know what *he* is. If you've seen the varlet's face it's enough. He's a villain. You could as soon break a mast in two with your fingers as to get me to do what he wants in this matter. *I'm* the judge."

"But surely I've got the right to make suggestions!" said Robert. "It was I who raised the moneys you've expended and in our position as agents, we're still equal. I ask you to let me see your account book and your lists of stores, showing how you have divided them between the ships."

Martin's voice rose again. "I tell you what it is! I never received no moneys on condition of you watching my accounts nor by any such agreement as you signed in London. I'm not beholden to Thomas Weston or any of his merchants. They're bloodsuckers all!"

Robert tried to orient himself to this twist of the wind. "Then where did the money come from you've spent?" he asked, cheeks flushing, mobile lips twitching. "Did it fly here from heaven or is it your own?"

"Don't sneer at me, sirrah!" screamed Chris. "I could have set out two ships for a voyage, myself, and never missed the money!"

It was like an argument with Mary which never by any

chance arrived at its proper destination. "I want but one thing," Cushman said. "I want to be convinced that the *Speedwell's* victualed for her full voyage."

"The *Speedwell!* The *Speedwell!*" squeaked Martin. "Why not make a ballad of it? I hear you're a poet! And hawk it on the quay to pay back your master, Thomas Weston! No! I'm going to control the pinnace through its belly in spite of your unthankfulness for my pains."

He snapped his fingers at Robert, whose sensitive face twitched at the affront. He bit his lip, utterly baffled. Martin, with a triumphant glance, started to leave the cabin and met the cabin boy carrying a huge jug of beer.

"The gentlemen are coming," announced the child, banging the jug on the table. He pulled down several tankards from the wall, stood them against the jug and pattered out. The elder and the deacon now arrived, John carrying a trencher of bread and cheese.

"Let us eat as we talk," suggested Brewster. "I went without supper last night, and have no mind to go empty till dinner." He smiled as he seated himself at the table and drew his knife. The others joined him.

"I hope you and Master Cushman have settled everything," said Carver to Chris.

"I've silenced Master Cushman," replied the governor and drank deep. "Still, he won't admit Reynolds is a knave—as knavish as he looks."

"I don't admit Reynolds is a knave either," exclaimed the elder. "He got his appointment from Pastor Robinson who vouched for the state of his soul. If he says he hasn't enough food, we must believe he speaks truth as he sees it."

"What food have we, Governor Martin?" asked Carver.

"Cheeses, unleavened bread, dried peas, salted and

smoked fish and meat and dried fruit," replied Chris promptly.

Carver's quick temper boiled over. "Don't play the fool! You know I mean how large are our provisions! By my troth—" He bit his lip and turned contritely toward Brewster. "Forgive me, William!" Then he looked fiercely at Chris. "Now then, let's see your lists, Governor."

"Yes, let's see your lists," agreed the elder.

Martin got excitedly to his feet. "So here we have the kernel of this hard nut! I'm to be examined for my honesty! Come, I'm a thief, am I? Then what?"

Brewster looked at the little man as he might have looked at a performing ape. Then he turned to Carver. "John, let us see your lists, prithee."

"I turned all my lists over to Christopher Martin," answered the deacon. "You know that Pastor Robinson sent for me to come over to Leyden last month and hearten those Pilgrims who were fainted of purpose. I only got back to Southampton in time to meet the *Mayflower* here."

"No, I didn't remember that." Brewster's large face began to take on heavy lines of something more than weariness. "I had a fearsome time getting here and I'm mortified to admit that all thoughts but my own safety left me. Who made estimates for provisions?"

"I did, for one, with Master Weston," replied Robert. "We were planning to make many of the purchases in Kent as prices were cheaper there than here. But then came the scolding letter from Leyden signed by Winslow, Fuller, Bradford and the pastor; and I was ordered to put all the provisioning in the hands of the deacon and Master Martin who were here in Southampton."

"They thought you were working too lovingly with the Merchant Adventurers," explained Carver, "though I told them they were fools when I learned what they'd done."

"They didn't believe you," remarked Cushman dryly.

"But Master Cushman had been insolent to me long before that letter," complained Martin, who was staring from one man to the other, anxious as well as angry.

"I tried to get Governor Martin to do me the honor of at least looking at my lists," explained Cushman. "But he would have counsel of no one. The insult, I suppose, was that I told him that a man in a society who won't regard counsel had better be a king than a consort. In short," leaning across the table, his blue eyes black with feeling, "unless we can beguile Christopher Martin into heeding advice and working according to the will of the majority, we leaders instead of being examples of patience and kindness will be examples of janglings and insultings and our plantation will end in the bottom of the Atlantic. That's what I care about, the plantation."

"The plantation can't fail, Robert," remarked the elder calmly. "The Lord has promised to lead us into Canaan. But I wish the janglings and insultings would cease. Your lists, prithee, Governor Martin."

"I have no lists," replied Martin sullenly. "I carry all in my head."

He looked like a man who was lying. The other three were baffled. Then Robert took his notebook from his pouch. "Perhaps there is another way to get at it," he suggested. "You've had twenty-eight hundred pounds from me, Governor. I sent you twenty hundred in June and eight hundred early in July."

"And you promised me six thousand!" cried Martin.

"The Merchant Adventurers promised it," returned

Robert. "As I pointed out yesterday, we lost twenty hundred when Sir George Farrer withdrew. We lost four hundred which Master Weston took back with him, and still another hundred through the failure of certain promised Pilgrims to come into the venture. But still you had enough to store both ships in a comely manner. That I know!"

"But I didn't though, did I, judging from all the mort of complaints?" demanded Martin, unabashed by the array of figures.

"Master Reynolds has a list of all he received in yesterday's loading," said Deacon Carver. "That will help us, surely. He says he needs particularly more meat and more beer."

"Beer!" Martin yelped as if someone had stepped on him. "Beer! Let him drink water and get worms!"

"Did Master Jones also take a roll of supplies?" asked Brewster.

"No," replied Robert. "As we've only chartered the ship, he's liable only for the crew's provisions. We've bought the *Speedwell*."

"I suppose it would delay us overlong to examine the *Mayflower's* stores," sighed John Carver. "There's six months' provisions for the colony stowed away, a grievous amount to move for the counting."

"Perhaps that's the only thing we can do," groaned Robert, "delay or no delay."

" 'Delay' has a portentous sound to me," remarked Brewster, somberly, "but if we must, we must!"

"If you do that," Martin spoke more quietly than any of them ever had heard him speak, "if you do that, I'll lead all my forty companions in the venture off the ship and back to Essex, so help me God."

There was silence broken by Reynolds walking in on them.  He sat down at the table, took his silver toothpick from behind his ear and put it in a corner of his mouth.

"Well, my masters," he began in his pleasant voice, "when do you propose to feed my lambs?"

"We're just discussing the matter," replied Brewster. "There's confusion about our lists."

"Here's my lists," said Reynolds, laying on the table the papers he was carrying.

Martin seized on them and carrying them to the window, looked at the totals.  Then he came back to thrust the sheets into the man's face.

"You're the father of liars!" he snarled.  "You have put down not a half of what I put aboard you."

Reynolds took his lists coolly and turned to the others. "If Master Martin really thinks that, he's a knavish fool! If he thinks we've enough to eat on the *Speedwell*, let him come aboard and eat it.  By God, that's the end!  Let Master and Mistress Martin sail aboard the pinnace!  He'll feed us then or we'll eat him."

"I'm assistant to Governor Martin," added Cushman, "so if he sails on the *Speedwell*, I will too."

"You'll stay on the *Mayflower* with me since you *are* my cursed assistant," shrilled Martin, giving Robert a vicious glance.

"As governor of the *Speedwell*, I go aboard today.  I hope you won't starve me!"  Carver's voice was half amused.

"I'm most flattered by all this clambering aboard my ship," grinned Reynolds, "but I want only Martin!  Martin or more provisions!"

"You forget," said Carver, "that the *Speedwell's* ours and that there are other masters to be got."

"Good!" exclaimed Reynolds. "Then pay me up and let me go. And don't forget the forty pound forfeit you'll owe me for breaking the contract, nor the shares I own in the venture."

There was an embarrassed pause. Everyone knew there was no money with which to get rid of Reynolds.

"We could only do that if you were willing to let us be in your debt for a while," admitted Robert.

"That makes a wise man laugh!" remarked the master of the pinnace. He was looking complacently from one to another.

William Brewster had been pursing his lip and blinking in a brown study and now he gave the result. "If I sail on the *Speedwell* with Deacon Carver, it will put both Master Reynolds' and Governor Martin's faith to the test. If there is a food shortage, we'll make the *Mayflower* tranship to us at sea. If there isn't and Master Reynolds has been cozening us for some reason of his own, why, that will be shown up too."

"But it's highly improper for our leader to sail in the lesser ship," protested Cushman, vehemently. "And who will conduct religious services on the *Mayflower?*"

"You will, Robert," replied the elder, promptly.

"But you and Deacon Carver both aboard the poor little *Speedwell!* It's absurd. Put Martin and me on her!" cried Robert.

"Come, let's argue no more! When can you be ready to sail, Master Reynolds?" asked Carver.

Reynolds used his toothpick thoughtfully and answered with a crafty look. "Under these new conditions, I'd want another day to prepare for my new and weighty passengers."

"If we grant you that, you'll stop this quarreling over the food?" asked Brewster.

"Oh, I'll endure anything aboard my ship that you will, elder!" Reynolds rose! "Welladay! What a pack of nonsense!" he grunted and abruptly walked out.

"I don't like it," sighed Robert. "Not any of it. It all seems mad; like a children's crusade."

"But after all, as you've said repeatedly," remarked John Carver, "nothing matters so much as our getting there. It can't be a voyage of more than a few weeks."

"You'll have our wives on your hands, Robert," said Brewster with a little grin. "They'd better remain in the *Mayflower*."

"I'm afraid Catherine will insist on coming with me!" Carver shook his head.

"You must be firm," the elder rose, "as I shall be. It's no place for women who can escape it, the *Speedwell*." He too walked out of the cabin.

"I'll do my best," said Carver, but without conviction. He took Cushman's arm. "Come, Robert, let me see you smile. I suppose the reason we find your smile so sweet is because we so rarely see it. And yet you love laughter!"

Robert permitted himself to be led toward the door. "You have only to mention this morning's scene at the washroom door any time you find me sad," he remarked. The two men looked into each other's eyes and burst into huge laughter.

Little Martin, biting his nails, looked at the two tall fellows with something wistful in his eyes and followed after them.

# VIII

## *In the Spinney*

I T was a heavenly morning and still only about six of
the clock. Some of the women were washing and the
main deck was full of clothes hung to dry. Forward,
several of the crew were tarring down the rigging and as
the deacon and Cushman emerged, one of the sailors sung
out a ribald remark about the women's occupation. The
others added comments of the same kind.

There had been a good deal of trouble with the crew
on the way down, on this score. Half of them were pressed
men, a low lot, even for sailors. The remainder were
rough and hard; chuck-farthing lads who could survive the
rigors of a sailor's life only because they were half brutish.

Jones, standing beside the mizzen, blew lustily on his
whistle. The bosun ran aft. "Will you flatten that scum,
his face for me—the first one who sang out—or shall I?"
roared the master in a voice that carried to the end of
the bowsprit. "And if you can find the others who spewed,
send them aft to me."

"Aye, aye, Master!" The bosun looked worried and returned forward.

"That's one of my best sailors, too," grumbled Jones to
the deacon and Robert. "By the grace of God, most of
the pressed men have escaped here in Hampton Waters.
I'm to have a new lot an hour before we sail. One thing is
certain, they can't be worse than the London batch. You
passengers have got to do your share. If one of the crew

is froward, knock him over, kick him, what you will."

Robert did not wait to see punishment administered.
He had seen enough of the bosun's fist and foot in the
previous week.

He went into the great cabin to write to Weston and
had settled to this, seated on the side of his bed, when
Will Bradford came up to him.

He was a sturdy-looking man of thirty, about five feet
ten in height, with a rather full face beneath black hair.
His eyes were dark too, with sleepy lids and extremely
heavy eyebrows.  His forehead was fine, his nose large and
his mouth full and firm with a protruding square chin.
He was well educated along certain lines, particularly in
Roman law and philosophy.  He had joined the Leyden
church when a mere lad and had put a good share of his
not inconsiderable property into the venture.  And as a
man of means, he dressed well.  His brown suit was of fine
cloth and the russet slashings were of silk as were his hosen.
He did not wear a ruff but one of the new high collars
called falling bands, which set off his ruddy face most
pleasantly.

"Ned Winslow and I have drawn up a letter to the
Merchants," explained Will, "which the elder, the deacon
and several others have approved.  We're going to send
it but the deacon thought you ought to know about it."

"I've had no talk with you at all since you arrived yesterday," said Robert.  "I'd like to speak of several matters, especially this one, with you, Will.  Shall we go
ashore where we can talk privily?"

Bradford nodded.  "Yes!  Though I warn you, I'm out
of all agreement with you."

"That's what I felt and is why I would like to speak
with you," returned Robert.  "You and I have always

been friends though we've not understood each other. Mayhap if we try to understand each other now, we may still be friends."

"Mayhap," said Will, doubtfully. "My wife would like the chance to go into the town, if there's room in the small boat."

"I'll ask my wife, too." Robert put away his portfolio. "Immediately, if you wish!" He went in search of Mary.

She was directing one of their servants at the cooking place and looked very pretty with her curly blond hair blowing from under her cap and her green skirts whipping about comely ankles.

"I'll go with a vim!" she exclaimed. "I feel as if I'd been clapped up in prison for a year, since yesterday. What was the conference in the poop cabin at dawn, Robert?" She sent the servant for her hood and proposed to improve the moment.

He had learned that it was wiser to tell Mary what he could. It was better to let her garble the truth than to make her stories up out of whole cloth, for tell stories she would!

"We're trying to satisfy Master Reynolds in the supplies for the *Speedwell*," he replied. "Where is Tommy?"

"Off again with Captain Standish! He worships that man even more than he does you. Come, there's Dorothy Bradford!"

Dorothy, a tall delicate woman with pale cheeks and sad blue eyes, came from the steerage, tying on her little pink hood.

"I must have a hood like that with a frontlet to shade my eyes," declared Mary. "She looks like a ghost. Still grieving because she must leave her babe behind. We can't have the cockboat. Desire Minter has already gone

ashore in that. No, I declare it's back again! Now, where
do you suppose she is? She told Mistress Carver she would
not go to the *Speedwell,* though Mistress Catherine is going. It wouldn't surprise me if she took herself back to
London."

"I hope not!" ejaculated Robert.

"And why should you care?" demanded Mary.

"I don't know, I'm sure," confessed Robert and the
servant arriving opportunely with the hood, he handed
Mary down the ladder where Dorothy already awaited her
in the boat.

"Now where do you suppose Desire Minter went all
alone into the town," Mary asked as the boat moved off,
"after that quarrel with her aunt?"

"But I was there. They didn't quarrel!" protested
Dorothy. "You do tell such tales!"

"But they did! Desire said—" began Mary, excitedly.

"It's none of our affair, Mary, prithee!" cried Robert.

Mary giggled. "Now, Robert, you know no one has
any private affairs among the Pilgrims! That's one of
the manifest advantages of being a Pilgrim, knowing all
about your neighbors; isn't it, Dorothy?"

"And that's why we're always in a hurly-burly," retorted
Dorothy.

Mary laughed and the two women fell to talking about
hoods and frontlets. It was a short ride to the quay and
their husbands left them there and were rowed up the
shore to the sands which had been the scene of yesterday's
debate. Near-by they found the log where Robert had
rested and seated themselves on it. The shade of the
little oak copse behind them was grateful and they took
off their hats; black head and yellow head against the
green of leaves.

"And now will you let me see the letter?" asked Cushman.

Without a word, Bradford took a folded paper from his pouch and passed it to his companion who read it.

"Beloved Friends! Sorry we are that there should be occasion of writing at all to you, partly because we expected to see the most of you here but especially because there should be any difference at all between us. But seeing it falls out that we cannot confer together, we think it meet to show you the just cause and reason of our differing from those articles last made by Robert Cushman without our commissions or knowledge. And though he might propound good ends to himself for doing it, yet it in no way justified him.

"Our main difference is in the fifth and ninth articles."

Here followed a restatement of the many arguments advanced the day before, then the letter continued:

"Judge therefore, we beseech you, impartially of things and if a fault has been committed, lay it where it is and not on us. We never gave Robert Cushman commission to make any one article for us but only sent him to receive moneys upon articles before agreed upon. Yet since you conceive yourselves wronged as well as we do, we thought it meet to add a branch to the agreement as first signed by us. That it may appear to all men that we are not lovers of ourselves only but desire also the good and enriching of our friends who have adventured your moneys with our persons, we have added a last article, promising you on behalf of the whole company that if large profits do not arise within the seven years we will continue together longer with you, if the Lord give a blessing. This we hope is sufficient to satisfy any in this case, especially friends."

The signature of the chief men among the Pilgrims followed.

Robert looked at Bradford. "They'll refuse the offer. I made it with all the assurance and vehemence at my command. They laughed at it. They said they wouldn't agree to tie up their moneys a day over the seven years."

The other's face fell but he set his chin obstinately. "It's a good and legal offer."

"What they want," reiterated Robert, "and what you offer are two different things, legal or no! Let's not debate the matter further, Will. We'll never agree. But I have a suggestion to make that may satisfy them. Let the agreement go. Let all of us who have property sign a statement that we hold ourselves responsible for the colony's debt to the Merchants."

"But only a dozen among us have property!" ejaculated Will. "That's not just."

"It's the largest justice for the very reason that we *are* the only ones with means," insisted Cushman. "That's God's kind of justice for the commonwealth of which the pastor preached. Need we be niggardly because we are fortunate?"

"But it would be a killing debt! It's overwhelming now and if the Merchant Adventurers keep their troth and supply us for a few years with necessities it will be as large as the King His Majesty's debt for masques," objected Will.

"But don't you see that the whole danger is that, having disgusted the Adventurers, they will repudiate us and we'll be starved in the wilderness?" Robert asked. "I've pointed that out again and again."

"But," reiterated Will, "we shall repay, though not by a few of us assuming the generality's debts. That would enmesh our personal honor, hopelessly."

"I tell you, the commonwealth's honor and our personal honor are one," urged Cushman.

"Commonwealth!" groaned Bradford. "I wish the parson could have heard his commonwealth yesterday; so fainted of purpose!"

Robert cleared his throat. His thoughts raced; his great, gleaming thoughts which marched like an army with banners to his very lips—and there turned back! England! England in the new world! England shorn of her brutalities, her short visions, her selfishness. Kind, hospitable England and free, free! A *new* England dedicated to the liberty of men's souls. This was the dream of the tiny commonwealth.

He cleared his throat again. Will could only look at him from under his heavy brows, his practical lips close pressed. Bradford was as careful and cautious as a Scot in all dreams that depended on moneys.

Robert swallowed the winged words and spoke prosaically. "But can you endure to go away from England, forever, leaving men to think you're dishonest?" he asked.

Bradford flushed. "I mislike your words, Master Cushman."

"I mean—" began Robert.

"You mean what you say, always," stiffly. "If this is all you have to tell me as to the letter, I'll tell you that I'll always pay my share to the Adventurers, regularly and lovingly. No more!" He rose. "And now I shall walk back to find my wife."

Robert rose too, to catch the younger man's hand. "Come, Will, I have enemies enough without you crowding onto the already full bench! I'm sorry to offend anyone as keenly honorable as you are. Let's agree to disagree on the agreement! Forgive me and tell me what in Bedlam to do with Chris Martin and our supplies."

Will suddenly smiled. "You are a dear fellow, Robert, but you are mad."

"I agree to both impeachments." Robert's eyes twinkled. "But do listen to the tale of the madness of Martin and Reynolds!"

Will listened with his most judicial expression. He pondered for a moment after Robert had finished and then delivered judgment.

"Martin's suspicions may be well founded. We know the temptation to piracy is all but overwhelming to the masters of ships trading far from English waters and not always far, either! Surely we'd be fond to ignore Martin's uneasiness. It seems to me that the elder's compromise outdoes Solomon's. I'll transfer to the *Speedwell* too, if he wishes it."

Robert ruffled his hair and looked at the dancing sea. The summer day was high. Laughter rang from the deck of the *Speedwell*, anchored opposite the wood. And suddenly Robert laughed too.

"I'm sorry I amuse you!" remarked Bradford.

"No, I'm laughing at myself," expostulated Robert. "I'm realizing that I've been trying to make our argosy with a Charon's fleet! And we are only Jasons in search of the golden fleece. We're no Pilgrims, Will."

"Now those are the very sayings that make you sound mad," frowned Will. Then, in a kind voice, "But for me, I don't doubt your loyalty to the colony, as some do who say you're for the Merchants first."

"Thank you, Will!" replied Robert a little grimly.

"And now let's go into the town," suggested Bradford.

"You go, Will," urged Cushman. "I'm going to return to the log and enjoy the novelty of loneliness."

Bradford nodded and started vigorously along the sands.

Robert watched him till he was lost in the crowds on the quay.

"And yet you will go to America!" exclaimed a voice behind him.

Cushman came to his feet and turned. Desire Minter was sitting in the low crotch of an oak, just within the spinney.

"I was here first." She smiled. "And you both ignored me. So I deliberately listened. I only wish I could have read the letter!"

Robert walked into the spinney. "It's a pity we didn't talk scandal about our friends," he remarked, seating himself on a stump close before her.

"What you talked of was scandalous enough," she retorted. "The King should have William Bradford in his privy council. He has neither imagination nor ambition."

"Nay, he has both," declared Robert. "And once we get over to New England he'll be one of the solid foundations of the colony, with his steadfast, sturdy mind and body. But for barking and worrying the people to the other side, they need a mad dog like me."

"You, mad?" Desire's voice was indignant. "Then it's a pity my uncle and the elder weren't touched by the same moon!"

Robert's pulse quickened. "You are a Dryad in your green gown, the bracken around you and—don't stir—a deer, peering from the thicket behind you."

"Now that," returned Desire, eyes liquid, cheeks vivid, "is very pretty and proper for a Puritan like Edmund Spenser but not at all proper for one of Pastor Robinson's Pilgrims!"

"I protest that a Pilgrim may find joy in whatever is good and lovely!" cried Robert. "In poetry, in music, in maids, in angels, in babes! Sir Philip Sidney proved that."

Desire clasped long, delicate fingers in her lap. "In my

grandmother's house in London where I have lived most of my life, we had music, organ music, and I play the *viola da gamba,* myself.  And now I live on the *Mayflower!*  You can't guess the horror of it."

"But I can!"  Robert leaned toward her.  "And so I tell you this.  I'm older than you are so I've learned more. I know that nothing, not exilement, nor distance, nor mis-understandings, can take beauty away from you for it derives from your own soul.  And, O dear my maid, there are beauties greater than music!  There are the visions which music conjures up!"

"Yes, but they are conjured only by music!" exclaimed Desire.  "And Uncle John wouldn't let me bring my viol."

"You shall have a viol, you shall have music, some day, in the great forests of America!  I promise you that," said Robert in a low voice.

Desire gave a little start and shook her head.  "So you dream too!  And such kindly dreams.  But you have your own life to care for and the lives of your wife and your son."

"But still I have room in my heart for a friend or two," smiled Robert.

"Friendship between a man and a woman," returned Desire lightly, "is possible only among the rich and the idle.  So gossamer and rare a thing requires leisure and the delicate touch of uncalloused fingers."

Robert felt a door close gently but firmly in his face.

He sat looking thoughtfully at Desire, remembering certain of his lifelong convictions about women.  First of all, on its mental side, he had no respect for the sex though he respected housewifery and motherhood and all the female craft for which Puritan women were supposed to be notable. Second and more important, he'd always looked on love between the sexes as a sin because he'd been taught that such love was mere lust. He was a sincere Puritan and had led a life of complete self-control and so of bitter inward struggle. For he was, he admitted, a man of strong passions and had a deep capacity for affection. Thus far he had succeeded in repressing all that pertained to love, probably, he thought, staring at Desire, because he'd never felt it for a particular woman. His first marriage had been arranged by his parents. He had undertaken his second himself, as a means of salvation from sin.

And now a female fifteen years younger than himself had quoted Shakespeare to him, had spoken of her quick love for England, had shown sympathy for his anxieties, and he, Robert Cushman, could feel the walls of his so painfully reared convictions shaking, nay, rocking! And to what end? He was a married man.

Desire was returning his gaze steadfastly. She was no gaping country lass. She was London bred and her mother's people were worldly. She was not looking at him coyly, he realized, but wisely, perhaps even tenderly.

"And so," he said slowly, "you will not be my friend?"

"I *may* not be your friend," she answered him.

"Friendship is a very comely affair," he went on, "quite above all human frailties."

"It is indeed!" She nodded her fine head. "But friendship isn't for you and me, Robert Cushman, and you know it. These aren't the days of Elizabeth nor is this her court where such attachment between men and women was possible."

Robert got to his feet and stood very straight before her. "All that you would warn me of I acknowledge," he said. "I shan't annoy you or bring a single oblique glance on your so lovely head. I shall scarcely speak to you. But still I am your very friend. And always in your loneliness and your rebellion against your fate, you may take what comfort you can out of the sure knowledge that a friend holds you very tenderly in his lonely heart."

Desire flushed, turned deadly pale, and rising too, returned him look for look. "Thank you, Master Cushman! And since you've promised not to presume, I'll confess that from the moment I beheld you with Master Jones and the foolish cabinet list, I knew we were of the same kind and I liked you. But this is all."

"Yes, this is all," nodded Robert.

The scent of the bracken touched him, delicately. And he was very happy with a sense of sudden enrichment and very unhappy in the pain of a sense of great loss.

"I think, since we might have been very friends," said Desire, "that I ought to tell you that I'm going to try not to go to America. I may run away!"

"No!" gasped Robert. "No! Not that!"

"I *can't* leave England," she explained. "No *person* keeps me here. It's this," touching the rough bark of the oak lovingly, "and this," stooping to lay her hand on the green sod at their feet. "These are me. And you who feel so too won't try to dissuade me."

"No!" he groaned. "Since you are you, I won't. But if you leave the venture, you leave me bereft as even Weston's going didn't. It's beyond strangeness that though this dream of planting the colony has been the greatest thing in my life for years, though it's been the light in God's hand, beckoning me on through such difficulty and contumely as you can't guess, yet when you say you shall desert the venture some of its beauty fades. And I never saw you till yesterday!"

"You said you'd not try to dissuade me!" exclaimed Desire, indignantly. "I won't listen to you!" She walked out of the spinney and then paused to look back at him, saying conversationally, "I know your Tom Weston! He was born to be a pirate and his silly father made him an ironmonger. Some day your Master Weston will seize His Majesty's *Royal Prince* and sail on it to Spain. There he'll make the King of Spain his prisoner for ransom!"

They both smiled and looked out at the great man-o'-war, *Royal Prince,* on which soldiers were being embarked from the quay. She was a glorious four-master with three plumes in gold over her stern gallery.

"It's a pity," she went on, as he joined her and they walked slowly along the sands toward the town, "that Master Weston isn't going to America with you. There's no one in all the two ships can compare with him for spirit unless it be Captain Standish. And Standish is no Pilgrim. He has a fiery temper of which he's very proud. He doesn't think of it as spleen, which it is, but as his soldier's courage, welling up from great depths and bursting all bonds!"

Robert laughed. "Yet he's the pleasantest man you can know."

"Isn't that just what I'm shewing you? Give me men who rant and swear and toy with their swords when they want something! Not those who flop to their knees and whine out a prayer!"

Throngs of soldiers were pouring out of the West Gate onto the quay, singing and shouting with a great gleam of pikes and arquebusses and shining helmets. Robert and Desire paused at the west end of the quay to let them pass.

"You ought to join Captain Standish's army," smiled

Cushman. "My fire-eating little son is his only recruit, so far. Look, yonder are my wife and Mistress Bradford!"

The two women were walking toward the cockboat with Will Bradford following them.

"My wife was very inquisitive about your errand ashore, this morning," Robert went on as they quickened their steps to join the others. "She'll be more so now."

Desire was amused. "How she'll envy me my place as eavesdropper!"

Mary hailed them shrilly from afar. "Where in the world did you find each other?"

"These wretched husbands of yours spoiled my retiring place in the spinney," answered Desire.

"I didn't see you," said Will bluntly, as he helped her into the boat.

"Nor did Master Cushman, till I hailed him," confessed Desire. "But I was sitting behind you and heard every word you said to each other."

"Never!" Bradford's voice was most annoyed.

"By my troth, yes!" with her sudden joyous laughter. "But I'll never tell a word, don't fear! Your colony is safe in my hands!"

Everybody joined in her mirth, even Will.

Mary said, "What a pity I wasn't there instead of you, Mistress Desire. I'd never have promised not to tell. Was it a very portentous conversation?"

"It was one of those utterly fond and footless conversations," replied Desire, "which men love to think are statesmanlike."

Dorothy and Mary giggled but Will and Robert looked at each other with something of chagrin in their smiles.

# IX

## Giles Heale

THERE was a mighty sound of hammering in the hold of the *Speedwell* as they rowed past her. The preparations for the "weighty passengers" were in progress. The others fell into talk about the discomforts the Brewsters and Carvers would endure in her but Robert did not join them. He was, in fact, struggling with another of the dizzy attacks which so annoyed him and mortified him too. He had always been a well man and had been very proud of the fact that at forty he was as fit for the wilderness life as any man of twenty-five. So now he said nothing of his feeling of illness and hoped that he was conquering it. But when they reached the *Mayflower's* deck, the great heat there, plus the smell of boiling fish from the galleys, smote him overwhelmingly. The deck rose blackly to meet him and he swooned.

When he came to himself, he was lying on his bed. He heard the linnet singing, then Mary's voice, "He's done this often of late. He goes without food, he meets with anxiety and then he swoons."

"But why does he go without food?" asked the doctor's young voice.

"He doesn't like Master Martin's choice of provisions, I suppose," was Mary's reply.

"But that's childish," protested the doctor.

"It's churlish insolence and he's well punished for it!" This was Chris Martin.

"Come, don't you be childish too, Governor," snapped Doctor Heale. "Now then, all of you go away! Out of the cabin! I'll sit with him till the medicine takes effect."

There was confusion for a moment, then quiet, and Robert dared open his eyes. He always recovered quickly from these spells and now he smiled at the doctor sitting at the foot of the bed. "Thank you, Giles! But my wife is mistaken. I've enjoyed the food."

Giles nodded. "I know Aunt Mary! What she meant was that *she* didn't enjoy Master Martin's diet. But you went into one of these swoons coming down the Thames, sir. I don't understand them. After all, you're no pale, puling miss of fifteen whose humors aren't worth noticing. I must find the source of your giddiness and attack it."

Robert looked at Giles with the pleasure his bright beauty always evoked. It was a young face, lean and regular of feature, with blue eyes under blond brows, a handsome, full mouth and with long auburn hair waving over his ruff. Even his black physician's cap could not detract seriously from the warmth and charm of that ruddy face and hair. He was not related to the Cushmans but Giles' father and Robert had been boyhood friends.

Giles rubbed his round chin thoughtfully. "Hum! Liver and spleen in a conspiracy! I shall have a cock cloven in two and laid fresh against the soles of your feet and a dose of spirits of amber every night."

"My good surgeon," protested Robert, "I don't want your cock's blood! They killed Prince Henry with that sort of physic."

The young doctor ignored the jibe. "I misdoubt me if you're fit for this mad voyage, Uncle Robert. It's a young man's venture."

Robert winced. "Don't be brazen in your pride of

youth, Giles! I am only two-and-forty, if I did sing 'Ride a cock horse' to you while you were still in petticoats."

"I'm not in petticoats now, though," grinned Giles, "and I tell you it's good that most of the Pilgrims are young like Edward Winslow. He's young and has a young wife whom he loves as a lover does a mistress. I ask you what braver front a man could present to the new world?"

"None!" agreed Cushman. "If a man has youth and his beloved, he can go singing to the very mouth of Hades."

"Whew!" breathed Giles. "And so even you have been in love in the long ago?"

"Don't be presumptuous!" said Robert crossly. "I'm hungry and if you'll remove yourself, I'll go get my dinner and pacify the governor as to the food."

"Not till we've tried the split cock," insisted the doctor.

"Well, if I must have the bird," grinned Cushman, "let's apply it well cooked and within, rather than without."

"Softly! I've given you amber and the splenic humor will soon be back in its own channel. I do wonder why it leaves its proper course! Did you have a shock this morning?" Giles scowled. "I've heard that anger or surprise will disturb the spleen."

"Mine is a shocking task." Robert's eyes were twinkling. "Consider the governor's high moods."

Giles laughed. "But seriously, dear Uncle Robert, nothing occurred that added to the weight above your heart about which you complained to me, the other day?"

Robert looked at Giles and said quietly, "Don't bother yourself, Giles. Not even you can plumb the depths of the pains and griefs of middle age."

The doctor returned the look, meditatively, and it was curious that he should have said after a time, "Tell me,

don't you think it's a shame and a pity that Mistress Minter should be removed to the *Speedwell?*"

"It will be a pity if she *is* removed," murmured Robert.

"She's not schooled to hardship as the other women
are," Giles went on. "When I think of her living 'tween
decks on the pinnace, I could weep for pity."

"Have you known Mistress Minter long?" asked Robert.

"Only since she came aboard this ship; a day; a century
ago! You know me as my own father knows me, Uncle
Robert. Tell me, am I worthy of her? Now don't say
there's no such thing as love at sight! Don't say she's a
year or so older than I. That's not gallant. And what
has age to do with love? 'There is a garden in her face,
Where roses and white lilies grow!' "

Robert suddenly felt very old. "Dear Giles," he
groaned, "do spare me your rhapsodies till I've eaten."

The young surgeon laughed apologetically. "Poor
Uncle Robert! Of course, you've forgotten the fond, silly
ways of lovers! Oh, it's glorious to be in love and with this
magnificent, mad voyage and a long life before me!"

"It must be! At the same time," smiling, "to boast over
the prostrate body of your aged patient isn't good for his
spleen or whatever may be the seat of his vile humor."

"True!" Giles flushed. "I'm a fool! Father always
said my tongue would undo all my physic wrought. Indeed, Uncle Robert, I never think of you as old."

"For this relief, much thanks," grunted Robert. He
sat up and swung his long legs over the edge of the bunk.
"Your amber's very potent, my good physician. I feel as
well as ever in my life."

Mistress Carver, hovering in the doorway, perceived
that the patient was up and hurried in, followed by her
several servants. "We must pack our clothing," she ex-

plained, "if all's well with you again, Master Cushman. Jasper More, run out and find Mistress Desire and bring her here and then help her as she directs you."

Jasper, a chubby little figure in dark blue, with hosen too long for him and doublet too short, pointed to Desire already entering the cabin, a steaming porringer in her hands.

She met Robert's glance for an instant, then looked down at her plump little aunt with her delightful wide smile. "Someone said you wanted me, Aunt Catherine! See how obedient I am? I come though I must bring my dinner with me!"

"Sit quiet for a moment, Uncle Robert," whispered Giles. "Let the amber do its full work."

"Finish your meal then, Desire," said Catherine briskly. "And after, Jasper and Elias will help you tie up your feather bed."

Mary Cushman drifted in with a trencher of fish and bread. Tommy followed with a tankard of beer.

"But," said Desire gently, "I'm not going over to the *Speedwell*, Auntie."

"Now, my good maid," crossly, "I can't fret myself—"

Desire interrupted firmly. "I don't want you to fret yourself, Aunt Catherine! It's quite right for you to go with Uncle John into this extra purgatory."

"Desire!" shrieked Catherine.

Giles nudged Robert.

"Well, worse than purgatory then, if you insist, dear Auntie." Desire's eyes were dancing. "What you forget is that I'm a woman grown and that while in my desperate need I've been docile so far"—this very slowly—"I can't be too docile. I shall stay on the *Mayflower*."

Robert said in a low voice, "Come, Mary and Tommy, I prefer to eat on deck."

"Don't disturb yourself, Master Cushman," smiled Desire. "We aren't going to quarrel."

"You may be seven and twenty, Desire Minter," cried Mistress Carver, "but as I reminded you this morning, you're unmarried! So you owe me reverence and obedience as your elder and your guardian. In my day, nay, even now, I wouldn't dare defy my elders as you do!"

"But these are modern times, Mistress Carver," cried Giles, rising, "and your niece—"

Little Mistress Carver turned on the young doctor fiercely. "Keep to your physic, Master Heale, of which I know a deal more than you do!" Giles collapsed beside Robert on the bed and Mary Cushman giggled. "As for you, Desire," Catherine swept on, "I'll be obliged to you if you'll tie up your feather bed."

"Not for the *Speedwell*, Auntie," said Desire gently. She perched herself on the feather bed in question and began to eat the stew which sent up a delectable odor from the porringer.

"Say something, Uncle Robert," whispered Giles.

"Not on my life and sword!" whispered Robert back.

Mary, sitting on the other side of Robert, had no such scruples. She clapped her hands. "It's like play acting! I went to hear the *Alchemist*—Ben Jonson, his play. Oh! I wore a mask! It was quite proper! We often went, at least when anything by Master Jonson or Master Shakespeare was played."

Catherine's attention was diverted for a moment. "And so while we toiled and waited, Robert Cushman dallied with Satan and bartered us into unrequited slavery!"

"Hoighty-toighty!" exclaimed a new voice. Deacon

Carver came slowly into the cabin. "Is our poor Robert being beaten again?"

"Aye! Help! Help!" cried Robert. "We're all getting a taste of the stick wielded by your wife. She's very firm in her discipline."

"Discipline!" sniffed Catherine, arms akimbo. "As if I'd presume to usurp you men your rights! My niece refuses to move to the *Speedwell,* John, and these others are interfering on her behalf. Do assert your authority!"

"Do you feel you need Desire's help on the pinnace?" asked Carver, looking affectionately down into his wife's anxious and indignant but always charming little face.

"Need her! Why, she's good only to read profane poetry and embroider herself shifts! I need her as I'd need Cleopatra's throne aboard the pinnace! What could your sister have been thinking about?"

John Carver's handsome eyes strayed to Desire's mischievous face, then to the window. Then he looked again at his wife. "You didn't know that the Bradfords are removing to the *Speedwell,* also. That makes us three married couples in the cabin and crowds it full. There'll be no room for Desire or young Jasper. We'll take but one servant with us."

"Thank heaven!" gasped Catherine.

"Have I fretted you so, Auntie?" cried Desire.

"Indeed you have, Desire," nodded Catherine. "I'm actually glad to have you off my hands for a while. Oh, it's not that you have been disobedient, really, except in the matter of the poetry. I'll admit that!"

Desire suddenly jumped to her feet and kissed her aunt, who reached up and touched Desire's cheek caressingly with her palm. "If you weren't so like your dearest mother, Desire," she sighed, "I could be severe with you."

"But I tremble at the mere sound of your voice, Aunt Catherine!" Desire kissed her again before returning to her porringer.

Robert had been eating throughout the conversation. The deacon turned to him to ask, "Robert, didn't you understand that Master Reynolds was merely delaying to make ready for the elder and me?"

"Yes, so he said," replied Robert.

"Well," sighed Carver, watching Catherine pack his clothing, "he's tearing out the very bowels of the pinnace, I should say. I can't see why. He won't tell me or the elder—is just his slippery, evasive self. Master Jones is in Southampton for the remainder of the day so he can't help us solve the riddle. Prithee, go over and see what you make of all the disturbance. That is if you feel well enough."

"Not so fast—" began Giles.

But Robert ignored him. "I'm perfectly recovered," he said. He put aside his trencher, glad of an excuse to escape from the cabin. It was true. He felt as well as ever.

On the main deck he encountered Martin in a new magenta-colored suit of fine cloth.

"Where are you going, Master Cushman?" demanded the governor.

Robert bit his lip and explained his errand.

Martin blinked rapidly. "You have nothing to do with the *Speedwell*. And you don't take commands from anyone but the governor of the *Mayflower*. You are not to talk to Reynolds. You are to remain in charge here while I go ashore. And—wait an instant—you've been so free demanding to see my accounts, let me see yours, sirrah!"

Robert stared. But it seemed to him when his flush of resentment had receded that Martin's was a fair enough demand and that if he gave the governor his account book, the governor certainly would not dare to refuse to hand over some sort of a statement in return.

"Good!" said Robert. He opened his leather pouch and taking out his notebook put it into Martin's clutching fingers. "You must remember, Governor, that the Merchant Adventurers are demanding from us a straight accounting of how every penny of their moneys has been spent. They've been very firm about it and claim they can have aid from the law if we don't comply."

"The law!" sneered Martin. He snapped his fingers. "That for the law! We go where there isn't no law."

"Wherever an Englishman goes, there goes English law!" declared Robert. "Don't forget that for a moment, my good governor."

Christopher squinted up at him, very pale. Robert thought that for the first time he had impressed the little man with some sense of the real gravity of his financial irregularities.

"As for my carrying out Deacon Carver's request," Robert went on, "you shall not prevent me. I must do all that I can to get the *Speedwell* moving. That is my duty as agent and you can't interfere. Stand out of my way!"

He shouted the last sentence and Martin jumped as if he'd been struck. Nor did he say more as Cushman strode across the deck. He pretended to be absorbed in the account book.

Robert made a quick crossing to the pinnace. From her hold rose terrific thuds, sharp hammering and unsubdued sea oaths. Reynolds stood at the open hatch, abaft the foremast, staring below and roaring orders. He paused to grin at Robert and say,

"I don't know what you thought you were buying when you bought this tub, Master Cushman."

Robert spoke shortly. "As you well know the ship was bought and equipped in Holland in my absence. But I know all about her. She's made many a long voyage on the high seas. She was known on all Thames side for her staunchness. What are you doing with her, now?"

To his surprise Reynolds replied without apparent reluctance, "Captain Jones said she was too much down by the stern which is true. I brought her by the stern before we left Holland but I admit it was a mistake. Now I'll try her trimmed down by the head. I stayed her masts too far forward, too."

"You won't unship the masts!" cried Robert in alarm.

"Don't bite yourself!" grinned Reynolds. "I'm only shifting the wedges between the mast and the partners to alter their rake. We won't touch the steps on the keelson."

Cushman threw up both hands. "You're pretending to be frank while you deliberately bewilder me!" he protested. "Look you, Master Reynolds, unless you've made it impossible, we *must* sail by the midnight tide if the wind continues fair."

"*Must?*" The silver toothpick again in evidence. "Come, you can't *must* a ship, if ye call this beer cask a ship. We'll sail when I'm ready."

"But, Master Reynolds, I don't understand," said Robert with what patience he could muster. "You lose as well as we by every day's delay. Every pound of food we consume, here, leaves us that much less for America where there'll be no crops for a year. And you signed for a year."

"Don't forget to add that the Merchant Adventurers

won't be sending supply ships, now," nodded Reynolds. He offered the toothpick to Robert and when Robert refused placed it carefully under the long black love lock which hung over his left ear. Then he went on in the other's own restrained manner. "When I signed my contract and took stock in this venture, I didn't understand the Pilgrims any better than I understood this pinnace. Now I know both and I don't like either, except yourself. You don't cozen yourself with holy words as the other chiefs do. Now, I can't improve your congregation, but by God's body, I can make the *Speedwell* do my will and she shall, if we remain here a week."

"You wrong us all!" protested Robert, not wishing to be drawn off the main point yet not willing to permit his friends to be so underestimated. "There may be hypocrites among our six score but—"

"But!" cackled Reynolds. "And what a world of difference! It's as good as a masque! Your handful of grand and reverend chiefs leading these wild Essex men who use you only as an escape from England!"

"Whatever they are," said Cushman shortly, "we shall lead them!" His blue eyes were half closed as he watched the yellow eyes opposite his. "And now, returning to the proper subject, let me remind you that you're under charter to sail the *Speedwell!*"

"Oh, I'll sail her! As long as you wish her to be sailed!" sneered the fat man. "It's a pity, though, you didn't force Chris Martin to come aboard her. I'd have drowned him for you with pleasure. As it is, watch him, Master Cushman! He's going about among your people, today, dropping a word here and there, and everyone who's heard the word believes you're in the pay of the Merchant Adventurers."

Robert shrugged his shoulders. "Oh, I've heard numerous hints on that theme, Master Reynolds. Don't bother to repeat them. Anyone with the sense of a fool must know they're groundless."

Reynolds cocked his absurd head on one side and gazed searchingly at Robert. "Groundless?" he repeated. "After all, who's to take care of the Adventurers' interests; see that they get their share of the beaver skins and cod? What will prevent Martin or Brewster or Bradford or Carver from trading for their private purses or for the Pilgrims, against the Adventurers?"

"Their honor—these men, their honor," replied Cushman quietly.

"Chris Martin's honor or Isaac Allerton's honor?" sneered Reynolds. "I know Allerton too. He's certain to trade on the sly."

"I won't listen to you!" cried Robert, his patience exhausted. "You're merely trying to keep me off the subject of the pinnace. When shall you be ready to sail, Master Reynolds?"

"I'll do my utmost to sail tonight," replied the master. "But Martin *is* cozening you. I could swear the reason he doesn't give me the food is because he hasn't bought enough. He can't have!"

Robert turned on his heel. "I shall tell Elder Brewster and the others to move themselves aboard at once," he said.

He saw a satisfied grin on the seaman's face as he was rowed away from the *Speedwell,* and wondered uneasily how he might have played into the fellow's hands.

# X

## The River of Ahava

JOHN CARVER and William Brewster were leaning over the *Mayflower's* bulwarks as Robert's boat approached. Their faces were anxious.

"Well, Robert? Well? Well?" queried Carver as Cushman came up the ladder.

"Reynolds says he'll sail on tonight's tide. He's been shifting the rake of his masts but it seems not to be a lengthy piece of business," he reported.

"Thank God for His mercies!" ejaculated the elder and turned away, his face working.

"We'll move our goods to the pinnace, now," said Carver. "The elder wishes us to have a combined service aboard this ship before we separate for the voyage. I'd say about eight o'clock this evening, then, since actually we sail tonight."

Robert nodded soberly. With Carver's words he was realizing that the much-longed-for, the greatly dreaded moment was very near when they must bid farewell to English soil. The people must be told. He spoke to John Alden standing near-by and asked him to spread the news. The young cooper ran eagerly among the groups dispersed over the ship and a little ripple of cheers followed him. A few of the women wept. There rose a clamor of excited voices. Many were for visiting the town once more. Governor Martin appeared and began his interminable wrangling again with the shore-goers. Master

Jones came aboard and immediately four young men borrowed his boat: Edward Winslow, Miles Standish, John Alden, and Giles Heale.

"Reynolds tells me he'll take the eight o'clock tide," said Jones, pausing to lean beside Robert against the bulwarks. "Never in God's world was there so lunatic a venture as this! Its men, its designs, its regiments are melancholy mad!" He shook his sandy head.

"But not *melancholy!*" said Cushman dryly. He pointed to the boatload of young men. They were singing lustily, "It was a lover and his lass!" at the top of very stout lungs. As the two men gazed, Standish's great sea oar caught him in the chest. He catapulted backward into Winslow's lap and both rolled over, fetching Giles, who was steering, a hearty kick in the stomach. In a second the cockboat was careering in the trough of the waves while the four young men rocked, helpless with laughter.

Jones guffawed. "Yes! You're right! Most of 'em are young and silly and that may save us."

"Where do they suppose they're going?" asked Robert, laughing also.

"Now, who would want to know?" cried Jones. "Winslow's the only Pilgrim in the boat, remember! I hope they *all* get sodden drunk, bless their silliness!"

"Sometimes, lately, I've wished I was sodden drunk myself," sighed Robert.

"You'll wish it many a time in the future," returned the sailor cheerfully. "Wait till we meet the west winds September will bring us! And that easterly current, out there, sometimes holds a westbound ship at a standstill for days. And I'm overloaded. I wish you could have got those charts from the Dutch of their soundings around Cape Cod and the Hudson."

"There was no hope after we refused to go to the Hudson," said Robert.

"Well, I've found those North Virginian shores, or as I should say, New England, once before and I'll find them again, God bless us and so forth," declared Jones.

"I'm certain you will," agreed Cushman heartily. "It's a gallant undertaking, Master! Thank God, it's going forward at long last."

"Aye! Who'd be a landsman with roots anchoring him in the soil?"

They both were silent, then Robert said, his eyes on Southampton, "And yet that's a comely, comfortable sort of a town, if one must stay at home, Master Jones."

"Aye!" the seaman nodded. "You'll never see ought so comely again, my friend."

Robert gave him a quizzical glance. "You do put heart in a man, Master!"

Jones' eyes twinkled, then suddenly he jerked his head forward. "Look! In that small hired boat! It's Mistress Minter with a bundle peeping from under her skirts and a cloak over all, this steaming day. She must have put off from the pinnace, the hussy! Do you suppose she's leaving us? Don't stand like a stork! Do you know?"

"I know she doesn't want to stay with us," replied Robert with a sinking heart.

"Go follow her, while I report to Deacon Carver," ejaculated the master.

Robert shook his head. "I promised her this morning I'd not interfere if she really decided to leave."

"Are you a fool?" demanded Jones. "Don't you know she's a natural chief among the women; that women are the very pox in a voyage and she can keep 'em in order? And besides that, she's a damned handsome, valiant hussy and is good luck to my ship. Now will you go after her?"

"No," replied Robert miserably.

"I'll see the deacon, and if I were ten years younger, wife or no wife, I'd thumb my nose at you all and take her to have and to hold!" Jones strode into the steerage.

Chis Martin was shrieking at the two Brewster lads who were climbing up the mainmast, and had almost reached the foretop. "Come down, ye imps, or I'll fetch your father!"

Wrestling's pink and white face, high above the deck, was turned downward long enough to put out a red tongue at the governor, then it was turned upward again. Martin darted toward the steerage, caught sight of Robert and paused.

"My good honest assistant!" He took Robert's little account book from his purse, opened it and after a moment's study pointed at an item he'd marked. "From T. Weston. 4 pounds, June 12, 1620." His finger was trembling. "Explain this to me and the people at large, for so you shall if I live!"

Robert replied wearily. "That's a personal loan. It has no connection with the Pilgrims."

"Did you repay him?" demanded the governor.

"I left my watch worth twenty pounds with him as a pledge," answered Robert wearily.

"So you say!" sneered the other. "So *you* say! But I say that your wife was wearing that very watch on a chain around her neck when she went into town with me and my wife yesterday. She said it was your watch. But mayhap, being a man of great affairs, you have two watches."

Robert pulled off his hat and rumpled his hair a little wildly. "Nay, I have only one watch which was willed to me by my father."

"So Mistress Cushman told us!" triumphantly. "Some people say you can't believe her but this time she spoke the truth. So you *are* in the pay of the Adventurers, my cursed, knavish assistant."

Robert's long arm shot out. He seized the governor by the ear and twisted it.

"For God's sake, you'll shame me before the people," gasped Chris, writhing.

"I hope so!" through set teeth.

"I'm sorry I accused you," muttered Martin.

"And my wife?"

" 'Twasn't meant."

Robert released him and wiped his fingers ostentatiously on his kerchief. Martin glanced anxiously around but for the moment the deck had been deserted. The episode had passed unnoticed unless Love and Wrestling had seen or a sailor on the forecastle who at that moment began to sing a song with a witching air:

> "Hey nonny no!
> Men are fools that wish to die!"

Love Brewster's delicate soprano voice joined in from high above.

Robert took the account book from Martin's unresisting fingers and returned it to his purse. The governor rushed into the steerage and Robert, ashamed of his flare of temper, turned again to the sea. Desire's boat had reached the quay.

But he felt no impulse to follow her. She was part and parcel of the almost universal frustrations of his life. Nothing could be more idle than an attempt to keep her near him. Let her return to her darling England. England!

There surged over him an engulfing agony of homesickness.  Suddenly he beckoned to a hovering small boat which awaited business near-by, and entering it, told the man to put him ashore at the spinney.  He was not proposing to pursue Desire.  He was going to be alone with England for the last time.

When he reached the sands before the copse, he told the boatman to return in an hour.  Then he walked northward among the trees until he was beyond the sound of the sea.  Here was bracken, knee-high and in an open glade, heather of a delicate pink and the odor of fern and flower combined, as he strolled through them, to ravish his heart as no other English beauty ever had ravished it.  Knee-deep in this loveliness he stared about him, looking and listening, striving to impress on his memory every outline of every tree, every tall spike of foxglove, every burst of melody from branch and bush.

And yet, he told himself, this was not what he was leaving with so much anguish.  That to which he was saying farewell was not written in this glade but in his heart; he was leaving behind him on this island not the mere forty-two years of his life but the thousand years of England which had preceded that life.

Beowulf, Chaucer, Alfred, Canute, Norman William, crusading Richard, Bloody Mary, gorgeous Elizabeth, Lyly, Sidney, Shakespeare, these were England!  And yet not all of England!  He gazed on the dreaming landscape.

> ". . . this fortress built by nature for herself
> Against infection and the hand of war,
> This happy breed of men, this little world,
> This precious stone set in a silver sea,

Which serves it in the office of a wall,
Or as a moat defensive to a house
Against the envy of less happier lands,
This blessed spot, this earth, this realm, this England—"

He paused, even these perfect words failing him. Then he whispered, "God! God! Comfort me! For only You are left!"

But comfort did not come. Instead, there rushed over him again the biting realization that England did not want him, that she denied him the most boasted possession of her citizens, freedom to be himself. She desired neither him nor his love, nor did she want that gallant crowd yonder on the two ships.

His dreams for the enlargement of England's glory, his loyalty, his admiration—she spurned them. He was outcast. These very trees he caressed so tenderly, already he was foreign to them. He was not wanted.

And then he cast himself downward in the heather and bracken, clutching the soil with both fists, and wept passionately, as he never before had wept.

The shadows were deep under the oaks when at last he rose. When he reached the shore the boatman grumbled that he'd been kept waiting overlong. Robert could see that the *Mayflower* and the *Speedwell* had been lashed together in preparation for the joint prayer service and he told the man to give way, quickly.

By the time he reached the deck of the *Mayflower*, the people were singing the evening hymn. Elder Brewster stood at the rail of the half deck, his lean figure elegant as usual and somehow comforting to look upon. The people crowded the main deck and spread back over the forecastle where they mingled with the sailors. Gulls sailed through the rigging. Trumpets sounded from the *Prince Henry* and as the hymn was finished, the watch called from the walls of Southampton and Elder Brewster's great voice rang out.

"I will read you again that part of Pastor Robinson's letter to us which I consider most needful for this moment of trial. For from the moment we put off to sea, you become a new people.

"'Lastly, whereas you are become a body politic, using amongst yourselves civil governments and are not furnished with any persons of special eminency above the rest to be chosen by you into the office of government, let your wisdom and godliness appear not only in choosing such persons as do entirely love and will promote the common good but also yielding them all due honor and obedience in their lawful administration. Not beholding in them the ordinariness of their persons but God's ordinance for your good. You know that the image of the Lord's power and authority which the magistrate bears is honorable in however mean a person. And this duty you may the more willingly and ought the more consciously to perform because you are, at least for the present, to have only them for your ordinary governors which you yourselves shall make choice of for that work.

"'These few things, I do earnestly commend to your care and conscience, joining therewith my daily incessant prayers unto the Lord that He Who has made the heavens and the earth, the sea and all the rivers of water and Whose Providence is over all His works, especially His dear children, for good, will guide you in your ways. As inwardly by His Spirit, so outwardly by the Hand of His power, all the days of your life. Fare you well in Him you trust and in Whom I rest. John Robinson.'"

"Amen," said John Carver.

"Ezra 8:21," read Elder Brewster. *"Then I proclaimed a fast there at the river of Ahava that we might afflict ourselves before God to seek of Him a right way for us and for our little ones and for all our substance. Psalm 107: They that go down to the sea in ships, that do business in great waters, these shall see the works of the Lord and His wonders in the great deep. For He commandeth and raiseth the stormy wind which lifteth the waves thereof. They mount up to heaven. They go down again to the depths. Their soul is melted because of trouble. . . . Then they cry unto the Lord in their trouble and He bringeth them out of their distress. He maketh the storm a calm so that the waves thereof are still. Then are they glad because they be quiet: so He bringeth them unto their desired haven. Amen."*

Brewster's face worked and he covered it with his hands. There was a sound of weeping from the people.

Then Master Jones' silver whistle piped. He was answered by the mate's and then the bosun's pipe. Sailors pushed through the thronging passengers to the capstan. To add to the confusion, two boatloads of pressed men appeared, who were shoved and dragged to the forecastle of the *Mayflower*, whither the two masters followed to divide them. *Mayflower* passengers clutched the less fortunate *Speedwell* folk in gloomy good-bys.

Robert was among the last to bid the elder and his little group Godspeed! He was thankful to Deacon Carver who cut all short by saying cheerfully, "We'll have the fires alight and the pot boiling for you when you reach New England, friends! Come, let's not try Master Reynolds' patience too far!" He led the way aboard the *Speedwell*. Sailors unlashed the two ships.

The sailors manning the capstan tramped round and round to their rough chantey: "Lustily, lustily, sail we forth—"

Sailors ran up the rigging and loosed the sails. Sailors on the decks braced the yards. The capstan clanked and the anchor rose. The wind caught the sails, the ship's stern swung round and with the shouts of the men at the braces, she picked up her headway and moved down the harbor.

Robert tried to soothe Mary who was sobbing inordinately. Christopher Martin was weeping on his Marie's comfortable bosom. Isaac Allerton, the tailor, stood with both hands clutching the rail, tears pouring down his cheeks. Thomas Blossom, frail but calm, patted his wife's hands.

But Edward Winslow, with reddened lids, sprang to the half-deck rail and shouted his own message above the clamor of the ship.

"Why the tears, good friends? Our beautiful ship is stout and spacious. The wind blows fair. The skies are clear. Our ship's master is tried and true. And yonder in the west beckons us all that man can desire: freedom, our own broad acres, mayhap gold and silver. We know there's beaver and fish in endless supply. And we shall live, work and pray with naught between us and our God but His own sweet Heavens. We're the most blessed Englishmen in the world, today! Why weep?"

His face was young and ardent, flushed and vivid. The people, gazing and listening, lost their frightened looks and broke into smiles. Someone cheered. And young Love Brewster, who with his brother had been left in Standish's care, broke into the entrancing air he'd learned that afternoon. A score of voices took it up.

"Hey nonny no!
Men are fools that wish to die.
Isn't it fine to dance and sing,
When the bells of death do ring?
And to sing Hey nonny no!
When the winds blow
And the seas flow.
Hey nonny no!"

"Now that's a precious text to start our fearful voyage with!" groaned Chris Martin. "Master Cushman, go shut them up!"

But Robert gave no heed to the governor. He was enjoying the song. And most of the people, arms interlocked, swaying to the music, continued to sing "Hey nonny no," as the walls of Southampton dropped behind them.

# XI

## *Hopeth All Things*

**M**ARY dried her tears. "I didn't think I could bring myself to the parting," she said brokenly. "God forgive you for putting me through it, Robert Cushman, for I can't."

"Ah, don't say that!" he cried.

"As if you care about my forgiveness!" she exclaimed. "You can't know how I suffer. No one on the ship does, except Desire Minter, and she can only guess at it. Poor maid! She remained below, for she said she couldn't trust herself not to go ashore, somehow, at the last."

"But she did go, two hours ago," said Robert.

"Nay, she returned with me just before the prayer service," insisted Mary. "I asked no questions for once in my life. But she had her bags with her when I came upon her at the quay."

Robert did not speak. He could not.

Mary caught sight of Tommy perched in the ratlines fifteen feet above the deck. "Do look at your son, Robert! That boy grows more like a monkey every day. You'd better fetch him before he breaks his neck. I feel queasy and shall go to bed."

Something had begun to glow warmly in Robert's heart. He swung himself up beside Tommy who was singing softly to himself, swaying as the ship swayed.

"Isn't it glorious?" shouted the boy. "Did you ever

think of being a ship's master, father?" He turned a
flushed, happy face to Cushman.

"Yes, very seriously at your age. But I liked farming
better when it came to a choice, later."

"We'll have a great farm in America!" nodded Tommy.
"I'll put cannons at the ends of the lanes and along the
walls to keep the savages out. We'll have a moated
manor house with a drawbridge. I'll work the drawbridge.
No more wool-combing for you, father! That's worth leaving England for, I say!" He began to sing lustily, "Hey
nonny no!"

Robert listened contentedly. It was heartening to realize that Tommy never would know the spiritual igno-
minies with which England shamed her home-keeping sons.
And that whatever hardships he was about to give the boy,
there would be in them nothing sordid. The struggle
would be set against a background of mighty daring.

The two remained in the rigging until the stars came
out and the ship acquired a pitch as well as a roll. Then,
with the rest of the passengers, they were glad to go to
bed.

The channel was rough and they had a wretched night.
Everyone in the great cabin was sick and the intimacy of
the crowded quarters was hateful to all. About dawn,
Mary fell asleep and Robert crept out to see how Tommy
had fared. The lad was sleeping soundly in the longboat.
The *Speedwell* could just be distinguished about a quarter
mile behind them. Robert stood shivering in the early
light. Master Jones, coming out of his cabin, grinned
broadly at his favorite passenger.

"Ye look like one dead of the plague for a week," he
shouted. "Come up here for a tumbler of brandy."

Robert managed to wave his hand and made shift to

reel to the starboard ladder, then with infinite labor to reach the half deck where the mate laughed at him. Jones hauled him into the poop cabin and handed him half a tumbler of raw liquor.  Robert tossed it off and promptly rushed for the window.  Having got rid of the drink, he wiped the sweat from his face and discovered that his seasickness was gone.

The master eyed him keenly.  Then he nodded. " 'Twill either kill or cure, that dose!  You'll not be seasick again, Master Cushman."

"You've saved me from worse than death and my gratitude's commensurate!" gasped Robert, more than half in earnest.

"Eat some of this," nodded the sailor, giving Cushman a lump of salt beef to gnaw, "and leave gratitude to those who are unfriends.  And whilst you chew, look aft at the *Speedwell.*"

Both put their heads out of the stern window.  Beneath was a great whirl of waters.  Spray drenched their hair. Now and again a wave swept to the sills of the great-cabin windows underneath.  But eastward, above the boil of the sea, one could now and again catch a glimpse of the reeling masts of the *Speedwell.*

"She's taking water, I fear," said Jones.  "See how sluggish she moves?"

"Is she in danger?" cried Cushman.

"Reynolds won't let himself drown," grunted the master.  "Lord, I mislike seeing a good seaman abuse a good ship!  That pinnace is as sweet a little craft as ever lived."

"She's especially sweet to us since our welfare in America depends on her," said Robert.

"If Reynolds was my man I'd burst his skull with a

marlinspike, the great up-ended hog trough!" remarked
the sailor.

"Aye, aye, sir!" nodded Robert. "But since unhappily
that may not be, what shall we do? Lay to and let her
overhaul us?"

"Not yet! He'll be lowering the topsails soon I hope,
and we'll see what she does then. Methinks she might be
overmasted. Now I wonder—" His voice died off in
thought as he eyed the troubled pinnace.

Robert finished the salt beef and began to feel his own
man again, and since he was helpless as to the *Speedwell*,
suddenly bethought him of the *Mayflower's* needs and
went below. He managed a toilet of sorts and then sought
Tommy. Tommy was on the forecastle top, with a look-
out man, happy as a born sailor can be. Robert dropped
down the ladder to the gun deck.

Giles Heale, that effulgent young surgeon, lay flat on the
deck, too ill to move to his bed. Miles Standish sat with
his back against the little cabinet he and Rose occupied.
The shallop was a shambles. The bunks gave forth
groans and protests. Passengers' belongings slid back
and forth across the deck mixed with ship's stores and
somewhat of water which sprayed in through the gun
ports. It looked, Robert thought, as if the place was
plague-stricken.

He couldn't brandy the lot of them, scarcely would have
dared to try Master Jones' furious remedy on the lads,
anyway, but at least he could give all of them a drink of
rum and water.

He went back to the master and asked for a bucket of
the decoction and a ladle and calling Tommy to help him,
once more entered the gun deck. Some of the men were
crawling about now, trying to adjust themselves to the

violent motion of the ship, to the immense amusement of a sailor on his way back to the steerage.  He paused over the recumbent Giles and called him a vile name.

Robert, at that moment, arrived with his potation.  "Get out!" he ordered the man, a sturdy, stocky specimen with one eye and that eye very bright and blue.

"I takes orders from no Brownists," sneered the sailor.

"But you'll take orders from me," returned Robert calmly.  "Get aft or wherever you're going and keep that foul mouth shut as you go!"

"And that I won't, ye sniveling lob-cock," grunted the man, thrusting his red face menacingly close to Robert. Robert promptly gave him a box on the ear which happily coincided with the arrival of a sliding cask of nails against the fellow's legs and sent him headlong.  He was up on his haunches in an instant, staring, obviously wondering if Cushman's blow had been as shrewd as it seemed.

There was something about that blue eye which Robert liked.  "Here," he said, "as you seem in no haste, help me dose these people!  The bucket's too much for my son with such a sea on.  You shall have a ladle or two for yourself at the end."

The man continued to stare at Robert who had spoken in a voice which was entirely friendly.  "You have a hard hand, Master," remarked the sailor.

"You mean you have a soft head!" jibed Cushman. "Come along!  Show these poor folk how easily a sailor rides this galloping deck."

"Damned if I don't!" exclaimed the man, seizing on the bucket.

They raised Giles and gave him the first draught, and after helped him to sit under the hatch where he could rest in the warmth of the sunlight.  Then they moved on to the

others. By the time they'd made half the rounds, Giles
was up and tottering to his bunk. Captain Standish took
a deep drink and announced that he was well enough to
carry his wife a ladleful. Others did not find the rum
helpful but quite the reverse. However, the Brewster lads
and John Billington and Bob Carter, who was Mullins'
servant, and Mullins, himself, shortly were able to keep
down the salt beef and bread which Tommy gave them,
and having dosed all, Robert felt that he could now turn
his attention to the great cabin.

He passed the brimming last ladleful to the sailor.
"Here you are, my lad! Now what's your name?"

"Jock Coombs, my master!" tossing off the rum and
water at a gulp.

"I thank you for your help, Jock," said Cushman
gravely.

The sailor pulled his forelock. "I'm well paid, Master,"
and started off, but returned to say with a jerk of his
thumb at Tommy, "I'd keep him out of the forecastle, sir!
He'll learn no good there." He rubbed his ear and moved
well out of Robert's reach. "You be the only greasy-
bellied Brownist I ever see that was a man!" Then he ran
for the steerage ladder.

Amused and not ungrateful, Robert made his way up
to the great cabin. Things were better here, with Winslow and one or two of the others able to help. There
was no sign or sound of life, though, from behind Desire
Minter's curtains. The More children had quite recovered and were playing at the table and Robert bade
Tommy take them out on deck. Mary still slept. After
he had done what he could, Robert too went on deck and
after an anxious look at the *Speedwell,* he lay down in

Tommy's bed in the longboat and fell into a dreamless sleep.

It was well into the afternoon when he woke. The wind had lessened and the sea had gone down and there were a number of passengers sitting or lying about the deck. Edward Winslow and his Elizabeth sat on the starboard ladder to the half deck. Both looked wan but indescribably happy. Elizabeth was exquisitely blond with masses of curly hair of the palest yellow. She was very small and of a dauntless energy. Even now she had a bit of sewing in her fingers.

Robert, feeling quite himself, went in to attend to Mary. She was fretful and begged him to leave her alone. Desire's curtains were still drawn. He went up to the poop to watch the *Speedwell*. She had lowered her topsails and wallowed less heavily. The poop deck proved a most pleasant spot, for the lateen and bonnet sails on the mizzenmast completely screened one here from the rest of the ship. It was a precious privilege to have such privacy and Robert leaned for a long time on the taffrail, hoping that no one would intrude on him. But at the end of the hour, Desire Minter very quietly joined his watch. He gave a great start and stared at her.

"You!" he exclaimed.

"Master Jones told me I'd find you here," she said, smiling.

"I was afraid you were very ill." Robert scrutinized her pale face. "You look as if you'd not enjoyed your twenty-four hours of seclusion."

"I didn't. But I'm well again. Master Jones came down to us an hour ago. He stood in the doorway and roared that we were to stop fighting the roll of the ship and *go* with it. Then he forced brandy on us and presto! Here am I! And Mistress Mary is better and wants you, so I offered to find you. She is anxious to be helped on deck. She says you'll carry her as Master Winslow did his wife."

"And so I will," agreed Robert. Then he added a little huskily, "I gave you up yesterday when I gave up England."

Her face was very gentle in the afterglow. "What do you mean, Master Cushman?"

"Master Jones and I thought you'd gone into Southampton, never to return," answered Robert.

"You shouldn't have sent him to my uncle," she said. "That made me a pox of trouble."

"I did nothing of the sort," protested Robert. "And I feel myself most virtuous because I refused to follow you at his command. But why did you return?"

Desire hesitated.

"Tell me, do!" he urged. "For you had taken your goods with you. We could see that."

She looked back at the *Speedwell* for a long time, then she said, soberly, "Well, I'll tell you why, Robert Cushman, and trust you not to misunderstand me. As I stood on the quay waiting for the person who was to accompany me back to London, I saw your yellow head as you strode across the sands to the spinney. And there was something very lonely about you and I had an impulse to follow you and discover what your new trouble might be. I knew that you must be going to the spinney to wrestle with some portentous problem. I thought you were meeting someone there as you had met Master Bradford. But you passed on into the copse and somehow I was fretted as the trees swallowed you. And so I did follow."

She paused, her hands on the rail beside Robert's. He

was quite unable either to move or speak.  Desire continued in a tense voice.

"And so, I saw your grief!  Your words to England, I heard, and I saw you weep and I dared not intrude.  It seemed to me too piteous a thing, that you should be so alone.  It was not endurable, that even I, whom you had asked to be your very friend, must not comfort you.  I came away.  And as I walked back to the quay, I thought of all I'd observed concerning you and I realized that you stood alone; that there was no one among all the Pilgrims upholding your so skillful hands."

She faltered a little, now, as she turned to look full into his eyes.  "If I'd been St. Paul writing to the Corinthians I'd never have prated of charity.  Nay, I'd have talked of friendship," her voice steadying, "that which you need more than anyone else on these two ships.  You need a friend."  Robert dared lay his hand on hers and she did not move as she added slowly, "Friendship is kind—vaunts not itself—seeketh not her own—thinketh no evil—beareth all things—hopeth all things—friendship never faileth. You said, I remembered, that I took Tom Weston's place. And so, even though I'd refused to fill Tom's niche, I returned to the ship."

He bowed his head on their clasped hands and when he raised it, he said, "Nothing matters, now!"  He dared to say no more and they stood in the silence of perfect communion.

Desire broke this by saying, "I was certain you'd understand."

"You've not only given me back my self-esteem," he exclaimed.  "You're making me proud and vain.  I *must* be a great man to have earned so limitless a reward!  And to think that the world looks on me as simple Robert Cushman!"

She gave a happy little laugh and freed her hands. "Come, then," she said. "We must go to Mistress Cushman."

He followed her down through the steerage.

Mary was sitting up in her bed, very large of eyes. "It took you a long time to find him!" was her greeting.

"Nay, I found him quickly enough on the poop deck," returned Desire, "but I held him there in talk. It was beautifully fresh after the hours in this kennel. I advise you all to crawl out into the breeze."

There came a hollow groan from Christopher Martin. Robert, who had persuaded him earlier to try the brandy cure with the most disastrous results, murmured, "Alas, poor Yorick!" and lifting Mary across his chest, carried her to the half deck. Desire, following, spread his great cloak in the shelter of the poop house and on this Robert seated Mary.

Master Jones peered from his quarters and cried heartily, "Another rescue! Jem, bring out the Madeira bottle and some bread! Now, Mistresses both, sop some bread in the wine and forget all the foul shore muck you've been eating. You are true sailors now eating good salt food on the good salt sea. Mistress Minter," taking Jem's tray in his own great hands, "seat yourself beside Mistress Cushman and you, Master Cushman, sit on the other side, that your wife may lean against your shoulder. But only the cold wall for your unmarried head, Mistress Minter!" Master Jones, enjoying his own quip immensely, poured the wine and returned to the study of his charts.

Mary leaned comfortably against her husband while she and Desire sipped wine and nibbled bread contentedly.

The stars came out. The first mate paced the half deck just beyond them, pausing now and again to look down through the hatch at the binnacle in the steerage and to give an order to the man at the helm. The lateen sail bellied above them and the great swell of the mainsail forward hardened as the wind freshened again. Desire, having finished her bread and wine, left the husband and wife together saying that she must put the little Mores to bed.

Said Mary, when Desire had gone, "In spite of all, I like the Martins! They're kind people. You must stop quarreling with Master Christopher, Robert."

"He must stop quarreling with me, who am only his poor underling," protested Cushman. "Our last quarrel, by the way, was concerned with my watch. How did you come by it, my dear?"

Mary sat up. "The silly tell-tale! I asked him not to speak of it to you. Tom Weston said I was to return it to you when we were well out at sea."

"Did you explain to Martin that it was a pledge?" asked Robert.

"Certainly not! I'm discreet, I hope! He's very prying. If I'd told him that he'd have asked me why we needed four pounds, and I'd have had to admit it was for clothes." Mary's voice was a little shrill.

Robert stiffened. "But not clothes! You know I put that money into buying shares in the venture. It was two months ago when it looked as if all must fail for lack of money."

"Then with what did you pay for our clothing?" obstinately.

"Those were paid for long since when we first went to

London, out of my savings. And that you knew also, Mary. Why such stupidity?"

"But I bought more this May," in a little rush of words. "A lovely durance petticoat and a gilt bodice and a handsome blue grogram gown lined with pink velvet. I do hope you were honorable enough to pay for them, Robert."

He mustered all his forbearance. "Don't dodge and hide, Mary," he said still gently. "You should have told me. And you must have known such gauds would be worthless in the forests."

"I know it now," she mourned, "but I thought you'd be a ruler or governor, or whatever it might be, of the colony. Now I know it's impossible because people say you're Tom Weston's and the Merchants' man."

"You deny it emphatically, I hope!" he exclaimed.

She hesitated. "I know how friendly they were to you and you to them. And how you used to eat great dinners with them and how you went to masques and the play with them. And I heard you'd drunk toasts with them. And I don't see any great harm if you are in their pay so long as you plant the colony honestly."

Robert was aghast. "Mary! You haven't said this to the others? To Chris Martin? Mary, you know I *couldn't* take a farthing from the Adventurers in wage! You're my wife and you *must* know me that well. Have you said this to Martin? The truth now, because I shall ask him."

"I—I answered his questions." She was frightened. "But for a certainty I know you couldn't do a dishonorable act, Robert, you are *too* strait-laced if anything. Merely to look at you proves that. But you will pay for my gowns, won't you, Robert?"

"Naturally," he answered sternly, and then was silent out of sheer helpless exasperation.

Then to his surprise Mary spoke freely. Perhaps her conscience for once was uneasy. "I was afraid to tell you. Sometimes I'm very afraid of you."

That somehow touched him. "Not afraid, Mary!" he protested. "I don't like a woman to fear me. Surely I'm kind to you!"

"Kind? Yes, in your way, which is a giving way. And you do give me everything but your love."

"Do you want my love?" he asked warily. A moment of such frankness between them never had occurred before.

"And if I did, could you give it?" she countered.

"Could you give me yours?" he returned.

"No!" she cried with curious vehemence. Then as if she would soften this, she added, "You and I can't even be friends."

"I don't see why you're so sure of that," remarked Robert, turning over in his mind the novel thought of Mary as his friend. The thought left him cold.

"There's no such thing as friendship between a man or a woman," she explained. "Either they're mere acquaintances or they are lovers. And of both, your Master Shakespeare says, 'Most friendship is feigning, Most loving mere folly.'"

The good moment had sped.

"You have a most unpleasant mind, Mary!" Robert felt extraordinarily indignant.

She yawned. "Mayhap I have! Help me back to bed, Robert. This knavish ship is bemusing me again."

A thousand times in their few years of marriage, it had been thus. She had outraged his most abiding sensibilities, then by her utter indifference had made either anger or resentment futile. He sometimes wondered at his own forbearance; as now. He lifted her, obediently. She was so slight and lay so easily across his heart, one arm around his neck. Aye, they were not lovers, indeed! The embrace held sweetness for neither of them. And yet he could be tender with her, for back of all the qualities he neither understood nor liked in her, he felt her utter dependence on him. He laid her in the bunk and saw Tommy to bed in the longboat. Then he fell to pacing the deserted decks, absorbed by his thoughts.

But he was not thinking of Mary. Serious as the consequences of her half lie to Martin about the watch might be, he thrust the thought of it aside. Time must take care of that canard. To straighten out the matter with Martin would be impossible. Ordinarily, such a scene as he had had with Mary would have upset him for hours, but not now. Desire's words at the taffrail filled his whole mind.

He was touched, he was moved, he was elated. No woman in his life had so reached his soul; no man ever had so filled him with joy.

And yet, for all the joy, he knew that the words Desire had spoken in the spinney after his meeting with Bradford and not those she had just uttered at the taffrail pronounced the real verdict on their friendship. It could not be. In her tenderness and her loyalty had she forgotten that her life was to be spent among Separatists? Or had she deluded herself into thinking their friendship could survive in such an environment?

Anything had seemed possible to both of them at that splendid moment an hour ago. But alone, on the windswept deck, Robert faced the cold truth. It could not be. Yet, just for one dangerous, joyous moment, he toyed with the dream of what might have been had his lot been

cast in the class to which Desire belonged and of which
he'd seen much in the years just past.

In London, in that group of men who called themselves
Merchant Adventurers, were gentlemen who lived at court,
rich men who wanted to live at court but could not and
a peer or two, one of whom was a patron of poets and
players, as the Earl of Southampton had been Shakespeare's patron.

It was more than mere money itch that had led several
of these Adventurers into the Pilgrim business.  Romance
called them, too, and Robert, who was hazarding all that
they would have liked to have hazarded themselves, had
for them something of an heroic quality.  They invited
him to their homes that they might have more than mere
business conversations with him and in these fine mansions
Robert caught glimpses of a life to which, by both nature
and taste, he belonged.  It was a life, it seemed to him, so
spacious, so beautiful as to belong to a fairy world.  And
not the least alluring of its charms was the one he was re-
calling now.  He had been a guest in several houses where
men and women did have true and sexless friendships
that were taken as a matter of course.

But these were London folk who had naught to do but
cultivate the graces of life; folk who read Virgil and Plato
as Puritans read their Bible; who could grow violent in
debate over the merits of the sonnet form as against the
madrigal; who if they spoke at all of the writings of the
Separatists or of the Church prelates, spoke with contempt; who looked on the plays of Jonson and Shakespeare
as true and magnificent forms of literature; and who could
spend a night in a lamentable, delectable wrangle on
beauty, its limitations and true definition.

But he *was* a Separatist.  And Desire, although of this

other class, had cast her lot in with Separatists. And to these, a woman was ever a female and a man a male. Christians though they tried to be, his fellow Pilgrims never would see his friendship for Desire in its actual purity and beauty.

A shadow began to loom terribly in his mind. Life, it seemed, was a series of losses, continuing until came loss of life itself. His children had been taken from him, and Sarah; then Weston, then England, and now Desire. There remained Tommy and the colony.

Giles Heale once had pointed out a discovered fact to him. Men deprived of certain senses grew proportionately stronger in the remaining senses. The blind man's ability to hear and to feel was greater than the whole man's. So, when domestic affection was lost to him with Sarah and the children, his capacity for friendship increased. But he and Weston were separated and friendship with Desire was impossible. With friendship wiped out, his love—for it seemed that love, itself, was indestructible—his love might have been given all to England. But since England could not, would not, accept it, the colony must receive the whole of the flood.

Aye, love was the most universal chemical in God's mysterious alchemy. Nor was it at all limited in its objects to persons or creatures. Did a man feel devotion to an idea, his pulse could leap at thought of it as at the sight of a loved woman's face. It should be purest joy to dream of the colony. And his heart did leap as he thought of his hopes for this which was to be so noble a plantation.

There they would, indeed, make a new England for God and the King. And their children's children, inheriting this new kingdom, thought Robert, would remember that their fathers were Englishmen who came over

the dread salt ocean-sea and created out of the wilderness
a nation in which each man toiled not for himself but for
all.

And thus with God's help one could transmute his love,
an alchemy of the soul which Christ Himself had experienced.

He was not happy but he was elated: not at peace but
inspired by what he knew to be a great and holy purpose.
And so as dawn pinked the sky, he went to bed.

# XII

## *The English Channel*

THERE was scarcely enough wind in the morning to give the ship steerageway. The *Speedwell* trailed behind at too great a distance to permit the *Mayflower* to speak to her. But she kept the greater ship's rate of progress and seemed not too sluggish in the water.

Robert spent a good part of the day in the master's quarters with the pilot Coppin and the mate Clarke, both of whom had crossed the Atlantic before. They were studying the North American coast to discover a landing place.

The ship was so sedate that the Pilgrims forgot their distress of the previous day and swarmed happily to the main deck, and as forward was forbidden territory, the male portion overflowed into the rigging, hung over the bulwarks and even crawled under the longboat. Robert caught an occasional glimpse of Desire. For a good part of the morning she held a school for the smaller children in the longboat. It made a quaint and not too awkward schoolroom and she seemed to be an easy mistress. There was much gurgling laughter from her pupils.

Captain Standish organized a game of skittles for the big boys with small cannon balls and staves of firewood. The men, at his behest, practiced at wrestling and throwing the discus. He even managed, 'tween decks, to evolve a crude form of football game and an abbreviated game of stool ball. The ship was a superb ground for hide and seek and in the afternoon, John Alden got them all into a glorious hunt.

The Leyden congregation was famed for its singing and toward the end of the day, Edward Winslow, who was a singer of no mean training, gathered the whole company of passengers, old and young together, as a singing class, and for an hour some very splendid music was wafted from beneath the sails of the *Mayflower* as she made her way down the Channel.

After the months of hurry and delays, of uncertainties and disturbances, debating and quarreling, this sudden peace was delightful and no one was more pleasured by it than Robert Cushman who had borne the brunt of everyone's complaints. Even Christopher Martin was peaceful and no Amen was quite so loud as his at evening prayer when Robert thanked God for the calm of the day.

The next morning, however, Martin was fully recovered from his bout with seasickness and returned to his usual form. The sound of his nagging and of the people's protests rose frequently over the ship. There were a good many complaints to Robert and he finally gathered himself together and asked Chris to cease his interfering.

"Why disturb yourself over little things, Governor?" he asked with what he hoped was tact. "Let Captain Standish keep order."

"I saw Isaac Allerton come to you and that fool Bob Carter. These Leyden Pilgrims all think they're masters," exclaimed Martin. "I'll have 'ee know they're beneath us Essex men for I am governor and represent those of Essex and we outnumber you."

"Nay, Governor, you represent us all!" protested Robert.

"Not the Leyden worms!" cried Chris. "And I'll have no complaints made to anyone but myself. 'Tis mutiny otherwise. They're a froward, waspish lot and you mustn't hear them."

"You're a fool, Christopher Martin!" exclaimed Cushman. "I wonder you've ever learned to read and write, with such a simple skull as yours." He turned on his heel.

To his pleased surprise, the governor did not follow him nor did he again address his assistant that day. Robert asked Mary that night if she had put the matter of the watch straight with the governor. She replied that she had.

Desire came and went in her own pursuits which seldom touched his. But he never was unconscious of her presence on the ship, never more so than when Giles Heale monopolized her as he frequently did. A dozen times a day their laughter rang out in unison, and more than all else he envied Giles her laughter.

The *Speedwell* rode farther behind them on the third day and lower in the sea. The *Mayflower's* officers thought she must be taking water heavily. As the winds continued light, she had again run up her topsails but even under these she now lagged more and more. Jones kept a constant watch on the little boat and Robert's last look at night and first in the morning was eastward. But it was not till the dawn of the fifth day that the pinnace asked for help. Robert had just joined the pilot on the poop when she lowered the St. Andrew's flag from her mainmast and ran it up again at half-mast. The pilot, staring through the spyglass, said she'd reversed the ensign.

"I wonder just how stricken she is," muttered Coppin and let out a roar for Master Jones.

Jones ran up in bare feet. After a prolonged stare through the glass he said, "We'll have to heave to and wait for her to overhaul us, Pilot." He ran down to the main deck and blew his whistle. The mate shouted, "Back the mainyard!" The coxswain's whistle blew. Sailors manned the main braces, the great-yards were swung and the *Mayflower* halted in her flight, sails flapping idly. The sudden stillness brought people up from 'tween decks and out from the cabin but it was nearly an hour before the *Speedwell* was within hailing distance.

"What's troubling ye, Master Reynolds?" roared Jones from the poop.

Reynolds' huge bulk loomed heavily against the white of his lateen sail.

"We've had the pumps going for three days but now we're nearly awash," he replied.

John Carver stood beside him on the poop and William Brewster in the waist with the people. As the pinnace crawled slowly toward them, the *Mayflower* folk could see how pale and weary her passengers looked.

"You should have kept those topsails off her. I told you they'd open her up! I hope you're satisfied!" snarled Master Jones.

"The topsail is the life of a ship," remarked Reynolds with fatuous dignity. "Any true sailor knows that."

"Are you drunk, you lobhead?" demanded Jones. "Tell me forthrightly what you require."

Reynolds put his toothpick between his lips. "I'm going to put into Dartmouth to be patched up. I wish you to escort me, in case we founder. That's what I require."

A murmur ran over the two ships.

Jones looked from Reynolds to the faint blue land to the north. "With this wind we'll be all day getting there."

"And I know that though I'm no sailor," said the master of the pinnace. "Heave to!" he called to his mate for he had now overhauled the *Mayflower*.

"Think well what you're doing, Master Reynolds!" Christopher Jones' honest voice was loud and stern. "This voyage was begun a month late. If you add a week or so of delay, we will be hulling many a bitter hour out there in the Atlantic in the westerly gales. These women and children—"

"Stow your sermon, my master!" snarled Reynolds, his dark face ugly. "I am making for Dartmouth. You can come or go."

Jones turned to consult with the pilot and the mate.

"Can't ye take us all aboard the *Mayflower?*" called a gaunt man from the waist of the pinnace. He was holding a tiny baby in his arms. "I would bide any crowding to get off this ill craft. She's haunted, I tell 'ee."

"Now, Edward Tilly," cried the elder, "I assured you yesterday and I assure you now that rats are not spirits."

"They might be!" said a woman. "And why should some of you be aboard the great ship in safety while us others sleep with death as a bedfellow here on the pinnace?"

"If I was you, Deacon Carver," shrilled Christopher Martin, "I'd allow no such familiar talk from the passengers."

The folk on the *Mayflower* shouted with laughter. "Don't you believe our bag of wind," called John Billington. "We are free men on this ship."

"I'll have you put in stocks, you—" began Martin.

"Stow your gab, everyone!" This from Master Jones. "Now then, Elder Brewster, what is your wish in this matter?"

The hush that followed was less at the master's command than it was because all knew the danger which threatened William Brewster if he returned to England.

"You must do whatever you feel is for the general good," replied Brewster coolly.

"Then we'll convoy the pinnace into Dartmouth," said Jones. "But I wish to declare to all and sundry that I consent with an anxious heart over the delay. When we make harbor, Master Reynolds, I propose to examine your hull myself."

"I'll be honored and be damned to you," retorted Reynolds. He turned to his helmsman who put the great tiller over.

Master Jones blew his whistle and the *Mayflower* crew sprang to life. Slowly, the two ships moved apart, the bulk of the people and the crews calling to each other gayly that they would meet in Dartmouth.

All the rest of the day the *Mayflower* maneuvered to keep within hailing distance of the *Speedwell*. The longboat was kept ready for a sudden launching. The wind was light and both vessels were obliged to take long tacks to make their northing. At noon, a calm fell and for three hours they drifted in a misty sun. Aboard the *Mayflower* they could hear the steady clank of the *Speedwell's* pumps.

Mid-afternoon, a breeze came up and shortly they sighted Mewstone and then Berry Head and the leadsman was put to work. Master Jones as well as the pilot did not leave the deck as the rope slipped through the sailor's hands.

In the first wide reaches of the Dart, as they slipped inside Start Point, another calm caught them. Reynolds, after an hour, got out his sweeps and this maneuver roused the wind which came cheerily along from the south.

Shortly now, they sailed between the two opposite castles which guarded the harbor and the full beauty of the famous haven burst upon them.

Mighty hills hemmed in the river closely. On either steep shore was perched a little thatch-roofed town, Kingswear to the east and Dartmouth to the west. Above the roofs, the hills rose green as living ivy against the blue of the harvest skies. The wheat fields high on the giant crests were patches of gold in which tiny men swung miniature scythes. The Dart here flowed down from the north around an emerald promontory and beneath this, on the Dartmouth side, the *Mayflower* dropped her anchor. A quarter of an hour later the *Speedwell* waddled up.

Master Jones, with the mate and pilot, immediately went aboard her. Robert would have gone with him had not Governor Martin immediately raised his usual protests over the people's going ashore.

"Why not let them go, for mercy's sake?" asked Cushman wearily.

"And have them never come back?" cried Chris.

"This isn't a slave-ship," retorted Robert. "We want only volunteers in America."

"Hie! Doctor Heale!" commanded Martin. "You're not to go ashore."

The main deck was crowded. Giles, who had had one foot on the accommodation ladder, stepped back to grin up at the little chapman on the half deck.

"I must go replenish my medicine chest, Governor," he said with excessive gravity. "As you are just, be merciful."

Richard Clarke, a young London cabinet-maker, stepped up beside Giles and said, "And I must renew my body linen. Alack, I spewed up my very only pair of drawers that first day out from Hampton."

Amid shouts of amusement, the young fellow joined Heale.

Robert foresaw trouble and went down to the main deck and said in a low voice to Clarke, "Master Martin is afraid you won't come back. Can't you set these others a good example and remain contented here?"

The young Londoner stared at him. "Does the chapman think he can keep forty of us mewed up here within a hundred yards of yonder pretty town? Look! There goes the *Speedwell's* passengers now and half the *Mayflower's* crew will be having shore leave!" He put his finger in his mouth and whistled to one of the several boatmen hovering near the ships.

"Where's Captain Standish?" yelled Martin. "Arrest me that man, Captain, that Richard Clarke!"

Richard Clarke thumbed his nose at the governor and dropped into the little boat. Miles Standish did not appear.

Giles Heale cried to Robert, "My dear old Nuncle, this can't be!"

Angry voices rose now. The doctor was pushed toward one of the half-deck ladders. "You speak for us, doctor," said John Goodman, a Leyden Pilgrim. "You live 'tween decks and you know us."

"Send Master Cushman back to the poop," called John Billington. "He'd make slaves of us too."

"No, your cause is just!" cried Robert. "I'll stay here and plead for you."

"Go up where you belong," insisted Billington, his sullen face very red and his great shoulders twitching. "We don't trust you any more than Chris Martin trusts us.

Tell 'em we're going ashore anyhow, Giles Heale, and why."

Several people came up the companionway from the great cabin and joined Martin at the half-deck rail. They were Desire Minter and Mary Cushman, Edward Winslow and Isaac Allerton. Marie Martin followed these and took her husband's arm. But he astounded everyone by shaking her off.

"That's right," called one of the sailors from the forecastle, "free your ferret, Mistress. He'll bite nastier out of the bag."

Martin turned purple.

Giles Heale's voice was very pleasant to hear. "Look you, Master Martin, let all of us go ashore. It will save your stores and our health. It's not according to nature and the will of God that we should live so close to one another except for dire necessity. Nobody intends to desert the ship. I'd stake my head on that."

"I know whereof I speak," asserted Martin loudly. "There's a round dozen among you who are out of joint with the venture."

"We're not out of joint with anything but your scurvy tongue and the burdens Master Cushman's put on us. A man would need to have the back of an ass to bear that!" This was Billington again. "Since Master Heale can't tell you the facts I can. We left England to be free. We *are* free! We'll go and come as we please. If you're going to play at tyranting, why you know what happens to tyrants."

Young Winslow stepped forward, very handsome in a new brown doublet slashed with green. The little governor thrust his elbow into Winslow's ribs.

"Don't interfere, Master! I'm governor of this ship by

the will of these my people and you know what the pastor wrote us."

"We never wanted you!" cried Thomas Blossom. "You're another of Pastor Robinson's bad jobs. He admitted Master Cushman was one, I heard, and if he'd see you now he'd know you was another."

Martin burst into one of his senseless tirades. Robert, jaw set, pushed through the crowd and mounted to the half deck. He put his arm firmly through Martin's and whispered in his ear, "They're saying down there they'll mischief you if you don't give way over this."

Chris jerked his head round to glare at Cushman. "They wouldn't dare!" he whispered back.

"See that group of sailors at the forecastle door?" Robert's voice was urgent. "You've interfered in their business lately and they're only waiting for an excuse to attack you. Master Jones and the mate, only, can control them and they're in the pinnace. Tell these people they may row up the Dart for a prayer service with Master Winslow. And say nothing about their returning by way of the town."

"I'll not do it," snorted Chris, swelling his chest again for it had dropped with Robert's first words.

"They'll not only mischief you but they'll unmake you as governor. I know it, Master Martin," insisted Robert, with all the vehemence to be got into a whisper.

The governor moistened his lips, swallowed, looked from Robert's grim face into the scowling faces below.

"What you should be thinking of is your wicked souls," shrilled Martin. "What I order you to do is this. Take boats, and with Master Winslow, row up the Dart to a meadow or spinney and hold a service, praying the Lord to make you less naughty and more obedient."

There was silence for a moment and then a great shout
of triumph echoed over the ship.  Edward Winslow, followed by Sarah and Isaac Allerton, ran down the ladder to
the main deck and took to a boat, and shortly groups of
Pilgrims still laughing at Martin were going over the
ship's side into waiting boats.

The governor turned to Robert again.  He was still red
in the eye.  He bit his nails and choked back a great sob
as he said, "You, Robert Cushman, treat me as if I was
nothing!  You think I'm only a peddler of gewgaws.  But
I tell you I'm a man of authority by my very nature.  I
have a paid spy in the gun deck and I know for sure that
near a quarter of the people there are ready, nay, eager
to desert, they so hate your agreement.  Let go my hand,
Marie, or, by God, I'll whip you."

The fat woman turned piteous eyes on Robert.

Mary and Desire had joined them and Desire held
Robert's eyes for a moment with a smile.  He turned to
Martin.

"Whatever you are or whatever you know, Governor,
you mustn't play the little tyrant with such men as these.
They can be led, but they can't be driven."

Chris tugged at his black beard.  "I've been elected for
a year.  I have authority."

Cushman shook his head.  "Since you are an elected
man, you have authority only as long as they concede it
to you.  An elected man must be the people's abject slave
unless he has an army which obeys him.  Captain Standish alone can't keep you governor!  Only the good will
of the Pilgrims can.  We're far from Pastor Robinson now
and I misdoubt if even he could force your nagging over
nothing down these men's throats."

Mary tugged at Cushman's sleeve.  "Robert, stop talk-

ing regiments and get in a boat.  You'll go up the Dart,
too, won't you, Mistress Desire?"

"I promised Master Heale to go with him to see the
little town," replied Desire.  "He will come back with his
medicines shortly."

"And you, Robert?" asked Mary.  "You're ready to go?"

"I must wait for Master Jones' opinion on the pinnace,"
answered Robert.  "Perchance Mistress Martin will go
with you."

Marie, who had been standing very pale and depressed
after her husband's rebuff, now recovered herself.  "Yes,
I'll go if Chris will come along to take care of us."

Chris cleared his throat.  "Do come, Master Martin,"
pleaded Mary.  "My husband is the most ungallant man
in the world.  Don't, prithee, take up his ways."

They all laughed and the governor, quite himself again,
smoothed his hosen and cocked his hat.  "Take charge
then, my good assistant, while I go see to the service up
the river."

And thus Robert and Desire were left alone for a few
precious moments; alone with the second mate, pacing
the deck near-by, and the forward end of the vessel swarm-
ing with the pressed men who could not go ashore.

They watched the little string of boats moving up the
reaches of the broad Dart.  They looked across to the
*Speedwell,* whence came the rough murmur of voices.

"I saw my aunt and uncle set off some time ago with
the Bradfords and Mistress Brewster," said Desire.  "I
suppose the poor elder won't put his nose out of the
cabin while he's here."

"It depends," returned Robert, "on whether or not he
feels it his duty to go.  He's the bravest man I know."

"Were the books he printed really seditious?" asked Desire.

"Yes, they were," admitted Robert. "His Majesty is logical enough. Since he's trying to suppress the kirk in Scotland and enforce Episcopacy there, it's seditious for an English citizen to print and smuggle into England a Scotsman's arguments against Episcopacy."

"What childishness!" sniffed Desire.

"Mayhap and on both sides," agreed Robert, "and it has put the whole venture in jeopardy. I have trembled for a year lest someone whisper in His Majesty's ear that William Brewster is a Pilgrim."

"Mayhap it's the bishop's business this pursuit, and the King His Majesty never heard of the elder," suggested Desire.

"Nay, he ordered by name that William Brewster, Brownist and printer of Leyden, be arrested and brought into his own presence," Robert told her, looking at her fine profile. "And to be brought before James on a religious charge is as near ruin as death. He rants. He roars. 'The devil take you away, both body and soul. You're a recusant!' they tell me he said to a poor Scot who was innocent as a babe of printing tracts. And he added for good measure, 'The devil rive your body and soul all in collops and cast them into hell!' He could prove nothing on the Scotsman. But he has the elder's books, types and press locked in their attic in Leyden. So he is on proved ground there."

"Then since death pursues William Brewster out of England," Desire turned to him now, with a little tender smile, "he's less brave in facing the wilderness than you, who could stay if you'd acknowledge Episcopacy."

Robert shook his head. "You know you're talking like

a childish female now. And you'd persuaded me that there was such a thing as a woman with a mind!"

"Thank you for naught!" she exclaimed. "You are behind the times. Your dearest Shakespeare believed in a Portia."

"Nay, he dreamed a Portia!" demurred Robert.

"But his women were all witty creatures! Even poor puling Ophelia was no fool. There must have been females of parts in Stratford—if that's where he lived—to tell him what women really are." She nodded her head vigorously.

"His mother was of fine family, I've heard. His father nothing much. But 'twas in London he met his splendid women among the happy free where ideas are without either maleness or femaleness." Robert looked at her wistfully.

"Where you and I both belong," she agreed.

"God has His reasons for what He is doing with us," said Robert, "but it's hard to be reconciled."

"Oh, don't be a Brownist," she cried, "in the only five minutes we may ever have alone! I despise your cant."

He flushed and said stiffly, "God is as real to me as you are, Mistress Desire. I'm no hypocrite."

"And so is He real to me," she retorted. "But I don't blame Him for all the unhappy events of my life. Most of them come from my own arrogance." Then her eyes which had been angry softened and her voice was unbelievably low and sweet as she added, "I know you're no hypocrite, Robin! Forgive me!"

He caught his breath. Could only look at her and grope for words which would not come.

"You are not really angry?" she asked a little anxiously.

"No! No! I only find it impossible to tell you how

dear your kindness is to me," he said. "Say what you will to me. I know how faulty I am."

"You don't know yourself, Robert!" She shook her dark head at him.

"And you have had no chance to learn me," he returned.

"Nor am I destined to," she said. "Master Jones is returning! And yonder is our young doctor. I shall go fetch my new hood to do him credit."

Jones came up the ladder, with a far less anxious face than he'd worn when he left. "She's opened up some of her seams but caulking will set that right. He's going to lower his topmasts. They are continual temptation to him to overcrowd the little ship."

"And how is the elder?" asked Robert.

"He is off up the river for the prayer service," answered Jones. "All on the pinnace are looking the worse for anxiety. He said I was to say he would see you at the prayer meeting."

But Robert had no intention of attending the meeting. He watched Giles and Desire set off and then he called a boat for himself. The chief craving of his soul was to be alone. The hills back of the town were sending him an invitation which could not be denied.

# XIII

## *The Dancing Bear*

THE harbor was very quiet. Perhaps a dozen ships of all sorts were anchored up and down the stream, with some fishing smacks tied to the quay.

Robert's boatman was an old fellow with a keen eye. He looked his passenger over with frank curiosity as he bent to his oars.

"I hear you're going to North Virginny, women and all. It's a marvelous unsavory land you're going to, my master, and a hard voyage. I know, for I sailed with the *Golden Hind*, I did."

"The *Golden Hind!*" ejaculated Robert, staring at this ruddy, bright-eyed old face.

"Aye!" grinned the sailor. "A hundred tons and a proper leaky old beer cask she was. I was a known man for a while after I got home. Bill Turtle's my name. Kissed the old Queen's hand, I have. She was such a prince as we'll never see again. Danish Ann to follow her!—nothing but rags and clouts compounded."

"Francis Drake and the *Golden Hind!*" repeated Cushman.

Turtle jerked his head. "Now, yonder's a ship!" He indicated a warship of about eight hundred tons. "She's a Frenchie but she do be a pretty ship. She took yonder little Spanish barque loaded with wines and silks and come in here bold as a walking mort to sell the goods in Dartmouth. I hear the Duke of Buckingham has ordered our Lord Mayor to stay both ships till His Grace discovers his own pleasure about them. Them was the words in the letter the mayor told. But the Frenchie will make a snout at that and now the barque's empty be off at next tide."

"And didn't Sir Humphrey Gilbert live near-by?" asked Robert.

"Aye, at Compton Castle. See yonder fat-bellied little galley about twenty ton, on our larboard? She come squittering in here last week and sold her whole cargo of lemons and oranges for eighty pounds. She drove a Frenchie ashore near Calais, a hundred-ton barque, and took her cargo. Us does those things!"

Cushman nodded. "And Sir Walter Raleigh lived on the Dart too. I knew Sir Walter, poor man!"

"I sailed on a voyage with him. Proper hard driver he was! Glad for once I was to get back to my old woman. Yonder tall ship is Captain Nutt's: the *Cushat Dove.* Should be the *Bloody Tiger,* I'd say. Don't stare too hard."

Robert glanced at the glorious three-master anchored mid-stream, a little south of the church tower. "Who's Captain Nutt?" he asked.

"Not so loud with names," Turtle protested. "And you're going to cross the ocean and don't know the name of the freebooter who scavenges this west coast? He's got our Newfoundland fishing fleet afraid to come home. His retreat's Torbay and Dartmouth's his market-place."

"Why does the Lord Mayor permit that last?" asked Robert.

Turtle grinned. "What can he do? Besides, Nutt comes in this time telling all he's suing for pardon. And he's just took a Colchester ship laden with sugar and wood, about ten thousand pounds' worth they say. And he's

brought it all here.  Our Devon vice-admiral has taken
fourteen chests of sugar out of her."

"Will he get his pardon?"  Robert smiled.

"He has it!  He was boasting in the town last night
about its large extent and that when it was handed to
him he was wearing the very clothes of the ship's master
he'd just plundered."  Turtle brought his boat skillfully
to the water steps and took his farthing fare.  "Shall I
tarry for you, Master?"

"If you're here in an hour I might use you," replied
Robert.  "Which road will take me to yonder hilltop,
friend Turtle?"

"Go past the mill, Master," Turtle told him, "and as
I hear you're a Brownist don't stop to preach anywhere.
Our town's for the King!"

"And so are we for the King!" exclaimed Robert, pausing on the steps.

Turtle pushed off.  "Ye can't be for the King and not
be for his church!" he cried and then added in a shout
as the tide caught him swiftly, "Not that *I* care which
church ye pray in.  Ye look a proper man to me."

Robert, gratified by this mild compliment, clambered
up to the little quay.  Right and left a low sea wall
ran along the front of the little town.  Back of this
and paralleling it was a road, and from the road, at
right angles up the hill, several winding lanes.  Cushman
took the one which passed the mill, then entered the path
along the brook which turned the ancient water wheels.

Up and up, he panted, past the high perched houses,
across a steep sloping field which led to an old church,
through the churchyard to a yet loftier field.  This one
entered over a stone stile and on the stile steps he rested
a while, enthralled by the view.

Devon lay fold on green fold below him; hill after perfect hill melting into the circumference of the skies. Far below, to his left, a tidal backwater gleamed through tall trees and he heard faintly the creak of yet another mill wheel. It was near eight o'clock and the shadows were grown long though the sun was still warm. The stiff climb had left him dizzy and after a long enchanted look about him, he lay down beside a spring which purled out of the hillside near-by.

The sound of church bells drifted to him. An exquisite blend of summer smells and summer sounds charmed nostril and ear while oak and beech and yew danced a slow gaillard across his bemused vision.

To be in England again, after the agony of that farewell in Southampton!

Although his breathing was difficult, it was not particularly painful. For a little while he brooded over this strange illness of his. He believed it to be serious but he knew of no treatment for it better than ignoring it. When God's time came for him he'd have to go, despite any doctor's remedies. And then as he began to feel easier it occurred to him that he was lying north and south and that the good earth currents were flowing through him. Aye, he was one with the very pulse of the land. He had been permitted to return for one more touch of the dust which had coined him!

Yet his fancy would not linger on this healing phantasy. It winged onward. If only Desire were here to brood with him over the loveliness of the land.

And then such a yearning for her presence seized him that he was startled. He sat up. Rumpled his hair. What did this mean? In all sincerity he had given up any hope or thought of ever achieving companionship with Desire. Then he sneered at himself. "But you've rushed up here like a lovesick boy the better to fancy that she is your companion!"

Had he dared, had he wished to believe there was more than friendship in Desire's words? No! He knew that she was only a friend. She was Giles Heale's friend, too. He wiped his forehead, and sat very still, focusing his eyes on the trees which now stood motionless in their proper places. Then he muttered, "God help me!" and got to his feet.

There was a precipitous twisting path down into the woods which bordered the tidal backwater. He thought that if one followed this, one might come to the banks of the Dart and there find the Pilgrims at their service. He set off, almost running away from his crowding thoughts.

It was shadowy and cool among the beeches. The path was bordered with bracken, waist-high. The water glanced below on his right, green-bronze. Swans floated there, entranced by their own reflections. He continued on his way rapidly until he heard voices ahead of him and recognized them. One was William Bradford's, the other Elder Brewster's. Suddenly he loathed the idea of meeting those two solemn men and answering their questions. He turned in among the trees and sat down on an ivy-covered log behind a holly bush.

Shortly, Brewster came slowly along the path, followed by Bradford. Then came Dorothy Bradford, moving languidly, and Mary Brewster.

"Shall you stop in the town, Dorothy?" called Mary Brewster.

"I don't know! This is a very far way round as the boatman warned us!" groaned Dorothy Bradford. The *Speedwell* hasn't fitted me for such a journey."

"You must see Doctor Heale and get something for your weariness," replied Mary Brewster. "That is if he can take his eyes from Desire long enough to observe your needs."

Both women giggled and their next sentences died out among the trees.

"Curse Giles Heale," whispered Robert fiercely as he rose.

And then, appalled, he caught himself. He was jealous of Giles. And why? He stood very still, acutely conscious of his surroundings (O sights and smells of perfect England!) and still more conscious of the fact that he despised himself.

The prayer meeting was over. He followed along the path after the others, his feet leaden billets, hanging from legs of straw.

The path was padded deep with moss. The low rays of the sun, striking past the beech and elm trunks and athwart this vernal carpet turned it to emerald shot with gold. He was walking through beauty. He might have been moving through a green sun-drenched sea so did the light on water below and trees above and on moss and bracken magic the scene.

So did it magic his soul for the unease lost something of its tinge of shame. Its darkness turned luminous under this unearthly radiance as though shame and sadness were impregnated with a mysterious joy. And next, without thought or volition, he knew the truth which ever since he had met Desire had pressed for recognition. It was not friendship alone he felt for her. He loved her.

And so caught and uplifted was Robert by the beauty around him that the beauty now revealed within him seemed a natural part of the loveliness of the world. Yes, he loved her. Thank God that this was so. Thank Him, although the love could never be fulfilled. Unless love were its own fulfillment! Mayhap it was. Mayhap it required nothing for its perfecting save that he recognize its existence in his own heart. A jewel was made no more perfect by its discovery. His love was set in the highest, most secret place of his soul. There it would remain, forever, high and secret in the sanctuary where only England had its place beside.

And who so blessed as he, with two such mistresses? Neither ever could be his, yet he was theirs, for ever. Neither ever would know of his passion, yet its very muteness would be the source of its vitality.

Just as the sun sank, Robert emerged from the beech wood. The path now continued as a pack road, on one side of which were fields and on the other a row of houses. In the valley below, the little town clustered round the square-towered church. He followed the road, looking now below him at the harbor; at the *Cushat Dove,* the *Mayflower,* the *Speedwell,* the *Gloire de France.* Now he gazed to the north, up the great Dart, now south beyond Dartmouth to the mighty spread of the Channel.

He was intensely happy. He was well and strong. And when the smell of roasting food blew in his face from the open door of one of the thatched houses, he realized that he was hungry and was thankful that a sign creaked from the doorpost, the Dancing Bear. He went in.

The room was small and low of beamed ceiling but well enough lighted, what with the afterglow and a fire before which a woman was basting fowls on a spit. To all this, however, Robert gave but a glance, for the company at once engrossed his attention. Ten of the Pilgrims were seated round the table and there were no other guests.

John Billington was there, also Thomas Tinker and Moses Fletcher. These last two being Leyden exiles, Cushman knew them well. The others were from London and Billerica and except for Billington they were only names to him. Young Richard Clarke, of course, had divulged something of himself earlier in the day. Richard was eighteen, small, ugly, with enormous ears, the apprentice's close-cropped hair and blue fustian clothes.

There was the last end of a veal pie on the table, a half-devoured loaf of bread and a great dish of pickled pilchards.

"And how did you know we were here, Master Cushman?" demanded John Billington, his great face lowering.

"If I'd known you were I'd never have come in," replied Robert. "But since I am here I'll ask the goodwife for my supper."

"Yes! Yes!" exclaimed the landlady, looking up from her birds. "I daren't leave these fowls for a breath. Fetch yourself a stool, Master, and fall to on the pie till these are ready for you all. There's ale in the black jug and the boy shall bring more."

Robert drew the stool up to the long table and seated himself next to Tinker.

"The prayer service didn't last long, I suppose," said Cushman pleasantly.

"Us came away early, if that's what you mean," returned young Clarke pertly.

"It was pretty to see the young ones in the meadow," drawled Tinker. "They were fit to eat it up, rolling in the grass, biting it and clutching up fists full."

"No sermons, Tom," protested one of the others. "We've had plenty of such physic from the elder."

"Don't 'ee dare call it so!" shouted a serious-looking

fellow who was going to the colony as a laborer. "The elder can rip the sinner's heart wide open. Look he don't start on 'ee for the wenching cuckoo 'ee be."

"Hard words break no bones," grinned the man thus admonished. "You're nothing but a drunken bezzle yourself most times. What I say is this and all of 'ee must listen for I have a strong rush of blood to my skull and can speak for once. And I say since the Lord has put this one of the chiefs in our hands, we must open his eyes to a thing or two. I'll begin on him."

"Nay, I called the meeting and I paid for the ale. I'll do the talking!" shouted Billington, leaning across the table. "Master Cushman, we don't like that covenant you've put on us. We weren't asked to that meeting on the sands at Southampton so you that calls yourselves leaders don't know what we think. Well, you've indentured us for seven years and many of us have just served our apprenticeship."

"You knew, all of you, of the seven years' indenture before you ever joined us," remarked Robert.

"I grant you that," nodded Billington, "but those who wasn't under Pastor Robinson's thumb was under the pastor's choice, Chris Martin. And the pastor treats common folks like little children and they obeys him. But there's going to be no more of that."

"What do you mean?" asked Robert, giving the great hulk of a man a clear glance.

"I mean, don't I, friends," looking round him, "that we beant a lot of women aboard the *Mayflower* and the *Speedwell,* praying and sniveling. If we don't like the course you chiefs take, why shouldn't we seize on the tiller ourselves?"

The others were silent but Cushman saw assent in their

faces. It was evidently an understood topic among them.
"You shouldn't because you don't understand navigation," was Robert's prompt reply.

Tom Tinker spoke when Billington hesitated over this.
He had soft brown eyes that were intelligent as well as
kind. "By navigation you mean governance, our regi-
menting. And who does understand that for a commonwealth? And who wants a commonwealth? We don't."

"It isn't the governance of the commonwealth that's
hard to learn," Robert looked from one half-scowling face
to another, "it's the governance of self. It's learning to
do one's duty to one's neighbor without regret or grudge.
And on the commonwealth's strength depends your very
life. Do you realize we must plow our fields with our
muskets on our backs? Until we're a fortified, regimented
body we must live only for one another. Seven years is
all too short a time to accomplish much security."

"I'll tell 'ee what," Dick Clarke's great ears were purple,
"I'll tell 'ee I'll do my duty by my neighbor if I'm fighting
for my own acres, not theirs, and I ain't going to work on
any but my own."

"Aye! Aye!" The murmur rose from all.

The landlady brought a great trencher of roasted fowls
to the table. Every man but Cushman grabbed at the
birds and there was quick hacking, with several knives
rending the same fowl and bitter complaints from those
left with the pope's nose who had reached for the wish-
bone.

"This, I suppose," remarked Robert, serving himself
with veal pie, "is a foretaste of what you hope for in the
colony. Snatch and root, some to guzzle and gobble while
others starve. A man like Tom Tinker, for instance, with
a head better than three of the rest of you but with a

weaker body, to starve with the pope's nose or nothing while John Billington, who can't keep his thoughts together from the door to the bedpost, waxes fatter yet on a whole bird."

John Billington choked. "Take it!" he snarled, throwing his loot onto Cushman's trencher. "I'd rather you'd stab me than give me a tongue lashing. If you want it, say so!"

Robert put the point of his knife into the fowl and placed it on the general trencher. "I want nothing at another man's loss," he remarked.

"You say that, Master, and yet dare you deny Master Weston hasn't given you promise of private trading chances with the colony's beaver in return for your tender care of the Merchants' stock?" It was young Clarke who asked this in his hostile voice.

Cushman felt his color rise.

"I dare deny it and I'll thank you, my lad, to let your elders and betters do the talking here."

"Betters! You hear that?" demanded Billington of the company. "Look 'ee, Robert Cushman, we be going to a free land where no man will be better than another except he prove it at the point of his knife or his musket. No one will rule me in North Virginia but myself."

Moses Fletcher, a young blacksmith of the Leyden group, even greater in stature and bulk than Billington, stretched out a great arm and took the much-traveled bird. "So! Eh, John? But you be wrong in one direction. The elder's a better man than any of us by his power in prayer. We need him. And so's Deacon Carver a better man by his greater wit. We need him. Master Cushman, we would need you, for you have the most farthest seeing head of those who call themselves chiefs, but you ain't for us. You're for Weston. So we daren't need you."

Robert was thinking rapidly. It was a curious thing that while he was thus thinking and fully recognizing the serious implications of this unruly talk, he was conscious that he loved Desire Minter. And he knew that never so long as he lived would he be without thrilling consciousness of it. Nor, at this moment, did this consciousness interfere with his clear perceptions of Billington's destructive influence.

Scarce a man at the table was yet thirty. All were without education. Only Tinker had deep religious convictions and all, excepting Tinker, were lusty and tough-fibered. They were fine material for the wilderness if they could be guided, but if not they would be a menace to the general welfare. Robert had warned Tom Weston that the Adventurers were not using wisdom in all their selections of colonists. But Tom was not a good judge of working men nor could he direct his associates.

Cushman said soberly to Moses Fletcher, "It's not for me to urge my services on you. I'm not in *anyone's* pay, publicly or privily. I'm as penniless, near, as any of you, for I've put my all into the stock of the colony, even borrowing from Master Weston for the purpose." He saw them glance at one another and knew that the story of the watch had spread. He went on, "Granted that you could do without me, do you think you can do without the Merchant Adventurers? Who will feed you and clothe you in New England till the first harvest is gathered, your first sheep sheared?"

"You mean you are the only one who could get their help now?" asked Tinker thoughtfully. "I heard some

say that. But if Pastor Robinson knew there was danger
we'd starve, why did he say not to sign that covenant?"

"Undoubtedly the pastor believed the Merchants would
give in," replied Cushman, "although I, who knew them
well, told him Nay. They *are* my friends, Master Weston
and all, because I stood up for their interests as well as
ours. And that's only common sense because our interest
is theirs and theirs is ours."

"But you admit you get moneys from Master Weston,"
grunted Clarke.

"Yes, and left him my father's watch till I could repay
him out of my share of the divisions, seven years hence,
unless meantime I shall inherit my father's estate. Master
Weston, because he loves me, sent me the watch by Mistress Cushman, trusting me to pay without the pledge.
I have some twenty shares in the colony. So how can you
think I shall not work my utmost to bring it to fruition?"

Several men nodded. Robert followed up his advantage. "As for the need for rules and regiment, let me tell
you I've talked with many men who've been in America,
even Sir Walter Raleigh and Captain John Smith themselves. They all tell the same story. Selfishness and laziness are worse enemies than savages or wilderness. In
every colony that's failed or is failing in Virginia, there's
been no chief strong enough to make the people work
and share. And in each there have been too many men
and women who won't work or if they do, only for themselves. And so they destroy not only themselves but the
generality. Therefore all matters considered deeply, the
covenant for seven years' common life under strict leaders
works both ways and both good. By clinging thus to law
and order and each other we repay the Adventurers and
we strengthen each other."

The others were listening intently but Billington, who had taken some rum, wiped his mouth on the back of his hand and remarked, "Talk! Talk! Well, I don't like you, Master Robert Cushman, with your high ways, so beware of me."

Cushman gazed at the younger man somberly. "You have a great fancy for yourself, Billington! I'm not afraid of you. And don't cozen yourself with thinking you're going to rule the colony. The colony is greater than you or any single man among us. Only by the best of us joining in harmony can any rule be maintained."

"That's so," nodded Moses Fletcher and several others.

Robert rose and asked the landlady for his score. Then he said to Tom Tinker, "Shall we return to the ship together?"

"He's afraid of me!" crowed Billington, also rising.

Robert gave the hostess his pennies, then very deliberately walked around the table to stand before the fellow. They were of the same height but John was the heavier, stronger man.

"Now just why should I fear you?" asked Cushman. "I have nothing to conceal. So you can't timid me with your tongue. You could easily knock me down. But suppose you did, it would only serve to put you out of the colony for I am one of the chiefs. Do you want that?"

Nobody at the table spoke. Billington ground his teeth audibly, but did not lift his great fists. Tom Tinker did not stir though he gave Robert an apologetic look.

"Good night, all!" remarked Cushman and walked out of the inn.

# XIV

## *Pilgrim Justice*

**T**HERE was a rising moon. It touched the harbor to iridescence. From the beech wood behind him rose a nightingale's song and Robert halted so caught up by beauty that all coherent thought was lost. He knew only that England and Desire were lovely. The bird's music expressed the inexpressible for him. He felt tears sting his eyes, but they were not tears of sadness; they were the overflow of a depth of love too great for his earthly body to compass.

After a time, loud voices in the Dancing Bear roused him and he went on down the hill, the nightingale's call pursuing him faintly. He was feeling keen and wide awake, by no means in a mood to retire to the stuffy darkness of the great cabin. He decided not to wait till morning for the report he must make to the elder and deacon of Billington's activities. He would rouse them both for a talk tonight.

There was but one Pilgrim on the quay when he reached it and that Pilgrim was a sorry sight! It was Bob Carter, the twenty-year-old servant of William Mullins. He was very drunk and to the admiration of a group of fishermen and Dartmouth youths, he was singing his evening hymn while he untrussed his points. It was bedtime for Bob and a pile of fish-nets appealed to him as an excellent bed.

Cushman observed Bill Turtle in the group of spectators.

"Help me to take him to the *Mayflower*," he whispered to the old sailor.

Turtle laughed. "Says he's going to marry his master's daughter, Priscilla! Listen to him! It's no longer a hymn!"

"Love and a hey nonny no!" warbled young Carter in a delightful tenor.

"Fetch him, quickly, with me, do!" urged Cushman. He pushed through the crowd followed by Turtle and took Bob's arm.

Bill took the other arm, saying, "Come along to your mistress, lad! She's sent for you."

"To Priscilla? I'll go, good sailor! Look ye, that's why I'm going to North Virginia, to be with beauteous she. Priscilla is my favorite and she—darling. I'm not drunk, I'm only happy."

"It's the same thing," sniggered Turtle.

"Bob, be quiet!" ordered Cushman. "Do you want your mistress' name bandied about the quay by common louts?"

The lad steadied himself against Turtle's shoulder. He had a round childish face and round eyes which he struggled to focus on Robert.

"Don't you talk about common fellers, Mashter Cushman. In Virginia, I won't be common. I'll get land. Be free. Be gentleman and never work. Don't shay common louts. Nobody common to himself. You ain't gentleman, Mashter Cushman, you look like one. Talk like one. But you work and gentlemen don't work. Mistress Mullins, I might wed her. She looks like a lady, but she ain't. I'm drunk and can shay what I think."

Bill Turtle was steadying Bob down the stairs now while Cushman held the boat. Much amused, Robert lifted the boy's legs over the gunwale and lowered him into the stern sheets.

"You'd better sit beside him, sir, and steady him or he'll be overboard," said the sailor, casting off the painter.

"It's a pleasure to find anyone in the world as happy as this," observed Cushman as he obeyed Turtle, "ungodly as drunkenness is! But you mustn't talk about women, Bob, when you've been drinking."

"I know, much thanks!" Bob went on confidingly. "Three unmarried wenches is all we're taking out to Virginia."

"Be quiet!" ordered Cushman sternly now.

"It's piteous," nodded Carter. "Desire Minter, Humility Cooper, Priscilla Mullins." He thrust Cushman's hand away when he would have put it over his lips. "All but three of us bachelors musht take to us savage maids. Filthy, Mashter Hopkins shays, and he's lived among 'em."

"Ahoy! Wait!" Quick steps on the stairs, a flying leap and Giles Heale landed in the boat. He peered at the head now resting on Robert's shoulder. "Bob Carter! You poor witless beetle-head! It's you I heard maundering! Haven't I warned you that even sweetened water would turn your head to vapor! So 'twas you bandying our maidens' names on the waterside! I'll put my dagger into you an you don't hold your foul tongue."

"And what are you so hoysed about, Dr. Hoddy-doddy?" hiccoughed Carter, cheerfully. "I'm drunk but you're drunk, too!"

"Liar!" snapped Giles. "For God's sake, row fast, boatman."

"You are alone, I see," observed Robert, curiously.

"You have good eyesight, Uncle Robert," said Giles savagely. "The Carvers didn't see fit to invite me to stay with them for supper ashore when they invited Desire."

"Rock-a-bye, baby!" sang Bob. "Dr. Hoddy-doddy, you'll never sing that in America. For why? For because there'll be only three wenches—"

"Put your hands over his mouth, both of you," urged Turtle. "We'll soon be passing the *Cushat Dove* and they're liable to press the lot of us. Short of men they be too. I rowed Captain Nutt ashore a while ago and he telled me so and he was full of questions about you Brownists."

"I'll hush this knave," said Giles. "If he's not quiet, I'll tell Mistress Priscilla Mullins all he did this day in Dartmouth."

"I'm dumb," declared Bob. And he was.

There were lights in the poop of the pirate vessel and a dark figure paced to and fro on the forecastle. They slipped past her stern in silence but a voice from the stern gallery called softly,

"Ahoy there, cockle boat, will ye take a passenger?"

"I'm taking three to the *Mayflower,* sir," answered Turtle. "I'll return for ye, shortly."

"But I want to go to the *Speedwell,*" said the voice. "Bring your cockle to the accommodation ladder. I'll join you instantly."

"Don't do it," whispered Giles. "It's a trap."

"It's Captain Nutt. I dursn't not," whispered Bill, swinging his boat round.

"It's no trap," protested Robert. "We could rouse the harbor with our shouts. Let's see whom he wants on the pinnace."

Turtle brought his heavy craft cleverly alongside and

in the moonlight they saw a small man waiting on the ladder. He dropped aboard the cockle and seated himself
facing the group in the stern. He was dark bearded and
wore a short cloak and a sword.

"Good evening, Masters," he said, staring.

"Good evening," returned Giles and Robert. Carter
only gaped.

"I was about to call for my own boat when I saw yours
and thought to get acquainted." He spoke gently and
in a not uneducated voice. "You," nodding at Giles,
"were in company with a very comely wench in Dartmouth market, today. And you, Master Cushman, were
at the Dancing Bear. I leaned in at the window beyond
the chimney and listened till I wearied of your patience
and then I came back to my ship. Did you finally put
your knife through Billington and eat him?"

"No!" smiled Robert. "No, I'm not fond of pork, Captain Nutt."

The other laughed. "So you recognize me! And you
may, for I have my pardon and I'm fit company for even
a Brownist now! It covered everything from my first
birching to my last business with Devon's vice-admiral."

"We're not Brownists," Robert corrected him. "But
we're glad to accommodate you, Captain, by whatever
name you call us, just so long as you don't make us out
disloyal."

"And what's disloyalty?" asked Nutt airily. "You desert
England. I relieve Frenchies of their goods and bring
it home to the gain of England. Who's the better Englishman?"

"I am!" said Bob Carter, giggling foolishly.

"Silence, beetle-head!" hissed Giles.

Robert had no wish to enter into debate with the pirate, but the man would have his answer.

"Who is the better Englishman?" he repeated.

*"You'*d be if you used your sword and your undoubted talents for the enlargement of England," Cushman replied. "Our colony in America, that's an enlargement of England."

"It won't be a comely enlargement if you suffer scum like Billington," remarked Nutt. "Put me aboard the *Speedwell,* boatman! I'll talk that matter further with you an' you're willing, some day, Master Cushman."

"At your pleasure," answered Robert. "I'm boarding the *Speedwell* also, Turtle. Pay him, Giles, and we'll settle afterwards. I must see Elder Brewster tonight. Send a boat for me in a half hour."

"You're not, perchance, following me?" Nutt suggested. "I'm going to see Master Reynolds, if that relieves you!"

Robert was not abashed. "My errand to Elder Brewster is a true one," he said.

Turtle ran alongside the pinnace and Robert caught the short rope ladder. Both men rose.

"Ha!" nodded the pirate. "You propose to tell him of the Dancing Bear talk, of course." He followed Robert to the deck of the pinnace.

Master Reynolds was standing on the poop watching but making no move to descend. William Brewster greeted Cushman from a seat on the main hatch combing, and bidding the pirate good night, Robert joined the elder.

He asked for Carver but Brewster explained that the deacon was spending the night ashore with an old friend. His wife and, he believed, his niece, were with him. Robert smiled to himself. Poor Giles! They chatted for

a moment of the voyage thus far on both ships and then
Robert told of his evening's experience in the Dancing
Bear.

The elder was more troubled than Cushman had ever
seen him.   He groaned, "Billington's the profanest man
among us!   Who in London shuffled him into our company?"

"Christopher Martin brought him as friend of a friend
and Master Weston accepted him for the venture," answered Cushman.

"Thomas Weston is not a careful judge at all times,"
mourned Brewster.   "What would you have me do,
Robert?"

"Call a meeting of the chiefs tomorrow, have Billington
before us and send him back to London with his wife and
children," answered Cushman promptly.

Brewster sighed again.   "It must be done but privily.
Ask Master Jones for his cabin at eight o'clock tomorrow
morning.   And secure Billington to come to us.   I'll explain to the deacon and Will Bradford.   You must tell
Edward Winslow and Martin."

Robert, who during all the recital had been watching
the poop, now said, "That was Captain Nutt who came
aboard with me.   He's the pirate."

Brewster nodded.   "I heard of him, this evening, from
Reynolds.   He's an old friend of Reynolds', it seems.   Yet,
Nutt was once a gentleman, poor fellow!"

"I don't like the friendship to be renewed at our possible expense," remarked Cushman, rising.   "But we can
only trust that to God."

"As you may, safely, I imagine," said the elder dryly.
"You must learn to trust Him more than you do your-

self, Robert." He followed to the ladder where the small boat waited.

"What little trust I had in myself, the pastor and the rest of you have lovingly removed, my dear elder," remarked Robert, with a one-sided smile as he went down the ladder.

"Trust and vanity are two differing matters!" cried Brewster leaning over the rail, eagerly.

He was quite capable, Cushman knew, of conversing an hour on this promising subject. "You are altogether in the right!" he hastened to assure the elder and bade the sailor shove off.

It was past midnight and on reaching the *Mayflower*, he went to bed and to sleep.

In the morning, he informed Martin of the impending meeting, just as the governor was preparing to go ashore. The little man received the news with dignity; was only too pleased, he said, to defer his own important affairs for matters of state.

Edward Winslow was finishing his morning ablutions when Robert found him.

"Alack!" said the young man. "Think of spending even one hour of this heaven-sent respite on that kennel-rat! Boot him out! There's my vote now! I'm off to our picnic!"

"Picnic?" repeated Robert. "I'd forgotten there were such pleasures."

"You are old before your time, poor Master Cushman!" smiled Winslow. "Yes, we are going to spend the day on a beautiful hill above the meadow where we held our service yesterday; Will Bradford and Dorothy, Giles Heale and Desire Minter, my Elizabeth and myself. I ought to add that the object of the jaunt will be to make

Will Bradford laugh!" He said this loudly, as Bradford
made his appearance.

"Still concerned with my welfare, Ned!" grunted Will,
as he crowded into the washroom. "I've come early to
make a proper toilet, for once. The washing place on the
pinnace is a pest-pit. I wish we'd never paused here. It
only prolongs our discomforts."

"I'll change places with you, gladly!" exclaimed Edward. "Elizabeth and I would like to experience everything on our voyage that the explorers did. And this great
ship is too comfortable to tell us what Raleigh or Cabot
endured."

Will shook his head with a sigh. "I wish I had your
gay heart, Ned! Nay, you're more useful on the *Mayflower* than I would be. Isn't that so, Master Cushman?"

"Yes, because he helps Standish so much with the discipline and training," agreed Robert frankly.

"I have no gift for that," admitted Bradford.

"What you should do, Will," laughed Winslow, "is to
retire to a private and recollected life and devote yourself to philosophy. For me, I'm just beginning to know
the real meaning of the word liberty."

"It has no real meaning," said Robert with a sardonic
smile. "I know."

"Seneca says," remarked Bradford, "that the great part
of liberty is a well-governed belly."

Both the others laughed but Will, insisting that he had
not meant to be witty, plunged his face into the wash
basin.

"Seriously then," jeered Edward as he pulled on his best
gold-colored doublet, "let's agree to make the session, this
morning, short and sharp like a donkey's trot."

"I, for one, won't prolong the agony," said Cushman,

and he went up to the poop to arrange for the use of the master's cabin.

By eight o'clock, a gentle rain was falling through a thick mist and the *Mayflower* was as isolated as the ark on Ararat. Even the cabin was misty and John Billington, seen only darkly, seemed more frowzy and unkempt than ever. He would have seated himself on a locker when he came in had the elder not called him to order, quickly.

"Stand up, my man, and tell us," Brewster said, "what was the meaning of your talk to Master Cushman, last night." The elder repeated the main points of Robert's report.

"I meant what I said," answered Billington, leaning against the wall and looking insolently from one man to another. "I work for no man."

"You eat, drink and sail the seas on moneys we others have found," said Carver. "How do you propose to make a return for your debt to us if you will work for no one but yourself?"

"Master Cushman signed the agreement without my consent," replied the man. "Let him pay my share."

Robert leaned forward from his seat under the stern window, his hair the brightest spot in the room. "I suggest that everyone at this meeting keep absolutely to the point. The point, as I see it, is this: John Billington despises the rules of the colony. Therefore he cannot want to live in the colony. Therefore let us arrange, to-day, to send him and his family back to London."

"I agree!" exclaimed Edward Winslow, looking eagerly out of the window where a momentary view of Dartmouth Church beckoned him.

"And so do I!" cried Martin. "This Billington has been insolent and unlawful ever since he boarded the ship.

If he's put his greasy fist under my nose once, he's put it under twenty times."

Billington snorted.

"Wait!" William Bradford's gray eyes under the heavy lids were keen. "This man, if he were right-minded, would make an excellent good colonist. He is very strong. He is young. He has his wife with him, a very decent woman, and so he'll be saved from the temptations of the flesh which will weaken so many of our young men. He is not a fool, though he acts one. I say, punish him and save him for the colony, if possible."

"And who are you to judge me as if I was a stallion you'd boughten?" exploded Billington.

"And how different are you from a stallion?" snapped John Carver. "Quite as unreasoning, just as strong—"

"And I'm no packhorse!" shouted Billington. "Listen, masters all, I'm my own man."

Again Robert brought them back to the point. "Will you put the matter to a vote, elder?" he urged. "This man has under his thumb a dozen other men. We may lose them all if you're not stern."

Brewster hesitated, his large face seamed with anxiety.

"If this is Christ's rule," jibed Billington, "give me the devil's!"

"Silence, blasphemer!" The elder's face hardened with purpose. "I agree with Master Cushman. This man must be sent away."

Billington for the first time looked startled. "Come, elder, you're not going to listen to Master Cushman! Nobody does! All that he's told you, you don't believe it?"

Brewster rapped on the table. "Deacon, your vote."

"Send him away!" exclaimed Carver.

"Governor?"

"Send him away," said Chris with great unction, but he did not look at the friend of his friend's friend as he spoke.

Will Bradford hesitated over his vote, then caught Winslow's impatient stare and said, after clearing his throat, "I still think we could use him, but I shall vote with the majority."

"We have your vote, Master Cushman," Brewster said, and turned to Billington, who, entirely dumbfounded, gasped a protest.

"But I haven't had a chance to say a word!" He was very white; all his bravado gone.

"Say it then, but no blasphemy," warned the elder. "And don't deny what you have said about your freedom. That's wasting time. We could gather in innumerable witnesses to corroborate what Master Cushman has told. He's a man of honor. We accuse you of planning to disrupt our rules and regiments and plunge us into the miseries of misrule in a savage wilderness. Now speak!"

There was a terrifying quality in Brewster's mighty voice which completely undid Billington. With a howl, he flung himself on his knees, hands clasped, arms outstretched.

"For God's sake, my masters, don't! Don't! I've been a sinner, I confess it! I've been wicked. But if you send me back to London, I'll starve and so will my wife and children. This is my only chance. I promised Master Weston I'd take it and be a credit to all. Don't do this, my masters. Put me in stocks for the rest of the voyage. But let me go with you. Put me in the *Speedwell*. Put me in the forecastle, here, a butt for the sailors. But don't cast me out!"

So the man was a mere blustering coward! Robert looked at the elder's face and groaned inwardly. Never had Brewster refused to forgive one who showed a contrite heart. Martin was biting his nails. There were tears in John Carver's handsome eyes. Bradford was nodding his black head, obstinate chin relaxed.

Edward Winslow murmured in Robert's ear, "It's all over! He'll stay! The elder and the deacon are going to pray over him and he knows it, the cur! I want to be off on my picnic."

William Brewster dropped to his knees and the others, perforce, followed his example. "O God," cried Brewster, "Thou knowest this man's heart! If in very truth, it has melted, let me be your instrument to shape him, to turn him to Your holy service! Look on him, Lord! Observe his mighty body which should be given to Thee."

"Amen! Amen!" groaned Billington.

"And Thou seest his black, sinful soul, brimming with lusts and cruelties and lies, empty it, O Great Jehovah, and fill it with Thy Holy Spirit! Amen!"

"It is emptied!" sobbed the culprit.

The elder put his hand on the gray fustian shoulder. "Leave him to me, brethren!" he exclaimed.

Robert set his teeth. "My dear elder," he dared to say, "nobody will be more pleased than I if this man prove contrite. But still I urge you to send him away."

"No!" protested Deacon Carver. "He *must* have his chance!"

Brewster rose, and now his hand was on Billington's bowed head. He looked reproachfully at Robert. "At this sacred moment—"

Robert lost all control of himself. "It's not a sacred moment!" he shouted. "Billington will do murder among us yet! It's not even a religious moment. This is a legal court sitting to try a traitor. We have found him guilty. You know he's guilty. Your long experience of men must have taught you his kind can't know true religious change."

"Stop!" Brewster was very red. "I put this charge to the vote again. Shall we send John Billington from us?"

Will Bradford, John Carver and, sullenly, Chris Martin, voted with the elder.

Edward Winslow bit his lip and said, "I vote with you, Elder Brewster, because in all things I will uphold your hands. But I fear, as Master Cushman does, that we may regret it."

"Your vote, Robert?" demanded Brewster.

"Cast him out!" said Cushman clearly.

Billington's hands now covered his face, but Robert felt his vicious gaze.

Through the window laughter drifted from the *Speedwell*. Smell of the sea . . . Desire . . . every drop of blood in his tired body rushed warmly and joyously to Robert's heart. . . .

He met William Brewster's cold gaze with sudden detachment. And answering the resentment he read there, Cushman said quietly, "It is only that I wish to save the colony and that only. If you understand this, you understand my every act. But since you've out-voted me, I leave Billington to you." He went out.

They had made a slide, the people, on the slippery main deck and were swooping from forecastle to steerage in a narrow line cleared of ropes and what-not. Robert paused in the steerage to watch them. How they roared and guffawed! Well, thank God for mirth!

As he stood, smiling in sympathy, an arm was thrust through his. It was young Winslow's.

"I know how you feel, Master Cushman!" he exclaimed.

"And for once, I'm in sympathy with you. But truly you take it all too gravely. These are all great boys, tickled with a slide and a bump on their seats and Billington's only one of them. He and they can be birched into good soldiers for our cause."

"Billington has murder in his heart," said Robert. "But if the rest of you can endure him, I can!"

"Endure being murdered?" The round brown eyes twinkled and then something very like admiration deepened in them as he studied Robert's face. "You had courage in there if you think that! But Billington's shown. he's a coward. Don't let him darken the voyage for you. It's such a splendid voyage and underneath all, a kind world! Look you, come on the picnic, you and Mistress Cushman! You've had too many of the cares of the company. Come and share some of its joys."

"In the rain?" smiled Robert.

"Aye, in the rain! That's just the point!" Winslow's dimples showed.

"We'll come!" exclaimed Cushman. "That is, if my wife is agreed. I must seek the governor out and get his permission."

"I tell you again," Edward's eyes were dancing, "you do take us all too seriously! What business is it of old Christopher's? Let him stew gallantly in his own spleen. See, they're gathering at the ladder now! Find Mistress Cushman. Nay, get into the small boat *now*, before anyone finds you! I've no trust in your conscience! Tommy? I'll speak to Captain Standish. I'll discover your wife." He was pushing Robert across the deck, laughing between words, and laughing with him. Robert allowed himself to be deposited in the boat. It was, as Edward said, a kind world.

# XV

## *Picnic at Dartmouth*

THE fine rain continued during the row up the river, but wrapped in their cloaks, the picnic party was indifferent to the moisture. The three younger men with Will Bradford at stroke rowed vigorously if erratically while Cushman steered and the four women made a more or less appreciative audience. In something less than a half hour, they landed in the low meadow from which Winslow had marked the spot whither he proposed to lead his friends. It was on a hilltop and the hill was now hidden by iridescent mists.

"You'll never find it, Ned!" remarked Will Bradford, hoisting a kettle to his shoulder.

Winslow gave him a scornful glance and cried, "Now, listen to me, friends, as confidently as you'd listen to Sir Humphrey Gilbert or Captain John Smith!"

"Or Master Marco Polo," suggested Robert.

"Or poor Master Columbus who never reached America at all," contributed Desire Minter.

Edward placed on the grass the basket of provisions with which Dorothy had laden him, swept off his hat with an elaborate bow, replaced it on his curly head, and said, as he lifted the basket, "I won't waste instructions on such frivolous minds." Then he led the way along a muddy path.

The women kilted up their skirts. They had left off their farthingales for the day's ardors and looked strangely

slender even with their bulky cloaks wrapped about them.
The path rose rapidly and shortly they crossed a stile into
a cart road which was completely over-canopied with hawthorn and ivy, a road so secret that not even the rain
had found it, and the dust rose under their feet. Here
they moved in couples. Giles Heale with Desire beside
him was next in front of Robert and Mary. Desire wore
a dark green cape over a paler green frock and had tied
a white kerchief over her hair and under her chin. Giles
kept his eyes on her in such open admiration that Mary
Cushman was moved to reprove him.

"You'll break your pretty neck, my worshipful physician," she called, "if you don't look at the road at least
once in a day!"

"I've no glances to spare, dear my aunt," retorted Giles,
unabashed and without taking his eyes from Desire's profile.

"How do you endure it, Mistress Desire!" exclaimed
Mary.

"Alas, what else may I do?" cried Desire, turning to
look at Mary. "You're looking far more worthy of any
man's gaze than I am, this morning, Mistress Cushman!"

Robert gave his wife a careless glance. It was true.
Desire looked pale and tired while Mary was ravishingly
pretty; red cloak, red kerchief over her hair and cheeks
brilliant. He smiled at Desire. She returned the smile.

"Take the right turn, friends!" called Ned Winslow.
"And save your breath for a steep climb."

They moved from under the may branches to find that
the rain had ceased and that they were in an upland field
from which the clouds were retreating.

"Yonder is our goal," said Winslow, pointing to a beech
copse on a rounded hilltop.

The road, grass-grown but deep-rutted, led along the edge of the field which was in wheat stubble, still up, for a good quarter mile, through a gate hung between high walls, over a last steep field where sheep were grazing, up and up to the beech spinney.

The sun burst out as they made the crest and the little group stood ravished by the beauty of the world beneath them; river and hill and far moorland beneath a glorious sky of white clouds racing over intensest blue.

"Well done, Marco Polo!" cried Giles Heale.

"Nay, he's Joshua and actually has got us to the Promised Land!" suggested Robert. "What do we do first, good Joshua?"

"We cook our dinner," proclaimed Winslow. "Husbands and wives are not to work together except Elizabeth and me. We never argue so *our* work will be done."

Violent protests met this exception and with much laughter, Ned was prevailed upon to include himself and Elizabeth in the realignment, silent, vivid little Elizabeth being paired off with Will Bradford. Dorothy Bradford was apportioned by the young Joshua to Giles Heale, while Ned himself chose Mary Cushman. Robert could scarcely believe his good fortune when Winslow ordered him and Desire to procure long pointed sticks on which to grill the rashers of bacon. Will Bradford and Elizabeth were to prepare the table, Giles and Dorothy to make the fire, Ned and Mary to do the cooking.

"Willow wands, very green, will be best, Master Cushman," cried Ned. "You will find a thicket of them below by the river. I observed them yesterday as we rowed by."

"They shall be produced, O master explorer!" said Robert gayly.

Desire hung her cloak on a bush and tossed off her

kerchief that her hair might dry. "The Merchant Adventurers," she exclaimed, "would not have worried themselves over the laziness of the Pilgrims, had they realized that Master Winslow was with us!"

Will Bradford bestirred himself. "It's not Master *Cushman* after all who'd have made slaves of us!"

Dorothy suddenly giggled. "Will's made a quip!"

"And you'll observe," was Mary Cushman's fling, "that Ned keeps the pleasantest, lightest task for himself!"

"Come, Master Cushman!" Desire smiled up at him. "You and I have the heaviest task of all and had better begin apace."

They walked to the brow of the hill. Far below the Dart was bordered by pollard willows. There were sheep tracks leading down the broad slopes. These were slippery with mud and very narrow. At Robert's suggestion they did not try to follow the tracks but descended zigzag over the grass.

"Can Ned Winslow possibly suspect what pleasure he's giving us?" asked Desire. "Somehow this seems more than a mere perchance!"

"I think that quite deliberately he's trying to pleasure me," replied Robert. "I was downed again in a critical decision by the chiefs this morning and for once Ned was in sympathy with me. I actually dare believe that he discovered, this morning, that I was truly and fully on the side of the Pilgrims. He brought me to the picnic to *frivol* me. And so," with a grin, "he gives me as a companion the lady whom all the others would have preferred!"

"My lady Frivol! How belittling!" her dimples showing. Then she added, serious again, "Tell me, what was

the decision that went against you? I will not repeat it
to any soul."

He complied, glad to have her opinion of the matter.
Desire listened intently, walking on the up side of the
hill from him so that she looked almost levelly into his
eyes from time to time. When he had finished, she gave
judgment.

"All we women are afraid of Billington. Instinct tells us
what a brute-beast he is. I shall get my uncle to tell me
this story over again so that I may be impertinent and in-
form him of what a pair of children he and the dear elder
are. Uncle John enjoys my impertinences even as he re-
proves me. And now, dearest of friends, I quite agree
with Ned that you need a dose of frivolity. Let's begin!"

"I could have frivoled well enough ten years ago,"
Robert assured her.

"And now that you're in your second childhood, grandfather, you should be light-minded and fond again!" she
assured him. "Grandfather! I'm not sure the title is
quite accurate. Your yellow hair is a boy's hair and gives
you the strangest look of youth!" Her glance was so impish that as she had intended, Robert burst out laughing.

"Ah, if you were only—" He caught himself and began
again. "Ah, if you and I could only do the things Tom
Weston and I did up and down Thameside, looking for
a proper ship. Was there ever a more delectable task! It
belonged to the very youth of the world, didn't it? To
Jason and Æneas and—young Marco Polo, if you please!"

"If I'd only known you, then!" sighed Desire, "I'd have
stolen along with you as your page boy. No, as your most
subdued and impressed secretary!"

"Secretaries are never impressed." Robert shook his
head. "Sir Robert Nauton is secretary to the King His

Majesty, and Sir Robert is beyond all doubt the most *un-*impressed man I ever beheld."

"Very well then!" Desire went on. "I'd have been a very congenial secretary and we'd have dined on the *Golden Hind* at its moorings in Deptford. What sacrilege to make an ordinary of that glorious little ship! And we'd not have devoted ourselves entirely to Thameside. We'd have found Ben Jonson's inn and listened to him and his court of mad poets."

"Not his plays but his poetry, only," amended Robert.

"But I like his plays," insisted Desire. "Shall we permit Master Shakespeare to be present?"

"No, we must give so precious a fancy some semblance to verity and he's been gone these four years while the *Golden Hind* was burned six years ago." Robert sighed.

Desire turned on him crossly. "You're no poet nor yet a sailor or you'd never hamper your fancy with verities! You'll be telling me next that this, our seeking after a ship, was in the reign of one James the First, when I know such seeking never belonged to him but to Elizabeth."

"I crave your pardon!" smiled Robert. "Yes, we made this famous junket when the old Queen was young. Not that she ever was old, either! She never gave in to the 'wreckful siege of battering years.' See how we always come back to him, my dear? I tell you he was the greatest of them all."

"Not greater as a love poet than Sidney," objected Desire.

"I saw you reading Sidney that first day!" exclaimed Robert. "I was angry because you ignored me."

"I didn't ignore you," contradicted Desire. "I was conscious of your every thought. But you mustn't be evasive!

Admit I'm right, that of all the old Queen's school of love poets, Sir Philip was the best."

"Nothing so fine as *'Let me not to the marriage of true minds'* was ever spoke with the pen," insisted Robert, doughtily.

"Cold words!" she said. "Cold and thoughtful which love cannot be. Look you, here are the willows!"

"Ah, thanks! Here are willows!" grimaced Robert, drawing his knife.

He cut a pile of wands quickly. Desire twisted a withy about them and Cushman took the bundle under his arm and looked up the hill, then glanced wistfully at Desire. "We must go back, I suppose, dear my secretary!"

Desire nodded. But she did not stir, only stood looking at him, her wide smile gay but her eyes sober.

Robert returned her gaze, the while he said to himself in warning, "You will say nothing to startle her. You will add nothing to her unhappiness. . . . But oh, how is she beautiful . . . !"

Desire started back up the hill. Her voice was casual. "Do you know that you are the object of Giles Heale's great adoration and that he is concerned about your health?"

Robert chuckled. "He says strange uncomely things about my spleen, that I know! The adoration is memory merely. He loved me when he was a little child."

"But you *are* feeling better?" asked Desire. "You are looking better than you did after your swoon."

"My health is well enough to carry me to New England and once I achieve that, my pains will be forgotten."

"Then you have pains!"

"At this moment," he replied, "I'm as strong as Sampson, as fleet of foot as Absalom—"

"And as mad as Saul!" Desire finished for him. "Mistress Cushman has my sympathy! Will you let me carry the willows for a little distance?"

"You're suspecting me of having shortness of breath! How insolent!" He could not help panting but he had thought no one could observe it. He quickened his pace.

Desire caught his free hand. "Robert Cushman, don't be a fond fool! Do you want to break my heart? Move slowly, I pray you!"

Robert would have clung to her fingers but she drew them away and they proceeded slowly and in silence up to the beeches. Hills were troublesome, he admitted to himself. By the time he reached the fireside and dropped his bundle of willows, the beech trees were doing the all too familiar gaillard. But by sheer force of will he kept himself erect, even answering the jibes about their slow return. Then he walked toward the trees and somehow found Giles Heale beside him as he leaned heavily against one of the great trunks.

"The bellows nearly bursted, that time!" remarked Robert.

Mary caught his arm. "Don't swoon, Robert!"

"But why should I?" he exclaimed. "Why this pother?"

"Because Mistress Desire rushed you up the hill, I suppose," answered Mary.

"Don't blame Mistress Desire for his own block-headedness!" snapped Giles. "I, myself, saw her pull him back when he quickened his pace."

"If I'm giddy, it's because of prolonged starvation," proclaimed Cushman, anxious to escape their attentions.

Desire had been watching him with a troubled face. She smiled a little now and said, "Master Cushman and I have risked our lives to finish our task. If you others were as hearty in your duty, Master Cushman wouldn't be starving."

"Come! This is too much insolence!" cried Winslow. "Back to the banquet table, friends!"

With relieved faces, the others returned to their tasks. Robert and Desire sat down beneath the beech.

"You will begin to take care of your health, will you not?" pleaded Desire in a low voice. "Dr. Heale says that if you'll only take the medicines he gives you, he'd cure you; but that you only laugh at him! If you don't trust his remedy, Master Cushman, why not take Sir Walter Raleigh's? The King's Majesty uses it and the Duke of Buckingham and they gave it to little Prince Charles for his poor thin legs."

"I know of it," nodded Robert. "It contains some score of drugs and I doubt me if we could have it compounded in Dartmouth. But if it is your wish, I'll take Giles' pills. I'd swallow spider legs and snake scales for you, dear my secretary!"

"How Giles will thank me!" she exclaimed.

"Don't tell Giles of the spider legs or he'll make a tincture of them for me!" he added.

Desire sprang to her feet and ran to join Giles and Mary at the fire. Robert sat contentedly gazing on what he found to be a compassionate as well as a beautiful world.

As usual, he recovered quickly from his giddy spell and was able to enjoy the dinner to which he was called shortly. After the prolonged meal was over, Ned set them all at a game of forfeits. Then they played puss-wants-a-corner and finally had a long bout of hide-and-seek. By supper time and sunset everyone was weary and ready for the return. At this meal, Will Bradford suggested that as they would reach the ships too late for evening service, Robert could hold it here. And so as the moon rose and the last of the afterglow lighted the tree tops, the young people knelt about him and Robert led them in the Lord's prayer. They sang "Come all ye faithful," and then repeated the ninety-first psalm.

*"He that dwelleth in the secret place of the most High shall abide under the shadow of the Almighty."*

And all about these, her children, worshiping on one of her most exquisite hilltops, England sent up her incense, subtle, nameless, enchanting.

# XVI

## *The Cushat Dove*

WHEN the moon was bright, they started home-
ward, moving swiftly down the hill and silent
except when they spoke of the marvel of the
night or of the goodness of God in vouchsafing them such
a day as had just passed.

The pack road under the hawthorn canopy was the
only unlighted spot in all the world, apparently, that
night. But this was black except for the arched gleam at
the far end. And even this gleam, as they were halfway
through, was obscured by the dark outline of a man on
horseback and they heard the patter of little hooves.

"We'd better retreat," said Robert.

"Too late!" exclaimed Will Bradford. "Draw up under the hedge, here, with the women behind us."

"Every man his dagger loosened," added Robert.

"And Master Cushman, be our spokesman," said Winslow. "I'll say too much and Will would quote Seneca on
bellies."

There was a little flurry of laughter and then the trot-
ting horse had reached them. Its rider halted the pack
train he was leading and unshuttered a lantern, sweeping
them with a finger of light.

"Master Cushman! And who are these? Ah, I see the
boy doctor and Mistress Minter!" It was Captain Nutt.

"These are fellow Pilgrims, Captain," replied Cushman.
"We've spent the day on the hilltop."

"In prayer, I suppose!" Nutt flashed his lantern back and forth. "I never knew a Puritan who wasn't as set for women as he was for prayer!"

There was a quick movement among the young men behind Robert. He put out his arm as if to hold them back and said, sternly, "You assured me last night, Captain Nutt, that you were now fit to associate *even with us!* But your remark is so vile, that I find you entirely unfit for *any* decent ears!"

There were men standing among the donkeys back of Nutt and they sniggered loudly.

"Silence, you!" snarled the Captain. "My good Cushman, I had no wish to insult you. . . . You're a brave man! . . . Now look you! I must talk to you and as I sail on the midnight tide, I have no time but the present. Let your friends go on. I'll speak you as I attend to my business and we'll carry you back to your ship when I return to mine."

"No! No!" whispered Mary Cushman, clasping her husband's arm.

"I may be a *boy* doctor," cried Giles, "but I have mind enough to know that Master Cushman has an illness of his breath and should climb no more hills tonight."

"I'm very well again, Giles," Robert assured him. He felt a little apprehension in regard to Nutt's motives but on the whole was glad to have an interview with him. He had not forgotten the pirate's call on Reynolds.

"Take me, also, Captain Nutt," suggested Will Bradford.

The pirate laughed in a pleased way. "So even you Leyden exiles feel called to fear Captain Nutt. Don't be afraid, my friends! I'll return your man to you, promptly and unharmed. As for Master Cushman's wind," he got off his horse, "come, mount this Ancient of Days, my master! She's just your pace, I trow."

"Don't go!" exclaimed Ned Winslow. "I'll take your place!"

"Content yourselves!" said Robert. "It's a proper move, this! I'm glad to make it. Will Bradford, take charge of my wife, will you?"

"But this is mad!" Desire cried suddenly. "How can you call yourselves men and give up the best man among you without a blow? Why don't you add, 'Thank you, Captain Nutt?' "

The pirate turned his lanthorn on her. "Ah, it's the *Mayflower* beauty speaking so stoutly. Well! Well! I think I'll take you with us to protect Master Cushman!"

"No! I'll refuse to go an you try such impudence!" shouted Robert.

Giles Heale made a leap toward Nutt. Mary Cushman began to scream and Will threw a stout arm around her. There was a confusion of expostulations from the Pilgrims and of oaths from the pirate. Robert seized Giles by the arm. "Don't be a fool!" he exclaimed.

"Dicken! Jock!" roared Nutt. "Walt! Mark!"

Two dark shapes thrust themselves between the captain and Giles. Two more separated Desire and Robert from the company. Robert found himself on Nutt's horse with Desire pillion-fashion behind him. Nutt flashed his lanthorn back and forth across the group of Pilgrims, disclosing angry, discomfited faces.

"Don't fret!" cried Desire, high glee in her voice. "Rather, envy us our adventure! For you'll return us at midnight, you promise, Captain?"

Nutt looked up at her. "Aye, you have my promise, Mistress! Come, there's been enough prittle-prattle!"

He pulled the reins over the horse's head and led him up the road. The line of laden donkeys fell in behind.

"We'll be waiting at the ladder of the *Cushat Dove* at midnight, Master Cushman!" shouted Edward Winslow.

"Wait at your own risk!" roared Nutt and broke into a run. "If you bring a single soul other than you three, I'll sink you!" And he continued to run until they emerged from the hawthorn arcade. Then he admonished all to be silent and settled to a rapid walk.

Desire's whisper came warm in Robert's ear. "What an unbelievable droll hazard! Your secretary, sir, accompanies you on a matter of mystery! Oh, Robert Cushman, what a jest! Marco Polo, what a tale!"

He turned his head (her warm cheek so close!). "Dearest of lion-hearts, what glorious luck! He dare not harm you!"

"Silence!" said Nutt hoarsely.

He turned into a turnip field and urged the pack train forward in the shadow of a hedge. They crossed a falling brook and entered a narrow road winding between steep banks and so to the ruins of an old farmhouse. In a cobblestoned stable yard, Nutt halted and remained with his double-laden horse while his men—there were six of them —drove the score of donkeys into the section of the stable which still retained a portion of thatch. Black in the silver light, ivy hung in enormous festoons over wall and crumbling chimney. Robert drew in long breaths of the ancient scents and bade himself live only in this fantastic, diverting moment.

With extraordinary dispatch and minimum of noise, the men did their work and returned to the yard. Nutt immediately turned the Ancient of Days and without a word, led the way back over the field. But they did not again enter the hawthorn arcade. They trotted down a steep pasture, then entered a long wood bordered far below by water and shortly in the black and silver of tree and moonlight, Robert recognized the path which had brought him to the Dancing Bear. And at the Dancing Bear they brought up. Here the donkeys were left and two of the men. The rest with Nutt descended to the harbor where at a spot well hid from the quay, there was a dory and Nutt ordered all aboard.

"I thank you for your silence!" he said, as with his men at the oars, he took the tiller. Robert and Desire were on either side of him.

"But," returned Desire, "we had been silly to have brought the watch on us. How could we have explained our presence in *your* company?"

"True!" chuckled the pirate. "And I hope you're all agog to know why you are with me."

"I am, indeed," she said. "But Master Cushman takes all things with calm—at least outwardly."

"Well," explained Robert, "I am so fain to talk to Captain Nutt and so pleased to be out of the hurly-burly, for an hour, with Mistress Minter that I wouldn't even rub my chin, lest it attract the watch."

Nutt laughed as he steered the dory skillfully among anchor cables. There was a sharp sea in the harbor. "It's pleasant to have contented guests! And so, prithee, silence again till we board my ship."

It was only a short row and in less than a quarter of an hour they were following him up the ladder of the *Cushat Dove*. She was twice the tonnage of the *Mayflower* with guns on all her decks. Except for the shadowy figures of the watch on forecastle and poop, she might have been deserted.

Nutt led the way at once to his cabin, an extremely comfortable room. Four lanthorns, all alight, hung from the beams. There were crimson cushions on the bed-lockers and silver dishes set forth a cold supper on the table. The cabin boy, asleep on the floor, jumped to his feet.

"Two more for supper, Pigs! Look lively, lad!" cried the captain.

"That isn't the poor boy's name?" exclaimed Desire.

"I don't know his name. So the sailors call him." The pirate was staring at Desire admiringly. She was disheveled after her long day but her cheeks were flushed, her dark eyes dancing, her white teeth flashing. "Damn my eyes, but I like thee, my handsome wench!" he ejaculated.

"I'm glad you do, Captain. Still, you deserve no great credit! Few people find me repulsive!" She pretended to speak seriously.

Black eyes dancing, Nutt tugged at his beard with one hand and with the other led her to a chair by the table. "It's only a half hour to midnight! Sit down here, Mistress, and you, Master Cushman, beside her, where I can see you both." He threw on the floor the knitted cap he'd been wearing, uncovering a mass of curly black hair, and took a third chair, facing them. Seen thus, his face was remarkable for very intelligent blue eyes and very full firm lips.

"Lookee, my friends, I have been in negotiation with your Master Reynolds, at his instance, and I have decided to refuse his proposal which was childish. So I can say this much to you. Under his hugeous layers of fat, Reynolds is a very frightened little man. He's not a bad man, except as some frightened men will be evil if their fear masters them."

"Precisely what does he fear?" asked Cushman, resting his chin on his cupped hands, elbows on table.

"That Master Martin means to drive him to mutiny by starvation and so get rid of him by dangling him at the end of a yardarm."

"But we'd never do that!" cried Desire.

"We'd hang a man if he earned hanging," declared Robert. "Why does Chris Martin want to be rid of Reynolds?"

"By fantastic chance, Reynolds knows some old but deep villainy of Martin's," answered the pirate.

Robert shook his head. "No, not deep villainy! Martin is a cozening coward. He'd not dare deep villainy. I can control him perfectly by dropping my hand on my knife and once he let me twist his ear."

"Why, Robert Cushman!" gasped Desire.

His smile was a little twisted. "Oh! We've met in the field of honor, Christopher and I!"

Nutt roared delightedly. "Passion of God, but the more I see of you the greater I like you, Robert Cushman! Enter, Pigs! Quick now! What have you?"

The child was staggering under a great tray of viands: cold fowl, cold roast pork, a tall bottle of wine, a jug of ale, a twist of wheat bread, a basket of figs and dates. Desire helped him place the load on the table.

"Why not have a servant at least old enough to place the dishes?" she asked indignantly.

"I'm a man, I am!" squeaked the lad.

"There's a Briton for you!" grinned Nutt. "His own mother left him with me and proud of the chance! Get out now, Sir Pigs! I'll call when I want you." The child ran away and the pirate went on, amiably, "If I could use such a poor bastard as Martin on the *Cushat Dove*, I'd press him for you. But since Master Cushman has learned how to intimidate him, we'll pass him by and continue to think of Reynolds. Help yourself, Mistress, to what you will."

"Have you known Reynolds long, Captain?" asked Desire, taking some bread and wine.

"Not too long," carving the fowl with enormous dexterity. "He will do something mad, now mark me. If I were your leader, Brewster, I'd return to the *Mayflower* and on the *Speedwell* put Martin and any others you're well shut of, like that sweet crew in the Dancing Bear, last night."

"What did Reynolds propose to you, Captain Nutt?" asked Robert.

"Since I refused, it's none of your affair," waving a well-shaped hand airily. "That's my first and last advice about him and the *Speedwell*."

"Did Master Reynolds explain to you," queried Desire, "that our very existence on the other side depends on the pinnace; for fishing and fur trading and at great need, for crossing the ocean back again?"

"No, he said nothing of that," replied the pirate thoughtfully. "However, that needn't interfere with your eating your supper."

"Nor does it!" smiled Desire.

"Which brings us to the real meat of the evening," said Nutt, pouring himself a glass of wine. "Silence, both of you, while I paint the picture! Master Cushman, I'd like ye to come with me on this voyage. You are going to Virginia or whatever part of that vile coast you make, for two reasons, to worship as it pleases you and to get yourself lands or riches. You will find the first. But the second! God help you for a witless lot of dreamers! If you outlive starvation, the savages will kill and eat you. And if you survive that, the wolves will devour you!

"Now, I'm off to Cathay! And I know for a certainty that I and my officers will return in a year's time with each a king's ransom in wealth. Cushman, there's your riches for you! As for freedom of worship—my Master, aboard the *Cushat Dove,* you may worship the devil, the saints, or the virgin or, like me, nothing at all. And now you are asking, Why do I want you? I reply that I am coming back to England to make a country gentleman of myself. I would have a tutor to teach me all this year, so that when I take my place, I will be one who has a little Latin, a little French, and the manners of a man who can kiss Her Majesty the Queen's hand without biting or slobbering!"

He paused and Robert, meeting those blue eyes, knew that this man liked him as Tom Weston had liked him. The knowledge warmed him, touched him.

"In other words," he remarked, "you and I, Captain, find that we might enjoy each other's company! I'm glad of that! Yet I cannot go with you to Cathay for I must go to North America."

"But why?" Nutt's voice rose a little. "Reynolds told me the people had repudiated you and your work for them!"

Robert flushed. "And that's why I must go! I must make them wipe out that repudiation so far as it concerns their debts to the men who have upheld them."

"You're a fool for your pains!" declared Nutt, setting down his half-finished glass.

"Nay, Captain Nutt!" Desire spoke eagerly. "Though they've disavowed some of his work, they unconsciously lean on him. They depend, all unknowing, on his steadfast guidance in matters of honorableness and good sense."

"Mayhap!" grunted Nutt. "But neither of you has given me a good reason for refusing Cathay."

"Tell him, Master Cushman," urged Desire.

Robert looked thoughtfully from one to the other. The *Cushat Dove* rolled heavily and tugged at her anchors against the rising tide. Mingled with the smell of food was the sharp tang of the sea, that sea of which Robert never was unconscious any more than he was of his love for Desire. And he thought now that the endless wash of the waves was like a persistent Greek chorus. It provided without cessation a background of terrible and magnificent implications to all that they of the Pilgrimage said or did.

Tell him—this freebooter—tell him his dream for a more noble England on America's shores? Display for him those splendid marching thoughts? Nay, he could not! And yet he truly liked this little man—this pirate who lied and robbed and killed! Certainly, Robert Cushman had a deep-seated kinship with sinners for Tom Weston too was potentially a freebooter! He looked helplessly at Desire.

She returned his look and then she said to the captain, "While Master Cushman ponders, will you tell me why you turned to piracy?"

"To procure fowl and wine and wheat bread in place of beer and black bread," he answered briefly. "And you, Mistress, are you going to America to wed the boy doctor as Reynolds said?"

"I go to procure even the black bread and beer," retorted Desire, flushing. "I am dependent on my uncle. I have no such lofty motives as Master Cushman who since this England will have none of him will make him an England of his own."

"He can get him a pardon, as I have," said Nutt. "It's a more useful document than the prayer service." He looked at Robert.

Robert shook his head. "All that I've ever thought and desired takes me to America just as your heart is set on Cathay." He said this with an earnestness that could not be ignored.

Nutt gave a sigh which was almost a groan and Desire tried to comfort him.

"Cathay! Its very sound is music," she said. "You choose to end your sea career with a stirring and beautiful adventure, Captain! When you return, make the *Cushat Dove* take a long tack and pause in America long enough to tell us the story."

The pirate's eyes blazed. "*You* come with me, Mistress! Passion of God, how have the landlubbers left you so long!"

Young Pigs appeared most opportunely at the door. "Some men are in a small boat at the gangway, sir, calling for you, loudly," he said to Cushman.

Robert and Desire rose at once. Nutt's eyes were half closed as he eyed Desire, but he had himself in hand again. "Aye, it's midnight!" he exclaimed. He helped Desire with her cloak. "And so, after all, it's farewell! A pity of the world!"

Robert held out his hand. "I would have liked the Cathay voyage on this noble ship and in your society, Captain, but—" he hesitated, then added lamely—"but your offer heartened me as you can't understand."

Nutt held Cushman's hand firmly. "If you'd sneered at the offer, I'd have drawn on you!" he said. "But you mean what you say; that you'd have liked the voyage. I knew that, though, before I asked you."

He led them out of the cabin and down to the gangway. The ship was no longer deserted. A group of the *Cushat Dove's* men were standing at the ladder. Below, Will Bradford, Edward Winslow and Giles Heale were looking up in the lanthorn and moonlight. Desire and Robert descended to the bobbing little craft.

No one spoke until they had pushed off. Then, "There's been a fearful to-do about you!" cried Ned. "But we have managed well. None but Master Jones besides our party knows of your junket so there'll be no gossip. Is all well with you?"

"He kept his word, absolutely," replied Robert, "as you have kept yours. I was afraid Captain Standish and his 'army' would come with you."

"We had enormous difficulty," said Giles, "but Master Jones took Nutt's part; said he was known to be a man of his word."

"Wait till we can all hear!" called Will Bradford. "The slap of the waves drowns everything!"

Under cover of the clamor of the sea, Robert said to Desire, "I have had a very dear happiness, today!"

She only looked at him and turned her head away.

Master Jones hailed them from the half deck of the *Mayflower*. "Is all well there? Come up and tell your story!"

"All's well, Master!" called Cushman.

Only Miles Standish was on the main deck. Desire hurried off to bed for it was long past midnight. The others followed Standish to the master's cabin. As the men mounted to the half deck, Jones said, "Look to the larboard, friends!"

In the fading moonlight, a great gray ship was moving down the harbor. It was the *Cushat Dove*, off for Cathay.

# XVII

## *The Ghost on the Speedwell*

ROBERT'S first task, the next morning, was to ease Mary's curiosity with regard to the events of the previous evening. He did his best to satisfy her while telling her as little as possible of the pirate's comments on Reynolds.

"I can't see why he chose Desire Minter rather than your wife," she said. "Is he a married man?"

"He didn't tell us," replied Robert, looking over the taffrail where they were leaning to observe the work on the *Speedwell*.

"I should think Desire would feel most immodest," Mary went on, "but she says she was only amused. And we had dreadful work with Christopher and Marie Martin when we got back. If only the younger people had gone, they wouldn't have minded. But since you and I went, they called themselves affronted."

"I hope you soothed him," yawned Cushman. He was feeling strangely weary. His bones ached and his mouth was parched. He nearly always felt thus, of late, after mental or bodily strain.

"I didn't try," returned Mary toploftily. "After all, Marie was only the wife of a farm laborer before she married a chapman. She was so hateful about Desire Minter, asking where was she and did she think herself equal to a married woman, until Giles Heale had to silence her."

"Giles can't cope with Marie, I'm afraid," said Cushman.

"If you'd heard him last night when you and Desire rode off so lovingly you'd not fear that. He was the peer of any ranting play-actor who tears up and down the stage of the Globe." Mary gave Robert one of her most innocent looks.

"It was so amusing!" she went on. "I hung to his arm. In all his fury he was most kind in helping me along the paths for Will forgot me, he was so busy lecturing about Captain Nutt. When Giles showed signs of calming down, I comforted him a bit. I told him that while you admired dark women, you did not admire women with brains and learning and that I was sure that as soon as you'd discovered to the pirate that Desire could read and write and that she'd admitted to studying Plato, he'd send her back. And then," with a giggle, "he turned on me and said Mistress Desire was not learned, that she had a smattering of this and that and such and such, but that she was no more capable of being really learned than any other women and he'd thank me to stop slurring her womanly nature. He was still in his frenzy when we got back to the *Mayflower* and Christopher Martin asked him for a dose of oil of stag's blood. And when Giles asked him what he meant by always complaining, Christopher explained, furiously, that if the doctor had been attending to his business, the governor would not have been suffering with the belly-ache. And Giles called him a *poor, quinching bag-pudding!*"

"No!" Robert's irritation vanished in amusement. "Did anyone hear the awful epithet?"

"All did! It was on the main deck and even the sailors shouted. Poor Christopher *was* in a way. Robert, did you use force to make the governor take back something he said about me? Love Brewster and his brother were in the rigging and they overheard you and Christopher quarreling and I overheard the two lads talking to each other about it."

"Yes, but it's all settled and better forgotten," answered Robert.

"The governor hasn't forgotten. He told me you'd insulted him and he hoped I'd remain his friend even so."

Robert wondered what in the world Mary was getting at. She so rarely followed any idea for more than a sentence or two that he was certain something serious had come up with the Martins; at least, serious in her opinion. "And what did you say to that?" he asked.

"I said nothing. What could I say?" She returned his keen look with one of round-eyed guilelessness. "But I think you had no right to keep from me what Martin said about me."

"Oh, I'll tell you!" he exclaimed, losing patience, and he retailed the sordid little passage to her.

A quick flush rose from her ruff to her hood frontlet. "But people *don't* say they can't believe me! Do they?"

"But they do," he replied very gently.

"Robert!" She was angry, resentful. "You've always been the only one to say such things about me!"

"Not *about* you, *to* you," he amended. "As you and I well know, the elder and Pastor Robinson have both labored with you on your besetting sin. You lied to them and to other people and they accused you of it before the congregation in Leyden. Now, how like a very babe it is of you to pretend that Martin's report was a falsehood! He had no business to speak so to me of my wife and I could have dragged his vile ear out by the roots for it.   But you and I both know he spoke truth."

"It wasn't truth!" declared Mary, teeth set.   "Nobody but you dislikes me.   Everyone on the two ships likes me except you."

"Likes and dislikes isn't what we're discussing," grunted Robert.   "It is lies and facts.   You've done me endless harm in the congregation and among the Pilgrims with your falsehoods!"

"If you liked me," with a little sob, "you wouldn't mind."

He looked at her now.   "I do like you," he said slowly, "and I do mind.   If you liked me, you'd cut out your tongue before you'd mave maligned me as you have.   It's the little things which you didn't think mattered; the pretended artless mention of our junketings in London, my fondness for the play and profane poetry, our clothes, our journey down to Canterbury.   All were entirely harmless yet you gave them a taint as if I'd been a sneak or a hypocrite or even dishonest, as in my borrowing from Tom Weston.   So for years you've helped to undermine the people's confidence in me and combined with their natural impatience and stupidity about the American venture, when the stressful moment came and they should have trusted me blindly, they repudiated me.   And so the Merchant Adventurers are disaffected and so Reynolds was put on the pinnace instead of good honest Thomas English, my choice.   And so if we starve in New England, it's your innuendoes and lies that are at the very uttermost bottom of it."

He never had turned on her before.   Mary, for once, was frightened.   She turned very pale.   "You're saying a horrible thing, Robert!" she whispered.

"Yes, a horrible thing!"   He was white now, also, and he trembled and his breathing troubled him a little.   "It's beyond villainy, what you have done to me and this gallant, lovely dream of the Pilgrims."

"But I didn't do it!   I didn't!" she gasped.

"You and God know you did," mercilessly.

She gave a little moan.   "How can you!   How can you!"

"I *must*," he said, "in a last attempt to save your soul. As for how *I* can—Mary, how could *you?*   Why did you? Perchance," feeling a little sorry for her, she was so frightened, "perchance, if you could discover *why* you lie about me, it would discover the key to all your lies and then—why then—" putting his hand over hers—"we'd throw the key away."

"But it's not so!"   She gave a little sob.

"But it is so!" sternly again and withdrawing his hand.

"But it's almost murder you're accusing me of!   I'll suffer eternal punishment for it.   You're wicked, wicked!"

"Yes, I am a great sinner.   But this particular sin is yours, not mine."

Mary twisted her hands together.   Then she screamed. Then in quick succession she laughed and sobbed and then screamed again, "Oh, Frank!   Oh, Frank!   Oh, Frank!"

Robert put his hand over her mouth.   Desire and Elizabeth Winslow came running up from the half deck.

"She's ill!" exclaimed Cushman.   "Will you help me get her to bed?"

Elizabeth pulled his hand away and with surprising skill put her handkerchief into Mary's mouth.   "Fetch a jug of cold water, Master Cushman!" she said.

He left the two women to get Mary down to the great cabin.   Here a dash of sea water brought her quickly to her senses.  Desire proceeded to clear the cabin of its other occupants and then Robert sat down beside his wife.

"Mary," he said uneasily, "who is Frank?"

"Nobody!  I don't know what you're talking about. You've almost killed me.  Aren't you satisfied?"  It was the old fretful voice.

But Robert would not free the struggling fingers. "Mary, for God's sake, let there be no more lies between us!  You needn't tell me who Frank is, but at least don't deny him.  If he's a friend, you're a very Judas to do that."

"Judas betrayed, Peter denied," whimpered Mary.

What a mere child she was!  "No more lies, Mary, my wife!  If there can't be love, there can be truth, at least, between us.  We can do without the one but not the other."

"There isn't any Frank!"  She caught her breath painfully.  "If there was, would you cast me off?"

(Ah, Desire!  So unconscious of his love, so much a part of him yet so infinitely remote!)

"Mary, never!  Always while I live, you shall be mine, be with me!  It's not been Robert who's tried to separate us, but Mary who would have stayed behind in Canterbury."

As he said the world "Canterbury" he knew!  Frank Bote, a yeoman farmer of their countryside.  Ah, poor little Mary!  Underneath the lies, what heartache and what courage!

She did not reply to this but she let her hand remain in his and lay motionless except for the occasional long-drawn sob.  The linnet sang happily in its cage.  The *Mayflower* rocked slowly.  From the main deck came the thudding ring of a game of quoits and shrieks of delight.  Mary at last lifted her swollen eyes to his.

"I'll try to stop my lies, Robert.  I don't know why I've told them, but all my life, I've thought so quickly of interesting things to say, both good and bad."

"I understand now," he said eagerly, "and when you had a chance to hurt me, you struck blindly at me because I am not the man you should have married and you've grown to hate me for it.  Oh, my dear, let's stop misunderstanding and hurting each other.  Our marriage can't be undone."

But she would not confide in him.  She only shook her head.  "I'll never understand you.  But I'll try to trust when I don't understand."

"Don't trust me too much, Mary," he whispered.  "I'm only a man and a sinner."

She did not reply but she laid her other hand on top of his and after a long silence he perceived that she was asleep.  He did not leave her at once.  He sat thinking back over the weeks at Canterbury but he could recall no moment that would cast a shadow on either Mary or Frank.  Well, God help them both!  Life was so cruel, so silly in its hazards, no wonder people fought so frantically to make sure of heaven!

*Life "but a tale told by an idiot, full of sound and fury . . ."*

Someone called to him softly from the doorway, and freeing his hand, Robert went out into the steerage. Christopher Martin awaited him there.

"Three several men have come from the *Speedwell*," he said, "to complain.  They declare they must see you which is insulting to me."

"Then I'll see them only in your presence," declared Robert.

"Aha!" triumphantly.  "Come!"  He rushed Cushman out to the gay sunlight and shadow of the main deck.

Moses Fletcher, Tom Tinker and John Goodman were standing in the shade of the longboat. Several sailors were grouped near the forecastle door.

"Good morning, friends," said Cushman. "If what you have to say is privy, this isn't a good place for saying it, is it?"

"The more that hears this, the better," grunted Moses. His young face was comically serious. "Only we aren't taking advice from Master Martin."

"I hope you remember the last part of Pastor Robinson's letter!" exclaimed Chris. "It says you are to yield those you choose into office due honor and obedience."

"And he also told us not to see in them the ordinariness of their persons," sniggered fat little John Goodman. "But the pastor hain't seen *you!*"

Cushman interposed. "Did you come to insult the governor? Is that your errand? I know better. Who's your spokesman?"

"I am, Master Cushman," replied Tom Tinker in his gentle voice. "There's a ghost on the pinnace. Us three has seen it and so have three several others. We want to move aboard the *Mayflower.*"

"What form does the ghost show?" asked Robert.

The three pinnace men and Martin crossed their fingers as Tom replied, "It's a hugeous great thing in black with one eye in its forehead. Round the eye is blue fire."

Christopher forgot that he'd been insulted. He leaned toward Tinker and whispered, "Do you guess what its intendment is?"

"Yes," answered Tom, "they say in years gone by there was a sailor murdered on the *Speedwell.* He's found out that for the first time there be godly folk on the ship and he's come back to ask for justice."

Cushman rubbed his head thoughtfully. Whether or not disembodied spirits wandered about this earth, he did not pretend to know. Most of the people he knew, high or low, believed they did. "When does the specter appear?" he asked.

"At night, in rough weather," answered Moses. "He was out last night, up and down the decks. I followed him till he floated into the poop cabin, for I had my courage all trussed up with a little cross I made myself of—of this and that—"

"That's popery!" sneered Christopher. "And you a Pilgrim!"

"I'm not a Pilgrim any more," declared Moses. "If I could get back the fortune I've put in this venture, I'd never more leave England."

"Nor me, neither," nodded Goodman. "Leaks! Leaks! Leaks! I've sozzled in salt water and bilge till my very guts reek. Please God, ever I get to North Virginia, I'll never behold the sea again!"

Martin gave Moses Fletcher a disdainful look which was difficult, for the young blacksmith stood a head taller than the governor. "Fortune!" squeaked Chris. "What fortune?"

"My father's and mine," answered Moses, stoutly. "The savings of our lifetimes, something over ten shillings!"

"Ten shillings!" screamed Martin. "You poor beetle! You purse-proud beggar, you and your father—"

He did not finish the sentence for Moses hit him in the midriff with a fist like an anvil hammer. The governor let out a mighty grunt and dropped. The sailors who had drawn near roared with delight. "Burst his craw for him, the strutting little cock!"

"Dismast him, lads!"

Christopher scrambled to his feet, and rendered lion-hearted by pain, he clawed one of the jibing seamen in the face. It was the signal for all the sailors to close on the little man and then many things happened with incredible swiftness.

"They'll kill him!" gasped Cushman. "Help him!"

"Let 'em!" ejaculated Moses Fletcher, not stirring.

John Goodman made pretense of plunging into the mêlée but kept carefully out of harm's reach.

Thomas Tinker said calmly, "A beating will do your governor good."

But Martin was in danger of serious injury and Robert leaped forward and with the world turning black around him, wrapped the governor in his arms.

Then he knew no more.

For a long, long time, he hovered in space, sometimes freely and gloriously, sometimes heavily and in agony, sometimes knowing that he was floating and again for long periods entirely extinct.

After he had been thus a century or so, he heard Desire's voice, "I'll watch with him, dear Mary, while you—"

He did not hear Mary's reply.

Long later Desire spoke again. "We'll brace him with pillows. Here is mine for his back."

No, he was not dead. He was living and so was Desire. And after he had come to this conclusion, he floated off again but came back to hear the linnet singing. Or was it Love Brewster's sweet voice? "Hey nonny, nonny, no!"

There were other familiar sounds, now: a riot of creaking and groaning of the ship's timbers, a tremendous rush of water, a ceaseless rolling of his bed which would not let him rest.

Something warm and soft rested against his cheek and a voice said in a whisper, yet he knew it was Desire's voice, "Come back, Robin!  Come back!  Come back!"

He made so great an effort that sweat broke out on him and lifted his eyelids.  Desire knelt beside his bunk, her face on his pillow, her cheek against his.  Warmth flowed through his cold body.  Life sang ecstatically in his brain. He was too weak to move his hand or speak but he never had been more alive.  Shortly, Desire lifted her head and stood erect.  Another face appeared within the curtains. It was Mary's.

"His eyes are open!" gasped Mary.  "I'll call Giles!" She disappeared.

Again Robert labored gigantically and a weak sound broke from his lips.  "Desire!"

"Yes!  Thank God!"  She touched his hair with her finger tips.

Giles' face appeared within the cabin.  He was smiling but his voice was anxious.  "Give him bread sopped in wine."

Robert floated away again.  But this time there accompanied him fragments of his life.  He and Desire looked at each other through the linnet's cage, prisoners, all three. There was new trouble brewing on the pinnace, absurd but real.  Captain Nutt's eyes were quizzical and his voice deliberate as he said, "I'd take her to have and to hold." No, Jones said that!  To have and to hold through eternity.  No, to have and to hold in England.  Moonlight . . . the oak spinney . . . this happy breed of men . . .

The next time he returned it was night and the ship was rolling more than ever.  Mary was with him in the bunk. The *Mayflower's* noises were terrific.  He felt almost well.

"Mary," he asked, "when did we sail?"

She put her head close to his. "Did you speak, Robert?"

"When did we sail?"

"Two days ago. You've been swooning for four days. Shall I get you a sip of wine, Robert?"

"No, my dear, wait until daylight. Did Martin get hurt?"

Mary patted him gently on the arm as one would soothe a child. "Not as you were hurt, though we can't discover where or who hurt you."

"No one hurt me," explained Robert. "I had one of my dizzy spells."

Before Mary could comment on this he dropped off to sleep.

When he woke, he felt completely recovered except for a little weakness and a slight tendency to pant. But his heart no longer roared in his ears. The *Mayflower* tossed violently and the floor was awash. Children's voices, shrill and gay, rose above the outcries of the troubled ship. The people were dressing behind their curtains, lowering their voices, he knew, because of his illness. Kind hearts, these.

And then he slipped back completely into life and his surroundings. *They had left Dartmouth. They were three days out on the Atlantic. England was behind them forever.* And that second parting he had so dreaded would not need to be. Thank God for His many mercies!

They were on the high seas at last! A great thrill of excitement and relief ran through him and gave him strength to sit up. Where were they? He must see Jones and his charts. What of the *Speedwell* and its ghost? After all, Elder Brewster was right. Nothing had been able to stop the pilgrimage.

Mary woke and sat up beside him, dim and shadowy, for the curtains darkened the bed.

"You must *not* move until Giles gives you permission, Robert! Oh, for once, don't be obdurate! You've caused us such unease!"

He patted her shoulder. "I'll be as motionless as a mast if you'll get me food, dear wife!"

"Food! You are well, then!" She began to pull her dress on over her head. "I can give you nothing hot, Robert. We've had no fire for a day, the waves are so high. Anyway, Giles said you were to have only wine-sop."

"And I could eat my own boot!" sighed Robert. "Mary, I think this illness has cleared my spleen of all its ill humors and I'm a well man again."

Mary buttoned her bodice and began to pull on her stockings. For a moment, the *Mayflower* hung poised and there was stillness in the cabin.

"Have I been hearing your voice, Master Cushman?" called Christopher Martin.

"Aye, governor!" returned Robert. "Are you recovered from your battle?"

"I'm battered and bruised, but thanks to you, no more. My left eye is—" But the *Mayflower* buried her nose in the sea, lifting her stern to the skies and pandemonium ruled again.

"Poor Chris!" Mary said in his ear. "He's so proud of his wounds! And he's really grateful to you."

"Grateful to me? Chris Martin?" Robert was mightily amused and cheered. Could a world which contained Desire be sad? And could a ship which housed Christopher Martin lack for comedy?

# XVIII

## *Interlude*

CHRISTOPHER MARTIN, later in the morning, braced himself on the edge of Robert's bed and recounted his woes.

"I thought my end was come. They tore my hosen and laid on with kicks and blows till the blood burst out in fountains. They dragged me up and down the deck by my hair. They gripped me by the weasand to tear it out as a mastiff roots at a bear's gullet. I was as helpless in their hands as a virgin among pirates."

"This was after I went senseless?" exclaimed Robert. "Did none try to rescue you?"

"Nay, this happened just before you rushed forward. You must have come with your eyes shut for I swear to the apostles all this took place just as I tell it!" His voice rose defiantly above the ship's noises.

Robert choked back his hilarity. This was a tale worth the hearing and one which evidently had been told often and received with incredulity. "Tell me the rest," he begged.

Christopher put his lips close to Robert's ear. "They screamed such obscene words at me as have obnubilated me ever since. Had you not grasped me round the waist, and even after you'd lost your senses, if you hadn't clung to me so that they couldn't beat me without beating you, I'd have gone to my Maker in a moment. That was a

224

shrewd blow they struck you and you paid heavily for it. But it saved my life."

"They didn't strike me, governor!" gasped Robert.

"But they did! I felt the blow through your body to mine and here's the bruise from it," displaying a dark spot among the hairs on his chest.

Robert gave up. "Well, I'm happy to have saved you!" he said meekly. "Tell me, governor, what was done to the sailors?"

"There you are!" groaned Martin. "If you can credit it, nothing! That sailor, Jock Coombs, rescued you and so me. He was not even thanked. Master Jones *laughed* at the matter when I took it to him."

"Alas and alack!" remarked Cushman. "And what became of the *Speedwell's* ghost?"

"The elder would have none of it and the deacon was very wroth when he heard the men had come to us. He talked very violently at prayer service against belief in abominations. Myself, I think that as governor of the *Speedwell*, he had been wise to ask those who were really afraid to shift places with those on the *Mayflower* who are not afraid. But the deacon is a very hasty man."

"Hasty, but in the long run, very just and impartial. Was there much of a to-do when we sailed?" Robert asked.

"Nay, we sailed at night when none but the ship's officers knew we were going and under cover of a mighty storm. So the sea absolves all for the length of the voyage." Martin sighed with relief.

Robert listened to the little chapman almost with liking. Perhaps during the voyage they two could actually come to an understanding about the venture's accounts. He let himself be cheered by the thought.

Christopher went away; to rest his wounds, he said.

Robert lay with his curtains open, watching the comings and goings in the cabin. The violent motion confined most of the women to their bunks where they sat with their children, if children they possessed, and their needlework. Mary established herself at the foot of their bed, mending stockings, putting her head occasionally around the partition to chat with Desire.

Toward noon, Mistress Billington, a sweet-faced young woman, made her appearance from her bunk, the curtains of which were still drawn. She had her baby under her left arm and with her right hand she was tugging at something. There came a shout from the bunk but Ellen Billington continued to tug. A great hand fetched her a box on the ear. She did not loosen her hold and a sudden twist of the *Mayflower* aiding her, John Billington plunged out onto the deck in time to catch the full wash of the brine which was ankle-deep on the even keel.

Billington rose and made for Ellen, but at that moment Captain Standish and Master Winslow entered the cabin and John pretended to be patting his baby's head.

Robert could just hear Standish's great shout. "You lazy loutish knave! Truss your points and get below for drill!"

Billington sullenly withdrew to finish dressing and Ellen, with an impish and contented smile, went to visit Marie Martin. Drill! How could the little soldier manage it with a sea like this? They must have great fun with it, 'tween decks.

Ned Winslow, removing a sodden russet cloak and shaking his dripping head, made his way to Robert's side.

"All's well then!" he exclaimed, taking Cushman's hand. "Praise God!"

"Amen!" said Robert. "And tell me what of the *Speedwell?*"

"We've had no sight of her since yesterday afternoon," answered Ned. "She was lusty enough then. What can I do for you, Master Cushman?"

"If you see Tommy, send him to me," replied Robert.

"I'll do that before I change into dry clothes," nodded Winslow. He disappeared into the steerage and came back shortly with the boy. Tommy was breathless as usual and wet to the skin. He kissed his father and whispered in his ear,

"I prayed for you, Father!"

"Thank you, Tommy! Dear my lad! Are you all swimming while you drill?"

"Not quite, Father! We've been playing hide-and-seek with the waves when Captain Standish or the mates don't stop us. You should see the decks all laced back and forth with life ropes! The main deck is awash and you hang to a line or go overboard!" He kissed his father again. "I have to go back to drill now."

"He might have spared you a moment," said Mary as Tommy plunged away.

"Children never know what to do with a sick person," Robert explained.

Mary shook her head.

Desire looked round the partition. "I've been reading my diary," she called, "and I've found such a beautiful quotation from an old tale by Thomas Nashe. I copied it years ago, never dreaming how close home it would come to me. Let me read it to you both?" She slipped round to sit beside Mary on the bed and opened the fat little book.

" 'The sea is the native soil of fishes. Take fishes from the sea, they take no joy nor thrive but perish, straight. So likewise, the birds removed from the air, the beasts from the earth and I, from England.  Can a lamb take delight to be suckled at the breasts of a she-wolf?—Believe me, no air, no bread, no fire, no water, doth a man any good out of his own country.  Cold fruits never prosper in a hot soil nor hot in a cold.  Let no man for any transitory pleasure sell away the inheritance he hath of breathing in the place where he was born.  Get thee home, my young lad.  Lay thy bones peaceably in the sepulcher of thy fathers.  Wax old in overlooking thy grounds.  Be at hand to close the eyes of thy kindred.  The devil and I are desperate, he of being restored to heaven, I of being called home.' "

"Now, is that a diplomatical piece to read us?" Robert asked in an amused voice.

Mary gave a little sob.

Desire looked from one to the other.  "But it's like the best poetry!  It's beautiful and it's true!  So one reads it with pleasure."

"It's *too* true!" sighed Robert.

"I've been thoughtless!" exclaimed Desire, taking Mary's hand.  "Do forgive me, Mary!"

"There's nothing to forgive, my sweet Desire!" said Mary, wiping her eyes.  "I think all the time of Canterbury and it's a relief to let my feelings speak for once."

"And when did you two begin to use each other's baptismal names?" asked Robert, anxious to steer the conversation into safer channels.

"When we were struggling to keep the breath in your obstinate body," replied Desire.  "There was no time for titles."

"So I feel now myself," said Robert, "at least among us three."

Mary laughed.  "He's not wandering again in his mind,

I suppose; only being subtle like the serpent or the ox!
It's time for you to take your first real food, Robert. We
have a cupboard in the steerage which Master Jones al-
lows us to use during this rough weather as a buttery.
There's only salt beef, smoked herring, beer, bread. It's a
pity, for you should have broth."

"My hunger will be broth enough," he assured her.
"Bring me bread and beef, Mary."

She left them. Desire gave Robert a gentle look and
then returned to her own quarters. He ate his lunch with
good appetite. Mary went visiting to the Martins' cabinet.
Winslow appeared from 'tween decks to invite all to come
below to sing. Everyone accepted save Robert. Even the
babes in arms were taken on the precarious journey! And
for a long hour or two, Robert and the now silent linnet
had the great cabin to themselves. Occasional bursts of
melody reached him. But for the most part, he listened
to the gigantic music of the sea and found an elusive but
magnificent pleasure in it.

Late in the afternoon, while he was still alone, Jim, the
master's boy, ran in lightly and steadily as a tightrope
juggler to ask if Master Jones could call.

"Tell him," exclaimed Cushman, "that no one could be
so welcome."

The child danced away and shortly in rolled the master,
legs aspraddle, throwing off a great wet cloak to perch on
the bed.

"What ho!" he grinned. "God bless us and so forth!
Decided you'd come back, did you? Where'd you go, eh?"

"You ask where I went and yet you must have seen the
bruises Chris Martin got clean through my helpless body!"
chuckled Robert, then he added soberly, "Have you
sighted the *Speedwell* yet, Master?"

Jones shook his rusty head. "But she's small and the waves are not small. Don't fret yourself! Reynolds will never let her founder! And she left Dartmouth tight as a lady's powder-closet."

"And Reynolds, himself?"

"Resigned to crossing the Atlantic with us," nodded Christopher. "He told me the reason he and Nutt exchanged visits was because they were boyhood friends. And they might have been! We're not worth a capture by Nutt, that I'm sure the freebooter must have learned."

"Unless Reynolds gives him the pinnace," suggested Robert.

Jones shook his head. "The only treasure he covets is Mistress Desire. I had a good talk with her today and got her to spin me the strands of the yarn you left out concerning your evening aboard the *Cushat Dove*."

"What a horrid fancy!" gasped Robert. "Does Mistress Minter think that Nutt might try—"

"Nay," interrupted the master, "she's humble at heart and she only laughed at me! Don't hoyse yourself, Master Cushman! Our lovely mistress and the *Speedwell* and the ghost, all are going to reach America safely. And now tell me when you shall be able to come up to the poop."

"Tomorrow I'll be myself again," answered Robert. "As a fact, I feel stronger than I've felt for weeks past. But Dr. Heale is vehement for me resting my spleen, so here I rest!"

"He's a good lad!" nodded Jones. "He and Mistress Desire make a handsome pair. 'Twas as good as a play to see them taking such care of you. Though I do think she's too good for a mere doctor's wife or for anyone's wife in the wilderness."

"So do I," agreed Robert. "The wilderness has no need

for what we chiefly admire in her—what you spoke of when you first saw her. In spite of her rich laughter she has that lovely and familiar gravity you described so fitly."

"I read it somewhere. I disremember where," admitted Jones. "I can't claim ownership of such choicy words!"

"You remembered them and so they became yours," Robert told him. "So language is built."

Jones looked pleased and the two men gazed at each other with affectionate understanding.

A sudden rush of laughing children from the steerage broke in on them and the master rose.

"Come as early as may be then, tomorrow," he said, wrapping his cloak around him again, "and have a look at the charts." He crossed the twisting deck as easily if not as gracefully as had Jim.

The people did not wait for darkness before going to bed. A storm at sea is utterly exhausting to body and nerves. The women tucked their children in before the weak afternoon light had waned. Mary Allerton, tiny and pug-nosed, made her young husband, Isaac, grin at some jibe as she hopped into their berth beyond the Winslows'. Priscilla Mullins appeared for a moment with her glorious hair in a braid down her back. She slept in the cabinet with Desire and the More children. Huge John Billington lunged into his bunk like a bull turning into his stall. There was something not uncomely in his very hugeness. But however much the elder and the deacon may have labored with him he was still sullen. Desire called good night as Mary closed their curtains.

Robert lay thinking of the half hour at the foot of the great hill at Dartmouth—he and Desire gathering willow wands—thinking with a deep sense of peace. He loved her! At last and for the first time in his life, he was in love!

He loved a woman who was not his wife! And yet he felt no sense of sin! Surely nothing sinful could be born of such exaltation of soul as had possessed him for nearly a fortnight. He was harming no one. Not Mary who loved another and frankly cared nothing for him. Not himself; for the rapture of his love was giving him moral strength to bear the heat and burden of the venture almost with calm. And surely not Desire, for she did not know, never would know that he loved her.

More at peace than he'd ever been in his life, he said his prayers and fell asleep.

# XIX

## Speedwell, Ahoy!

THE storm continued during the night but with dawn the wind fell and rest became possible for the turmoiled passengers. Robert, however, after his five days in bed, could endure no more of the great cabin and with the first ray of light, he dressed and went into the steerage. There were four men at the tiller which still fought fiercely with a following sea. The waist of the ship was under water, but the first mate standing by the binnacle assured Cushman that by noon she'd be riding the billows light as a gull.

With great difficulty, Robert clambered up the companionway to the half deck. The second mate was lashed to the mizzenmast, his head and hair white with salt. He grinned at Robert and waved his hand as a green wall of water lifted high above the poop. Robert leaped for the cabin and reached it just before the deluge broke.

Master Jones was pulling on his sea boots. His face, too, was salt-crusted and his eyes were bloodshot but he was cheerful as usual.

"Ought to sight the pinnace soon," he said. "Sea'll drop fast now and I'll be getting some rags of sail on my old lady. Haven't been able to use the cross-staff since we left Dartmouth and it's a riddle where we are! Mayhap ninety leagues off Land's End. Drink you a tankard of ale, friend Cushman."

"Thanks," said Robert gratefully, but obeying with

difficulty for the motion of the ship in this lofty cabin seemed twice that on the deck below. "It must have been horrible aboard the *Speedwell* during the gale. The women will have suffered specially."

"Oh! the pinnace could be a very snug little ship if properly handled," Jones answered him, "though she lacks the comfort and space of my ship."

"Let's pray Master Reynolds is handling her properly, then!" exclaimed Cushman.

The pilot, coming in wearily, heard Robert's words. "Prayers are a proper thing at sea." He began to work his boots off. "Even a modest gale like this gives you to think of your Maker." He rolled himself in a blanket on the larboard locker and closed his eyes. Almost instantly, he was snoring.

"He's over-young to be a pilot," remarked Robert, scanning the aquiline face with respect.

"He's crossed to Virginia three several times." Jones filled a tankard for himself. "He was born weatherwise. Take the spyglass, Master Cushman, and settle yourself at the stern window to watch for the *Speedwell*. I've no time for the charts now."

Robert took the instrument eagerly and established himself as the master had ordered. But for a long time the glass was all but useless. The window was coated with brine and the high seas prevented his opening the sash. But he had learned somewhat of the seaman's patience and continued at his post and as the hours wore on, he had a partial reward for the sea dropped rapidly and he began at shorter and shorter intervals to catch glimpses of the horizon. About the middle of the morning, the pilot went on duty again and Giles Heale appeared. He came to protest against his patient's leaving his bed but finding him quite fit, the young man remained to gossip. Robert, who preferred his own thoughts to Giles' chatter, finally suggested that the doctor was neglecting his other sick folk.

"Now just what sick have I besides yourself, dear Nuncle?" demanded Giles.

"There's our poor governor," replied Robert, "who claims to be worse off than Job with wounds and sores."

Giles gave a great laugh, "Oh, but he really is wounded now, Uncle Robert! He came below this morning to wrangle with Captain Standish about drill. Chris thinks he should be an officer. I won't shock your ears by telling you the office the captain offered him! But it made our good Christopher so drunken mad that he let go a life rope and knocked his nose against a sword young Dicky Clarke was waving about in this so famous drill. I had to tie him up his poor snout and what a precious sight is our poor governor! Even Captain Standish forgot to drill us while he guffawed!"

Robert roared and Giles, very pleased with himself as a raconteur, rambled on. "How can you bear to sit gazing at naught but the sea? I'd far rather gaze down John Billington's gullet or at Priscilla Mullins' pretty tongue when she complains of megrim." He took a look through the glass as Cushman relinquished it, but handed it back at once. "Mind you stay quiet up here, sir, and do nothing to make you pant. I am going down to rest my eyes with a sight of Mistress Minter." He went away.

There was blue sky now and a brilliant sun. At noon, the master got a reading with his cross-staff and after a long wrestling with his chart and compass announced that they were one hundred leagues off Land's End.

"And now let me look for the pinnace," he said, taking the glass from Cushman. And as if he had summoned them, like a genie, from the depths, two masts carrying square sails rose in the northeast. "There she rides!" shouted Jones. "By God, he's put up his topsails again! Is he mad? The foreordained fool! The fellow's a villain!"

"But he'd agreed to remove them!" cried Robert.

"I'll *agree* him!" snarled Jones. "I'll let him overhaul us this afternoon and I'll board the pinnace and make dog meat of the fat knave. If she doesn't sink before she overhauls us!" he added darkly.

"Is she very low in the water?" asked Robert anxiously. "Or is the distance and my own fear deceiving me?"

"Aye, she's deep enough to satisfy even Reynolds. Yet see her sail! Ah, my beauty, you're in the hands of your ravisher but still you can run like a stricken deer!" He stood with the glass to his eye talking now to the pinnace and now to Robert, or whom it might or might not concern, as the mates came in and out. . . . "I didn't actually see her with those topmasts off. I spent that last day on a tour up the coast to Brixham to see an old shipmate. It was dark when I returned and the gale was rising. I came in a trawler, sent word to Reynolds we must be off at high tide, storm or no, and I haven't seen her since. For aught I know he could have remained in Dartmouth long enough to work any villainy he pleased on the poor little ship. Those topmasts are murder, willful murder!"

Pilot Coppin appeared at the door. "The Newfoundland fleet is off our starboard bow, sir," he announced.

"Aye! Now you shall see *sailormen!*" shouted Jones, rushing out. Robert followed him to the half-deck rail.

There remained only a choppy sea with a long, slow swell. The whole populace of the *Mayflower* crowded the decks and rigging. To the west and nearing them rapidly, was a fleet of sails of every variety known to fishermen and all so small in the vasty deep that they might have been mistaken for gulls by less knowledgeable eyes than seamen's. Jones called off a few of their names as they grew larger against sea and sky: yawls and trawlers, dandies, smacks, luggers, cats, shallops and gigs. "Everything there," declared the mate, "except ships! Not more than a score of the ten score are full-decked!"

Shortly the *Mayflower* was surrounded by the tiny sails and there was an enormous confusion of voices as the *Mayflower* and the fleet exchanged their greetings. The little boats, loaded with their harvest of fish, rode low in the water. All were storm battered. One which passed under the great ship's stern had ropes passed round it to hold the hull together. Few of the boats had achieved the dignity of pumps and were being continually bailed. All had flags! English, Dutch, French, Portuguese, and as many tongues returned the shouts from the *Mayflower*. It was impossible to understand what was said in such a pandemonium and the boats were passing quickly. Master Jones blew his whistle violently for silence and finally was able to exchange a few sentences with the master of a Brixham trawler. Where was the *Mayflower* going? To America, with colonists for northern Virginia. Could Jones do aught for the trawler or fleet? Nay, they were nearly home now after a good season. Very cold on the Banks. What news of Captain Nutt? asked the trawler. Cathay! Huzza! . . . and they were gone, their ragged, rugged owners waving nonchalant hands as they melted into the east.

"I sailed thrice with that fleet," said the pilot casually to Cushman. "That was my sea-school, my horn book and birchen rod!"

"I'd be prouder of that fact than of a knighthood," exclaimed Robert.

"Any lazy knave with a few pounds can feel the King's sword on his shoulder," growled Christopher Jones. "But no money can buy a man what Coppin's got from the fury of the deep." He turned his spyglass on the *Speedwell*.

Under foresail and lateen, the *Mayflower* was making only half the speed of the pinnace and slowly but surely the *Speedwell* approached them until, just before the sun sank, the two ships were moving side by side. The pumps were going on the *Speedwell*.

"Heave to!" shouted Reynolds from the poop. "I'm coming aboard you!"

"What's the trouble now?" returned Jones, looking down sourly on the master of the pinnace. "You lied to me about those topmasts, you fool!"

There was a breathless pause as this exchange took place, passengers and crews in anxious silence. And above the sough of wave and wind, the pumps on the pinnace spoke.

"Who's the master of this bastard ship?" inquired Reynolds. "Keep a civil tongue in your head. This is a matter of life and death. We're sinking, if you want the truth in a gulp."

Jones blew his whistle. The mate shouted. Sailors ran thither and yon and the *Mayflower* lay with idle sails. The pinnace also hove to and a small boat put off from her, bearing her master, the elder and the deacon. The *Mayflower* Pilgrims, overwhelmed by this sudden disaster, stood in a silent crowd through which the three visitors scarcely could make their way to the poop.

"We shall require Master Cushman and Governor Martin," said Brewster as he crossed the half deck. Robert immediately followed to the poop cabin where Martin joined them a moment later.

"Be seated, my masters," said Jones gruffly, perching himself on his favorite seat on the edge of the table and pushing the Monmouth cap over his right ear.

William Brewster looked haggard. John Carver was pale and there was a plaster on his forehead. Reynolds' yellow doublet was, if possible, a little dirtier than ever and his huge cheeks were covered with a week's stubble. Undoubtedly the *Speedwell* had returned evil for evil.

"I wish to say—" began Reynolds, taking the inevitable toothpick from its perch.

"Put that foul besom of yours up, or I'll be sick again!" ordered Carver.

Reynolds thrust the toothpick back behind his ear.

"Let me speak, prithee!" Brewster's great voice was hoarse. "There are six inches of water in the great cabin of the pinnace. The very bunks are sodden, 'tween decks, and for three days and three nights, every man of us has taken his turn at the pumps. We have been thrown about like pebbles in a babe's rattle. Master Carver was severely cut by a flying rope end. All this though is endurable and our people have not complained overmuch. But today, three of John Billington's men have refused to aid at the pumps and neither Governor Carver nor I have been able to move them. There have been two general fights between the Billington men and the sailors so that five of our people lie gashed and bruised in their hammocks and Master Reynolds refuses to discipline the culprits."

"Culprits!" scoffed Reynolds.

"Yes! For the quarrel began with your sailors railing at our poor people for their vomiting and retching during the gale. A dog would have had more pity than you or they showed on board." Brewster's voice had dropped to its usual gentle cadence and was the more impressive for that reason. "It is for this cause I have come to you, Master Jones, who keep order and decency on your ship."

"You need Master Cushman!" ejaculated Jones. "He put his fist to Jock Coombs' jaw the first day out from Hampton and has had no trouble since."

Brewster gave Cushman a surprised glance and smiled a little. Then he said, "Master Cushman is needed as spiritual leader here. He cannot go to the pinnace. Will you lend us an officer who will control the sailors since Master Reynolds cannot?"

"What?" demanded Reynolds. "You dare?"

"And why shouldn't he dare?" inquired Jones truculently, his great jaw thrust forward. "Before I reply to you, elder, though, I'll hear Master Reynolds' plaint."

"Thanks!" using the toothpick. "The pinnace must put back to Plymouth for repairs, if ever she can be repaired. And the *Mayflower* must go with us to save us if we sink!"

"Never shall either ship put back!" shouted Robert.

Reynolds went on, blandly, "And you must give us some provisions. We have had some spoiled by sea water and haven't enough to take us to Plymouth."

"But of what use is it to give you food to be spoiled in the water your topmasts pump in?" asked Cushman.

"Right!" exploded Jones. "Now heed me, Reynolds."

"Nay, I'll not heed you!" shouted Reynolds. "Back we go!"

Clank! Clank! Clank! sounded the *Speedwell's* pumps.

Robert thought rapidly. At any cost, Reynolds must be got rid of. The only way to do this was for all to return to Plymouth, somehow raise money to pay him off and then put Coppin or Clarke, the first mate, aboard the *Speedwell*. The season was late for their trip. The people were impatient and discouraged. This new delay would break the resolution of many. Well, a purging of the weakest would be excellent for the body politic. When they left Plymouth, he himself would insist on going aboard the pinnace to assist Carver. The people might not like him. They might believe him to be Tom Weston's man but he knew he could control them.

He rose suddenly in his place, the evening glow striking athwart his head and giving it a sort of splendor which even in that desperate hour his companions could not help noting.

"My friends," said Robert, "of what avail is anger when the sea presents her bitter facts? The pinnace cannot cross the waters as she is. She is essential to our colony. We will put back into Plymouth and have her mended. Master Reynolds fears to sail on her, be she sick or well. Excellent! We will pay him what we owe him, in Plymouth, beg Master Jones to let us have his pilot or mate to master the pinnace, store her with her fair third of our provisions and then though the autumn storm scream immortal defiance, yet shall we sail! Yet shall we reach New England! Yet shall we plant our God and our King on that waiting shore!"

"By the passion of heaven," breathed Jones, "that's the talk a true sailor can understand!"

"But we'll go hungry if we part with a third of our food!" bleated Martin.

Robert wheeled on him. "And in Plymouth, sir, we shall list every pound of food we possess. If you have faulted, you shall make it good."

John Carver spoke. "I am with Master Cushman! Put

it to the vote, William, and stop the gap, for sweet pity's sake!  I'm weary of the human voice, including mine own!"

Brewster turned to Reynolds.  "Will you give up your control under these conditions, Master?"

"With pleasure!" Reynolds exclaimed.  "I'd sooner move Bedlam itself over the Atlantic as the *Speedwell* full of Separatists!  Don't forget the forty-pound penalty besides my wage!"

"That is to be given only in case the pinnace through no fault of ours—" began Brewster.

"Forgive me, elder," said Robert, "but let us discuss that when we reach Plymouth.  Who is the leader of your insubordinates, sir?"

"A mere child!  That young blacksmith, Moses Fletcher," replied Brewster.  "Thomas Tinker is his companion."

Robert nodded and turned to Jones.  "How long do you say it is to Plymouth, Master?"

"We're logging about two miles an hour," announced Jones.  "It depends on the wind.  If this remains average fair, we can make it in four or five days."  He raised his eyebrows at Reynolds who nodded.

"It will be mid-September before we get to sea again!" gasped John Carver.  "Our poor, poor people!  Who will break the news to them?"

"I will," said the elder.

"Or I," offered Robert and Martin together.

"I will!" grinned Reynolds.

"Will you have three or four of my lusty men to ease yours at the pumps?" asked Jones of Reynolds.

"Take 'em gladly," nodded the master of the pinnace.

"Send Jock Coombs over, if I may suggest, Master

Jones," said Robert. "And," turning to Carver, "let us have Moses Fletcher and Tom Tinker in the *Mayflower*. Perhaps we can win them to better heart."

"God bless you!" cried Carver. "And in return I'll bear the burden of telling the people the bad news."

"No, it's my task, John!" The elder rose a little heavily.

Robert told himself that if Reynolds had even a spark of humanity in him, the bewilderment and trouble shown by the two older men would touch him to at least a vague regret. But the fat face of the sailor reflected only a complete satisfaction. As he was following the others out of the cabin, however, Reynolds' sleeve was caught by Christopher Jones. And Christopher burst into an oration of such fury concerning Reynolds' missailing of the pinnace that bitter as he was over the situation, Robert, for one, was glad to move out of hearing. He closed the cabin door behind him.

The people were waiting and Brewster had no need to clear his throat. Looking five years older, he stepped to the railing, and in a single sentence broke the news to them.

There came a long, deep sigh, a muffled groan, from the close-packed Pilgrims.

"This will ruin us!" called Sam Fuller.

"There's an ill omen followed us. It's the ghost!" exclaimed Isaac Allerton.

"It'll be over here yet, that ghost!" Bob Carter spoke from a group of serving lads, grouped together.

"Don't be babes!" cried Desire Minter. She was standing near the mainmast. "Any ghost on the *Speedwell* must be drowned by now! And if you men are frightened by all this chopping and changing, give us women charge!

As for me, I didn't near finish my fairing in Dartmouth. I shall be glad to purchase a few more ribbands."

There was quick applause from the women and laughter, in which, one by one, the men joined.

"Count on us, elder!" called Ned Winslow.

"As far as Plymouth only for me," said a voice from near the longboat.

"Shame! Shame!" The disaffected voice was quickly drowned.

"We'll never give up! We're going to America, Father!" It was Wrestling Brewster, high in the mizzen rigging.

"So am I!" yelled Tommy Cushman. "I'm a soldier!"

"My army is loyal!" shouted Captain Standish.

Hearty laughter greeted this sally for all knew of Tommy's adoration and aspirations.

Master Reynolds rushed out of the cabin and down the ladder, his face purple. "Aboard the small boat, masters both! We've no time for prayers now."

"You'd think you owned the pinnace and us too," roared Bob Carter, "you great tub of . . ." Someone clapped a hand over his mouth.

Brewster and Carver followed Reynolds to the boat. It was as well that there should be no loitering, no further debate, no renewed farewells. Nor did Brewster have to break the news a second time. While the boat was moving between the ships, the *Mayflower* folk called the decision across to the *Speedwell*. A woman on the pinnace shrieked but otherwise those on the greater ship heard no comment made by those on the sister ship.

The *Mayflower's* boatswain was called aft by the mate and after a short conference, four sailors, including Coombs, all very sulky, tumbled into the boat and were rowed to the pinnace. The cockle brought back Moses Fletcher and Tom Tinker with his wife and baby son. A load of fish and bread in casks which had been broken out from the *Mayflower's* hold was sent to the *Speedwell*. Then the ships parted once more.

# XX

## *Becalmed*

IN the twilight when the *Mayflower* was well under way
again, Robert called the Pilgrims to evening service.
He opened his Bible to the sixteenth Psalm and read
from it:

" 'Preserve me, O God, for in Thee do I put my
trust. . . . The Lord is the portion of mine inheritance
and of my cup; Thou maintainest my lot. The lines are
fallen unto me in pleasant places; yea, I have a goodly
heritage.' "

He looked the people over from his place on the half
deck. Desire was just below him. He looked into her
eyes and then away to the mainmast where Tom Tinker
stood with his baby son in his arms.

"I wish Pastor Robinson were here tonight to preach
to you," said Robert. "He could tell you what he would
be feeling about our voyage while I find it next to impossible to discover words for my thoughts. I am dis-
appointed, impatient, turmoiled, distressed. But look
you! With a prayer on my lips for guidance, I opened
my Bible just now and the Almighty God whispers to me,
'Your lives have fallen you in pleasant places. Yea, you
have a goodly heritage.'

"And I ask God, 'Where, oh, where?' I look about me.
I see the stout *Mayflower* with the stoutest and loyalest of
masters on the poop. And then I think of the pitiful

*Speedwell* and the lot of those who must sail in her. 'Where, Lord?' do I say?

" 'Why, here,' answers God, 'on the spacious, stately *Mayflower,* is one of your pleasant places. But only one!'

"And so I look further. And I see Plymouth, that town of such comely repute which harbored Raleigh and Drake and Gilbert and which I know contains dear friends to our cause and especially to Elder Brewster, a very blessed hot-bed of Puritanism and Separatism. 'Hither,' whispers God, 'I am sending you for one further purging of your members, one final look at your darling motherland, one more chance to repair the fainted state of your business with the Merchant Adventurers. Nor is Plymouth the last or the greatest of your pleasant places,' says God. 'Your goodly heritage is not here but yonder across the inexpressible sea. There shall you be such Englishmen as no longer exist in England. There shall you be free, erect, with work for all and all for work, calling no man your master save the King and serving the commonwealth; a commonwealth of simple men who love one another.' . . . Aye, we have a goodly heritage."

He came to an end.

"Let's sing 'The Lord is my Shepherd,' " cried Ned Winslow.

They sang. How they sang! The very sailors joined them.

Afterward, when he was standing alone at the taffrail, Desire came to Robert. She stood beside him in silence for a little while and then she exclaimed, "You spoke well! The people are saying so, below. Some of them are wondering if Pastor Robinson wasn't mistaken when he said the things he did!"

Her beauty was like star beauty, he thought, just so clear

and remote.   Aloud he remarked, "I possess a mort of weaknesses and faults but it seems to me the pastor declaimed on those I don't possess!   Perhaps, though, that's merely my hurt feeling that he should have discovered more!"

"You talk like a very Separatist!" she complained.   "If you must have a fever of religion, why not suffer it as the King His Majesty does, with great ragings and snortings and richly ornamented oaths?   I despise you puling Christians!"

"Am I puling?" he gasped.   "Come, dear my maid, religion is not an illness nor will a dose of aloes effect it. Moreover, everyone knows that the true poet confines his ragings, snortings and rich oaths to the one great fever— love!"

"Meaning, mayhap, that Robert Cushman is a poet and James I is not!" laughed Desire.

"To the extent that I love, I'm a poet," answered Robert.

"And how does Mistress Mary enjoy the snortings?" inquired Desire.

"But one needn't make poetry to be a poet!   How ignorant you are!" he complained in his turn.   "I have been afraid you were learned and until I met you, I despised a learned woman.   What a sweet deliverance!"

"Deliverance from what, dear my poet?" inquired Desire.

He caught his breath but, after a second, tossed the ball back again.   "From wisdom, my secretary of the stars!"

"Indeed and indeed, you are right," she replied.   "Wisdom is only another name for sadness."

They were both silent and then Desire added, "What brought me seeking you, besides the wish to tell you how we felt about your little sermon, was to ask you if you remembered that Sir Fernando Gorges, who is obtaining a patent for himself for all the lands you call New England, will establish his company at Plymouth?"

"I know of Sir Fernando. In truth, I know the man himself, but I didn't know about Plymouth," answered Robert. "Are you certain of your news?"

"I had it from Master James Shirley, one of Master Weston's good friends," replied Desire, "just before I left London. I hadn't thought of it again until now."

"Yes, Shirley has put huge sums into this venture of ours," Robert said, thoughtfully. "We were inclined to appeal to this Sir Fernando's company for our patent but his grant from the King was in an uncertain state, in spite of Sir Fernando's great talk, and many of our people were furiously opposed to going so far north as his share of Virginia is. So, finally, we got our patent from the old Virginia Company."

"But if Sir Fernando obtains a part of the Virginia Company's lands, what becomes of your patent, since you are to be in New England, the very lands he takes?" asked Desire.

"He must honor our patent, certainly! But," admitted Robert, "I am not secure in my mind about it. Tom Weston wasn't either. Tom will look to it and keep us informed. But what a blessing if we find the Gorges company established in Plymouth when we reach there! My first effort will be to discover if they have obtained a monopoly of the fishing, for then we must obtain a license to catch our cod and bass."

"Mayhap 'twere better if you sailed on to America in ignorance!" suggested Desire. "I suppose licenses are a matter of money. News travels slowly across this ocean-sea and by the time Sir Fernando writes you that you may not fish, you'll have caught enough fish to pay for the license!"

Robert was much amused. "Most logical! No, we'd best know the worst before leaving. I see God's hand in this."

"Spoken like a true Separatist!" moaned Desire.

"Meaning I'm a puling Christian, I suppose," suggested Robert cheerfully.

They laughed heartily and Desire left him for bed. Robert pondered for a little while on the news she had brought him but shortly his mind reverted to Desire herself. He stood with teeth set for a moment in a surge of unutterable loneliness and then he, too, went down to the great cabin.

Mary was awake. He thought she had been weeping and he touched her cheek very gently with his fingers. He heard her draw a quick breath.

"Robert," she whispered, "I'm afraid!"

"Of what, dear Mary?" he asked.

"Of going back to Plymouth! No good can come of it. I tell you, no good." She began to shudder.

He threw his arm across her and suddenly she turned and buried her face on his shoulder. "Oh, Robert! Robert! How shall I ever endure leaving England again! If only we'd kept straight on when we left Hampton Waters, I'd have been better by now. At Dartmouth— you don't know! And now again at Plymouth. . . . Oh, you don't know!"

"What don't I know?" If only she would confide in him. If only he could confide in her and all could be clear, however tragic between them. But he dared not trust her poor tattling little tongue. Yet it would be quite safe for her to confide in him and so he told her. "Let me help you, Mary. Don't fear to tell me anything. I *will* help you, now, even though I've not been all I should be to you before."

"You've been all you ever can be to me," she sobbed. "I can never tell you—what England means to me! Don't ask me questions, Robert, just let me feel your good, good arm across me."

"Good! Poor Mary!" he murmured. But he made no more queries and so the two lay quiet until sleep came to give them release.

In the morning, the Pilgrims found the ship becalmed. The *Speedwell* with drooping main and lateen sails—Reynolds at last had furled his topsails—lay a quarter mile to their larboard.

It was August twenty-fourth.

The heat was horrible. It was impossible to say whether it was hotter on deck or between decks. The sailors went half naked and doused one another with buckets of sea water. Captain Standish, taking this hint, shifted his military drill to a rough game he named Wash-buckets All! He established a squad of youngsters at the rail drawing up water and a second squad in the ship's waist who splashed all male comers till the main deck ran floods. Fishing was popular with the women who were excluded from this cooling sport. The little children fished, too, the mothers clinging to their offsprings' hosen or clouts while they dangled lines baited with pork rinds or bits of red wool.

Singing palled in the heat. Desire Minter told stories and nursery rhymes to children who ordinarily would have scoffed at such childish nonsense. And it was amusing to hear great lads like Tommy and the Brewster boys, lying on the deck, wet but happy, chanting "Multiplication is vexation" in voices that were getting ready to change.

On the whole, this first day of the calm, the people were patient enough. Robert put in the entire day in the poop cabin, searching the maps for possible landing places in New England. It was late in the afternoon, returning to the great cabin for his notes from Captain Smith's book of travels in New England, that he found Tom Tinker in conversation with John Billington. The place was so inordinately warm that all others had deserted it.

Billington had not spoken to Cushman since the day of his "trial" in the master's cabin. But now, as Robert paused before the berth where the two men were sitting, Billington said rudely,

"We want no truck with you, Master Cushman!"

"Now! Now! Don't 'ee, John!" protested Tom, his brown eyes apologetically on Cushman. "Deacon Carver said you was the kind friend who got me brought to the *Mayflower*. Thank you, master!" Tinker had risen respectfully.

"I desire no thanks," returned Robert. "Thank your fault in friendship with John Billington. I wanted to win you from him, for we need you badly, we chiefs of the colony, Tom. And to win you, I must have you here, risking Billington's soliciting of you."

"That's like the rest of the lies—" began John.

Robert interrupted him. "If you care to talk to me later, John, without abuse, as man to man, I'll be glad to hear you. But now, if Tom Tinker will come up to the half deck, we'll tell over a few facts together."

Billington, still stretched in the bunk, leered at him. He looked larger than ever without his doublet, his beautiful great chest padded with muscles and quite hairless.

"I wouldn't walk with you nor yet talk with you," sneered John, "if you gave me half Virginia for a garden. I'm more likely to have you arrested."

"Arrested!" Robert was greatly diverted by the idea. "But for what?"

"For stealing money from the Pilgrims to clothe yourself and your silly wife—"

Tom Tinker hastily thrust himself between the two men. Robert swept him aside and moved close to the bulky brute on the bed. His hands itched for the fool's throat. But even though he reduced Billington's body to a cowering jelly by drawing his dagger on him, Robert knew this would not subdue Billington's tongue.

"Go find Masters Edward Winslow, Samuel Fuller and Christopher Martin," he told Tinker. "Tell them I require their help here. After they come to me, gather in the rest of the great cabin passengers."

Tom hesitated.

"Aye," grunted John, wagging his head, "he dassn't touch me without help."

"You'd best fetch them yourself, sir," said Tom. "I won't leave you alone here."

Robert laughed sardonically. "The fellow won't put a finger on me, Tom! Nor do I want my friends' fists. I want their judgments. Hurry!"

Reluctantly, Tinker went out, smoothing his gray fustian hosen as if he felt the importance of his errand.

Billington grew a little pale. "You think I'm afraid?"

"I know you'll never stand up to a strong man. You consort only with feeble folk, like poor Tom," declared Cushman. "I'm going to show you that you can't insult a *man* and go unscathed by something heavier than a sword or a fist. I'm going to hold a court here."

Billington sniggered. "The assizes, a hundred leagues from a county town!"

"Yes!" nodded Robert. "The King His Majesty has given us power to regiment ourselves at our good discretion and as near as possible to the statutes and governments of his own realm of England."

The mighty words, as Robert had hoped, made John's jaw drop.

Ned Winslow hurried in, followed by Fuller and Martin. Sam was a quiet, kind man, but very ready in a controversy.

"What's the trouble?" cried the governor.

"Tom, go call all here," ordered Robert. Then he turned to the three men grouped against the long table. "Here's John Billington, saying he's going to have me arrested for stealing from the Pilgrims' funds to clothe myself and my wife. I want him to make his accusations in legal form. Let Captain Standish, if he's the proper person in your estimation, arrest me and let a picked jury hear the case tried. If I'm found not guilty, I'll then have Billington arrested and tried for libel."

While Robert was making his explanation, the cabin was packing with passengers from both decks.

"What I want all the people to understand," he went on, "is that wherever an Englishman settles, there settles the English law. For the moment, our realm is the ship *Mayflower,* our ruler is Governor Martin, our militia is Captain Standish. In my long endeavor to procure our patent, I learned that the King His Majesty gives his colonists power to organize themselves into a governing body of all branches."

Chris Martin cleared his throat loudly. "Correct in every sentence, my good assistant!" he said.

"Is this your understanding?" asked Robert, looking at Ned and Sam.

Deacon Fuller said, "Yes, Master Cushman!" very loudly.

"We all know you're giving us common sense as well as fact," observed Ned, in his clear voice. "We must have stocks made and set up here on the ship for Captain Standish complains that mutinous speeches and carriages are not uncommon with certain men."

"I suppose the trial can be held with Governor Martin presiding as judge," Robert continued. "He was elected by the people. Let him appoint a man such as Thomas Tinker, who can write, as foreman of the jury."

"No, the jurors must be drawn by lot from the whole body of us," objected Edward.

"You can all save your breaths," shouted John Billington, suddenly. "I take back what I said about Master Cushman."

"That's not enough," Deacon Fuller said still loudly. "Billington's too free with his foul beast's tongue just because he's overstrong."

A murmur of assent rose from the people. But Dick Clarke cried, "I never heard of no trials and juries when I agreed to come. I was asked if I wanted to be rid of English jails, stocks and pillories and all the curse of English Law. That's why I come!"

"You'd better stop off for good and all then, when we land at Plymouth," smiled Robert. "You have been cozened! You should have joined Captain Nutt!"

"He'd have found law there too, at the end of Nutt's sword or at the end of a yardarm!" contributed Sam Fuller, his ruddy face half humorous, half earnest. "They told me that if you even nose a mast on the *Cushat Dove*, you lose an ear or mayhap that same nose. Now," soberly, "I say Billington should be put in stocks for a day or so for his lying and insults."

"No!" Robert shook his head. "Billington's withdrawn his libel. That's enough, this time."

"But is that in your hands? The governor should say!" remarked little Martin, very throaty as to voice and very straight as to back.

"Don't take away little cockalorum's chance to strut!" called someone.

"Who said that?" Robert whirled in the direction of the voice.

No one answered. The *Mayflower* rolled a little and a moist breath of air moved in the cabin.

"A breeze! A breeze!" shrilled a girl's voice from without.

Edward Winslow laughed. "Huzza! That's what we need most, a breeze." He burst into the chantey, "Lustily! Lustily! Let the winds blow!" and with a gay eye on Robert, he led the way out to the decks.

Miles Standish and Cushman stood at the stern window after the others had gone and watched the light squall coming up from the southeast.

"I didn't say anything for the generality to hear, Master Cushman," Standish pulled at his great yellow mustache, "but I doubt me if Governor Martin would have been a proper person to sit over your case. He's been whispering that very lie in folks' ears ever since Dartmouth, at least."

"That I know," admitted Robert soberly. "I didn't force this scene to show Martin up. But I did realize, as we talked, that he'd show his unfitness for his position quicker in a jury trial than any other way. No people are going to tolerate a silly judge if they can be rid of him.

They'll endure a tyrant king more tolerantly. Martin's supposed to have been fairly elected. He's their man, then. Let them learn that if they choose a fool and keep him, he represents fools. And let them realize in a commonwealth the most simple man needs wisdom or he votes himself into slavery."

Standish gazed keenly up into Robert's thin face. "I think the people haven't got to the depth of you yet, sir. What this colony would be without you, I loathe to think."

"So do I!" Cushman flushed with pleasure. Compliments were rare in his experience. "Though not because I'm valuable but because the colony is my very heart!"

The *Mayflower* was motionless again, the squall had passed. From without rose a strange shrill medley of whistles.

"What can that be?" exclaimed Robert.

"My 'tween-decks lads are whistling for a breeze," replied Miles.

He cocked his hat over one ear and, whistling himself, marched out to join in the fun.

# XXI

## *Plymouth*

**B**UT although the shrill chorus, interspersed with much
laughter, was continued at intervals during the evening; although one of the sailors stole the cook's
best hosen and hung them conspicuously on the point of
the *Mayflower's* beak, although at the suggestion of the
boatswain, a row of delighted children spat vociferously
into the sea, no wind disturbed the shining calm of the
Atlantic until dawn of the following day. Then as the
sun rolled above the horizon, a southerly wind suddenly
filled the sails and the patient ship again began to beat her
zigzag way back to the English coast.

During the morning, Robert sought out Captain Standish and asked him to give Tom Tinker some sort of an
official position.

"But the fellow doesn't know a sword from a musket,"
objected the soldier. "And he's thick with the Billington
crowd."

"That's why," nodded Cushman. "You must have
learned in your military experience that putting authority
in a thinking man's hands will subdue him as nothing else
will. Tinker's a thinking man. He's thinking about Billington's ideas of the colony now. It would be better for
the colony if he'd thought about yours."

Miles scratched his head. "But what can he do besides
carry that babe of his about? He plays quoits best of any

on the two ships.  Let me see—let me see."  He wandered
off thoughtfully.

Robert settled to a book on the half deck.  About half
an hour later, he saw Tinker with several of the half-
grown boys, tossing quoits.  Mistress Tinker perched herself and her pale baby in the longboat to watch.  The
three little girls among the Pilgrims joined her.  And for
the first time was seen on Mistress Tinker's young face
an expression of pleasure and peace.  Robert began to be
hopeful about Tom Tinker.

The southerly wind lasted three days, then it shifted to
the northeast.  The pinnace which had struggled along
always just in sight of the *Mayflower,* now disappeared
from view although Captain Jones said she ought to have
had less difficulty making her way to windward than
the great square-rigged *Mayflower.*  There was a period
of keen anxiety and of debate whether or not to turn and
seek the *Speedwell* but just as the *Mayflower's* officers had
made up their minds to 'bout ship, the pinnace appeared
on the horizon from a northerly tack.

All day and the next the two ships played at "I spy"
but gradually they worked their way northeast and on the
afternoon of August thirtieth, the man in the maintop
sighted land.  The leadsman was set to work.  Slowly they
crawled.  Just before sunset, they sighted Rame Head,
the western outpost of Plymouth Harbor.  Then the wind
died again and all that night there was not a ripple on the
deep.  The next morning a fog hung low for hours, then
a head wind blew it away.  The two ships, a half mile
apart, waited all day for a fair breeze.  None came; only a
calm and more fog at night.

With land so near the Pilgrims finally and for the first
time completely lost their patience and there rose such

complaints and wailings as had not been heard since the ship left Southampton. Master Jones was highly incensed and exploded to Robert and Ned Winslow who were lounging in the poop cabin with him.

"Bedlamites! They declare they'll endure all the torture and toil of the wilderness with good cheer. Yet they burst with insultings at my navigation when they have to remain an extra day or two in the comforts of a ship like mine! Look at my sailors! They're very scum and yet not a murmur from them!"

"But they're hardened to the contrariness of winds in making harbor," said Ned. "One of them told me he'd been a week sometimes waiting for a fair wind into Plymouth."

"I've waited more than that," growled Jones, his quick wrath evaporated. "Well, I haven't whistled yet myself. I'll see what I can bring about." He thrust his red head out of the stern window and began to pipe a gentle little ditty.

"Very seductive!" whispered Ned, eyes dancing.

"Let's hope the rain hears," Robert returned. "We mustn't smile. He believes in his power, perhaps."

It might have been full five minutes that the master continued his mysterious communing with the sky and the deep. At the end of that time he turned his head and said, "You two, come here!"

They crowded into the window beside him. To the south, the rim of a black cloud was showing. It mounted the sky with incredible rapidity. The master himself looked awe-struck, as if he were overwhelmed by the brilliancy of his own gifts. His companions were dumb.

The first mate shouted from the half deck for two more men to man the tiller. "Furl the mainsail," roared the pilot. Jones rushed from the cabin and there followed the hurly-burly of snugging the ship down for a storm.

Robert grinned at Ned. "He whistled at least three minutes longer than wisdom demanded!"

"That was mere vanity, I fear!" Winslow's brown eyes were very bright. Then, suddenly sobering, "The poor *Speedwell!*"

They hastened out to the deck. The southern half of the sky was black now and shot with lightning and the wind came with cannon ball velocity. The *Mayflower* stuck her nose deep, lifted it and was off like a duck scooting over a barn-yard wall to a pond. The *Speedwell* with only her sprit and her lateen set moved slowly after them. Then as an infuriate rain came down, they lost sight of her.

Robert and Ned returned to the great cabin. Its full complement of passengers was there. The linnet was fluttering wildly and someone flung a shawl over his cage.

Robert sat down by Mary. Tommy rushed in and crouched close to his father. "One of the sailors said we'd drive on the rocks!" he panted, clinging to Robert's hand. "There are hugeous great rocks in the opening of the haven, hard to miss on a fair day, and he said he hoped we'd split in half on Mewlstone and drown every damned Pilgrim be—"

"Don't swear, Tommy. We needn't fear. God gave us a wonderful seaman in Master Jones," said his father.

"Why aren't you down with your sweetest Captain Standish?" demanded Mary. "We don't love your 'tween-decks ways up here."

"I like Tommy, 'tween-decks or no!" Robert hugged the lad. "But I don't like cursing."

"I don't curse myself, Father. I was just telling what

the sailor said." Tommy's voice was aggrieved. "I hardly see you once a day, sir."

"You'll be seeing overmuch of me when we reach New England and are at work chopping trees," Robert reminded him.

"It won't be overmuch," stoutly from the boy.

Desire was talking to the More children. "And so Jesus walked on the water. He said—" The din of the storm drowned her voice. The ship lurched and quivered throughout her length.

The master's silver whistle pierced the riot of the storm. There were shouts from the steerage. The ship lay almost on her beam end. Children shrieked. Governor Martin shouted, "Let us pray!" But no one moved to obey! They could only cling helplessly to whatever was at hand.

Then slowly, very slowly, the ship began to right herself and although the noise, above, of the storm was unabated, the *Mayflower* began to ride on an even keel. And then they heard the clank of anchor chains.

There was a rush for the decks. But both doors into the steerage had been bolted from without. Panic-stricken, a woman beat on the panels. Someone screamed, "We're trapped to drown! Let us out, you brutes!"

"Don't be fools!" cried Sam Fuller. *"We're safe anchored!"*

As he spoke, the bolts were withdrawn and the doors were pushed wide. The Pilgrims poured out into the open air. The rain still was falling heavily but the waves were stilled. High and faintly, beyond the bow, occasional lights were twinkling. These were not stars, the boatswain told them, but beacons on Plymouth Hoe. They were safe in Plymouth Harbor.

What of the *Speedwell?*

No one could answer this query which was on every lip. For hours, the people waited, listening, hoping, praying, but at last, one by one went off to bed. Desire was among the last to go for she was consumed with anxiety over her aunt and uncle. However, Mary Cushman toward midnight persuaded her to come down to the great cabin. Giles Heale advised Robert to do likewise.

But Robert would not. "My breath frets me when I lie down, today," he told Giles, "but not at all when I am erect. I couldn't sleep anyhow for I have a sense of depression as if something portentous were coming."

"Good God! Don't say that!" pleaded the young man; then he added impressively, "Though of course it's only your spleen!"

Grim as he felt, Robert could but laugh and Giles stamped off indignantly. Cushman, left alone, climbed to the poop cabin and found all save the second mate preparing for a night's sleep. He would not disturb them, so he fetched his cloak from his bed and found shelter under the lee of the longboat where he could keep watch for the pinnace. It was not precisely a dry spot but he was sheltered from the full drive of the rain and he crouched on a coil of rope content only to be alone.

But there were others besides Cushman who bore the *Speedwell* too heavily on their hearts to forget her in sleep. Men and women prowled at intervals from their beds to ask questions of the watch and when they discovered Robert's whereabouts, they paused to speculate with him about the fate of their tiny consort.

Tom Tinker, Priscilla Mullins, Marie Martin, Sam Fuller, Mary Cushman, the Winslows and a dozen others came to the longboat, shivered, ejaculated and returned to their beds only to appear shortly again with the inevitable, "Where can she be!"

Desire came among others, but she scarcely paused in her anxiety. Robert saw her several times pacing the deck, a shadow among many shadows. Mary made him a second visit about two in the morning and brought Desire with her.

"Do come to your rest, Robert," Mary begged him. "If you'd only realize how stern an illness you had!"

"But I'm well now," replied Robert, "and you've found yourself that bed is useless tonight. Look! It's dry enough if you can crowd back under the boat. I'll arrange seats for you and you both can join my vigil."

"It's very cold," said Desire, "but anything is better than the great cabin. Let's do it, Mary."

Mary consented, but without eagerness, and Robert established the two with what comfort he could.

"Suppose the *Speedwell* is lost," suggested Mary as he wrapped her cloak about her. "Then we'd have to give up the venture, wouldn't we?"

"No, terribly as we'd grieve, we'd find more people and go on," replied Cushman.

"But how can you?" cried Desire. "Don't these six-score people and these ships embrace the utmost you could do in three years' effort?"

"Yes, they do," admitted Robert, "but still I know that we shall sail to America."

He heard his wife give a soft moan and he touched her gently. "It must be, Mary," he said.

"I've been getting more reconciled to the venture as our difficulties and obstructions increase. It never lacks for amusement, this passage to Utopia!" Desire was close on the other side of Robert. "You can well believe it's a holy cause because Satan takes such pains to ruin it."

"It ought to be very holy to compensate for all the suffering it's causing!" Mary exclaimed.

"There would have been more suffering if we'd remained in Leyden," commented Cushman.

"Now that's mere cant, isn't it?" demanded Desire. "You would suffer poverty if you returned to Leyden but if you gave up your enmity to the Established Church, you could live happily in England!"

"I'm no enemy to the Church—" began Robert.

Mary interrupted. "Must I listen at this hour and this place to a dissertation on the sins of the Church? I wish I'd been born a savage, then I'd have missed all this pother about religion."

"But the savages have a most insistent religion," objected Robert.

"Alack!" groaned Mary, "then how can one flee from religion's everlasting trammels? I have it! Will Bradford tells that the Greeks had a religion of joy. I'd be a Greek."

"Helen of Troy?" asked Robert.

"Mayhap! I wonder if she was as beautiful as the men thought her!"

"Probably not," said Desire.

Both women laughed.

"Suppose we could stay in England, Desire," asked Mary, "what would you do unless you lived with your relations?"

"Hum!" mused Desire. "I'd try to find some notable family who would let me be a female tutor to its daughters. Not a nurse, mind you, but a tutor, like a man."

"But how?" cried Mary. "One would need great connections."

"I have none, certainly," confessed Desire. "But why shouldn't I seek a patroness as educated young men seek a patron? I wager I can write as good verse as many a gosling poet who's gaping this moment at Ben Jonson! I'd be a precious secretary to Lady Falkland, for example!"

Mary's voice was now cheerful as she shook Robert's arm and said, "You see what company you keep! Helen of Troy and the secretary to the learned Lady Falkland!"

"Aye, it's enough to dither a plain man like me!" admitted Robert.

"You're laughing at us but with a superior note in your voice," said Desire. "Men are all alike, Mary. They feel superior to us."

Mary giggled. "Well, Robert *is* my superior. I admit it. And I don't care!"

"Never, never admit it!" admonished Desire. "And, Master Cushman, don't you sit like a gaping fledgling and swallow that worm!"

"I haven't swallowed it, never fear," returned Robert. "Women never mean what they say."

"Certainly, they don't!" agreed Desire. "Now tell us what *you'd* best love to be in life."

"No, I can't," he replied, "because men do mean what they say."

"Not always, I hope!" cried Mary.

"Then," keenly from Desire, "your best wish is not to establish a new England on the Virginian coast, for you've told us that freely."

"This is getting to be a most uncomely game, like Giles Heale probing one's gullet in search of his dearest spleen!" Robert remarked.

"Don't be disgusting, Robert," protested Mary.

"And don't *you* be!—giving me Helen of Troy and the

secretary to Lady Falkland and expecting the true Robert Cushman in return!" He chuckled again. "I can't give you him but I can give you Captain Bob, the pirate, sailing in the good ship '*Dreams of Avarice*' for Zanzibar with Tom Weston as master."

Both women laughed, then Mary said, with a quaver in her voice, "I'd rather have a certain little farm in Kent than all the beauty, all the learning, all the treasure in the world."

"Not for me your Kentish farm!" Robert spoke soberly now.

"Ah! But I haven't invited you to the little farm," explained Mary. "You wouldn't be happy there. You must go to London where there are poets and plays and great strivings concerning England."

"You aren't speaking like a proper Separatist wife!" Desire's voice was mock solemn.

"I'm not one of those poor creatures. I'm only a Puritan, the wife of a Separatist," said Mary, crossly. "A Puritan is a human being. Sir Philip Sidney, Robert told me, wrote beautiful poems to another man's wife and nobody thought the worse of him. Nay, he was the darling of England. But that's because he was of noble family. We Separatists' wives must say we love our husbands even if we hate them."

"What *are* you telling, Mary!" Robert put a firm hand on her knee.

She flung it off. "I'm saying what Desire, since she isn't a Separatist, will admit, that wives don't always want to be every minute with their husbands and she thinks no sin of it. Here on the *Mayflower,* do you see how Ellen Billington avoids her John and how Mary Cushman—"

Desire interrupted firmly. "No, I'm not married so I

don't fret myself over such things. Shall we go to bed, Mary?"

"Nay," she answered. "But I won't be horrid any more. It's this voyage, this dreadful, this ridiculous, this unending voyage which makes a fool of me."

The rain beat more and more lightly. Robert sat pondering on Mary's state of mind. It was as if for the first time in her life she had laid hold on truth and was finding in its utterance a wild relief. What must Desire think of her, though? How could he explain so that his wife should not seem sinful and weak?

But Desire required no explanations. She said, "Perhaps love between man and wife isn't really needed to make a pleasant home and happy children which is the true purpose of marriage."

"I'm not talking of the generality." Mary spoke quietly but her voice was hard. "I'm not one of your lofty folk who can talk endlessly about the world. I'm interested only in me and mine. It's all very well for you to talk, Desire; you don't know what love is."

"Do you?" asked Desire abruptly.

Mary gave a great sob and jumping to her feet, rushed down the deck into the dimly lighted steerage.

Desire, after a moment, rose too. "I'm sorry I asked that," she said. "I had no thought it would hurt her. She seems in such trouble. I love her and pity her."

"She's very unhappy," sighed Robert, "but she won't let me help her."

"It's very unfitting for her to be a Separatist. One must be born with a mind and conscience that can endure its narrow limits and she was not born so. Nor were you." Desire spoke thoughtfully.

"I'm inherently a Separatist in most things," insisted

Robert. "I admit, though, that in a few matters, I find it hard to remain within the boundaries set by Parson Robinson."

"And who would not?" she cried.

"Many people make no difficulty of them. To name a few, there are Elder Brewster, Will Bradford and your uncle. They live blameless lives and without a struggle."

"Mere cant!" said Desire very vehemently. "No one is good without a struggle. There's no honest Puritan, let alone Separatist, who doesn't feel his sins tearing like a tiger at his Puritan metes and bounds. Even Elder Brewster has his tiger or else he's not fit to understand other human beings."

"He owns no such tiger as mine!" groaned Robert.

"My tiger—" began Desire and paused.

"Aye, your tiger, dear my secretary?" He touched her hand. "Didn't I see you fighting him that first day as we talked through the linnet cage?"

"I thought he was a tiger then, but since I've learned he was only a tame puss-cat in comparison. Oh, this is hopeless nonsense! I am going to follow Mary!" But she stood looking down at him.

He dared not speak, did not trust himself to speak. But he dared to lift her hand to his lips and this she suffered. Then she left him.

But just as she reached the square of light which marked the steerage door, there reached the ship faintly but clearly a familiar sound, "Clank! Clank! Clank!"

"A ship's pump going, astern of us!" called the man on the forecastle.

"Listen, fool!" cried the mate.

Louder, louder, "Clank! Clank!" It was a piteous sound, labored, weary.

"Wave a lanthorn there on the forecastle," roared the mate. "Ahoy! Is that the *Speedwell?* This is the *Mayflower.*"

"Ahoy, *Mayflower!*" Reynolds' voice. "Send us over some men to keep our pump going till dawn."

"Aye! Aye! Are ye all safe?"

"Safe enough, if we don't sink before I can beach this coffin." The *Speedwell's* riding lights could now be seen.

"Shall we take your passengers off now?" It was Master Jones' voice.

"Morning will be soon enough. Send us men for the pump and we'll do!" called Reynolds.

The *Mayflower's* people were crowding the waist now and for a little time they exchanged greetings with their unseen friends on the pinnace. The *Speedwell* passengers were too glad to be safe to do much complaining. They said that Reynolds had locked the great cabin and battened down the hatches until they made the harbor. There had been a mort of seasickness. In response to an anxious query from Desire, John Carver's rich voice came through the drizzle. "Nay, we're battered and sodden, but well. And now that we're safe, I'm going to my bed although it may float out through a porthole!"

There was general approval of this sentiment and once more the weary people sought their rest.

# XXII

## *"That Flesh Is Heir to—"*

IT was clear and cool in the morning and the Pilgrims were on deck with the sun for their first view of famous old Plymouth.

The town lay on a green bluff side to the north with low hills behind it, stretching upward to the far horizon where Dartmoor dreamed against the skies. Broad arms of the sea stretched from the outer harbor to embrace the bluff on the east and west so that, from the deck of the *Mayflower,* Plymouth looked to be set on a lofty island.

As became the chief harbor of England's West Country, the town was well fortified. The bluff side—Plymouth Hoe—was fortified along its seafront by a towered wall which bristled with cannon. Plymouth itself, lying north and east of the Hoe, was enclosed in yet another wall with towers and at the southwest corner there was a great castle. This fine citadel protected the entrance to the inner harbor which was formed by the easterly arm of the sea and here a barbican in the lower wall opened on a quay from which a chain could be stretched to a wall on the opposite shore in time of emergency.

It was to this inner harbor, known as Sutton Pool, that the *Speedwell* would be obliged to go for repairs. Wharfage would be an expensive business so the *Mayflower,* Master Jones decided, would work up toward the barbican as far as permissible and there anchor.

When Robert came on deck the sun was just above

the hills, yet already the passengers had been transferred from the pinnace and with her sweeps out, pump still going, the *Speedwell* was moving toward the Pool.

A stranger might well have supposed, Cushman thought, that Plymouth was the final goal of the Pilgrims, that every danger had been passed, every problem solved, so gayly did the passengers from the two vessels greet and mingle. Even when Elder Brewster hushed them for a thanksgiving service, there was a reprehensible restlessness and surreptitious gaping at the shining roofs of Plymouth! Deacon Carver perhaps had sympathy for the people in this lack of seriousness, for when the last Amen had been said, he remarked to them all with a smile on his good-looking face,

"It's a sweetly pretty place, is it not? The home of the sea-dogs who broke the Armada's back! Let's all get ashore as soon as we can! But," turning to Martin, "shall they all not agree to be back by noon for then we hope to learn where my *Speedwell* people are to sleep and when we shall sail?"

"All passengers be aboard this ship by twelve of the clock!" announced Governor Martin, importantly.

For once a pronouncement by Martin was received with cheerfulness. Everyone wanted to get ashore at once and there was a chorus of cries for boats accompanied by a confusion of running comments.

"To the west those hills are Cornwall! Here, you coracle!"

"This is Sir Francis Drake's town. Up there he played bowls on the Hoe! Hie, boatman!"

"Come along! Come along! My cramped legs want to run a league! There's a man will boat us!"

"All my clothes are soaked with brine. How can I be seen without shame?"

"What, in this little town lost in the West? They still wear Great Harry's styles and will think your wrinkled skirts the latest London fashion."

"I need a ruff or shall I buy one of the new falling bands?"

Tommy touched his father's arm. "Are we going ashore now, Father?"

"Not yet, lad! We must arrange three several matters first. I suppose your craving to climb the Hoe is almost more than you can bear!"

Tommy's dark eyes sparkled. "I can bear it, sir, if by waiting a while I can go with you. Or I can go with John Alden or Tom Tinker or Captain Standish. I have a mort of friends!"

Robert took a farthing from his purse and gave it to the boy. "Go with any of them, my dear, but be back here at noon. And keep your friends, Tom. They're the only things that really help a man to bear his life."

Tommy nodded casually and ran away.

Mary was off in an early boatload with Dorothy Bradford. It was a curious friendship, Dorothy so sad, so staid, and Mary so frivolous. And yet, thinking thus, Robert brought himself up short. Was Mary as shallow as he had thought her? Might not there be depths in her of which he'd never dreamed?

Will Bradford broke in on his thoughts. "The elder requires us in the poop cabin, Master Cushman!"

Bradford was looking thin and very tired. His eyes under the curious drooping lids were bloodshot and his lips pale.

"But since you *can't* make a sailor of yourself, Will,"

exclaimed Robert, as they walked toward the poop together, "why not be sensible and let me take your place on the *Speedwell?*"

"Thanks," replied Bradford, his obstinate lip stiff, "but I'm going to overcome this seasickness or die in the attempt."

Martin and Winslow, Carver and Brewster and Cushman—it was the old group gathered after what seemed a five months' instead of five days' separation.

"Well," remarked the deacon, "I, for one, feel as if I'd returned from the very bowels of the deep! Your *Mayflower* washroom was the gratefulest spot in the seven seas, this morning. Elder, you look like a Christian again and not a pirate fellow with a salty rheum of the face!"

The two older men smiled at each other.

"I do wish I might go in the *Speedwell* in your place, Elder!" exclaimed Winslow. "It's very unfitting for you to be suffering so unnecessarily."

"It's good for me," replied Brewster, quite simply.

"All that I need is sleep," said the deacon. "And we can't *all* get that on the *Mayflower*. Some of us must find a few days' lodging in the town."

"I have friends here with whom my family and I can stay," said the elder. "I shall risk leaving the ship, this far from London. But we are only four out of thirty-odd."

"You think the pinnace will be long in repairing?" asked Cushman, anxiously.

"Reynolds said if we were recalked in a week it would be a wonder," answered Carver. "My thought was, Where is the money to be found!"

"Can't we sell more stock in the venture here in Plymouth?" suggested Winslow, with an uncomfortable glance at Cushman.

"Perhaps it might be difficult in consideration of our differences with the Adventurers." Carver also had one eye on Robert who smiled inwardly. The deacon went on, "You were sure the Lord would show you the way, Robert."

"He hasn't yet." Cushman shook his head. "I've been asking myself if it would be wise to visit Sir Fernando Gorges' secretary here. At least, I suppose he has one in Plymouth, for I was told that he was getting himself a King's charter calling his company as of Plymouth, in Devonshire."

"Do you think Sir Fernando would take stock?" asked Chris Martin eagerly.

"No one ever knows what he will do," answered Cushman. "He is a man who speaks so loudly that it's difficult to hear what he says. But there's another matter that concerns him and us." He reminded them of the rumors that Sir Fernando was seeking a fishing monopoly.

"Look you, Robert," said John Carver, "take this matter into your own judgment, will you? You know how to treat with these noble Adventurers better than the rest of us."

Cushman hesitated and then replied, "But I can't undertake that now. You've all lost your trust in me and that, with absolute injustice as far as my honor's concerned."

"Nay," cried Ned, his boyish face a little sheepish, "your honor was always safe in our estimation. It was your judgment we disparaged. And as I was a leader in disparagement, it's fitting I should say I've lost faith in my own judgment—since I've been so much with you—and have gained faith in yours."

Robert could feel himself flushing like a girl. Martin and Will Bradford said nothing but the elder nodded his great head. "Yes, see to it for us, Robert! And now," as cheerfully as if the money were already in their purses, "what do we do about sleeping our great family?"

"Let's do nothing till we know the extent of the *Speedwell's* injuries," suggested Winslow, rising and waving his hand at someone, through the door. It was Elizabeth, of course. "Whatever you all wish to do, so do I. But prithee, I want to get off the ship and into Plymouth!"

"Get on with your fairing, Edward," laughed Carver. "We understand. We, too, have been in Arcady." Ned turned pink and bolted. "And you, Will," John went on, "go to bed in the blessed quiet and comfort of the *Mayflower's* great cabin. It will be all but empty, now."

"There's nothing more to be considered until noon, I think," said the elder. "Robert, since you'll be going into Plymouth on this business, will you bring back the report on the *Speedwell?* I would like to go at once to seek my old friends. Will you come with me, John?"

"Thank you, William," shaking his iron-gray head, "but my wife and my niece also are waiting for me to look at the Hoe with them. And I confess I too—" He was already following after Winslow.

"But we can take a boat together!" called Brewster and he rushed in pursuit of his friend.

Robert and Martin looked at each other. "Children!" groaned Martin. "Mere children! They know we'll be here a week at least. Tonight will crowd on the heels of this noon. Where will the people sleep?"

"Do you know anyone in Plymouth?" asked Robert.

The governor nodded. "Yes, if he still is in the land

of the living, a merchant I used to buy from when he visited London, yearly. He's a good Puritan."

"If he's a man of understanding, call on him and ask him for a list of three several families who each might take in some of our Pilgrims," advised Robert.

"Excellent! I'll start at once. What would these fools do without my head and influence! Will you share a boat with Marie and me?" Martin, too, was chafing to be off.

Robert thanked him and they went below together.

The Carvers and Brewsters were just going down the gangway and Robert had a glimpse of Desire in a rose-colored dress which flowed about her in long graceful lines. Marie Martin, too, was waiting for her husband, dressed for the fairing in a handsome black silk with falling bands of an exquisite sheerness. She was very condescending to Robert and the three made the trip ashore in the most complete harmony.

They were rowed to the barbican and landed on the quay under the castle wall. The Pool was an extremely busy spot, crowded with shipping, and the quay was piled high with freight of every variety. Sir Richard Hawkins was preparing his fleet of twenty sail for his attempt against the Turks of Algiers. The storm had driven a number of ships into Plymouth for protection and repairs and Martin suggested cheerfully, as they parted, that the pinnace would have to pay by the nose for the shipwrights would scorn so small a business.

Robert was glad to be rid of them all and to be alone with the glamor of Plymouth and his own thoughts. For a little while he walked along the quay looking up the little streets which opened on the water front and wound up to the heights of the great west walls. And he dreamed of Drake and his fleet of little ships sailing from this very

Pool to compass the earth.  And he swept the distant hills
with a wistful glance, then made his way, after some in-
quiring, to the Guild Hall for information regarding
Gorges' Plymouth Company.  The Town Recorder was
able to give him very exact information.  Sir Fernando
Gorges' secretary for the Plymouth Company had left for
London the day before and would not return till God
knew when; for Sir Fernando was having a great fret with
the King His Majesty about the fishing monopoly which
perhaps would not be allowed.  No, there was no other
soul in Devon, so far as the Recorder knew, who would
know aught of Sir Fernando's affairs.

Robert descended the steep stairway to the street wearing a half-wry smile.  After all his superiority, they must
do as Desire had suggested and sail to America ignorant
of their rights in the matter of fishing!  As for Sir Fernando or his friends helping the Pilgrims financially, well,
since the secretary was gone, that hope also was dashed.

The market was in full swing in the arcade under the
Guild Hall.  Robert observed some of the Pilgrims gaping at the stalls, waved his hand at Mary who was clinging
to Dorothy's arm as they stood before a tub of periwinkles,
and made his way back to the water front.

It was busier and more crowded than ever here but
people spared a glance for this tall man of so erect carriage, his hair so yellow above his ruff.  A butcher's boy
directed him to the shipyard at the north end of the Pool
and here he found the pinnace, thrust well up on the
beach and braced to an even keel by odds and ends of
masts and spars.  Her sailors were dropping over her side
on shore leave as Robert reached her.  He wondered if
any of them would be seen again in spite of the fact that
they'd receive no wages unless they completed the voyage.

However, they were a poor lot, easily replaced in a port such as this.

One of the men stopped to speak with Robert. It was Jock Coombs in bright blue hosen and a black leather jerkin.

"Good morning, Master!" he said. "Could I have a word with you?"

"Gladly," answered Cushman. "There's no man I'd like better to put a few questions to. Where can we go?"

Jock looked about him. There were in the yard half a dozen small ships on ways and one large merchant vessel. These swarmed with workmen. Along the beach were débris and wreckage of all sorts among which children and ancients were scavenging. It would not be easy to speak privily in this place! But Coombs jerked his well-greased head toward a large rock lying above the tide mark and said as he led the way toward it, "What I have to tell 'ee won't bear hearin'!"

He seated Cushman on the rock facing the Pool, and stood before him, his one blue eye brilliantly clear.

"They sailormen would drown me an they knowed I tell 'ee this, but—" He hesitated, looking at the other wistfully.

"But you and I are friends so you feel you ought to tell me and you know you can trust me not to give you away!" Robert finished the sentence for him.

"Right 'ee be, Master!" with his irresistible wink. "Now then, square your yards to this breeze. When in Dartmouth a shipwright overhauled the pinnace. That man was an ancient shipmate of Captain Nutt's and so was Master Reynolds. And how he worked it I don't know, nor yet do the *Speedwell* sailors. But while they was seeming to repair the hull of the pinnace, they changed her ballast so that her tail drooped and every wave that followed was fit to poop her."

"Reynolds is a villain!" gasped Cushman.

"That's one!" Jock held up a huge, tar-stained finger. "Now here's another. Reynolds had her remasted at Delfthaven with larger sails and longer masts, all at the expense of the Leyden people who knew not what he was doing, only believed what Reynolds told them, that the pinnace needed much repairing. Not that he planned then not to go to Ameriky nor that he was too good a sailor not to know that to put topmasts on her might be very dangerous. But he feared to be left by the *Mayflower*. He learned in crossing to Hampton that she was too much pressed with sails and he would have corrected her in Southampton, if he hadn't fell afoul of Master Martin. Then he decided he'd never go to Ameriky and his mind was all on how he could get out and save his fine and his wages. This he told the first mate. And the cabin boy heard all and told the forecastle for he hates the master's guts. You'll never get the pinnace to Ameriky, Master Cushman."

"We shall if we restore her to her proper trim and get rid of Reynolds." Robert's voice was stubborn.

Jock rubbed his nose on his sleeve. "The crew won't never come back to her, even though most of 'em knows now that Master Reynolds was the ghost that haunted us. She's got a bad name. If you get another crew, you'll have to press 'em. Me, I'll never put foot on her again, the wallowing dirty little sow, be she made over from stem to stern and keel to peak."

"But you'll come back to the *Mayflower*, Jock!" exclaimed Cushman.

"Nay," shaking his head slowly, "nay, if I be going to

take so perilous a journey, I go as a freebooter where there's a chance of treasure for my pains."

"But after the crew's hired year with us, there are beaver, fish—"

Jock waved his huge paw. "Gold is the only bait that would lure men aboard your ship, Master Cushman! What have you to offer? A hard voyage. Where? Nobody knows. What at the other end? A year's slavery. Master, only as great fools as they Pilgrims would go!"

"The reason they go is because they're not fools," declared Cushman. "They see treasure in America that fools like the rest of you never would see, Jock. As for risks, what kind of risks have we compared with those Newfoundland fishing boats?"

"Aye, but that's a short shift of a few months and share and share alike in what each boat takes. I beant going to Ameriky, Master."

"I shall miss you, Jock."

Jock twisted his shoulders. "Nay, I'm not going."

Robert held out his hand. "Then it's good-by! And I thank you, truly, Jock, for telling me this."

"What be you going to do about it?" The sailor touched Robert's hand shyly.

"I don't know," he replied dejectedly.

"Why do 'ee go to they savage lands, Master? England, now what does England lack for 'ee?"

"It lacks room for me, Jock," grimly.

"More fool England then!" Jock jerked his head, cleared his throat and rolled off.

Only the details of what the sailor had told him were new to Robert but these were so very discomforting that he sat for a little while collecting his thoughts and looking with pitying eyes on the ravished little craft. And for the first time since its inception, a distaste for the whole venture swept over Robert.   He wished that a vicious wave would sweep up Sutton Pool and irretrievably wreck the *Speedwell*.   And worse than this, he felt a sudden loathing for himself, for his sick spleen—if it was his spleen—for his whole traitor body, for his way of life, for the absurdities which he knew as well as the King His Majesty knew, tainted the Separatist's theology.   He loathed the Merchant Adventurers and their pound of flesh.   Aye, and he loathed more than that, life, itself, which was so dank and ugly a business, life which could separate Mary from Frank and Robert from Desire, life which could make the so stupid devil which resided in the King's so clever head, use Christ as a sword with which to slay good citizens; how he hated life!

And even such a poor thing as was this, his own life, how close he was to wrecking it, with the voyage so near to disaster, his honor impugned with the Merchant Adventurers and most perilous of all, with his passionate love for Desire so growing that any moment it might break bounds, carry himself and Desire to destruction and taint the name of Pilgrim before the cynical, malicious, watching world.   The loathing was so intense that it became physical.   He felt as if he must tear off his flesh, slough off "this muddy vestment of decay."   But to what end? Aye, to what end?

"Robert!"

It was Desire who spoke.   She was standing before him, gazing at him with startled dark eyes.

"Are you in such pain again?" she gasped.

"You!" he ejaculated.   "I didn't see you coming.   Yet I'd have sworn I'd feel your presence from your place in heaven down into my very hell!"

She turned very pale. "You *are* ill then! I'll find help for you. You look agonized."

He put out his hand to stay her. Now he would tell her! By all that was truth, such love as his carried its own absolution with it. He would tell her he loved her.

He felt her cool, slender fingers grasp his and he looked up into her great candid, tragic eyes and at her chaste, warm mouth and it seemed to him that it was only the Christ within him which helped him to say,

"I'm not ill, dearest Desire, except with contempt for myself. What brought you here?"

She did not reply immediately but stood returning his gaze.

The Pool was full of sea gulls. One swept lightly down and stood awkwardly at their feet. A sailor's chantey sounded faintly from an outbound galley. From Desire's fingers there flowed through Robert's body a thrill of perfect happiness. Poor body! He must not loathe it utterly since it could carry so dear a message to him. And poor Pilgrim venture, he must hold it sacred for without it he had not known the ecstasy of love.

"Desire," he said aloud, "Desire, what was it brought you to me at my moment of need?"

"It was as if you called me," she answered simply. "I was coming along the quay with my aunt and uncle. We saw you sitting here and were afraid you were dizzy again. I ran ahead of them."

The Carvers hurried up, faces concerned. Desire turned to them, Robert's hand still in hers. "He looked like death when I reached him but he says he's not ill."

Robert smiled. "I was merely gathering up courage to go aboard the *Speedwell* to learn its fate." He rose and Desire released his hand.

"I believe you should return to the *Mayflower* and lie down," remarked Catherine, peering up into his face anxiously. "I don't think greatly of your looks."

"That's piteous hearing," Robert tried to speak gayly, "for they're my very best, donned for the trip ashore!"

"Well, you're no court beauty at any time." John was grinning in his turn. "Still I've seen you look less as if you'd just passed under the headsman's ax. . . . I saw poor Raleigh's head," he added irrelevantly.

Catherine made him a disgusted little mouth. "What if you did! I should hope poor Robert— Alack, I never do see where you get your ideas, John!"

They all laughed.

"Where are you three going?" asked Robert. "I suppose," eyes twinkling, "you wouldn't care to visit the *Speedwell?*"

"I tell you, if I were the master of the pinnace, I'd build a proper high poop and house the people in that," exclaimed Catherine. "Then it wouldn't matter how deep her precious stern rode in the water!"

"Tell the shipwright that, Robert!" cried John, with huge enjoyment. "And while you do so, we shall go see the Guild Hall and the room Drake used when he was mayor."

Robert watched them depart. They took his bad moment with them for now only the thought of Desire sang happily in his heart. He walked briskly down the sands to the *Speedwell.*

# XXIII

## *Hey Nonny No!*

EXCEPT for the sulky mate sitting on the poop, the pinnace's deck was deserted. But as Robert would have dropped down into the hold, Master Jones came up the ladder, followed by his mate Clarke, then Reynolds and the shipwright. The last was a stockily built, middle-aged man, very swarthy, with quick, deep-set black eyes.

Reynolds was looking less supercilious than usual. His fat cheeks sagged and his famous yellow doublet was almost unrecognizable, what with salt water stains and general uncleanliness. He would have led the way to the great cabin but Christopher Jones protested.

"No, don't take us indoors! Phew! What a fearsome jakes that hold of yours is! I'm for the fresh air on deck. Send that mate of yours ashore—he looks as if he'd lost his wife—and we can talk as it pleases us."

Reynolds signaled to the man who, transformed by a grin, jumped to the sands and as if he feared Reynolds might change his mind, ran like a rabbit toward the quay.

The shipwright looked questioningly at Cushman.

"I'm a passenger on the *Mayflower*," Robert explained.

"Aye, he's well enough here, Master Hawkes." Reynolds spoke for the first time. "He's one of the cursed fathers of this cursed junket!" But there was no rancor in his voice. There need not be, thought Robert. Shortly he'd be free of the *Speedwell*.

"I'd want to let the bilge all run out of her," began the shipwright. "But I can say, right now, that a month will be none too long to repair her."

Jones whistled. Robert gaped at Hawkes in despair. "But that would bring us to America in the winter! Impossible!"

Hawkes returned his look. "Sorry, Master, but this little ship has had bad treatment. She needs a mort of work on her."

"Bad treatment! What do you mean?" cried Reynolds.

"Go to, you beetle-headed fool!" shouted Jones, his florid face turning purple. "Don't try that with sailormen!"

"I risked my life—!" screamed Reynolds.

"And everyone else's!" added Mate Clarke.

"You risked your granny's great toe," said Christopher Jones through his teeth. "You bursten-bellied sot, you—"

"Stop!" Robert walked between the two masters. "No brawling! This is too serious!" He turned to the shipwright. "Master Hawkes, not only is the pinnace overpressed with sail, but she's had the rake of her masts shifted to keep her down by the stern. I'm not a sailor so I don't express myself clearly, perhaps."

"Clear enough!" Hawkes' black eyes gleamed. "I'll look into that, also."

"And what will all this cost, prithee?" asked Robert, his anxiety growing by leaps and bounds.

"I can only guess," answered Hawkes. "With laborers getting four shillings for carrying a mere thousand billets of wood and eight shillings to fill a ship with a thousand gallons of drinking water and three shillings a ton to move ballast and a boy six shillings a day—"

"This means nothing to me," interrupted Cushman. "Give me a rude estimate."

"Forty pounds!" said Hawkes.

"Forty pounds!" Robert scarcely breathed the words. They were ruined! All the resources in cash of all the Pilgrims scarcely reached that sum.

The others were watching him. He hoped his face did not reveal his panic and tried to say, naturally, "It's a larger sum of money than we thought we'd have to lay out after our voyage actually began. I shall have to consult with my brethren. But if you will, as you suggest, run off the bilge and get at the calking, I'll return to you tomorrow morning empowered to make some sort of an agreement with you!"

Hawkes' black eyes bored into Cushman's blue ones. "And what surety have I that I'll be paid even for the calking?" he asked.

"I have three pounds in my possession I'll bring to you in another hour," answered Robert. "That will cover any work you may do today or tomorrow."

"Assuredly," nodded Hawkes. "I'll be back here then with my workmen at eleven of the clock." He nodded to the others, clambered over the bulwarks and disappeared.

Robert turned to Reynolds and said with an anger too righteous and too deep for vehemence, "The burthen and grief you've put on us shall not destroy us but it will you. The Lord works slowly but surely." Then he flung up his hands. "I can't talk to you!"

"Leave him to me, Master Cushman," growled Christopher. "I'll warm the up-ended hog trough, the blue-bellied sturgeon for 'ee; the—"

But Robert for once found no amusement in the seaman's power of invective. He walked to the ship's side and dropping to the sands, walked back to the quay.

To the north, above the Pool, spacious houses were set in gardens—secure and serene in the September sun. Robert looked at them hungrily as he passed.

At the quay he called a boat and was rowed out to the *Mayflower*.

His little bag of coins was hid under the feather bed, next the wall. It represented absolutely the end of his cash and would have gone toward paying Tom Weston had Tom not been so vehement in insisting that it was dangerous to leave England without a penny in the pocket. How right Tom had been, as usual!

Robert sat for a moment on the edge of his bed. The great cabin seemed almost homelike and very comforting to a homeless man. He put up his hand and touched one of the huge beams. Good ship. Dear ship. Built of the very fiber of England. Never would she fail them. Nor would the pinnace have failed them had she not been betrayed.

He put the money bag under his cloak and returned to the shipyard. He found Jones on the sands talking with Hawkes. Cushman handed the money to the shipwright who counted it and gave a receipt, which he had waiting, and went aboard the pinnace. Reynolds was not to be seen.

"I've sent the first mate back to the *Mayflower* with the small boat," said Christopher Jones. "Pay off your boatman, Master Cushman, and have a chat with me."

Robert noted for the first time that the seaman wore a doublet of cream-colored velvet under his old cloak and that although he was wet to the knee, his stockings were of silk. Instead of the precious Monmouth cap, he wore a felt hat with a wide brim and a plume set rakishly on end.

"Surely you weren't wearing that hat when I saw you on the *Speedwell* just now!" Robert's eyes twinkled. "It's indecorous to look so seductive at your age!"

Jones clapped Robert on the shoulder. "I left this hat in the small boat, wrapped in a kerchief. Reynolds would have been like a ravening wolf if he'd seen my shore-going headpiece. You're a gallant lad, Master, and I love you! Come along to the Admiral Inn, tucked so sweetly under the hill, yonder. I'm enhungered and so are you, God bless us, and so forth. So cheerily we go!"

"Meaning, to my landsman's ears, with a hey nonny no!" agreed Robert. "Yes, I'll come with thanks."

He followed the master as he led the way at a half trot around new-laid keels, past gaping idlers, through a wide gate and out into a country road where, a stride or two up the green hill, lay a low, gray-thatched inn. There was a watering trough before the door where a little boy and a donkey drank together. But within, the tiny parlor was empty. There was a little table and some chairs in the bow window and here they seated themselves. They waited for a moment, then Jones bellowed for the landlord. A tall Cornishman came in an unhurried manner and the master demanded to be told instantly what was preparing for dinner.

"A pasty, sir, of best beef, hot in the oven now, oozing gravy, or a dish of fresh roasted pig ribs. My mistress has just drawn out a baking of bread and—"

"Don't stand there babbling while my mouth runs fountains!" cried Jones. "Fetch everything you have and the best wine in the house!"

The landlord looked gratified and left the parlor at a run.

The sailor turned to the window. "We're starved for green fields," he said, "and we find ourselves a window which shows us only the sea."

It was true! They were looking over the shipyard and down the Pool to the blue waters of the Sound. Ships, sails and then more ships.

"Did you succeed in making Reynolds repent?" asked Cushman.

"Being old in wisdom, I never tried for that! I held a mirror up to him. That was my purpose. And though he put up a goodly show of words, I silenced him. I'm a traveled man and I'm a reading man. I know my Marlowe and my Marprelate and my Nashe. They be the greatest yielders of succulent words in all England. Also I have a natural talent for cursing that's always stood by me in time of need. My father before me had it and his father. There are forms we've handed down from father to son which are peculiar to our family, the Jones family!" His eyes were dancing.

"It's a gift!" agreed Robert with great solemnity. "If I had it, I'd be a true poet."

"It's sweet to be admired!" nodded the sailor.

They were still laughing when the landlord strode in carrying a mighty pasty which erupted steam and exuded gravy with such an odor as haunts one's hungry moments for a lifetime. His wife, anxious-eyed, followed with the platter of ribs, brown and covered with crackle, and a little boy with the warm loaf and the wine brought up the rear.

Robert never had felt so ravenous before. Wise Master Jones! They literally seized on the food and neither spoke till the first craving was satisfied. This was when the whole of the pasty and half of the ribs had been cleared up with a loaf of bread. Then Jones poured the wine and they leaned back in their chairs to look at each other appreciatively.

"I never thought you a beautiful fellow before, Admiral Jones!" remarked Cushman. "But now!"

Christopher tried to arrange his hard jaw in a smirk and the effort sent Robert off in peals of mirth.

"With a hey nonny no!" nodded the master. "God knows that was a meal! I could face the King His Majesty now."

"No one could appreciate the Jones taste in curses more, I'm certain, than our good James!" Cushman looked affectionately at the red head opposite.

"Which brings us back to Reynolds!" Jones sighed. "You must gather your chiefs together and I'll give you all my opinion then."

Robert nodded. "In the meantime, I'll tell you the tale Jock Coombs told me this morning."

"Aye, your henchman you subdued so lustily! I suppose he's surly because we'd put him on the *Speedwell*."

"He didn't say so. He spoke of Reynolds." Robert gave Jones his tale.

The master was not surprised. "If we could get Coombs and some of the other sailors to face Reynolds with that, before competent witnesses, methinks you'll have no great effort on his part to obtain wages. I doubt me if the men will dare, though!"

"Whether they dare or not," declared Robert, "I shall do my utmost to see that he receives justice."

"Which would be the hangman's noose! And you know your gentle Brewster couldn't hang a pussy-cat," grumbled Jones.

"We've no time to tarry in England hanging villains!" Robert said with a shrug. "My trouble's no longer with

Reynolds. Somehow we shall be rid of him. My chiefest fright now is about the costs on the pinnace. I gave Hawkes the last farthing in my purse. Had we not disaffected the Merchant Adventurers, I could have sent a post-rider to London and have obtained the needed moneys from them. But as it is, much as I'm sure of his love, I dare not ask even Master Weston."

"Don't forget to pour that vinegar into your chiefs' wounds!" cried Christopher. "I could lend you money myself but I have a family to support and my all is in the *Mayflower*."

"I hope that Elder Brewster's friends here will buy shares in the enterprise," Robert said.

Jones scratched his poll, beginning with the crown and working carefully down to his ears. "Well, don't let it disaffect your meat pasty to say naught of the crackle! Go along to the Hoe and watch your betters playing at bowls and then get you a good night's sleep and the morning will bring wisdom. By-the-by, did you save enough out of that purse to pay an oarsman back to the *Mayflower?*"

Robert turned red. He hated to appear a fool. "What a babe you think me! And I believed you admired me!" As a matter of fact he had only just realized that his last farthing had gone to paying the last boatman!

"Many was the good meal I got from you and Master Weston in London. It's my turn now!" Jones gave his passenger a quizzical and affectionate glance, called the landlord and paid him.

Robert thanked him but said no more. Jones understood.

It was half after eleven o'clock. They walked along the water front to the castle, admired this vasty pile, and then up through a great arched gate to the Hoe. This was a broad open common, with a magnificent view of Plymouth Sound beyond the walls. Here the master left Robert and hurried off on whatever private business had demanded the noble effort in costume.

Robert strolled aimlessly about, his mind tussling with the money problem. There were other of the passengers to be seen here and there but none to whom he wished to talk and he was alone with his thoughts until Tom Tinker came up to him.

"I hope you find yourself in good health, sir," said Tom, standing very stiff and straight. He had bought new-fangled hosen which were full and reached to the knee, making his thin shanks look ridiculous.

"I'm very well, Tom! How is Mistress Tinker enjoying the holiday?"

"She's keeping the baby quiet, in a little tavern below, Master! I came up for the view. What news of the pinnace, sir?"

"Not good news, I'm afraid," answered Robert. "The shipwright says proper repairs will take a month!"

"A month! Nay, that's impossible!" cried Tinker. "Why, we'd eat up the very ship! And the people would —nay, as far as that's concerned, Captain Standish and I could keep the people straight."

"Could you!" ejaculated Robert, more gratified than he cared to show Tinker.

The sallow fellow turned a little red. "I was a fool to listen to John Billington, sir. Er—did Captain Standish tell you he's training me for drill-master?"

Robert shook his head. "I've scarcely seen him for a day. But I felt sure he could rely on you. How's my young Tommy? Giving you any trouble?"

"None—that is—none beyond his years. As for Billington, you know, Master Cushman, he makes out he's gone into Elder Brewster's fold and is a saved lamb! But he needs to be watched, sir! And especially now he can talk freely with the *Speedwell* crowd."

"Have you told the elder or Deacon Carver this?" asked Robert.

"I told the elder, this morning, and he told me to go pray to be forgiven for my doubts of a struggling Christian. And that beant sense!" He looked up at the sun. "Suppose we'd best be getting back to the ship."

Robert nodded. "I'll inquire into Billington's Christianity, Tom. Keep a hand on those lads," pointing to half a dozen 'tween-decks youngsters who were playing follow the leader across the Hoe.

Tinker hurried off. Robert with a pleased smile watched him bring the lads to order, then he walked slowly down to the landing place.

The people were gathering along the quay, some of them hiring their own boats, but most of them waiting for the ship's boats which were tardy. Christopher Martin hurried up to him. "I found my friend and he is most interested and kind. He will discover sleeping places among the brethren for a dozen people!"

"Then we are well cared for!" said Elder Brewster who appeared at this moment, with Mary fine in a wine-colored gown. "My friend must meet yours, governor! Mine spoke of forming a committee to meet us here on the quay at mid-afternoon and apportion the people! A score, he said!"

"But that was my task!" protested Martin. "Master Cushman assigned it to me."

"Don't be aggrieved," said Robert impatiently.

"There's work for all of us and more! The shipwright wants a month and forty pounds!"

Brewster and Martin gasped. Edward Winslow, joining them with Elizabeth on his arm, asked if there was bad news. "Your faces look like death," he added.

Martin told him. "Impossible!" Ned cried. "We can't make this a winter voyage with the women and children."

"But you shan't leave us behind!" Elizabeth's voice was very firm. Mary Brewster added a vehement, "No, indeed!" to this.

"What did you tell the shipwright, Robert?" asked the elder.

"To get his workmen at the calking and I'd consult you all as to time and money. We have none of either, I know! Still, I couldn't tell him that."

"Let us get back to the ship," said the elder. "The *Mayflower* seems a very haunt of peace to me. What a confusion the people do make! One would think it was a 'prentices' holiday. Look at those serving men!" Young Bob Carter and Robert's two servants were playing at leap frog at the extreme end of the quay.

"They'll tumble over in a moment!" exclaimed Mary Brewster.

"And a good thing if they did!" Winslow remarked.

And in a moment, they did pitch over with an enormous splash, to the inordinate joy of the crowd and the ruin of their holiday finery.

"I think Frankford is wearing my second best silk stockings," groaned Robert comically as one of the dripping figures emerged from the water.

Samuel Mullins gave Bob Carter a hand up the steps, then a good beating with his cane and this also delighted the audience.

Mary Cushman, Mistress Martin and Dorothy Bradford now joined the group and on their heels came the Carvers with Desire and Giles Heale. They had dined together at an inn. The doctor had abandoned his black physician's dress and looked like a courtier in bright blue satin, a broad-brimmed hat on his curls. There could be no doubt that he and Desire made a superb pair. Cushman, looking at them, felt old and tired.

The boats arrived and began to ferry the people out to the *Mayflower*. The chiefs were carried first and reaching the ship gathered at once in the deserted poop cabin. A list must be prepared of those they felt were worthy of the hospitality of the Plymouth friends. Ordinarily such a task would have been attended by endless debate and wrangling. But the sense of worry flattened even Martin, and the elder, though with a hurt look, gave in at once when Cushman and Winslow stood together against including the Billingtons with their two young sons in the list. When Martin spoke wistfully of the invitation from Master Fallon, the merchant, to Marie and himself, Robert urged him to accept, saying that he would take the governor's place on the ship, for he had no zest for visiting. John Carver was so cast down that he pleaded he could never make the effort to be a proper guest. And poor Brewster who had been so delighted to stretch his legs in freedom was so depressed by his companion's depression that he declared that he too would not leave the ship.

At this Carver roused himself. "Nay, William!" he cried. "You must go! You've been denied polite intercourse for more than a year. Go get your last sip of it! There's nothing you can do here—"

"Among the impolite?" suggested Robert, making a wan effort to lighten the gloom.

"Well, we're not precisely fine society, are we?" jibed the deacon.

"Finest in the world," declared Ned stoutly. "And it's certain that if the Pilgrims are judged by the elder's manners, they'll leave a most comely reputation in Plymouth."

Brewster finally agreed to go and as Robert and the deacon were remaining, it was decided that Ned and Will also should use the opportunity to broaden the Pilgrim acquaintance and influence. Will, having been wakened, now came in and was told the news. His heavy eyelids flickered as if he'd received a physical blow, but he said in his calm way, "When Cæsar came to the Rhine in flood, everyone undoubtedly told him he'd never get across. But he *bridged* the river, and Seneca—"

"Listen!" interrupted Brewster.

The boats were still ferrying the passengers and through the windows sounded a familiar chorus:

> ". . . And sing hey nonny no!
> When the winds blow and the seas flow,
> Hey nonny no!"

"Now this is unseemly!" cried the elder. "Somebody stop them!"

"Nay, elder, prithee!" Winslow's boyish cheeks were flushing. "Be thankful we can sing. I say we—for I'm one of the young ones too! And to us who have no years to weigh us down, these difficulties merely add to our relish of the voyage."

"You can't hey nonny no forty pounds out of the sea nor save us a month's time with it," said Carver unhappily.

"But it's a harmless banner to fleck in the face of Satan,"

insisted Ned, "when he threatens us who have a living God."

"You're right, Ned!" exclaimed Robert. "I take your lesson to myself. I've been too cast down by small obstacles."

"Yes, you have been," agreed Winslow cheerfully.

"Well," Carver straightened his fine shoulders, "since our two infants, Ned and Will, think our news is not bad, let's keep it from the generality until we've solved the problem. Let the generality go carefree as long as possible—poor young things! But they should gather on the *Mayflower* each day at noon to learn of our progress and wishes."

All agreed with this and then Martin was sent out to read the list to the congregation.

# XXIV

## *The Pinnace Again*

"In spite of youth and glory," John Carver sighed, "we must discuss moneys for the *Speedwell*. Would Master Weston advance us more, Robert? I think a post might ride to London and back in a month."

"But we *can't* be here a month!" cried Cushman. "We *can't* take the women and children into starving winter on the other side!"

"Let's go without the pinnace," boldly and baldly from Ned Winslow.

"Are you mad?" shouted Carver.

"Come, Ned, this is too much hey nonny no!" objected Robert.

The elder shook his gray head.

Will Bradford said thoughtfully, "Certes! Why not?"

Then no one spoke and Ned wriggled like an embarrassed child.

Cushman ran his fingers through his hair. And again despair touched him coldly. Back of Winslow's half careless suggestion lay something menacing, something that since the shipwright had made his declaration, had leered at him remotely. He tried to thrust it aside and turning to Carver answered his first query.

"As for the Merchant Adventurers, it would require a bolder heart than mine to ask them for help after all that has passed."

Will Bradford cleared his throat. "A long, strong

lever has been put into your hands, Master Cushman.  I
mean the dire needs of the pinnace may force us, you hope,
into signing—"

But here, fortunately, Christopher Martin burst into the
cabin, crying, "Here's John Billington swears he'll be one
of the guests and that ten of his friends must be too!  He's
a little drunk and he swears that he's a free man and that
I must shut myself of my position so's he can be governor!"

"So Billington's backslid!" ejaculated the elder heavily
and as if this were a last straw.  He looked sadly at Carver.

"Put Captain Standish on him," said Cushman
promptly.

"Billington is a knave," remarked Bradford.

Billington strode into the cabin on these words.  He
looked not unhandsome in his heavy sullen way.  He wore
a green doublet and hosen of fine cloth and black stockings
on his massive legs.  He paused beside the table and
shouted, "If you don't treat us better we'll take the business in our own hands."

"Take off your hat in the presence of your betters,"
ordered the elder, his thin lips working.

"Don't excite him!" moaned Chris, edging toward the
door.

"What's troubling you, John?" asked the deacon sooth-
ingly.

"Everything you chiefs do troubles me!  You're jelly,
my beautiful deacon, and yonder villain, he—" pointing at
Robert and trying to form a word which between drunkenness and hate would not come.

"But this is intolerable insolence!"  Winslow rose.
"Put him in stocks."

Robert caught the drunken man's eye.  "Give him a
moment, Ned, and he'll tell us all we want to know!"

"I'll not!" said Billington through his teeth. "It's a secret plot. Only five of us know it. You wait till we get on the high seas. Or mayhap not till we land if the sea is high, rushing over the deck like loads of wool packs. And you'll be the first to go!" thrusting his chin at Cushman.

"I'm flattered!" responded Robert. "I suppose you'll be governor of the colony."

"You'll wonder why you have to call me Excellency—hic —now then, tell me where me and my privy council is to sleep o' nights!"

Captain Standish came in, his very mustache bristling with wrath.

Billington grinned at him. "Hic—hail, my little body-guard! Kiss my hand, varlet, and call me 'Excellency!' "

Robert caught Miles' wrist before he exploded. "Do try to humor him, Captain," he whispered, "till we learn all."

Standish swallowed hard and managed to say with apparent calm, "And what's your will, Excellency?"

"Sh-h!" lurching toward the soldier to say very loudly behind his hand, "Sh-h! I be governor of the colony!"

"Let's go very secretly into a corner of the gun deck and talk about it," Standish suggested.

Billington nodded and permitted the captain to lead him away.

"That villain should be sent back to London at once!" exclaimed Ned. "Master Cushman was right about him."

"Yes, he was!" agreed Will Bradford.

"I think he should be whipped," cried Carver. "But who will undertake the task?"

The elder rose. "This isn't Christian. I grant you that the man seems possessed of a devil. But that only

gives us a greater opportunity to serve God.  I ask you all
—and I never before have asked a favor of you—to leave
him to me.  Don't, indeed, permit him to visit anyone
ashore but let him come each day to me for instruction.
Let me do my utmost to save him.  He can't overthrow
this venture.  No man living can do that.  I will go to
him now.  Only grant me this one favor."

In the face of such pleading even Martin was silenced.
But after Brewster had left the cabin, the governor uttered
a shrill protest.

"Billington ought to be driven at the end of a cart from
here to London and whipped every step of the way.  He
called me a crawling lick-spiggot!"

Robert, Carver and Ned roared, but Will with an interested face said to Martin, "Do you know the Romans
used such epithets and—"

"Nay, Will!" cried Carver with huge enjoyment.  "Don't
contaminate us further!  Our good governor treated this
ribaldry with silent contempt.  You needn't give him
words."

"Silent?  Not I!" exclaimed Martin indignantly.  "I
told him he had a face like a bladder of taffety!"

"Come! this grows unseemly!"  Carver stopped his
laughter.  "After all, this is a council room, not a pudding
house.  We must solve the riddle of the pinnace.  Can we
raise the money out of our private means?  I have six
pounds to which the colony is welcome."

"I have four," said Winslow.  "I will have no more for
a year."

Will added two pounds.  Robert explained that he'd
already given all that he had.  Only Martin was silent.

"Governor," said Cushman very courteously, "you told

me you could set out two ships the size of this. Won't you put in for the common weal?"

"Mind your business, assistant!" snapped Chris. "Do you think I carry my savings in my purse? All I have with me is thirty shillings which I'll lend ye."

"But if we remain a fortnight you could send to Southampton for your savings!" Robert tried to catch Martin's eye but could not.

"I don't know what you're talking about," turning a sickly green.

"You do and yet you don't," Robert said sternly. "What you don't know is that the rest of us are giving to the venture our honor and all our material as well as our spiritual possessions."

"But at Southampton," sneered Chris, "you and Tom Martin said that you, Robert Cushman, was the only Pilgrim possessing honor."

"Isn't it possible," asked Will Bradford, "for us to consult together without this senseless bickering? I despise it. You usually start it, Master Cushman. Surely, the governor knows his own purse better than you do."

"I'm truly sorry to be a troublemaker," sighed Robert. "But I do believe that if Master Martin's accounts were properly examined, it would be discovered he owes the Pilgrims a substantial sum. I had thought to let this matter lie till we reached New England when his responsibilities might have developed a loving heart toward us. But now our need is so dire that I daren't foreslow my suspicions."

"This is a very serious accusation, Robert!" exclaimed the deacon. "What proof have you?"

"I have no proof," answered Robert. "But I shall pursue Governor Martin till he proves me wrong."

"You would have arrested Billington for just such an insulting!" Martin shook his fist at Cushman.

"An arrest and trial would clear this up," nodded Robert.

"I wouldn't stoop so low!" Martin said in a tone of great superiority. "I tell 'ee again, I'll submit my accounts to none. But out of the sheer goodness of my heart and my natural loving-kindness, I will *give* the venture the thirty shillings."

Robert ventured one more shaft. "Reynolds might be induced to help us in this."

Martin turned very white and jumped to his feet. "I'll not remain in the same ship with Master Cushman until he withdraws his vile words!" He stalked out.

"But you should have warned us of your suspicions long ago, Master Cushman!" exclaimed Winslow.

"Warn you! Did I do anything in Hampton but warn you and visit you with objections till I was a hated man?"

"Not hated, Robert," said Carver gently.

Robert's smile was a little bitter. "Even you who *knew* the truth of my fault finding were impatient of my harping on one string."

"If you think there's hope of our getting cash from our pleasing little chapman, let's be about it," cried Ned impatiently.

"Our chief hope lies in getting hold of the list of his expenditures for the Pilgrims—in fact we must have it for the Adventurers' accounts—and comparing it with the moneys I sent him and for which I have his receipt." Robert still managed to speak patiently.

"Have I your permission to try to win these from him?" asked Ned, glancing from one to another.

They all consented.

Will Bradford now said in his deliberate way, "But if we dare not stay here a month for the repair of the pinnace and if she will not be seaworthy without the month's repairs, why this immediate pother about money? As far as Chris Martin's concerned, Robert Cushman was wise enough when he decided to let the governor rest until we reached our destination. Could we hope to exchange the *Speedwell* for a sound ship by adding the moneys we've just raised, and to which the elder will add a few pounds, we know? And I'm certain Isaac Allerton and William Mullins and several others will put in their moiety."

"Don't be too sure of that," remarked Winslow. "They're all feeling screwed to the last farthing. But Will's suggestion is good so far as what we've already raised goes."

All sat thoughtful. Robert, as doubtless did the others, felt hope rising in his heart, even though better than his companions, he knew the difficulty of laying hands on a proper ship.

"Master Jones had better be consulted on this," he suggested.

"We'll trust you to take charge of the matter, Robert!" John Carver smiled at him. "None of us must forget that while others were bungling in Holland in the matter of the *Speedwell*, you were discovering this blessed *Mayflower* for us. I even have faith that yet you'll find the moneys for us."

There was a murmur of approval. Robert felt his eyes smart and he covered his confusion by rising and saying, "I'll show my gratitude by being off at once! It's mid-afternoon already and I don't know where Master Jones may be, so I'll first consult with the shipwright."

Tommy and Mary were watching for him on the half deck, Mary very pretty in a new lace hood.

"This stupid boy says you're taking him into the town this afternoon," she cried. "I want to go with you, Robert, and he'll be such a nuisance!"

Cushman, sharing Tommy's hurt at this rude speech, put his hand on the boy's shoulder. "You may come with us and welcome, Mary, but I'm not sure you'll enjoy yourself. I must see the shipwright and make the round of the Pool, seeking information."

"As to what? Don't be mysterious!" exclaimed Mary.

"About the pinnace," replied Robert. Then he added with a half smile, "You're very cross with Tommy and me and we try so hard to be dutiful!"

Mary looked up into his face and her fine eyes slowly filled with tears. "This renewed touch with England is killing me," she said.

He was moved at once. "Aye! Who should know better than I! I dare not let myself realize that this is England. Will you come with us, Mary? It will be very pleasant, rambling among ships."

"Nay, you two have your junket," she said in a softened voice. "I'll remain with Desire Minter. Don't let your father overdo himself, Tommy." She turned away.

"I don't understand women-folk," remarked Tommy gloomily.

They found Master Hawkes sitting on a rock near the *Speedwell,* marking in his notebook. Tommy walked on to investigate the shipyard and Robert sat down beside Hawkes.

"And what say your friends, my master?" asked the shipwright, vivid dark eyes on the other's sensitive face.

"We wonder if we could exchange the pinnace for a more seaworthy ship, by giving something to boot?"

Robert returned Hawkes' gaze, wondering if those keen eyes were honest.

The shipwright laughed. "I wouldn't exchange a cock-boat for her. She's a sieve! She's old. She'd fall to pieces if I pressed my thumb on her."

"But after she's repaired?"

"Her proper repair would mean a new hull!"

Robert bit his lip.

"Master Reynolds thinks very poorly of your enterprise," said Hawkes conversationally. "And his feeling is to be understood. I'm a Puritan, myself, but I can't say I'd cross the North Atlantic sea merely to show my contempt for the rotten clergy. But we digest our religion in divers ways, thank God! And because we're both Puritans, I offer you two pounds for the pinnace."

"Do you consider that a fair offer?" gasped Robert.

"It's a gift!" retorted Hawkes.

"Thanks, but we pay for what we get!" Robert spoke stiffly. "Two pounds and no pinnace leaves us nowhere. I must continue round the Pool and see if everyone's as ill-disposed to our poor *Speedwell* as you are!"

Hawkes shrugged his shoulders. "And what shall my calkers do tomorrow?"

"Let them go on calking," replied Robert, in desperation. "You'll hear from us in the morning."

"Good day, then!" Again the shipwright shrugged.

Robert called Tommy and they returned to the quay and after an inquiry or two began the search for a vessel. It was a familiar task, this, and had not Hawkes all but convinced him that it was hopeless, he would have enjoyed it keenly. Tommy's pleasure and interest helped keep up his flagging spirits, though, and he faithfully pursued his quest till darkness ended it.

# XXV

## *Truth, Bittersweet*

T HEY found the Carvers and Desire waiting supper
for them in the poop cabin. Never before had the
women-folk been admitted to its sacred portal.

"How did it ever happen?" cried Robert as he and
Tommy entered in response to the deacon's hail.

"Desire asked for the use of it," answered Mary. "I
admit it took courage but the ship was almost deserted
and we are so weary of the great cabin! Master Clarke
gave it to us. He was going ashore in his best clothes and
I think he was sorry for us, remaining on the ship."

"What a boon to eat in quiet and comfort!" sighed
Robert. "Tommy, my lad, sup quickly and be off to bed."

"May I take my supper below, please?" asked Tommy,
always glad to slip away from his stepmother.

They loaded a trencher for him with bread and cheese,
pickled pilchards and beer. Tommy kissed his father and
was off.

"You do spoil him, Robert," complained Mary as the
door closed. "He should have eaten here with proper
manners for once."

"I think he's the prettiest mannered of any child on the
ship," remarked Catherine Carver. "Love and Wrestling
Brewster are as saucy as young parrots. I tell Mary
Brewster often she spares the rod too much."

"Tommy's father won't beat him," Mary went on fret-
fully.

"Nay, *you* beat him if you want it done!" Robert nodded.

"Will you tell us what of the pinnace, Master Cushman?" asked Desire. She was sitting opposite him, between her aunt and uncle, her green gown and her hair both shadowed with bronze in the flickering candlelight. There were curls over her ears, falling to her ruff, and her cheeks were brilliant.

"Master Martin told Marie and me about the meeting this afternoon," said Mary. "He's very insulted with you, Robert. It's such a pity, for you were growing to be friends and Marie was saying kind things about your yellow hair and elegant carriage."

"She's a fool!" exclaimed Robert.

"But tell us of the *Speedwell!*" urged Catherine Carver, as she handed round the cheese.

"The poor pinnace is in very bad odor, I'm afraid," sighed Robert. "Her evil reputation's spread the length of the Pool already!" And he told them of the afternoon's efforts. "They all knew all about her," he added. "The veriest ancient sitting on a bit of wreckage knew she's haunted and that's a far more serious ailment than her unseaworthiness. And the whole Poolside has heard that Reynolds considers her an unlucky ship. He and his men must have been very busy talking, today!"

"Plymouth is a small place," suggested Desire, "and for all her knowledge of ships, ours is a strange errand, as Master Hawkes told you. You didn't see Master Reynolds?"

"Nay, I was very weary and I had nothing new to say to him," replied Robert.

The little group continued with supper but in a troubled way.

The harbor was very quiet and the *Mayflower* quite motionless. From below came the murmur of voices and the 'tween-decks lads were singing themselves to sleep with nursery rhymes:

> "Hush-a-bye, baby, on the tree top,
> When the wind blows, the cradle will rock—"

Suddenly Desire thrust her trencher aside and looking at Robert said, "Why not take Edward Winslow's suggestion and leave the pinnace behind, going alone with the *Mayflower?*"

Robert stiffened. "Do you realize what you're saying?"

"Certainly, I do," she answered. "I was thinking that if Master Jones would spare us half of this huge poop cabin and if we could build a few more cabinets 'tween decks we could accommodate everybody on the *Mayflower.*"

"And end all the pother!" nodded Catherine. "The knavish little ship has cost us over two weeks' time now."

"You women don't understand," said John Carver. "If we got into too serious trouble in New England, and the *Mayflower* had left us, we could come home again in the pinnace—some of us—for help. This, besides her usefulness as a trading boat. If we have no pinnace, we shall be cut off from Europe completely."

"We shall be anyway," remarked Mary Cushman, pushing restlessly back from the table.

"And the *Speedwell* is ruining us," added Desire. Then, her dark eyes suddenly anxious, she exclaimed, "You're *very* tired, Master Cushman!"

"Too tired to argue with anyone about the *Speedwell!*" admitted Robert. "The only hope I have now is to find more money, by a miracle, and buy us another pinnace."

"Do you hope, then, to get something substantial from

Christopher Martin?" asked Catherine, her round face very anxious.

Robert rubbed his head. He was literally too weary to think.

John Carver who had been watching him, now rose, saying in a light tone which still was peremptory, "Put him to bed, Mary. We let him work too hard, mayhap."

"Mayhap!" ejaculated Desire. "You're *killing* him with frets and burdens!"

"Good lack!" laughed Mary. "She'll be having us arrested for murder!"

They all started for the door, save Cushman. "I can't sleep," he told them, "until I've consulted with Master Jones. I'll just lie here on a locker and rest and wait. Do you go off like good friends and let me have my way."

"Come!" John nodded. "Once a year it's wise to let a married man have his way. It gives him back his self-conceit. And Robert's feathers have been drooping for weeks!" He marshaled the three women out.

Robert stretched himself on the stern locker. A little breeze was wandering in at the window carrying a smell of the land with it. Of Devon! . . . A sweep of red cliffs crowned with green—sheep feeding—a blue sea—the cuckoo —the lark—sentinel foxgloves— The moments passed.

A dear voice spoke from the doorway. "Robert, may I come in?"

He looked at her, convinced that he was asleep. He remained motionless, lest he waken himself.

Desire crossed the room to seat herself in the master's chair, near the locker. Robert put out his hand and touched her knee. Then he swung his feet to the floor. "It's really you!" he exclaimed, suddenly more widely awake than ever he'd been in his life.

Her white teeth flashed, then she was very serious. "Mary and I've been talking this quarter hour. And I made up my mind that though it blast my reputation, I was coming to speak to you while I could find you actually alone. I have left the door open and the second mate says he'll see we are not interrupted."

Robert smiled. "What is it, Desire?"

"I want you not to pursue the Christopher Martin matter further. It can only bring trouble and humiliation to you."

"What do you mean?" exclaimed Robert.

She swallowed and moistened her lips. "Mary told Martin, today, that you and Tom Weston had boughten a forty ton fishing boat which would go next year to fish in New England waters. She said she couldn't see why you didn't substitute that for the pinnace."

"That's a lie," said Robert through his teeth.

"What made her tell it?" asked Desire quickly.

"I don't know!" He sat scowling and puzzled.

"Do you mind if I say—you won't think me too indelicate—" She flushed painfully.

"For God's sake, say what you please! If you only knew how rare and bittersweet truth sounds in my ears!"

"Well then," Desire spoke slowly, "I notice that when Mary departs from the truth it's always to win her way about something. Can you think of anything this lie would win Mary?"

He shook his head dejectedly. "Why she told it is less important now than that she be made to tell Martin that it is a lie."

"She'll never do that and if you push the money suspicion with Chris Martin, he'll spread her story abroad, if he hasn't already." She was looking at him with such sympathy in her great eyes that in his heart he blessed her.

But he spoke harshly. "You mean I must make a vile bargain with Martin as if I were a cheating knave like himself?"

"Oh!" she burst forth, "how can you say that to me?" Then she paused. "But I suppose that's what it amounts to. I didn't think! Forgive me, Robert! But tell me, tell me, what can you do?"

"Make Mary confess to Martin. Yet, no, that won't do. She'll know you've told me."

Desire straightened her shoulder. "You may tell her I told! I can pacify Mary, never fear! In fact, I tried to make her come to you now to face you with your sly dealing," with a little grimace, "but she was very angry and went off to bed. I didn't try to pacify her then for I was angry, myself."

"You mean Mary knows you've come up to me with this?" he asked incredulously.

"She must guess it, though I didn't *say* I was coming alone," nodded Desire.

"You are a most gallant friend!" he ejaculated. "How can I repay you?"

"You can put me in *your* debt by talking to Mary of this in my presence. I think I can help her. She will be troubled and I do love her."

"Nay, we're best alone. I shall say nothing tonight, nor till I'm less angry." He spoke as firmly as he felt.

Desire sighed. "Well, my errand's done!" She rose and moved toward the door, then paused to look back at him as he stood erect by the locker. During the instant that their gaze held, she moved to lean with both hands on the table. Lovely shadows from the lanthorn played on her face.

"I can't bear it!" she murmured.  "You are so alone."

He held himself in leash.  "We're all alone, aren't we?" he asked.

"None in this ship as much as you," she insisted, her voice very deep and soft.  "I can't bear it.  I am your very friend so I see you as you are but I must say nothing, do nothing, share with you nothing of all that fills my heart. Robert, it is a heavy trouble for me."

He kept his hand rigid at his side.  "Desire," he pleaded, "tell me a little of what fills your heart!  Something that will give me a staff to go on with!"

Her face worked.  "I can't!" she said brokenly and again turned to the door.

"Stop!" he whispered but he did not move from his place.

She looked at him over her shoulder, hesitated, returned to the table and there were unheeded tears on her cheeks.

"I can tell you all that's in *my* heart," he whispered, "in three words.  I love you."

Waves splashed lightly against the *Mayflower*.  The night wind brought the fields in at the window.  Desire gave a long sigh, once more turned and without again looking back, walked out of the cabin.

Robert dropped to the locker, buried his face in his hands and let his world tumble about his head.

After a time, the weight above his heart oppressed him and he lay down.  But this time, no merciful unconsciousness gave him surcease from either mental or physical pain.  He was acutely alive.

So—he had made this friendship impossible!  Nothing else mattered, not the pinnace, not Reynolds, not Chris Martin, not Mary's lie, not the whole Pilgrim venture.

In all his life he had had only England and Desire and he had deprived himself of both.

The Puritan in him whispered that he had sinned and was being punished for his sin. He had assured himself that so long as his was an untold love, it was not sinful. Perhaps he had been correct in this. But now the Puritan told him that as soon as he confessed to Desire—a married man professing love to a maiden—he sinned and very deep.

But there was a man in him who was not Puritan, a man who found in Philip Sidney an ideal and in Sidney's unfulfilled love for Stella the uttermost height of passion and beauty. This man did not judge his love from the theological standpoint. Was his love beautiful, was it pure, was it of delicate texture, was it the sole and supreme passion of his manhood, did it find expression in thoughts and deeds that were good, even noble, and always lovely? These were the questions Robert's other man asked and to all these the answer was Yes!

Yet this man said, also, that never should he have confessed to Desire. Not that this was either moral or immoral, but because it was not kind. Desire was no Stella bred in Elizabeth's school of love. She was not a Pilgrim, either, but her lines had fallen in the Pilgrim place and she must live by Pilgrim standards. So he had made their friendship impossible.

He started to his feet. Bah! It had been impossible from the beginning; a hole and corner relationship which belittled something which should have been open and comely and admired by all. It was as well that he had killed it.

He fell to pacing the floor.

At one o'clock, he realized how weary he was and leaned

his aching head against the window while he gazed at Plymouth, asleep on her little hills. Beyond and beyond and beyond lay "this England, this blessed spot—this earth —this realm—this happy breed of men" such as his own fathers, who had tilled their acres and begot their sons. They were the stones which formed the moat defensive to the house of England.

He, Robert, was the first of their line to leave. Did England's sons weaken the moat defensive when they departed forever from her house? Or would they always be sons though building other houses? Romans had always been Romans even when Rome straddled the world. But Rome had fallen. What was he doing for England with his beloved colony?

Smell of harvest fields. The lap, lap of little waves.

Oh, Desire! Desire! Desire!

# XXVI

## *The Family of Lies*

Eventually Robert fell asleep on the locker and did not waken until he heard Master Jones order Jem to produce his Monmouth cap. It was morning. A delicate fog shimmered in the window. It would be a fine day.

Then he remembered everything!

But after all, he was reckoned a man and not a puling child! He summoned all that was in him of will power and rose with a smile for his friend.

Master Jones was tying the points of his familiar purple doublet. "How now, Master Cushman! You were waiting for me overlong, I'm afraid!" This, with his broad honest grin.

"I'm sorry to have cozened you out of your bed, Master!"

Jones gave him a sudden keen look. "You are well?"

"Very well, thanks, though needing to wash and comb myself. I was wanting to ask your advice."

Jones pushed a tankard toward Robert and took one himself. "I've already seen Mistress Minter," he observed. "She told me of the proposal to find a new pinnace and of your discouragement in the matter. It's a good motion. I'll see what I can discover for you, today, though I tell you, now, I'm not over hopeful. There's a fearsome dearth of little ships and as you have found, prices are very high. Sir Richard Hawkins' enterprise has put the cap on everything here. This was what you waited to speak to me?"

Robert nodded and cooled his aching throat with the ale.

The seaman gave him another keen look. "You are very down in the mouth, eh? Be a philosopher, sir. You are the best man of the sixscore and you've given them your best. The Almighty knows that and so does Christopher Jones, if they don't!"

"Master Jones," Robert put his hand on the other's huge shoulder, "if God judges a man by his secret thoughts, by his mind's advances and retreats, alarums and excursions, I'm the most cowardly, the most boneless poor thing in the *Mayflower's* whole company."

"Mayhap God does judge so," nodded Jones, "but I'm only a man! Yet I'm no blind fool and I find ye gallant. Now for the sake of Judas priest, get out and let me write a letter to my wife and babe!"

Robert went below and what with the master's sympathy, the ale, a wash and a shave, he emerged from the steerage a half hour later, his own man.

John Carver was still a-bed. Tommy said his stepmother had gone to walk on the sands soon after sunrise. She had refused to let him go with her. She had said the Martins were meeting her later and they were going to take her to see Master Fallon's gardens.

Robert left a note for Carver and went ashore to find Mary. If she were not on the sands, he would follow to the Fallons' house. But she was on a quiet bit of beach, near the Hoe, searching for sea-shells. As he approached, she stood up, her hands full of delicate sea-treasures, her lovely eyes defiant.

"I suppose that hussy did tell you! I can see by your

holier-than-thou expression." Mary's opening words were not encouraging.

"She had to tell me for all our sakes," he returned. "It was a particularly harmful lie, Mary. Come over to this ledge of rock and let's get to the bottom of the story."

"It's not a lie," she shrieked. "You did make plans with Tom Weston! I heard you. The name of the ship was the *Sparrow*."

"The Merchant Adventurers were going to send the *Sparrow* next year with provisions for us," explained Cushman. "But I had naught to do with it, either with moneys or profit. I suppose the *Sparrow* won't go now, because we are at outs with the Adventurers. You knew that, Mary. Why did you twist the facts? Did you want to rouse the people against me again?"

"Yes, just enough so they'd throw you out and you'd have to stay in England!" She rushed from him to throw herself down on the ledge of rock and bury her face in her hands.

There was no one on the beach so early. He let her weep for a few minutes. It was a so familiar formula; crimination and recrimination, defiance, tears and sometimes confession but more often sullen denial till he was worn out and dropped the matter. Only this time, he must persist.

"But what a childish scheme!" he said, at last. "Not worthy even of Tommy. This lie thrusts you into the men's business, into the men's world and it's a hard, tearless world. You have got to tell the two Martins that you've lied."

"No! No! You've got to stay in England! I can't go, I can't!" Her face was hidden in her red cloak.

For a moment he was tempted to bribe her; to tell her

that if she would clear up the falsehood she could go back to Canterbury. But for the sake of her immortal soul and his own he durst not.

"You don't understand," she wailed. "You're so cold, so sure, you can't understand an ordinary sinful human being like me! I'm *too* homesick, I tell you! People do die of it. I shall die of it."

What if he told her that he did understand and that his heart ached in sympathy? Nay, that would be to shame her. She must keep her tragic secret as he kept his. But she must be made to confess the lie to the wretched Martins.

"Many times, lately," he said, "I've felt there were worse things than death. To live with one's honor besmirched by a wife's lie is worse than death to a man."

She gave a great gasp and ceased to sob, though she kept her face buried. Robert sat down beside her.

The tide was rising. Ships were loosing their sails. The sea! The sea! It owned men, body and soul. He drew a deep breath and felt its mordant savor bite into his lungs. The infinite deep, Mary's lie, Robert's heartache, in the long, long end, the deep would have them all.

"Mary! Mary!" he pleaded. "You were going to be through hurting me with falsehoods. You've been so different in the week since we left Dartmouth that I thought we were growing toward friendship. Let's cut this sore out quickly and rejoin the edges! Mary!" He touched her shoulder.

"How can you ask me to shame myself before the Martins?" she demanded. "And what of that jade, Desire? And what of her going to the poop cabin at midnight to be alone with you?"

Little red motes danced before Robert's eyes. He pulled

the red cloak away and taking Mary's face between his palms, forced her to look at him. She turned so pale she might have been fainting.

"If you dare," he said with deadly quiet, "if you dare to breathe a word that shall cast the remotest doubt on the purpose of Desire's visit to me, I shall whip you as I would a wicked child." He moistened his lips. "You and I," his voice husky, "are not fit to speak her name. Do you understand me, Mary?"

She did not answer. He kept his palms firmly on her cheeks and went on. "I have endured with what patience I could, your false tongue when it confined its nastiness to me, but when you couple Desire's name to mine—guard yourself, Mary!"

Still she did not speak and it dawned on him that she was too frightened to do so. He freed her and said gently, "What is your reply?"

"I will never mention her visit," she whispered, watching him with eyes that were still dilated with terror.

"What of the other matter?" he insisted.

She turned her head away. He rose so that he could stoop over her and still peer into her eyes. She shrank as though he had struck her, though never in her life had she had aught but gentleness from him. The gesture added to his fury and yet in his fury, he could have wept over her— Mary, so unhappy—so weak—so unfit to cope with her secret—

"What of the other matter?" he repeated harshly.

"I'll tell them!" she muttered. Then, with a sudden return of color to her face, "There they are now, thank heaven!" And she slipped past him and ran up the path to the approaching Martins.

Robert followed rapidly.   Mary threw herself on Marie's great bulwark of a bosom and Chris patted her shoulder.

"What's this!   What's this!" spluttered the governor. "Can't you quarrel with your wife without frightening her to death!   Now Marie and I fight by the hour but I wouldn't think of frightening her.   That's not gallant, my good assistant."

"I'll admit to the lack of chivalry," returned Cushman heavily.   "Come over here to this rocky shelf and I'll tell you why, unless Mistress Cushman will."

Mary withdrew her tall self from Marie's arms and the three followed Robert.   They seated themselves on the ledge with Cushman standing before them, he thought, like a birch-wielding schoolmaster.   He hated the part.

"Prithee, tell them, Mary," he said.

"No, Robert, you tell them," she implored.

He bit his lip but wasted no time.   "My wife reported to you that Master Weston and I had bought the *Sparrow* for our private profit, next year.   This is entirely false. I have not had nor do I plan to have aught to do with that enterprise.   I had no wish and no money.   Mary, I have told this truly?"

"Yes," she replied faintly.

"Have you scared her into admitting she lied when she didn't?" demanded Marie, her lower lip stuck out.

Robert turned to Chris.   "You know me well now, governor.   What do you think, yourself, of my wife's story?"

"If you hadn't told that pack of nonsense about me yesterday," answered little Martin in an aggrieved voice, "I'd have told Mistress Cushman she was silly.   But if you are mean enough to say that about me, you're mean enough to make your wife a liar and your scapegoat."

"My wife a scapegoat!" cried Robert.   "My poor wife

whom I know to be half ill with her own griefs! Now just what sort of a man would I be to use her for a scapegoat? The sort you've met in me?"

Marie was studying Robert as though she saw him for the first time. He was holding his hat under his arm. The early sun was on his hair. His blue eyes in which the past few weeks had written something Marie could feel while she could not read it, were fastened on Mary.

Marie said, abruptly, "I'll not forget to my dying day, how of all the people on the ship, you were the only one who ran to save my goodman's life."

His life never had been in danger, thought Robert, but let Marie think so if it could help in this crisis!

She went on, "And you made them all call him governor and you give him due honor yourself. Now will you tell me why you dishonored him, yesterday?"

"Because I suspect that you and he made profit out of the buying of our provisions. We are now in dire straits for money." Robert let them have it, straitly.

"Did Reynolds first give you that idea?" demanded Chris.

"Why do you think so?" returned Cushman.

"Because Reynolds bought butter at fifty pounds the firkin and tried to sell it to me for the Pilgrims at sixty pounds. And I told him he was a swilling pirate. And he said if I told on him, he'd tell that once he'd seen me in stocks in Billerica which I was but for an unjust cause and I'll never tell 'ee what it was because it makes me weep for shame whenever I think on't."

"But if your accounts are honest, why not let me or someone else examine them?" pursued Robert.

Chris hesitated and glanced at Marie.

"Go on," she ordered him, "or I will. I'm sick of the trouble over it."

"The truth is," stuttered the governor, his stomach sagging, "the er—truth is that I'm something unlettered and so is my goodwife and I've always kept my business in my head with Marie helping with her head and so we haven't got any accounts! And in Southampton we hired a scholarly man to take down all we conjointly remembered but it didn't make sense. And—and—!" He drew a deep breath, his sallow face turned orange and he fairly roared the rest,

"We don't know whether we owe the Pilgrims or the Pilgrims owe us. I drew all I had from the counting house in Southampton and I put that in but still we couldn't clear the muddy waters. All I know is that everything's gone, the moneys you gave me, and mine own moneys! Now this is truth, whether you believe it or not."

Robert knew it was truth. He gazed at the two Martins in utter consternation. His last hope for raising immediate cash was gone.

"You don't believe him?" shrilled Marie.

"Alas, yes! I know we've got truth at last," groaned Robert. Abruptly he sat down beside the fat woman and put his hand on hers. She was something solid to touch even if she was a money-fool. "But how horrible a truth! What is to become of us?"

Martin had a queer little smile on his lean face. "Ye hoped we were cozening knaves!"

Robert returned the smile in kind. "It seems I did! Governor, what shall we do? I'm pooped, completely, by this final great following wave!"

There was a disconsolate pause. Mary, sitting between

Marie and Chris, spoke first. "But at any rate, a whole family of lies has been cleared up!"

"Two families!" Marie reminded her.

"But that doesn't make a new pinnace," moaned the governor. "You being women can't see how that kills our best hopes."

"I suppose we'll have to explain all to the other chiefs!" Marie shuddered.

"I'll do it, very gently, for you if you ask me to," suggested Cushman.

The two nodded.

Robert went on, "And is all clear between us as to my having no share in the *Sparrow?*"

"I told Chris, last night, that that was just one of Mistress Mary's fables," explained Marie.

Mary started to speak, blushed and was silent.

"We shall have to come to a decision quickly about the pinnace," said Robert. "We will gather at noon, on the *Mayflower*. And if you'll be a little tardy arriving, I'll make my little explanation to the others before you get there." He got to his feet.

"Where are you going?" Mary asked him.

He rubbed his aching head. "I suppose to the shipyard."

"Nay, Robert, go out to the ship and sleep until noon. You do look so tired!" Mary's voice was almost affectionate.

He looked at her. "Well," he said hesitatingly, "perhaps I ought to. I lack sleep."

"There!" remarked Marie. "That's one of the pleasures of quarreling with your spouse. You know you're always going to make it up!"

# XXVII

## *The Deserters*

ROBERT slept for several hours, then went to the meeting. They sat out on the poop deck for the day was exquisite and Robert told Martin's tale.

The other four were still silently turning it over in their minds, when Brewster cleared his throat and delivered judgment. "Thanks be to the all just God! We suspected Christopher Martin of being a thief. Now we know that he's only been ignorant and silly. Praise God, I say!"

"And I will ask forgiveness for my heavy share in the suspicions," said Robert. "But this doesn't lessen our anxiety about the pinnace."

"What a fool he's been!" exclaimed Bradford. "The brainless ass might just as well have been a villain! The result's the same for us!"

"But not the same for his immortal soul!" The elder's voice was stern.

"But it is for our mortal bodies!" grunted John Carver. "It looks as if *they* were destined to starve. Martin should be punished," his big voice rising angrily.

"So say I!" cried Ned Winslow. "The strutting little braggart! Think what we've all put up with from him! In my estimation one might as well be a fool as a knave. Our poor moneys! It seems we must go into the wilderness almost as naked as we came into the world!"

"It's no use locking backward on Martin's beetle-headedness," Robert sighed. "A year in the stocks wouldn't bring back what he's squandered. What of the pinnace?"

"Yesterday, you didn't think my idea worth a reply, that we set out without a consort," said Ned. "Today sings so different a tune that perchance you'll consider it."

His companions looked at him heavily. Will Bradford said, looking toward the barbican, "Yonder comes Master Jones. Perhaps he's found us a new ship!"

"But give me the courtesy of a comment, at least," urged Ned, jumping from his perch on the taffrail to lay his hand on Bradford's arm.

Bradford looked at the elder. Brewster said, "Wait for Master Jones' report. Anyway, we couldn't decide so weighty a matter among us chiefs. We'd have to lay it before all the people."

"And then guide them to abide by *our* decision," remarked Will, his drooping eyelids lifted briefly as he watched the effect of his comment on John Carver, for the two seldom agreed. "The perfect democracy will never exist. The best minds will always rule the lesser."

"Best minds! Like Chris Martin's, I suppose!" began the deacon.

"Hush!" Brewster raised his hand. "Here comes the governor with Master Jones!"

And so it was. The master was bringing Chris and Marie and Mary Cushman back with him. The two men came at once to the poop, Martin dragging his feet like an unhappy schoolboy. The elder rose to meet him and putting his hand on the governor's shoulder looked down on the little man from his great height with a very gentle, humble expression on his long face.

"We all seek your forgiveness, Governor," he said.

"But—but—I've wasted our moneys! You understand that?" mumbled Chris.

"Yes, you've been weak and silly but you haven't been a thief which is what we all feared! Sit down and let's be at work."

Martin wiped his eyes and nose on his sleeve and seated himself on the deck beside Robert, crying softly like a little lad who's been badly frightened. While he was gathering himself together, Carver explained the cause of this display of grief to Jones.

That philosopher scratched his red head and blurted out, "It's just as well then that I've been able to find nothing for you at less than a hundred pounds including the *Speedwell's* self."

"Come! Let's be sailing! We'll build us a fishing boat when we reach New England," cried Ned.

"There's not a shipwright in our company," Carver reminded him. "Thomas Weston was to try to find us one. Their wages are so high in England that the wilderness has no enticement for them."

"Will Weston continue his search, think you?" Ned asked Robert.

"You know his mood when he left Hampton," Cushman replied with a shrug of his shoulders.

"If only *you* could talk to him now!" sighed the young man. "What fools we've been!"

"Come, don't dream the undoable!" boomed Jones. "Make up your minds to let the pinnace go. Weed out Billington and his breed and the weaklings and complainers and that will leave room for all on our faithful *Mayflower* and food for all. Then up anchor and away!"

"How shall we fish and trade in America?" asked Robert.

"Our melancholy Jacques, as usual!" groaned Ned. "You must risk greatly if you'd gain greatly, in this life. We must continue westward! Can you think of returning to London, tail between our legs, beaten by the coward knave, Reynolds?"

"So your vote, Ned, is toward the setting sun!" nodded the elder with a sudden smile. "And yours, Will?"

"I'm with Ned," squaring the good shoulders under the brown doublet. "After my week on the *Speedwell*, I declare she deserves to be abandoned! Perhaps though we can sell her for something."

"Not in Plymouth!" from Jones who was leaning on the taffrail and looking from one man to the other as though comparing their worth. "You might back in the Thames where her reputation is still good."

"What do you say, John?" Brewster looked at his friend who was sitting on the deck, gazing with sad pleasure at his handsome legs stretched at length before him.

Carver lifted his splendid head and said clearly, "I say the pinnace has been Satan from the beginning; that we're well rid of her and Reynolds; that God will enable."

"Governor Martin?" nodding at Chris whose chest was up again and whose eyes, though red, were very determined.

"I say I know how Master Cushman feels. There are women and babes dependent on us and as Master Bradford once said, we must fear the grim and grisly face of hunger coming on us like an armed man. And it's piteous to see your babies starve. Most of the people we have with us have stared once and again at starvation's bony skull. If we tell 'em to give up the pinnace they'll remember what hunger is and be afeared. So we must decide for them, which is to leave the *Speedwell* and sail at once."

"And a lion-hearted speech that is, my good Chris!" cried Carver.

"Robert?" asked William Brewster.

All eyes turned on Cushman with anxious interest.

"I don't think this is a matter for debate," he replied. "We *must* plant our colony in America! Clearly as my better judgment tells me we're foolhardy to go without our consort, I'd as soon give up life itself as not continue our voyage. We have no option, my friends. God wills the *Mayflower* and us to America."

"Thank the Almighty!" cried Brewster.

Everyone was motionless, moved beyond words by the portentousness of their decision.

A little string of boats was putting off from the shore. The people were returning for the noon meeting. Gayly on the breeze came their chorus:

> "When the winds blow
> And the seas flow,
> Hey nonny no!"

"And that's the way they'll take it!" cried Ned. "With carefree zest!"

But again Winslow was wrong in his judgment.

The people, when they had gathered in the ship's waist, received the pronouncement from the half deck with a fury of resentment. A hubbub of imprecations drowned every effort of the elder to call them to order. They denounced Reynolds, the pinnace and those in Leyden who had bought the pinnace. They denounced the chiefs for their ill management. And Brewster finally let them have their way.

It was Billington's mighty roar that finally brought a modicum of silence. "We can't all pack into the *May-*

*flower!* Who's going to stay behind? Not me or mine!"

"Don't let that worrit nobody!" called one of the young married men. "We can pack us all in. I've only got my goodwife and myself and my baby. We can take a couple of children to sleep at our feet."

"Well, anybody can have my place that wants it," sneered one of Billington's friends, a thin man with a harelip. "This here voyage is without head nor tail. Nobody knows nothing about nothing. And now they've secured it so we'll starve in America and if we don't starve, we'll make no money, for we can't trade nor fish."

"Very well, Jacob!" called Robert Cushman. "I'll write you down first of those to go back." He took out his notebook.

A woman screamed, "But, Jacob, I'm not going back to starve in London! I'm going to have a new chance. That's how Master Weston says it'll be."

"Shut your gab, wench!" snarled Jacob.

A woman who had been on the *Speedwell* from the very first cried, "I'll go back. I'll return to London in the plague and thankful after the pinnace. And so will my man! He's often wished for the chance."

"Do you agree, Saul?" demanded Cushman.

"And thankful I be!" agreed Saul.

The people were silent now.

"We'll go back," said a young farm laborer stolidly, though his face was red. "This is a fool's work, run by fools."

"Shame!" exclaimed Marie Martin.

"Shut your mouth, ye common scold!" snapped the laborer.

"Write us down, too, in your Doomsday Book," called another man.

"And back I goes too!" a woman from Billerica.

And then a little panic swept the people. Ten, twelve, fifteen names, Robert wrote down with an increasing sense of apprehension. Were only the thirty-five from Leyden to remain steadfast? Nay, even two of these were deserting!

The elder and the deacon were consulting anxiously together. Winslow was standing by the mizzenmast, his eyes dancing with excitement but evidently confused and a little alarmed. Will Bradford had joined Dorothy on the main deck. It was a moment of such fear and doubt as had not visited the Pilgrims before.

"It's ruin, deep ruin," whispered Martin to Cushman. "I doubt if even the elder can halt them. There won't be a score left if something isn't done." He was panting as if he'd been running.

And then another woman took up the cry of "Shame! Shame!" It was Desire. "Shame, you Pilgrim men!" she cried. By its sheer beauty, her voice got their attention. She was standing with Mary Cushman by the longboat and they turned to look at her. She tossed her head.

"Men! At least fifteen *men* have turned cowards this day but only two women. Well, go back to your safe hiding places, brothers! We, your sisters, are going to the new world with the true men of the venture. Aren't we, Priscilla Mullins and Humility Cooper and Marie Martin? We're going with as high hearts as ever sent great Raleigh over the ocean-sea! Get back behind the skirts of discretion and safety, brothers! As for us, we prefer the folly of the high waves and the wilderness."

Chin in air, violet eyes blazing, she paused. The women clapped their hands and crowded about her.

Ned Winslow took off his hat and waved it. "Good-by,

old *Speedwell*. We've broken your evil spell. It's up anchor and away now. That is"—with a glance of mock alarm at Desire and her group—"if the women-folk will permit us to go on *their* ship."

There was a ripple of amusement.

"She's right!" cried Tom Tinker. "We've talked over-much about danger. Why, who cares for danger? We've lived for years in the shadow of the jail and the ax! We can share our beds, turn and turn about, if we'll sleep in watches like the sailors!"

"Right, old Tom!"

"So we can!"

"Just so we're careful to make the proper shifts!" This from Bob Carter. "I'd weep to find a damsel oversleeping into my watch a-bed."

"Shame!" and much laughter.

"Tell them," whispered Cushman to Martin, "that we'll let them know shortly about getting those who are leaving, back to London."

The governor shook his head. "I want no more Billington! You do it!"

Robert complied but the people gave him only a glance. They were talking excitedly among themselves.

Jones, who had been leaning against the cabin all this time, watching with keen eyes and an out-thrust jaw, now said to Robert, "You'd better go clear up matters with Reynolds. I saw him this morning. He's had a mighty spree, is over it and says he's going to force a settlement from you all, today. I was to tell you, you'd find him aboard the pinnace. And take Mistress Minter with you! As I've said before, she's the best chief among you."

Robert followed his nod. Desire was laughing up into Giles Heale's face.

"That boy's no fit mate for her," grumbled the master, "except for his comeliness!"

Robert rumpled his hair. The other four now joined them. "What of that list of names?" asked the deacon.

"All it lacks is Billington," replied Cushman. "Just the purging we needed, this."

"Not Billington," said Brewster quietly.

"If ye have the sense of ducks in a pond," Jones spoke with great earnestness, "you'll send Billington and his spawn back if ye have to manacle 'em."

"No!" Brewster's voice was of an unalterable obstinacy. "No!"

Jones shrugged his shoulders. "Ye'll live to regret it!" He went into his cabin.

Robert set off for the *Speedwell*.

Reynolds, sitting on the poop, saw Robert on the sands and waved a hand at him. Then with a fat man's agility, he dropped over the ship's side.

"The noise of the calkers is not to be endured," he said as Robert came up. "Let us go to the Admiral where we can talk in comfort." He spoke with all the assurance of an untroubled conscience.

"Since it's bound to be an uncomfortable interview," returned Robert dryly, "we may as well be comfortable during its course," and they started across the shipyard.

Reynolds, on reaching the Admiral, asked the landlord for the use of the little parlor, off the barroom. This was scarcely larger than a cupboard, with a stone floor, ceiling beamed with old spars and a tiny mullioned window which gave on the stable yard. They ordered ale and when he had put a dripping jug with pewter tankards on the table, the landlord opened the window and went out, closing the door after him.

"Well, Master Reynolds," said Robert, "you've achieved your purpose! We go to America untended by a consort."

"I had no such purpose, Master Cushman." The fat seaman's voice was airy. His little eyes and his long nose, which so contradicted his huge good-natured cheeks, were turned up to the ceiling as if asking heaven to endorse his innocency.

"Look you," Cushman leaned on the table and spoke in a leisurely manner, "look you, Master Reynolds. I know you well now. You are a cozening coward. And because you are that, you've all but wrecked a venture of such pith as you're unable to understand. You're not only a cheat and a coward but you're an ingrate and that's worst of all. No, don't bother to draw your dagger! I'm not afraid of your dagger any more than I am of the ghost by which you gave your ship a bad name. I have been afraid of your villainy but no more. That's a bill which has been rendered and recognized and need not be feared. Only paid."

Reynolds breathed deep through his nose, then sat back on his stool gazing at Cushman from under his eyebrows.

"You mentioned," he drawled, "that I'm ungrateful."

"Yes, to Pastor Robinson and those kind fools in Leyden who put you on your feet, gave you a share in the pinnace and set you over her because they so trusted you."

"And then tried to starve me," snapped the master, flinging his hat to the floor and slapping the table in approved bravo manner.

"Don't say *starve* again. I'm cloyed with the word!" Robert ignored the gesture. "And let's have no more chatter. I know what you think of us and you know what we think of you. My advice is that you keep away from our angry young men and make your way back to London with whatever speed you find suits you."

The sailor bit his lip, glared at Cushman, met an amused glance which turned him purple, then said in a very mild voice, "I'll leave as soon as you pay me my moneys."

"And I'll pay you your moneys," returned Robert promptly, "when you pay us the price of the pinnace you ruined."

They sat and stared at each other. Curious, Robert thought, that he couldn't hate the scoundrel.

Beyond Reynolds' small head, he saw three musicians file under the archway into the stable yard. They were mere ragged boys in dirty gray fustian but two of them carried lutes and the third began to sing very sweetly to their accompaniment. It was that most popular air, "Hey nonny no!"

"You know that never will I pay," said Reynolds, "and for two reasons. You have no cause and I have no money."

"I could prove my cause in court!" Robert lifted his tankard to his lips. The day was taking its toll of him. He had the familiar sensation of parched tongue and vaguely aching bones. The ale was delicious in his tired throat.

"But you'll be in America," grinned the other, "unless you're among those who elect to stay behind as three several have told me they shall."

"Fifteen men have so elected, to be exact," nodded Robert.

Reynolds got up from his stool and with a single stride crossed the tiny room to the fireplace where he stood warming his enormous seat at an imaginary fire.

"Master Cushman," as he took his silver toothpick from his ear, "you've said some harsh words to me. Has it occurred to you that I've curbed myself beyond what any Christian would be expected to do? I've done you all a many secret kindness. There was Captain Nutt. He was all hoysed about Mistress Minter and ready to steal her from the *Mayflower* as soon as she left the English Channel. But I beguiled him off."

"Did you, indeed!" Robert smiled dryly. "A liar is always a fool."

"You don't believe me!" loudly.

"You forget that Mistress Minter and I had an hour of Captain Nutt's society before he sailed from Dartmouth."

The lads still made their pretty music without the window. It was piercing sweet. Robert thought, "Never again will I hear minstrels—only the wild noises of savages and waters—"

Reynolds tried another tack. "Well then, jibes aside, Master Cushman, this is what I would suggest for the salvation of your venture. The Pilgrims must go to America, it seems, without proper means of support. The only people who can help them are those to whom they owe money. The only man in all the Pilgrim crowd who could get the Adventurers to equip a ship forthrightly and send it to keep alive their poor mad debtors, is yourself. If you really wish to plant your colony, if you really wish to keep your people from famine, go up to London, yourself, and remain there at anchor to the windward for your Bedlamites."

"How dare you suggest such a thing?" demanded Robert, angry now.

"Softly! Softly!" urged Reynolds. "This idea is gathering weight in my brain! Have them calk the *Speedwell* but let be the rest. I can work the old tub back up to the Thames with your deserters between decks and

you, sir, in the great cabin with me.  Let the *Mayflower*
proceed to America.  At Deptford, you can easily sell the
pinnace, or I can for you, pay me up and then devote your
great skill to procuring proper supplies and support for
the colony."

"Never!" repeated Robert.

"Think it over, sir!" implored Reynolds, an unusual
note of sincerity in his raucous voice.  "Your decision
means the difference between success and failure to your
people."

Robert forgot that he despised this seaman.  He only
felt that curious liking, as if he were arguing with a friend.
He said, "Laying aside my lifelong eagerness to do such
a work as this for England, laying aside my craving for
the sea and ships which only this voyage can allay, there
still remains the greatest necessity of all.  It is incumbent
on my personal honor to see that they repay the Merchant
Adventurers."

"But it's only from London that means can be got to
fill their bellies so they can work and so repay.  And that
requires a proper ship.  And no one will send the proper
ship unless it be you and Master Weston."  Reynolds
nodded knowingly.

"No!  Urge me no longer, Master Reynolds.  But I will
concede this.  Your idea of selling the pinnace at Deptford
is excellent.  I will send a letter by you to Master Weston
and he will attend to the sale and to settling with you."
Robert felt relieved.

"And who will be responsible for that misbegotten
crowd between decks?" asked Reynolds.

"We'll find someone," Robert replied.  "I suppose
you'll be satisfied to let Master Weston settle your account
with you?"

The seaman gave him an inscrutable look. "Since he's *your* friend, yes. And that we may sell the pinnace for a fair price, I'll get back and see that the calking is well done. That's to my interest, now," he added shamelessly.

He thrust his toothpick behind his ear, cocked his hat on his stringy black curls and went out. Robert heard him argue over the score with the landlord, then the outer door slammed.

Robert finished his ale slowly. After all, the interview so dreaded had ended satisfactorily.

# XXVIII

## *Supper in a Garden*

O N the quay, Robert met Giles Heale.
"I was sent to watch for you!" explained Giles.
"We have an invitation to supper, Uncle Robert.
It's from Master Fallon, the host to Governor Martin and
his Marie. The Martins being unaccountably full of the
milk of human kindness have arranged for you and Aunt
Mary to take supper in the Fallons' garden, and Aunt
Mary, having made up a quarrel with Mistress Desire, has
got Desire included and because we two make such graceful garden ornaments, I've been asked to accompany my
beautiful mistress. Not that she's admitted yet that she's
mine but I'm sure she will. She's softened to me markedly,
today."

Robert, who had been hovering between acceptance and
refusal, now said with set jaws, "I'll come. Although," he
added with a sudden twinkle, "you look like a flock of
butterflies and I, like a flight of rooks!"

Giles gayly smoothed down his brown silk thighs. "The
Fallons are only shopkeepers, but you understand, Uncle,
I have so few chances to cut a figure before Mistress Desire! And you always look most elegant," he finished
kindly.

Robert chuckled as he took Giles' arm. "Come! Is
the company already gathered?"

"Yes, it's just a step up along the High Street. I've
waited for you a long time. Mistress Desire, though, was

sure I'd waylay you if I stood by the small boat which was to meet you."

"Mistress Desire!" exclaimed Robert in such a voice that the young doctor looked at him curiously. "She is very thoughtful," Robert went on more coolly.

"Something wonderful!" cried Giles. "There's no one like her. You saw, today, how even the women love her." And they proceeded up the narrow street singing Desire's praises with the greatest harmony between them.

A long, thatch-roofed house lay behind a gray stone wall on which moss and ivy grew thick. A little gate let into the place from the roadway. They opened this and followed a narrow stone path under latticed windows to the garden. It was not a large garden; only two squares of lawn enclosed in masses of flowers and in one of the lawns an acacia tree under which the supper table was spread.

The hosts, Master and Mistress Fallon, were chatting with the other guests near the lavender hedge. Master Fallon wore a little prim pointed beard and clothing of fine black, with a small ruff, lace-edged. He was short and stout and Mistress Fallon was short and slender. She was dressed in cherry-colored silk, and a large lace collar, wired to stand high at the back of her head, gave her a very smart appearance.

Desire in her rose-colored muslin made Robert a little curtsey and went on talking to Master Fallon after the introductions had been made.

The arrival of Cushman and the doctor was the signal for Mistress Fallon's little maid to place a huge pork pie on the table which was already loaded with breads, cakes, jellies, fruits and wines. Robert stood a little apart, steadying himself for what must be a trying evening. He wondered, as he realized this, why he'd been so weak as to come.

There was a white cloth on the table. The oak benches were black against it. The grass was of intensest, living green. The women's bright gowns trailing on its velvet perfection, the yellows, oranges, purples, pinks, of the flower borders, the soft notes of birds; it was the essence of all the homes these Pilgrims never would see again, Cushman told himself.

Mistress Fallon called them to the meal. Mary in pale green and very lovely, too, sat beside Robert. Desire, sitting opposite him, scarcely glanced at him during the meal which was prolonged till sundown. Fallon had a brother in Kent and Mistress Fallon was an Essex woman. They were intensely interested in the Pilgrim enterprise, knowing much of the section from which the Martins' group derived. The table talk centered on Pilgrims, their problems, until Robert, at least, was weary of it and so it seemed was Desire, for at the end of the meal, she asked permission to walk in the orchard. This, gorgeous with ripening apples, lay beyond the lavender hedge. She scarcely had disappeared when Giles cried, "She's forgot her hood and the dew is falling!" He picked up the bit of rose silk from Desire's bench and ran after her.

"There!" smiled Marie. "Love will find a way!"

"Is it so!" exclaimed Mistress Fallon. "What a notable pair to be sure!"

"It seems to me, though," Master Fallon picked his teeth thoughtfully, "that the hardships of the wilderness may be too much for a lady like Mistress Minter."

"But she's not a lady," protested Marie. "At least, no more than Mistress Cushman."

Robert got up from his place. "Will you show me your

kitchen garden, friend Fallon?" he asked. "It will be a long time before I'll see a well-ordered garden again."

"Gladly! and my pig also! He's the most advantageable creature in my possession. Fowls, dogs, horses, cows! You may have them all, but leave me my pig!" He nodded waggishly and led Cushman off behind the house where, built into a great hawthorn hedge, was a cave-like stone structure giving into the rear of the orchard. This was the advantageable creature's sty.

The two men leaned on the door, admiring the huge beast for a slow quarter of an hour. The afterglow turned the sty to pink marble. The rows of cabbage and turnip sported leaves of gold.

"It's an old place as such things go," murmured Fallon as he rubbed the porker's back. "My great-grandfather had this sty built. I suspicion he borrowed the stone from God! At least they're not native and they match those in the church tower yonder, which was building then. No wonder I have marvelous good pigs!"

They both chuckled and fell silent. A companionable man, Peter Fallon. After a time, Fallon heaved a sigh. "I must go fetch Master Martin. He'll think we avoid him. Stay till I come back and I'll show you both my spring house and my little red cow."

He returned to the flower garden. Crickets chirped, a belated dove alighted on its cote and cooed.

And then the door which led from the sty into the orchard was pushed open and Giles Heale vaulted over muck and pig to the door on which Robert still leaned. Robert stepped back, opening the door, and Giles coming out said in an anguished voice,

"It's all over with me! And yet she wept! And yet she would have none of me!" He rushed away.

Robert's self-control crumbled like a mud dike on which
the floods are sweeping.   He reversed Giles' route.   He
leaped the pig and the muck and strode through the door
into the orchard.

Very ancient, this orchard, with trunks and branches
and uttermost twigs coated with gray-green lichen.   Green
leaves, fruit gold and crimson and pale yellow, and at the
far end, where peach trees pressed fanwise against a tall
gray wall, the slender figure in pale rose.

"Desire!"   Robert paused before her.   "Desire, say
that you'll forgive me for last night!   If you order me so,
I'll never address you again but say that you don't despise
me!   Or if you do despise me that you'll not refuse me
absolution!"

She was leaning against the trunk of a tree and she did
not stir except to turn her head from the peach trees toward him.   Yes, she had been crying!

But she tried to be gay.   "This isn't a pleasant supper
party, after all!   And I thought that, though I could find
no place in the *Mayflower* to weep privily, I had surely
found such a weeping place here!"

Robert could not smile.   "I have no quips left, Desire!
I can only plea for grace.   Truly I had pledged the very
faith of my soul in myself, that never should you know.
Poor fool, I saw myself a sort of Philip Sidney!"

"But Stella knew!"   Desire's voice was very gentle.
"Stella knew and the world was immortally enriched by the
words with which Sir Philip told her."

"You mean—?"   He paused, not daring to take an un-
bidden step.

But she did not help him.   He thought she could not.
Her pulse beat so rapidly in her throat that he could
see the white flesh throbbing.   And so he tried again.

"You mean that if I had words— Oh, for dear Christ's sake, Desire, tell me what you mean! In all eternity we may have only these few minutes alone together."

"No!" cried Desire. "One can only live by believing that in heaven, although there'll be no marriage, there'll be love and that those who were good here on earth and loved but could never be even friends may find that God has something nobler, more chaste, more glorious, than marriage for them. It must be so or one couldn't go on living."

"You mean you love me?" Robert's voice was very quiet.

"Yes," replied Desire.

A little wind crept through the trees and there followed a soft thudding of apples to the turf.

"I'm wholly to blame," said Robert, "wholly. If I'd gone to God with it when it began with me in Hampton Waters, He'd have helped me destroy the sin, there and then."

"Sin?" Desire spoke indignantly. "You affront me, now. Thank heaven, I'm no canting Separatist calling so beautiful a gift as this by a hard name. I'm a child of that world which doesn't see sin where God himself sees none. God is love. And no love He gives His creatures is purer than mine for you, Robert Cushman."

He clenched his fist to keep from touching her. "Aye, dearest, dearest Desire of my heart! But however am I to go on living in the same great cabin with you, in the same forest with you and this same tide ever rising in my soul, yet never again intimating to you that it is there; never by a glance, nay, by a thought unexpressed, letting others dream of what I feel?"

"But that's the very glory and mystery of it!" she cried. "Never to yield to it as common people do!"

Robert shook his head. "No giant could hope to conceal a love like mine. And I have no giant soul. I'm a plain man, trying to cope with something greater than myself; a poor little field mouse contending against a mastiff."

"You're not flattering!" Desire tried to speak lightly again.

His smile was not happy. "I'm only comparing my feeble will with the strength of my love. I resolved with invincible firmness never to tell you of it. I told. I resolved with the strength of mountains never to seek you out again. Yet when Giles told me you'd refused him, I leaped like a mad man to reach you, to be alone with you. This love of mine goes on from strength to strength. I fear for it, dear my secretary!"

"Fear for it?" she repeated wonderingly. "Why, Robin, since you told me you loved me, I've been a god! Every impulse in me has been ennobled. Today, at that meeting on the ship, I had only to look at you and I could have overturned the ship! Our love shall never do anything but bring a thousandfold more good to the Pilgrims than as though we'd never loved."

She put out her hand. He took it, laid his cheek against the palm and said brokenly, "I never can hide from the world this which I feel. God help me! God forgive me! Aye, only good shall come to the Pilgrims from this but at what cost I tremble to think!"

"What do you fear?" she asked.

He lifted his head, clasping her hand warmly in both of his. The deepening night was hiding their faces from each other but he knew every expression of her candid eyes, her generous mouth, and he knew she was staring puzzled at him like an honest child.

"I'm fifteen years older than you," he answered her. "And life has taught me much about men and women. Desire, I haven't the strength to go on with it."

"Why? But you are the strongest man I know!" she said uneasily.

Then she withdrew her hand for voices were rising from the pig sty. "Master Cushman! Ho! Mistress Minter! Doctor Giles!"

"Coming!" called Robert. "Mistress Minter is with me but not the doctor!"

They started back and Fallon and Martin met them. Robert went on, "Dr. Heale rushed by me ten minutes ago and I came in to chat with Mistress Desire. I'm sorry if we've troubled anyone."

"Mistress Fallon must think Pilgrims make strange guests," said Governor Martin severely.

"So she must! How long have I been in the orchard?" cried Desire.

"Only a half hour," replied their host comfortably. "My wife admires lovers. Did you and your young man quarrel?"

"We disagreed," admitted Desire. "I'm sure he'll return to make amends to Mistress Fallon!"

They now had reached the vegetable garden and shortly were making explanations and apologies to the three wives who were strolling on the lawns.

"It's naughty of you to remain talking in the orchard with a maiden," said Mistress Fallon somewhat severely to Robert. "But if your wife doesn't complain, I shan't."

"And if I complained, then what?" laughed Mary.

"Then you'd have to kiss and make up," declared Marie.

"My Chris is a marvelous amorous man with the maidens but it doesn't fret me!"

Mary laughed more heartily still. "My husband as an amorous man is fabulous! Robert, do you think you ought to go find Giles and remind him of his manners? Do go see if the silly gander has thrown himself off the Hoe!"

"If he's a gander, he can't drown!" exclaimed Master Fallon. "But that's no errand for an assistant governor!"

"Nor for any man!" agreed Cushman. He turned to Mistress Fallon prepared to make amends for his neglect of her. "And so you are from Kent, Mistress! Have you been to Canterbury?"

"Nay," answered his hostess. "I never left Westerham till I was married. But I had a second cousin who lived near Canterbury. He was killed a month ago. Mayhap you knew him, Frank Bote? He owned a large freehold farm near the town."

Mary gave a little cry.

Robert said quickly, "He was our friend and neighbor, and when we saw him last June he was in excellent health."

"His horse kicked him in the head and that was his end," explained Fallon. "Frank being unmarried, my lad inherits. So there's always a balm in Gilead."

Robert was thankful that in the starlight no one could see Mary's face. He went on quickly, "Mayhap for you but for us it's grievous to lose so good a friend. He was a silent man but we always liked to have him arrive of an evening with his tobacco pipe."

"Why now! Mistress Cushman is weeping!" exclaimed Marie Martin. "He was a dear neighbor then?"

"Yes," replied Mary brokenly. "I've known him since I was born."

"Well," the governor spoke briskly, "he's with the angels now, that is, I hope he is if he was a pious man."

"Certainly, he was pious!" Mistress Fallon's voice was a little indignant. Then her tone softened. "Ah, here comes poor Doctor Heale!"

Giles crossed the lawn and joined the little circle. "I remembered suddenly," he said to Master Fallon, "that one of my 'tween-decks men was likely to have a fit and so I rushed away to find him. Will you forgive me my bad manners?"

"Indeed, I will!" Fallon patted the young man's arm. "And now, wife, take us into your warm kitchen and cheer us with your elderberry wine."

In the great kitchen where the settles on either side of the fireplace held them all, the guests under Desire's leadership made such an ardent effort to be amusing that their hosts, who perhaps had been looking a little mazed by their vagaries, now rocked with laughter. It was not until eleven, after wine and cakes, that they made their adieus.

In the street, Giles offered his arm to Mary. "My dear aunt, do walk with me," he pleaded. "I must tell you about my poor man with fits."

"And I must hear about him!" cried Mary. "Give Desire your arm, Robert," and off she sailed with Giles.

Desire put her hand on his doublet sleeve and they moved together down the street.

Desire pressed close to him and looked up into his face. "Tell me again," she whispered, "for all the long years ahead."

"I love you!" he told her in a voice that he could not hold steady.

She gave a little sob. "You may have my Philip Sidney!

His heights are not for me.   You shall give me your Shakespeare to have and to hold when the years part us.   He understood the human heart better than Sidney."

"You may have all of him but these four lines."   Robert touched her fingers with his and repeated Shakespeare's words:

> "As easy might I from myself depart
> As from my soul, which in thy breast doth lie.
> That is my home of love: if I have ranged
> Like him that travels, I return again—"

She was silent for a moment, then she said and with anguish in her voice, "So this is what it comes to—after all the years of my girlhood and womanhood, keeping myself for the lover I knew existed somewhere—it comes to this, that I see him only across the deck of a ship or through a wilderness of trees!   If we had never told each other, it would have been endurable."

Robert groaned.   "Mea culpa!"

"No, don't blame yourself, my Robin!   God meant this to happen.   It's our task to discover why, so that only good may come of it."

"That good may come of it," he repeated harshly. "Tell me again—Desire of my heart!"

They were almost on the quay.   She paused and said in tones whose cadence he never was to forget, "Robert, I love you."

Sutton Pool, star-spangled, was a confusion of quivering reflections, masts, lights and rigging.

Giles had found a boatman.   The four spoke little on the row out to the *Mayflower*.

# XXIX

## *Completion*

GILES went below at once. Robert waited on deck for Mary and Desire to get to bed and then Master Jones accosted him:

"So you're back, Master Cushman! I saw Reynolds, to-night. You did well! The *Speedwell* ought to fetch a fair price in Deptford. As you were not to be found, I took it on myself to speak to Deacon Carver and he was sure the other chiefs would be complaisant, and so I'll build the few extra bunks in the *Mayflower* tomorrow, and by the next day, we should be off. As to his other suggestion to you about your going to London, I would say—"

"Not tonight, for God's sake!" pleaded Cushman. "I will talk to you of it when I'm not so weary!" He put his hand on the other's arm.

"Yes! Yes! My poor friend, I know how you love the voyage and all! Well then, in the morning!"

Robert went down to Mary.

She was motionless, lying as far as possible from his side of the bed. The great cabin was horrible, full of snores and puffings and muttered dreams. Now a babe cried out in its sleep. Now a man moaned. When the ship was in motion there was at least a semblance of seclusion.

Robert thought a full hour must have passed when he felt Mary's hand creep out to clutch his sleeve. He waited a moment and then moved toward her to whisper in her ear,

"Dearest Mary, can I help you? I know what you're feeling."

He felt her stiffen. Then she whispered back, "What do you know?"

"About Frank, that day in Dartmouth when you had hysterics, you called his name."

"I feared I had! And so you hate me! I don't blame you."

"Hate you?" He put his arm under her and drew her head to rest on his shoulder. "Have I acted as if I hated you?"

"No, unless it was when I lied about the *Sparrow.* Oh, Robert! This is my payment for that sin! Why wasn't I killed, not Frank! Oh! He was good, good! He never so much as touched my hand! He never knew about my lies. He thought I was as good as he. Robert, will you believe me if I say that never, never will a lie pass my lips? My lies killed him. I know it as clearly as if God told me."

He whispered with an aching throat, "Mary, my sin is heavier than yours."

"No, you're good, like Frank! But I'll never be afraid of you again. In all the world now, I have only you. We must try to love each other a little. There in the wilderness, I'll try to be less selfish, Robert. Go to sleep, you're very weary."

She moved away from him and with a heart and a conscience as heavy as millstones, he closed his eyes and for very exhaustion did actually fall asleep.

Morning dawned clear and from five o'clock on, all was bustle and excitement aboard the *Mayflower.* The ship's carpenter began work on the extra beds as soon as the people were dressed. Everyone was very gay as they

moved into their contracted quarters. The extra crowding had become a game.

The poop cabin was the one quiet spot in the ship and
here, about six o'clock, Robert found the master at work
over his charts. "That island of New England," said
Jones, "may be a very pleasant land on its western side
but certainly on the east, there's little but sand and sickly
trees which look as if many a tide had over-raked them."

"Do you think you could sail round the island?" asked
Cushman, looking over the master's shoulder.

"I'll try," replied Jones, pushing aside the map and
staring at his friend. "I've got a word to say that's like
drawing my gullet out with pincers, so I'll say it short
and rough which is a sailor's way. I think it's your duty,
Master Cushman, to stay in London as agent for these
helpless people."

Robert responded with a fury that surprised himself as
much as it did the *Mayflower's* master. *"You* say this to
*me? I* am to stay! Not Deacon Carver, nor Mullins, nor
Allerton! I, because I'm hated. I, because more than any
other I'd fain plant the colony. I—"

"Softly! Softly, Master Cushman!" gasped Jones.

"Softly! While you rend my living heartstrings. Master Jones, I shall proceed to America on the *Mayflower* and
no man shall stay me." And yet, even as he raved, he
knew that his outcry was futile.

He beat the table with his fist and, turning, strode out
of the cabin. Desire and John Carver were standing on
the half deck. They must have heard him for they were
looking at him queerly, or were they? Was it the deck,
the rigging— He was fainting. He heard Desire cry,
"Robert!" and then the familiar whirling blackness caught
him.

But he fought against it with the greatest desperation and after an instant actually conquered it. When his eyes cleared, he was sitting on the deck, his back against the cabin. Desire was chafing his hands and murmuring his name, tenderly. John Carver was gazing at his niece with astonishment and disapproval.

"Desire," said the deacon sternly, "go below!"

Robert freed his hands and somehow got to his feet. Desire, meanwhile, turned and went down the companionway.

"Thanks, deacon," Robert said. "I'm well again. I must finish my talk with the master."

John turned away with a shrug. Just for an instant, Robert steadied himself against the rail. And in that instant, he realized that Desire had divulged her secret to her uncle and that he must submit himself to that solution of their problem which had been pressing for recognition since the moment in the orchard when Desire had acknowledged that she loved him.

He walked firmly into Jones' cabin and said, casually, "I'll go back to London in the *Speedwell*."

The master got up from the table, rested one hand on a French map of Virginia and said, "Good!" Then looking into Robert's eyes, he drew his sleeve across his own. "I know how dear it is to ye, this damnable voyage of Bedlamites!"

Robert regarded him not calmly but with a curiously high quality of self-control. He was conscious of the same sense of exaltation that had come to him in the Dartmouth hills when he had discovered that he loved Desire. It was as if his, again, was an untold love; as if a sin had been blotted from something exquisite, ennobling, chaste.

"We must tell the others—get their consent," Robert said.

"Consent to what?" asked a familiar voice. Brewster was coming in. "You are recovered, Robert?"

"Entirely," replied Cushman. "I want your advice on a vital matter, elder. You know the outcome of my talk with Reynolds, yesterday?"

"Yes," nodded Brewster. "John told me, last night. You did well."

"Master Jones," Robert turned to the seaman, "mayhap you'll tell the elder of Reynolds' suggestion." He sat down on a bunk.

Jones nodded his sandy head. "Reynolds tried to persuade Master Cushman to remain in London as your agent, for, as he said to me, unless he or a man his equal in parts, reinstated you with the Merchant Adventurers or some other men with moneys, you'd be doomed as Jamestown was doomed."

The elder dropped down in the master's great oak chair and stared at Robert. The *Mayflower* rocked at her anchorage very gently. Up on the Hoe the huge guns gleamed. England was very secure.

"This is painful!" Brewster's great voice was husky. "And yet, Robert, we've all thought for some time that your health—"

"Spare me that, my dear elder," protested Robert. "I've already decided to remain if you all wish it. But I do not desire to be present when you discuss this with the others. I am sated with talk."

For the first time in the ten years he'd known him, Cushman beheld William Brewster speechless, and taking advantage of the poor man's helpless state, he walked out of the cabin.

Aye, at least he would escape the everlasting considerations! Martin had been making more than a mere jibe when he declared that any four Pilgrims could talk the Houses of Parliament out of existence. He, himself, had always been one of the worst offenders in this matter. But now, he told himself, he'd hide in the Admiral Inn to avoid the hour of debate which must follow his declaration to the elder.

But first, he must discover what had passed between Carver and Desire. He went into the great cabin. Desire was not there. Mary was sitting sadly over a bit of sewing.

"Why aren't you up in the poop cabin?" she asked. "They just sent for Deacon Carver and the governor. I suppose the world's to be turned wrong side out again!"

"Where are all the others?" asked Robert.

"Desire went to fetch her cloak from the Fallons'. I haven't seen any of the others. When do we sail, Robert?"

"I'll tell you later," he replied. Desire must know of his resolution, first. He went ashore and to the Fallons'. She had been there and gone for a walk in the town. For an hour, he sought her, up and down the streets, only at last to discover her on the rocks below the Hoe, in conversation with John Carver.

Then the session in the poop cabin must have been a short one and John must be telling her of his decision. He made his way hurriedly down the rocks and was panting when he reached them.

Desire, very pale, did not return his greeting. Her eyes looked as if they were fixed on his corpse.

"We were speaking of you, Robert," Carver told him. "I have been telling Desire of your resolve to abide in London and that we all approved."

Robert looked at him closely. "None of you must fail

to understand that I remain with a weary sense of loss and failure."

"You've done your duty, no more and no less," said the deacon harshly. "From what Desire has told me, there was nothing else you could do."

"You shan't speak so, Uncle John," said Desire. "You don't know what you're doing to him."

"Wait, Desire!" Robert touched her hand. "The deacon, too, is doing his duty."

John Carver eyed him keenly, and then as Robert had seen it do a hundred times before, his quick anger gave way to a mood of utter generosity and sweetness.

"Ah, Robert! Robert!" he exclaimed. "I know what this sacrifice means to you! Why did you ever make it necessary?"

Cushman looked off to the sea—the bitter, estranging sea. Carver continued to stare at him.

"Robert, I know you so well! You and I have been through so much together—man, I love you—look'ee, I'm not all brute. I have lived in the world a long time, ten years longer than you, and I know what you've overcome and put aside. For Desire is rare among women. I've been harsh but I thought it was needed. Now I see that I might have trusted you. Yet it was only by the grace of heaven that there was no one within hearing of Desire's cries when you fainted. She told all in her sobs."

"It has all been my fault, mine alone," said Robert.

"No. I loved you from the moment you came down into the great cabin at Southampton," declared Desire clearly.

Carver looked from one fine, anguished face to the other and his own face quivered. "I shall walk up the path," he said, "and you may follow slowly." He moved away.

"Desire! Desire! What can I say?" whispered Robert.

"That you forgive me!" she exclaimed. "I blurted forth my love before the very ship when you fainted and you knew then I was not to be trusted."

"It was inevitable," he said. "Sooner or later, one of us was bound to break out. There's nothing to forgive."

"I see it now. You tried to make me see it, last night. And so, for that reason, you remain. You give up your dearest plan. You abide in the England which doesn't want you." She bit her lips, then went on. "Nay, I'm not going to add a pennyweight to it, Robin—dear, dear Robin! I shall go to America, thanking God that I am loved by one having so great a nature as yours!"

"Great in nothing but my love for you," he whispered. "Can you understand when I say that since my decision was made, I seem to have achieved the very perfectness of love? The perfect communion through the perfect sacrifice!"

"Yes!" She answered him in a voice hardly audible. "And so a special grace comes to the Pilgrims because you and I love each other and on that we must rest."

He touched her hand again. "No! We rest on our love which is a completed and eternal fact."

They walked on in silence. Then as they neared the deacon, Robert said, "God keep you, Desire! Desire of my heart!"

They reached the deacon. Robert bowed, put his hat back on his head and walked rapidly away.

# XXX

## *Yonder Sails the Mayflower*

H<small>E</small> wandered without purpose for a time, but eventually he found himself in the shipyard. Master Reynolds was standing under the beak of the *Speedwell* watching the workmen with an eagle eye.

He beamed on Robert. "I've heard the news, sir! Worth pounds to me, not to be left to Master Weston's mercies! And," soberly, "with the difference between starvation and food to the Pilgrims."

"When will you be ready to sail?" asked Robert.

"Tomorrow, as ever was," he replied. "These robbers shall give the full worth of your money, I'll warrant you! Will you come aboard and tell me where you and your family will sleep?"

"I'll leave that to you," said Cushman indifferently. "When shall we send our possessions aboard?"

"Tomorrow morning," very briskly. "I can take the passengers tonight."

Robert gave the pinnace a glance of extreme distaste and asked to be rowed out to the *Mayflower*.

The tide was against them, so it was not a short trip and during its progress, Cushman was able to orient himself again. His brain was clearer than it had been since he left Southampton. He was more his own man than he'd ever been in his life. This he did not understand but he was grateful that his tragedy had been healing somehow; had not destroyed him.

They were eating dinner on the *Mayflower,* but everyone paused to stare at Robert. They knew then that he was returning to London!

He found Mary and Tom in their favorite place in the longboat and Mary sent Tom to bid the servant bring his father's dinner. During the boy's short absence, she said, "You should have told me, Robert— No, no!" as he looked at her pleadingly. "I'll not utter a word to add to your care! Only, I'm so thankful! So joyful!"

"Poor Tommy! I suppose he's heartbroken!" sighed Cushman.

"He was at first, but—you'll scarcely credit this—I've managed to comfort him! You shall not find me ungrateful, my dear husband! I talked with Dorothy Bradford and she says she and Will shall be glad to take care of Tommy if you wish to send him over with them."

Tommy and the servant arrived. Robert, with his trencher on his knees, looked from his wife to his son. "I need you, Tommy," he said. "Remain with me another year, until you're fourteen. Then, if all is well with the colony, you shall go to Master Bradford."

*"Must* I stay here?" Tommy's eyes were so swollen from tears that they were mere slits.

Robert was utterly tired of making great decisions. "No, you shall do as you wish," he replied quietly.

Tommy took a huge bite of pork and slowly chewed it. When his mouth was partially emptied, he said, "The other lads have all been laughing at me. Captain Standish, too, would take me. Why do you need me, Father?"

"You'll have to take my word for it. I could never explain. But you are very dear to me—" He broke off.

Tommy scratched his chin and heaved a great sigh.

"Well, I'll stay and I'll eat your pork for you, if you don't care for it."

"Nay, young vulture!" smiled his father. "I'm hungry, myself!"

"Finish mine, Tommy," suggested Mary. "I'm too excited to eat. They are saying, some of them, Robert, that you're afraid to go. They don't say it twice in my hearing."

"I gave Love Brewster a black eye. My father's just as brave as his father." Tommy wolfed down Mary's dinner. Governor Martin came up. "I'm very heavy over this, Master Cushman!"

"Don't fret yourself, Governor!" exclaimed Robert. "I'm heartily weary of the whole subject and the less that's said the better I'll like it. But I fear we'll have to go over money matters to the extent of letting me know how much you'll all think I should find for you. Perhaps I can help you reckon roughly what's been spent and that will be my guide."

Martin nodded. "I must go home to Master Fallon's for my dinner. Perhaps you'll come there, anon, where we can have quiet."

"Yes," agreed Robert. Martin disappeared.

"Shall I pack our things, shortly?" asked Mary.

"Have them ready for the pinnace tomorrow morning," replied Cushman.

"Will I not!" she cried. "Oh, Robert, in spite of all, you've made me happy."

"Thank God for that!" he said and he meant it.

He finished the meal and shortly went ashore again. He was very restless. On the quay, he met Brewster.

"I was just coming to find you," said the elder. "But this is better. Will you walk with me on the sands?"

Robert accepted the invitation without eagerness. More talk! But if Brewster sensed his dullness he did not heed it. He took the younger man's arm and they made their way along the path under the cliffs.

"We had a strange session, this morning," began the elder. "Carver was quite distraught. He left the meeting in its midst, was gone an hour, came back calm but very sad. He spoke then most movingly of you as our loving friend. Poor Martin wept again saying it was all his fault and that he'd be the one to remain. That was worse than foolish, as we pointed out to him, showing him his lacks and faults. Edward Winslow admitted to all your virtues and values but couldn't understand how you could quit the voyage. Nor could Will Bradford see but there was cowardice in it."

"They think I've lost heart in the venture! Surely you beguiled them from that, elder!"

"I did my best," answered the other, "but both are young and so their judgments are narrow."

Robert's voice was bitter. "And so I must be writ in the Pilgrim books as one who deserted the venture because of delays and crosses! This grieves me more than anything."

"That will pass," said the elder quietly.

But Robert observed that he did not contradict the statement. Aye, none understood but Desire and Carver who could not speak.

"All misunderstandings do pass with time." William Brewster continued. "Even the King is less biting than he was against those who would purify the Church! So my friends here tell me. He has overstepped himself in his vindictiveness and has so strengthened the parliamentary Puritans that now he is finding it convenient to overlook some against whom he's been most violent. I don't say that it would be safe for me to return to London, but it will be for you. You may be even more open than you have been. Nay, I want you to go farther."

"Farther?" Robert replied, bewildered.

"Yes, Robert. This is for your private ear. I am not the villager who left Scrooby with other villagers. My Leyden experiences taught me much. I can see now the beauties of the Church of England and I look on our separation from it as our inevitable tragedy, not our glory. Only for the persecuting bishops do I lack affection. I subscribe wholly, as you must subscribe, to the confession of faith published by the Church and I acknowledge the authority of the present bishops as they derive it from the King. I wish you to make this known in England, Robert. I wish you to mingle with people who are fain to speak of us as traitors and prove to them by your own life and faith that we are as deep lovers of England as any bishop who ever lived. How you are to do this, I don't know! But I trust to your large mindedness and your knowledge of the world."

Cushman, as the full significance of the elder's words sank in on him, came to a halt and turning from that sea which could no longer claim him, swept with a long glance the hills of Cornwall, the cliffs of Devon.

*They were his once more.*

He had lost Desire. He had lost the venture. He had gained England. Surely God had forgiven him!

"No man ever had a nobler task given him!" he exclaimed.

" 'Tis true!" agreed the elder. "England needs you to interpret us, her own sons, to her, lest she lose them utterly when she needs them most." He put his arm across Robert's shoulders.

"You've given me life again! The earth and the fullness thereof!" Robert could say no more.

They walked on in silence.

Later, Cushman went to meet Chris Martin. He found him at the table under the acacia tree, gazing forlornly at a blank sheet of paper and a quill pen which lay before him. Desire Minter and Mistress Martin disappeared into the orchard as Robert crossed the lawn. Chris explained that Desire was staying with them until the *Mayflower* sailed.

Robert nodded. "Let's begin."

But it was no good! An hour later, he dropped the pen and said with a smile, "I'll fret you no more, Governor! Let's say that in God our accounts balance and I'll use my own judgment and experience as to your future needs. I would impress this on you. Send the *Mayflower* back as quickly as possible from America. If you find trees and can send her loaded with clapboard, we can sell it and this will be an earnest to the Adventurers of our intentions. This will incline them toward us."

"Trust me!" cried Martin, immensely cheered. "Trading is my own business. I *can* carry that in my poor head."

They talked a little longer about the hope of getting beaver furs from the savages, then, hearing the women returning, Robert made his adieus.

When he got back to the *Mayflower,* he found that the carpenter had completed the additional bunks, that the luggage had been taken out of the hold ready to transfer to the *Speedwell* and that the ship was in comparative quiet for most people had gone ashore. Although it was not yet dusk, Robert went to his bed and instantly fell

into a more profound slumber than he'd experienced in
weeks. He did not waken when Mary came to bed nor
until the linnet's piping finally roused him in the dawn.

And with the opening of his eyes, he was conscious of
the stupendous fact that he no longer was an exile. He
was needed in England! And this being so, he could go
through the parting with Desire and the venture with a
man's fortitude.

There was a fair wind. Jones called down to him from
the poop that they'd sail with the high tide at nine, if all
the beetle-headed people returned as they should.

They did return. The Brewsters and all the chiefs save
the Martins had come back the previous night. By eight
all the others were aboard except the Martins and Desire
who arrived a little later. Robert had hoped to get off
before Desire returned but Carver and Jones held him in
last consultations.

Somehow and finally, though, he got Mary and Tommy
into the cockboat and was about to descend the ladder
himself, when Marie Martin rushed forward and kissed
him soundly. Catherine Carver did likewise. Mary
Brewster's tired eyes were full of tears. "We can't afford
not to have you with us, Robert," she said and gave him
both her hands. He bent his yellow head and kissed them.
Then he took Desire's dear fingers and pressed his lips
upon them and after this he was conscious only that he
was seated in the cockboat and that a row of faces, many
of them scornful, was looking down upon them.

The *Speedwell* was anchored at the quayside. Mary and
Tommy went aboard at once but Robert remained on the
quay that he might be alone when the *Mayflower* sailed.

He saw the sailors run up the rigging, saw the white
sails loosed, saw them back the foreyards and brace the

main and mizzen.   They had manned the capstan.   Faintly came the chantey, "Lustily!   Lustily!   Sail we forth!" They had raised the anchor.

The ship gathered sternway as the sails began to fill; turning, hesitating, picking up headway, she moved rapidly and lightly toward the open sea.

A cheer burst forth from the *Speedwell* and from a small group of spectators.   A little boy, fishing from the wharf, looked up casually and said to another little boy,

"Yonder sails the *Mayflower*."

Then he gave his attention to his lines.

Robert went aboard the pinnace and to his berth in the master's cabin and there he remained alone while the *Speedwell* got under way.

## Partial List of Books Studied

THE STORY OF THE PILGRIM FATHERS, *Edward Arber.* Boston, 1897.

HISTORY OF THE PLYMOUTH PLANTATION, *William Bradford.*

THE PILGRIM FATHERS, *W. H. Bartlett.* London, 1863.

WILLIAM BREWSTER. LETTER BOOK. Boston, 1794.

NATHANIEL MORTON. NEW ENGLAND MEMORIAL. London, 1669.

THE ENGLAND AND HOLLAND OF THE PILGRIMS, *H. M. and M. Dexter.* Boston, 1906.

NAVAL WORTHIES OF ELIZABETH'S REIGN, *John Barrow.* London, 1845.

PRINCIPAL VOYAGES OF THE ENGLISH NATION, VOL. I, *Richard Hakluyt.* London, 1589.

PURITANISM AND ART, *Joseph Crouch.* London, 1910.

SOCIAL LIFE UNDER THE STUARTS, *Elizabeth Godfrey.* London, 1904.

VOYAGES AND TRAVELS, *C. R. Beazley.* London, 1877.

TRUE TRAVELS, ETC., *John Smith.* London, 1630.

THE BEGINNINGS OF NEW ENGLAND, *John Fiske.* London, 1889.

HISTORY OF PLYMOUTH, *A. L. Salmon.* London, 1920.

HISTORY OF DEVON, *Thos. Moore.* 1826.

DEVONSHIRE IN 1630, *Thos. Westcote.* London, 1845.

DARTMOUTH AND SOUTH DEVON. Ward Lock and Co.

COSTUME IN ENGLAND, *F. W. Fairchild.* London, 1860.

SAILING SHIPS, THEIR HISTORY AND DEVELOPMENT, *S. S. Laird Clowes.* 1932.

LAND HO! 1620, *W. S. Nickerson.* Boston, 1931.

ENGLISH ANCESTRY AND HOMES OF THE PILGRIMS, *C. E. Banks.* New York, 1929.

HISTORY OF ENGLAND, VOLS. I, II, III, *S. R. Gardiner.* London, 1883.

HOME LIFE UNDER THE STUARTS, *E. Godfrey.* London, 1903.

THE PAPERS OF THOS. BOWERY. Hakluyt Society, London, 1927.